THE KING'S SHADOW

Cheryl Sawyer

Copyright © 2016 Cheryl Anne Hingley

Cheryl Hingley has asserted her rights under the Copyright, Design and Patents Act, 1988, to be identified as the author of this work.

First published by Endeavour Press Ltd in 2016.

To our summer princess:

Clara Joy Hingley

In tribute to my grandparents:

Rupert Harry Sawyer
Alice Mabel Sawyer (née Skill)
Thomas Charles Denton
and in loving memory of
Helen May Denton (née Baker)

Terror & Awe: England's Revolution

This trilogy begins in 1642, when Charles I and Parliament first clashed in the Civil War, and ends in 1660, with the return of Charles II.

The first volume is *The Winter Prince*, a compelling account of the fierce military duel between Prince Rupert of the Rhine and Parliament's commander at the time, the Earl of Essex. The second volume *Farewell, Cavaliers*, is set in 1652, when Oliver Cromwell struggles for ultimate power over England and his avenger stalks the streets of London. This final volume, *The King's Shadow*, begins on New Year's morning, 1660, at the village of Coldstream, as General George Monck's army crosses the border into England and begins its long, risky, ominous march towards London—are they marching to restore King Charles II?

Notwithstanding the opposition of the soldiery and other great factions, yet was the king brought into his own kingdom, city of London and parliament ... without the power of one dog that durst open his mouth, or the loss of one drop of bloodshed in the whole kingdom. A main instrument of our deliverance was General Monck ... desiring to join with the consent of the best in the nation who petitioned him for a free parliament, all the way as he came out of Scotland.

Alice Thornton 1626-1707

COLDSTREAM
New Year, 1660

The colonel had travelled a long way in the last few days but he was still in Scotland and still riding through snow as he entered Coldstream, a mean village on the Tweed. As he and two troopers clattered down the only street, he saw the unquiet river gleaming at the end of it like molten pewter. Coldstream itself seemed frozen solid. It was well after midnight and if General Monck and his officers had seen the New Year in with any toasts at the hearthsides, no smoke lingered over the snow-laden roofs and not a light showed, even behind the shutters of the general's quarters, which turned out to be a low stone building of dismal aspect. Uneven hummocks, white with snow, were piled on each side of the front door.

Since early December, an army under George Monck, Commander-in-Chief and Governor of Scotland, had been camped for five miles along the banks of the river that formed the border with England. Colonel Mark Denton had spent the last few weeks in Scotland on reconnaissance for Monck and during the hard journey south he had heard a rumour that Monck was about to march his entire army over the border. The news inspired in Denton a fiery response that might have been either hope or dread; not even he could define it. If 6000 Englishmen were about to cross the Tweed he wanted to know why.

The escort roused the guard by hammering on the door. Denton glanced back at his corporal and two spare mounts, one horse bearing a pack. The beasts twitched their sodden coats and looked about them with a morose air.

'Colonel Denton reporting to General Monck,' said the escort.

The guard, half asleep, looked up and touched his hand to his brow. 'The general's expecting you, sir.'

Denton slid to the ground and passed the reins of his horse to the escort. 'The stables?' he said to the guard.

'Back up the street and to the right there, colonel. It's but a barn—'

Denton said to his corporal: 'Take care of the horses, Hales. Whoever's there, tell them to feed you.' He nodded to the escort, walked past the guard and entered the dwelling.

It was darker than the night outside and, if possible, colder. The guard clapped the door to, muttered an apology to Denton, stumbled ahead without a light and went through to a kitchen where embers in the fireplace shed a faint glow onto a flagged floor. The guard grabbed a candle and bent to light it in the grate.

'I've orders to wake the general, sir, and it may take a moment …' He gave a respectful nod, turned to knock on a door that led towards the back of the house and stepped out of sight.

There was not enough warmth from the embers to thaw the stiffness caused by a day's ride through the depths of winter, so Mark Denton did not approach the hearth. He took in the dim room, which held an unadorned fireplace, table and chairs and a tall dresser. Monck in his many victorious years as a parliamentary commander had shared the hardships of his staff and his men when necessary. What necessity now drove him on from Coldstream? In December the Parliament had begged Monck to march south and quell a major rebellion masterminded by several army leaders. Now the rebellion was over and his forces were arguably no longer needed in London. If the general crossed the border tomorrow, he must be doing so against Parliament's wishes. Why?

George Monck emerged from his chamber and Denton, bowing, could see he must have lain down fully clothed. Heavy-featured and with a rounded form, Monck was a short man, but his presence filled the room as he ordered his guard to place sack, bread and cheese on the table, light more candles, stoke the fire and pile it with the local coal.

Monck left Denton standing by the door until they were alone, then sat down and ran his eye over him. Mark was weary but did not betray it; he simply examined the general in his turn. Whatever the company, it was his habit to take a long look at them before he spoke, indifferent as to whom this might irritate or disconcert.

'Be seated, colonel,' the general said. Denton slid his riding cloak off his shoulders and over a chairback, and laid down the broad-brimmed hat that he had been holding against his thigh. 'You'll eat?'

Denton shook his head, sat down, raised a cup of sack and caught Monck's eye as though toasting him. 'Thank you, sir.'

Monck's first question was delivered in his rolling Devon accent. 'Glencairn?'

'As discontented a spirit as ever and despondent that you refused his offer of 20,000 men.' Mark's delivery was deep and deliberate, which emphasised the rich vowels of his Yorkshire speech. 'On the other hand, he is mighty pleased to be wearing his sword again and permitted to arm his servants.'

'Argyll?'

'None could more disaffect English interests, but he won't show his hand against us at present.'

'Huntly?'

Mark examined Monck's expression as he said: 'Quiescent. You've so arranged it, sir, that Highlanders or Lowlanders who favour Charles Stuart have had no room to move for many a year. If they're shifting their feet now, it's for two reasons: they're avid to hear whether you're about to march to London; and they'd like to know what you'll do when you get there.'

Monck nodded, imperturbable. 'Let them wait. Stirlingshire pledges to stay quiet. Tell me about Edinburgh.'

Mark gave the rest of his report, the product of a thorough investigation into the preparedness for rebellion that might arise in Scotland should Monck remove from it a good part of his army of occupation. Five years before, the late Oliver Cromwell had given Monck the task of subduing the country and he had more than fulfilled his commission; numerous garrisons across the country served as reminders of his supremacy.

Mark, having divulged as much information as he had ever committed to memory in his life, wished the general would be as revelatory in return, but Monck was taciturn. He never answered impromptu questions or asked for opinions unless in meetings with his officers and revealed no ideas except when giving orders. However, Mark expected his report to be a relief to him because it justified the general's turning his back on the Scots to march south. This afforded a slim chance to find out why.

'Sir, being on the move for you has deprived me of news from London. Has Parliament crushed the army rebels?'

Monck frowned. 'In London, yes. In the North, we still have to contend with that fanatical reprobate, Major General Lambert.' Monck leaned back, lowering his massive chin to stare at the tabletop, his heavy features and dark eyes retaining a pugnacious look even in repose. 'Thank you for your report, colonel. You are the most rigorous defender of Parliament under my command, which is why I sent you to assess the situation in Scotland—I knew I would get an honest report. You've convinced me that Scotland is not about to descend into chaos. England, however ...'

He paused, and Mark held his breath. Monck's most powerful characteristic was his dedication to order—in the army and in the body politic. The general had found the recent rebellion alarming: Parliament governed England with the support of its army and if factions of that army tried to supplant it, order could no longer prevail. In the early stages of the civil war, Monck had fought for the king and there were people in England at this moment who believed the only way of upholding representative government was to bring back Charles II, currently in exile. It was at least possible that Monck, seeing Parliament weak and the army in crisis, had secretly changed allegiances. Was he taking his forces south for Parliament's sake—or to persuade it to bring back the king?

But Monck did not finish his sentence: he gave an order. 'We ford the Tweed tomorrow—that is, today. You'll cross with the infantry.'

Mark, seized by a sudden dizziness, did not reply.

Monck went on ponderously, 'You'll cross with the infantry, but once over the border I want you out after Lambert. I need to know exactly where he is, and the news has been too vague. He's left Newcastle with an unknown force, heading westward. The defeat of the rebels in London has not slowed him down and he still has one ally—your Governor Lilburne in York. If Lambert aims to lurk between here and York, I need to know.'

The militia regiment of cavalry that Mark Denton commanded was in York and Governor Lilburne had requested him to return to it once he had finished Monck's commission amongst the Scots. But he would rather serve under the general—and discover his intentions.

'Sir, will you inform Governor Lilburne that I'm still under your orders?'

'I have already done so. Your information is vital, colonel—I need to know whether Lambert is a threat. You'll reconnoitre his position and his strength, then rejoin me on the march, where and when you can. I'd prefer Morpeth.'

Lambert had been in the North for some time and Monck's intelligence was excellent. Mark wondered why Monck was not relying on his usual scouts to trace the rebel general's movements. 'With respect, sir, I understood you were in correspondence with some of Lambert's officers. Is their information not enough?'

'No. Lambert's army is in confusion and leaking away from desertion. We've a host of his on this side the Tweed and we're glad to have them. Meanwhile his money's melting faster than snow. I've been parleying for weeks and I've stayed put so he doesn't have to face us, and he's been doing the same. God be thanked, we've had the weather to divide us. I'd rather not put my men in the field against their old comrades, colonel. If he's a spent force, we will let him slip away. But I need to know in which direction he goes and how many he has with him.'

'I'll find out for you as speedily as I can, sir.'

Monck rose. 'You're quartered with Colonel Knight. The house is back up the street—you'll know it by the artillery wagon outside. You've no need to report to me at six with the others. Get some sleep. The infantry moves out at nine.'

'Thank you, sir.' Mark rose, threw on his sodden cloak and bowed with a flourish of his ruined hat.

Monck's full lips were faintly smiling. 'I hope you're not reluctant to go scurrying about Northumberland for me, colonel. Is there somewhere else you'd rather be?'

Mark was too tired to prevaricate. 'I'm honoured to carry out your orders, sir. And glad to move with you to York. After that, with your leave, I'd march to London. If you go there, I'd like my men at your side.'

Monck's smile faded and the great black bars of his eyebrows drew together as he said with solemn emphasis: 'I understand you, colonel. Your aim is mine: to stand by and sustain this present Parliament.'

Mark bowed once more and left.

Furnished with a lantern by the guard, he went first to the stables and found Corporal Hales asleep in a pile of straw, under a horse blanket. One of the general's troopers, couched on a pallet in a corner, woke at once with a challenge, but Mark bade him lower his voice so as not to disturb Hales.

'What's that piled on each side of the general's door?' Mark said.

'Dung, sir.'

Mark examined his mounts; they had been brushed down and covers had been found. He went up the street to Colonel Ralph Knight's quarters and banged on the door.

Knight unbolted the door himself. Mark had last seen him in Dunbar, where Monck had given Mark his instructions for darting about Scotland. Knight was colonel of his own regiment and major of Monck's cavalry regiment. He and Mark treated each other with respect, beneath which a cautious friendship had begun to grow, but on this singular morning, courtesy was laid aside.

'Thank God,' Knight said. 'What kept you? I've been waking at every sound and cursing you until the next. I've had five minutes' sleep all night.'

'The snow,' Mark said, and stepped inside. The house was even smaller than Monck's and he found himself in a room that was kitchen, parlour and sty in one. The odour of pig emanated from an empty enclosure in the corner.

'Welcome to Coldstream,' Knight said. 'There's another room, with two apologies for beds but no fire. Have you eaten?'

Mark shook his head. 'I'd sooner sleep.' He flung his cloak over the settle by the fireplace, dropped his hat on the seat, divested himself of cavalry sword and belt and began unfastening the leather buff coat that he wore over his doublet.

Knight—a tall, well-built gentleman with tousled hair—was fully clothed. 'I'd leave the rest on.' He gestured towards the open door behind him. 'Allow me to show you the apology.'

Mark wrestled off the buff coat. 'The general claims the present Parliament needs his aid. What did he mean? Lambert and the rest might have thrown Parliament out, but it's back in power. It doesn't need Monck at all. What's he up to?'

Knight said: 'He received a dispatch yesterday. It was from Parliament—I know that much. But what it might have begged him to do, I have no idea. And nor has anyone else.'

Mark's head was buzzing, but he said evenly, 'We're marching into England today.'

'Yes. Infantry today, cavalry tomorrow.'

'Consider this: it may be that Parliament has just written to him with instructions to keep his army out of England. If we cross the Tweed tomorrow, it means that George Monck takes no orders but his own.'

He watched Knight, hoping to prompt an incautious reply, but the older man said: 'I'll be up before you—I'm sent ahead to make sure Newcastle is secure.'

'Do you have any idea what the hell is going on?'

'I know we're marching to London.'

'For what? Parliament or the return of the king?'

Knight looked genuinely shocked. 'How do you expect me to answer that?'

'You must have asked yourself the same question, surely. What is Monck playing at?'

Knight said curtly: 'We can talk of this again after I've finished in Newcastle. I counsel you to sleep on it.'

Mark looked at him with irony and after a moment Knight shrugged and turned. 'This way, colonel.'

BRUSSELS
New Year's Morning, 1660

Charles Stuart, by the grace of God King of Scotland and by heredity and ambition King of England and Ireland, woke in a warm bed and felt fingers gliding through his hair, an agreeable enough way to begin the New Year. Nearly 30 and he still had a luxuriant crown of hair—and did not have the pox, somewhat of a miracle considering the women he could at present afford to entertain. He slid an arm under the owner of the fingers and pulled her to him in mental apology; Catherine Pegge was no whore, she was the lively and willing daughter of one of his most devoted supporters in exile. She did not even deserve the name of courtesan, for he had been the first to debauch her and she showed no signs of wanting to make a career of it; she was content with him and touchingly grateful for his unspectacular presents. Keeping his eyes closed, he fondled her so lightly that she grew ticklish and giggled.

His standards had no doubt slipped during more than a decade of exile, but tupping duchesses was a kingly pleasure that he had been denied along with many another, and he was meanwhile obliged to stay in practice for his eventual queen. He sighed at the vision of her, and Cate moved to lie over him and slide her hand down his belly. From whatever corner of Europe his bride might come, her characteristics were tragically predictable: an overbred princess, a virgin—perhaps a venerable virgin kept on the shelf in expectation of a powerful match—and an innocent. Of little use to him in bed, of none at court. He groaned, and Cate began seriously to caress him.

His bride would be outmanoeuvred, as his poor mother had been when she came as France's Catholic princess to marry his father in London. Though pretty as a little picture, she had not found a way to woo the king at first. He had banished her French ladies-in-waiting and she had wept. Then the king had lost his best friend, the Duke of Buckingham, and he had wept—and when she comforted him, they fell in love. So she became the helpmeet, the confidante, the 'warrior queen' in the struggle with Parliament that had cost the king his head.

No, he did not wish to be exposed to that kind of innocence. Not yet. He concentrated on the willing flesh to hand.

Later, dressed in a doublet and breeches of French velvet, he held court to an audience of one who was a comfort to him in other ways. He had grown up with Mary Villiers, dowager Duchess of Richmond and Lennox. Ten years his senior, she was brought to court as his father's ward when a child and she and her brothers had been his companions during the war with Parliament. Sparkling, merry and airily affectionate, Mary was still an attractive woman.

Since the death of her husband James five years before, she had devoted herself to Charles's mother, Queen Henrietta-Maria, and lived at Colombes with her two young children. Although she had been lady in waiting to the queen since her youth, and married to the king's devoted cousin, Mary was never suspected by Parliament of harbouring political grudges or ambitions. Despite being a Stuart by marriage she was not considered a 'delinquent', so visits to England were not denied her.

Charles always welcomed Mary for two reasons: she cheered him; and she shared with him valuable information from royalist conspirators at home. This morning he had got rid of all attendants so they could talk alone.

He said with a smile: 'Thank you for bringing Mam's news. And the lace cravats. I've ordered some new wigs that will set them off. If I'd known you were coming here so soon, I'd have waited for you at Colombes. As it is, we've both got here before the wigs.'

'By heaven,' she said, 'you're not shaving all that beautiful hair for a wig?'

'For several, my dear.'

'I never would have thought you'd succumb so to French fashion.'

'Why not? I've got precious little else out of France and the same goes for Spain.'

Her blue eyes darkened. 'You really don't expect *anything* from Spain? What happened at the treaty talks?'

He had softened his failures when talking to his mother. With Mary he could be frank. 'I went all the way to the Pyrenees for nothing. If I'm to lay hands on more troops or funds, they won't come from France or Spain. And I'll never receive anything more from the Scots than bargains they won't keep.'

She winced, but he found he could not stop. 'My personal debt stands at around £60,000 and there's more owed to my pitiful numbers of troops. My counsellors and servants are alike unpaid—they've sold off their silver and we're down to eating off pewter and wood. We've contemplated rationing ourselves to one meal a day.'

She feigned to take this lightly. 'When does one hunt in Flanders? If this is the right season, you might dine off one wild boar a day. Would that suffice?'

'You must ask Chancellor Hyde,' he said without warmth. 'Tell, me, madam, why you are come to Brussels.'

'To see you, Your Majesty,' she said with a lovely, unperturbed smile that melted him at once. She was standing by the window that looked down on a narrow paved street, beside a table covered by a tasselled carpet. She had placed on it an object wrapped in felt which she indicated with her tapering fingers. 'I've brought you something. And I came to talk to a physician recommended to me by Sir William Harvey. I needed advice about the children—especially Esmé; his health worries me terribly. I've paid the physician a ridiculous fee to go to Colombes and see both the children. He leaves tomorrow. And when you're tired of me, I shall be off, too.'

'Please sit down.' He approached and took the chair on one side of the table as she sank gracefully into the other. 'What about Cobham? How long since you were there?'

She gave him a veiled look. He might have asked her while he was on his way through Colombes, where his mother lived, but there had been no opportunity to sound her about her infrequent visits to Cobham, the seat of her Stuart family in Kent. He made the question more personal. 'Mall, how do you get on? Whom do you see? Who are your intimates now?'

With a tiny spark of amusement in her eyes, she obliged him. They talked for an hour, of people and places dear to them both or important for other, more strategic, reasons. He relaxed. By contrast with his faithful military and political advisers, who succumbed in the worst of times to giving him false hope, Mary had always been devastatingly candid. In return he found himself explaining his diplomatic setbacks in more detail.

'So you see,' he concluded, 'abandoned as I am by every power on earth, my return to England can only be accomplished by the English.'

'No bad thing,' she said at once, looking him straight in the eye.

'I agree. What are my chances?'

She gave him a thoughtful smile. 'How does one take the pulse of a nation? I'm seldom in London, but I think I know Kent. And I'm not devoid of news from elsewhere.' She paused, smoothing the cloth package that lay in front of her. She was never entirely still. 'It's my feeling that Cromwell finally sickened the whole country of the army when he put the major-generals in every corner. To do so in a time of so-called peace offended the spirits of men and women everywhere. The major-generals are gone and so is Cromwell, but no one has forgiven them. As for parliament, it summoned the strength to murder our dear sovereign, but it has shown itself a weakling ever since. It barely holds its own against the army—the dog that it bred but cannot keep to heel.'

It was scarcely a pragmatic picture, but then Mary was a poet and alive to human feeling in a way that intrigued him. 'The counties?'

'Desire your return.'

'The City?'

'Likewise, but it's not yet ready to admit it.'

He rose. 'And *no one* is ready to act.'

'That's unfair. Only four months ago, Sir George Booth declared for you in the northwest.'

'Declared for me? He took care not to mention my name! And he was left without support, which allowed Lambert to put him to rout. Meanwhile, I was led to expect uprisings in all quarters. The Sealed Knot, the Trust, Sir John Mordaunt, convinced me to wait at Dieppe for the tide to turn. What trash. Everyone delayed and Booth was crushed. Whilst I—' he said quickly, forestalling any comment as he paced the floor, '*I was* prepared. I sounded everyone. For a time I even thought I might have Monck's ear. We dug his brother out of Devon to send to Scotland as ambassador. He's a reverend and as loyal a man as one could wish. Through him, I offered Monck £100,000.'

Mary gasped but refrained from saying '*That's £100,000 you do not have*'. 'When was this?'

'Last July. Monck was reluctant even to receive his own brother and wouldn't open my letter. But he did respond. Ambiguously. He turned down the offer but not the idea of a secret compact. Still, in the end he acted just like our so-called allies: he delayed until it was too late. He sat around in Scotland until August and Booth was left to perdition.'

Mary raised her beautifully arched eyebrows. 'You don't trust Monck?'

'I don't trust anyone.'

Her gaze fell. 'That's a pity. I come with a plea from brother George.'

He did not reply. He was rather sick of George Villiers, Duke of Buckingham. George was as charming and brilliant as his late father, who had been the bedfellow of King James I and beloved friend of Charles I, and whose assassination had brought the Villiers children to court. George seemed to have inherited all the wayward Buckingham blood. He too had fought for Charles and accompanied him into exile; however, he picked a quarrel and went back to England. His wife was none other than the daughter of Thomas Fairfax, former Lord General of Parliament's army; but George made himself unpopular with Parliament and had been locked in the Tower. He was currently free but still in bad odour.

'George is in Yorkshire,' Mary said into the frosty silence, 'and conveys his deepest homage to Your Majesty. He begs me to let you know that, placed as he is in the closest intimacy with Lord Fairfax, he means to imprint the honour and justice of Your Majesty's cause upon his lordship's heart. If Your Majesty wishes to bring a person of power to your banner, there is no stronger arm in England than that of Lord Fairfax.'

One of the spaniels began to nibble at the leather bow on Charles's right shoe and he bent, scooped it up and held the little face close to his own, saying into its soft brown eyes: 'Can you really imagine Black Tom Fairfax taking counsel from a Buckingham?'

Mary's light voice continued. 'If Fairfax is prepared to come out of retirement and gather forces from the region and secure York, then there is a chance for the rest of the North to declare for you. Do you *not* wish George to prosecute all this, in your name?'

'If, if, if and if,' Charles said pleasantly, and sat down opposite her again with the dog on his lap. 'So, what did you bring me?'

She slid it across. 'It was a gift to me from your father. A little treasure from Whitehall that he presented to me in Oxford one Christmas. You were there, and James, and little James, and George, and Prince Rupert, and we were very ruby-cheeked and jolly over mulled wine.'

He slid it from the covering and exclaimed: 'Of course I remember!'

It was a small painting by Holbein, unsigned. Unlike other Holbein masterpieces from the king's broken and dispersed collection, it was not a portrait but a view of a Dutch garden from a window. It was an unpretentious, domestic garden, such as one might create in the back yard of this house in Brussels, with fruit trees and evergreens clustered together and a path leading away around a bushy corner.

'Do with it what you will,' she said. 'Keep it and take it back to Whitehall when your day comes—it travels lightly enough. Or sell it. It occurred to me that this is just the city in which to get your best price.'

'I'll keep it. You teased my father that Christmas.' Charles put it at arm's length to keep it from the spaniel in his lap. 'You said he'd discovered it was not by Holbein after all, and so he passed it to you. You made us all laugh.'

Unfortunately his voice cracked on the last word, and that set Mary off—she was only too susceptible to emotion. They sat in silence with the painting on the table between them, looking at each other through their tears.

MARSTON MOOR
New Year's Day

Lucinda Selby hid in Wilstrop Wood after riding up to the moor in the morning, but if scouts prowling for either side came closer, there was still the risk that she might be spied amongst the thicket of bare branches, despite the camouflage of her grey cloak and the dappled hide of the mare that had brought her the seven miles from York. The mare, hating the cold, stamped a hoof now and then, puffing out uneven breaths that vanished swiftly amongst the rimed branches.

Below, between the villages of Tockwith and Long Marston, armed men milled about and riders darted back and forth across the frozen ground. Marston Moor was familiar to her, since her family's former lands were only a few miles to the west, but this mass of troops turned it into foreign territory. It looked almost as though the carapaced men had broken forth from the snow-bound earth in a mysterious eruption, released by an inhuman power. They had a purpose, but they did not yet have a direction.

Back in town, when word had reached her about these forces, she had not been able to resist coming, to witness the beginning of the end—the blessed deliverance of York. Lucinda had been two years of age when Charles I began his war with Parliament. Two years after that the largest battle on English soil had taken place on this very spot, ending in a parliamentary victory that proved a bloody harbinger of the king's downfall. Ever since, York had been a garrison for Parliament. Throughout the twenty years of her life, Lucinda had been hemmed in by troops—and it thrilled her that today, for the first time, she was looking at armed men prepared to support the royal cause. Their plan was to gather under Lord Fairfax and march to York to relieve Governor Lilburne of his command and his troops. Their real aim was more ambitious: rumour had it that Fairfax believed England's parliament should be persuaded to bring back the king.

She calculated that well over 1500 men were strung out across the shallow vale. It was impossible to pick out any commanders. She looked for George, Duke of Buckingham, seeking his dashing figure, flowing red hair and fine Barbary horse, but even in the crisp winter air, the riders were blurred by distance. The only person she had a chance of identifying was Lord Fairfax, should he consent to lead these motley forces, because he could not come on horseback; he was racked with illness and would require a coach.

It was at forbidding Marston Moor that Thomas Fairfax had fought the hardest victory of his career. This was the place where York's elite royalist infantry, the White Coats, had refused to surrender and had been smashed to the earth only a few hundred yards from where she hid. Across a rabbit warren to Lucinda's right, now buried in snow, Cromwell's Ironsides had battered their way into Prince Rupert's cavalry until long after the light had gone from the sky, and skewed the prince's army back over its own ground so that the remnants ended up streaming away in the night, Lucinda's father amongst them, leaving 4000 dead and 1500 prisoners. Marston Moor. The very name spelled the death of hope.

Then she saw it, crawling into view over the white lip of the landscape: a coach pulled by four horses and surrounded by heavy-clad cavalrymen who jostled one another on the uneven ground where hundreds of hooves had turned the deep snow into slush. The massed men below congealed into attention. Black Tom Fairfax had come, to lead them to York.

****

Lucinda returned home unseen, or at any rate unchallenged, keeping to overgrown gullies scoured by rainwater that led down off the moor, then sunken lanes bordered by hedges where country girls drove cows to pasture in spring and summer. Since childhood, when she used to ride far afield with her brother, she had been able to name the tenants and small farmers of the wide stretch of land between her family's former properties and York. Even of late, when she rode out from the city, she would greet these people as she passed, but in this harsh season there was not a soul to be seen in the fields.

There was no question of her entering the city by Micklegate, at which she would be recognised by the guards. In the long years of Parliament's rule, during which royalists had suffered dispossession, surveillance and persecution, Lucinda and her brother had conducted all their crucial business in secret. One of their father's tenant farmers, thrown off when the properties were seized by Parliament, had set up market gardens at Saint Mary Bishop and he had one or two entries through buildings set directly against the town walls. Lucinda relied on Geoffrey Paget whenever she left town, and paid him to keep her mare in a stable with the mules that pulled his carts to market.

He apologised today as he saw the mare to her stall and piled up feed. ''Tis all I can do, my lady. I maun stay within the walls, now. York's to be sealed up and the curfew kept and there'll be nowt on the streets but troops until this bout's over.'

Lucinda nodded, pulled her hood about her face and followed him through the smallholdings that led towards the river. When they neared prosperous Middle Street, which joined York's one bridge across the Ouse river, she paused to take leave of Geoffrey. It was not yet three o'clock but already the winter sun had deserted the rooftops and darkness had gathered at the ends of the street, which was flanked by tall houses and places of business.

'Shall I escort you home, my lady?' Geoffrey asked, his face creased with anxiety.

'Thank you, but it's safer if we part. If a guard shouts at me to get along indoors I'll be very happy to oblige him. Take this until we meet again.' She slipped double the usual coins into his hand.

His fingers closed around them. 'Can you tell me, my lady ... does Lord Fairfax come?'

It should not trouble her that he had guessed where she had been. If she could not trust Geoffrey Paget, she must cease to trust anyone. 'I believe so.'

'God be praised,' he said, then ducked his head to her and hurried away.

The Selby townhouse was in the Coppergate, one of the principal streets just across the bridge, so Lucinda had not far to go, but the town as it cloaked itself in dusk offered no welcome. Business and houses were shuttered. There were few carts or tradesmen's benches outside the shopfronts and the only people she saw were householders darting out to bring possessions indoors. She met no one on Middle Street nor was she challenged by guards as she crossed the bridge.

She walked briskly along the Coppergate and knocked at the front door of the Selby house. The servant, Edward Bird, opened it to her a second later and with an apology slammed it to when she was scarcely inside. His nervousness touched her on the raw.

'Is everyone here?'

'Yes, my lady.' Bird's eyes were wide and his mane of hair, always untidy, seemed to stand up in alarm.

'You will tell them there is no cause for panic,' she said. 'No one is to leave the house. If anyone comes to the door you'll find out politely who they are and come and let me or Sir Maurice know. Do you have any questions?'

Bird stretched out his hand: 'May I take your cloak, my lady?'

'Thank you.' She shrugged it off and put it over his arm. 'And please set some more light upon the stairs; we needn't live like moles just because York stands at siege.'

'Siege?' the servant breathed.

Suddenly, she smiled at him. 'Be of good cheer, Bird. Whatever comes, any change must be for the better.' She ran up the stairs.

When she entered the great chamber she found her brother where she had left him, before a fire piled in the marble-mantled hearth, but he was not dozing; his high-coloured face beneath the burnished fair hair was contorted with anger. 'You broke your promise! Gone hours, without telling me.'

She came to a stop in the middle of the room. 'You were asleep and I didn't want to wake you. I'm sorry you've been anxious.'

He struggled to his feet, grimaced and had to support his weight on the back of the chair as he examined her—the hair escaping from the knot at the back of her head, the sodden hems of her riding dress, the stockings slashed at the ankles by briars. 'By heaven, I knew it: you went to Marston.' Only then did he notice how she shivered. 'Come to the fire.'

She obeyed and stood facing him. 'I hoped you'd be glad to hear the truth, one way or the other. Fairfax is bringing an army. I saw them. They're coming.'

At that moment an alarm bell began tolling at the Minster and within seconds it was echoed by others across the town.

Maurice reached out and took her hand, then let it go. 'Did they see you? By God, you're cold.'

She shook her head, then crouched on her knees, dropped her gloves on the rug and held her palms towards the flames. The news she brought back made up for everything; it would teach them both to live again.

Maurice had known nothing but injury and failure ever since the royalist uprising in the west was crushed four months before.

'There are nearly 2000 of them. Not enough to take the city by assault, but no mean threat. Lilburne must parley the moment they appear at the gates.'

His frown admonished her for treating him to a military lecture. She smiled. 'It's exactly what you hoped for. If you were fit, wouldn't you join them?'

'Fairfax? You have a strange idea of my honour if you can imagine me at that man's side, crippled or whole.' But he sat down again and stared into the fire. When she put her hand on his knee he cupped it briefly and said, 'Reckless! You need wine and food—ring for them and then come back here. Where I can see you.'

She sprang up to do so, then returned to the other chair by the hearth. As they spoke, warmth began to return to her body. She loved Maurice too much to be at odds with him. Since the death of their mother, when she was eight and he was ten, her brother had had a special care of her. After the battle at Marston Moor their father had tried to defend Selby Manor against a parliamentarian raid, but he was taken prisoner and all his lands were confiscated. Sir John Selby's health had been undermined by his imprisonment and when he died in the York townhouse after his release, Maurice and Lucinda had had no one to depend on but each other.

They had gone through a dangerous period after Maurice had ridden in secret across the country to join the doomed royalist uprising near Chester. He was seriously wounded and escaped with his life only through a daring rescue by an unknown king's man who had had him spirited back to York. Disillusioned by the crushing of Sir George Booth's rebellion, unable to show himself in York in case the governor guessed that he had been injured there, Maurice felt helpless in confinement.

'Maurice,' she said, 'only think. In a few days' time you may be able to walk free. No need for concealment. Fairfax will control the city and he brings royalists with him. Whether he's for the king or not, his allies are.'

He reached over the small table between them to pour more wine into his glass. 'Perhaps you're right.' He raised the glass, his eyes lighting up. 'A Fairfax!'

She raised her own. 'The Lord Fairfax, and may he prosper. I wonder what he really intends.'

'Luce, he has been ill for years. He's laid low by gout and the stone. What else would bring him out of retirement but a complete change of heart? He's sickened by ruin and chaos and wants the return of the king.'

'I grant you he's sickened,' she said with an ironical smile. 'He must despise Lilburne for collaborating with the rebels. If Fairfax wants to take over York, it's in the name of the army he once led. But is he really doing this for the king?'

Maurice was silent for a moment. Watching the heat come and go in his sister's flawless cheeks, seeing the flashes of hope in her blue eyes, was like catching himself in a mirror that had shattered four months before. For the rest, she was his opposite: her hair as black as his was fair; her lips as red and pliant as if she had just been kissing someone instead of riding about the countryside; her body slim and graceful, even in the worn garments she had piled on against the cold. He had tasted the dregs of life over the past months—and she with him.

At last he replied: 'If Fairfax takes York, then I think we'll go forth with the rest of the city and see what he has to say.'

He got up and went to the windows to draw curtains against the cold and to muffle the frenzied tolling of the bells. He fancied that he had managed to cross the room without showing any sign of the constant ache in his right leg. He was nearly whole again, because of Lucinda and through the help of a mysterious rider who had lifted him half-conscious from the bloody aftermath of Booth's defeat.

It was as though she caught the idea from him. 'I wonder if the King's Shadow rides with Fairfax? He is a king's man, after all. And a northerner, judging by his field of action.'

'Not everyone is ready to trumpet their allegiance so soon. Was the Duke of Buckingham on the moor today? I'll wager he wasn't.'

'I didn't see him.' Then she said, with a blush perhaps caused by the fire: 'Have you ever thought that he might be the Shadow?'

He laughed. 'George Villiers? Ye Gods. I'm sorry to disappoint you, Luce, but no. The Shadow is taller—even I could see that, though I caught precious little else in my state. I'd more easily recognise his horse—a big grey brute. The man's reputed to be over 6ft, as lofty as Charles Stuart, and wears black hair past the shoulders—which is why he's called the King's Shadow, my dear. Ten to one it's a wig. Combine it with the mask and he could be anyone beneath—except George Villiers.'

'His voice? How does he speak, Yorkshire or southern?'

'I didn't hear much—he uttered a dozen words in as many miles. He left me at a safe farmhouse that might have been at Bate Heath or Bucklow Hill; I've no more idea than a babe in arms. From there he has clandestine connections right across the Pennines or he'd never have got me conveyed here in one piece. A man like that does not come out in the open for a trifle.' He gave her a teasing smile. 'Not even for you.'

THE PICTS' WALL
January 2

Over the last few miles Mark tracked Lambert alone. It was after dusk and therefore not easy, but it was the way he preferred it. As a boy, running through the dales after game or as a young soldier scouting for the advance guard before battle, he had been most alert and alive in that crisp instant of decision when, alone at a crucial spot, he searched all the evidence for his right direction. It was this self-sufficiency, this confidence in his own dangerous choices, that had propelled Mark to command in the army. He relied on it now to prompt him along a path towards farm buildings perched at the head of a shallow dale, a few miles from the Picts' Wall.

Yesterday morning he had thought that searching for Lambert would be like chasing a feather in the wind, but Monck had given him a little more information. The general admitted, to Mark's inward surprise, that he had been in communication with Lord Fairfax for some time. About what, he did not say.

Mark had said, testing: 'My first thought, sir, was that Lambert might move south, to reinforce Governor Lilburne at York. But only if he has enough men.'

'And if he hasn't, colonel, he'd do well to stay out of our way. So you'll direct yourself southwest, if you please, keeping parallel with the border. We may depend upon it Lambert won't cross into Scotland, and if he seeks a ship to take him out of England altogether he must go into Cumberland. Don't lose him.'

I've not found him yet, Mark had thought grimly. But he was fiercely gratified to have the task. Proving himself once again to Monck might ensure that he could take his militia regiment all the way to London.

Monck said, 'You'll rejoin me at once and tell me where he is and how many he has with him. You know him; no one could give me clearer picture.'

The picture that Mark could see as he approached the farm had the eerie stillness endowed by moonlight. The leafless hedges on either side stood out like black, open basketwork on the white fields. The low byres, stables and barns around the farmhouse were hunched against the slopes, softened into their winter shapes by drifts of snow. Mark was familiar with the place and knew that its humble appearance was deceptive, for there was ample accommodation behind its thick stone walls for man as well as beast. Farmer Gerrold's sheep had long been brought in from the folds to join the cows, poultry and pigs in the barns, but alongside the animals were warm corners where fugitive troopers might lie down for the night, leaving just a few comrades awake in the cold to watch against strangers.

Mark had traced Lambert across country by dint of hard riding and soft questioning. At a place called Haltwhistle he had left Corporal Hales with the other horses and spurred his black stallion northwest, close enough behind Lambert's force now to spy the marks of his passing. If that force were holed up in Gerrold Farm they were mighty quiet about it—but quiet they had cause to be.

On approach, there had been no point in trying to leave the beaten track and scout on foot to detect how many might be hiding there for the night. For more than a month, snow had blanketed the north of England. The drifts were too deep for reconnaissance across country except on the most frequently used thoroughfares and the track to Gerrold's was not one of them. The body of riders that had trodden it down into this state must number at least 20.

Mark whistled as he went with a sound that, as he neared the farm gates, reverberated jauntily off the dark walls of two barns that flanked the big yard. It was a signal that over the years he had employed with Gerrold and a select number of farmers in the region—a tune called 'The Jovial Crew' or 'A Beggar, a beggar, a beggar I'll be'. He had convinced them that if he came alone he was a beggar for intelligence only and not worth a bullet in the head as he rode near. They all had their own allegiances, which he was careful not to inquire after too closely. So far none had seen fit to publicly mistrust his own.

He remained in the saddle, his horse fidgeting, eager to be moving again.

Gerrold took his time. In silence, Mark watched him clump over the yard, a thick-clad form in calf boots and nightcap with lantern swinging in one mittened hand. When the farmer got to the gate, he raised the lantern and examined Mark, the light glancing off a jaw like flint and catching a spark in each deeply sunken eye.

Neither spoke. Indeed, there was not a great deal to be said. If Lambert had only twenty men with him, he was a spent force—at least in the North. And Gerrold would have his own reasons for telling the troopers to keep their heads down and their mouths shut.

At last Gerrold said; 'How goes it, colonel? I've not seen 'ee these past months.'

'No cause. Until tonight.'

'You're alone?' Gerrold shot a look down the track behind Mark but he already knew the answer to his own question. His dogs had heralded Mark's coming ten minutes before but Mark had noted that Gerrold had been able to stop their barking almost at once. This would have told the farmer that there was no danger; if troops had been gathering to surround the farm, the animals would have gone wild.

Mark said nothing. The glow from the lantern, hazy in the moist, cold air, obscured his view of the yard and outbuildings. He glimpsed a faint light from a chink by the farmhouse window and no other. There was something unnatural about the hush that extended over the courtyard from the barns full of slumbering beasts. There were men there, too, eyes wide open, staring into the dark; or sighting along a musket barrel that pointed straight at his head, around which Gerrold's lantern shed a convenient halo.

He had to assume that they would fire only on Lambert's orders.

But was Lambert with them?

He glanced to his left where in daylight and better weather one could see a path made by Gerrold's flocks leading around the homestead and onto higher ground that stretched towards the Wall across heathland, scrub and patches of good pasture. Tonight the way looked smooth— almost. The horsemen had certainly not ridden on. Or not *en masse*.

'Aye,' Mark said at last. 'Passing through.'

Gerrold, relieved not to be ordered to open his gate, allowed himself a small grimace that in other circumstances would have been a smile.

Mark's glance flicked to the top of the slope. 'What's the going like up there?'

'Solitary.' Gerrold stepped back and the lantern swung to his side. The two men might not be overheard but the farmer could not risk the appearance of giving the visitor information.

'I'll not stop,' Mark said, his voice deep and clear against the stone walls. 'Tarltons' is not far to go. I bid you goodnight.' He pulled the stallion away before Gerrold had time to complete his farewell.

In snow that came up to the horse's knees, Mark had to find the path up the slope by memory and clouds were sliding across the moon, so it took some time to get out of range of pistol, then carbine and finally musket. The suspense was unpleasant but he had no choice. If there were marksmen observing him he might have been recognised, having served under John Lambert for several years. If they were locals it was even more likely. As a militia colonel during the rule of Cromwell's major-generals, Mark had been the most effective commissioner in the North, a scourge to seditious royalists and ruthless in the application of order. He and his troops had penetrated to every corner of the region and where he was known he was feared. Those who had seen his former dedication to Lambert would find it hard to believe that he was in the hunt for him now. Those who had watched him pass many a time along the byways of the West Country would be prepared to credit that for some disciplinary reason he was on his way to the Tarltons' property.

Gerrold's one proffered clue—'solitary'—convinced Mark that Lambert was ahead and alone. The general would not go near the Tarltons, a royalist family. There was just one place of shelter ahead: a sheepfold a few miles across the upland, formed by the remains of an ancient guardhouse that straddled the great wall the Romans had built across England. Mark was intrigued. There was no particular reason why Lambert should relish spending the night cramped in the farmhouse with the numerous family, but still it was hard to imagine a good excuse for his bivouacking in a ruin. Unless he needed time alone to think—which hinted at an unquiet mind.

Mark's black stallion picked its way across the upland. The moon came out once more and played over an almost featureless scene. The turf beneath a covering of fresh snow was patched here and there with soft mounds that indicated heath or bracken. The snow must have been scattered across the grass by a sharp wind, for it had collected only ankle deep.

The terrain was the same all the way to the Wall and Mark would have no chance of concealment as he got near it. The faint tracks of a single horse across the land told him that Lambert was near.

It was vital to the security of Monck's army that he assess Lambert's intentions but he was not looking forward to the meeting—he had thought too highly of John Lambert in the past.

As a lad of fifteen, searching for something to believe in, Mark had joined the Model Army on the day when his father died at Marston Moor. He had loved his father and in his grief he had taken up his father's cause. He was the eldest son but he left the running of the family lands, at Denton Moor and in Swaledale, to his mother and his younger brothers, whom he seldom saw. The army became his home, and its purpose—the defence of parliament—became his religion. He looked for guidance from its leaders, learning what he could from those he most admired. But such worship could not outlive certain experiences. Mark had adored his father, and his father had been killed. He had found another mentor, Thomas Fairfax, and had watched him step down and hand the fruits of victory to Oliver Cromwell. It was Cromwell who had cut off the bargaining over the fate of Charles I, brought the king to execution and fought to discipline Parliament into forming a sound government for England. In that last mighty task, Cromwell had had Mark's allegiance.

Mark had served high commanders like John Lambert with a determination and flair that had made him colonel of a cavalry regiment at 21. And yet his system of belief had gradually crumbled. It was in 1653, when Oliver Cromwell accepted the office of Lord Protector and put himself above Parliament, that Mark Denton made a cruel admission to himself: the army was not the sacred cause he had willed it to be. In fact he sensed that it had not even done its worst yet.

This conclusion had hurt, and still did, because his belief had been passionate and nothing had come to take its place. Mark's mission from Monck made him willing to undertake this encounter with Lambert but his heart shrank as he rode towards it. He had only to think back to one battle amongst the many that he had fought under Lambert—the crushing victory over Charles Stuart at Worcester in 1651—to remember his brilliance as a leader, his skills as a strategist and his relentless courage. But Lambert had been pushed off the public stage by Cromwell and now he had joined the ill-prepared rebellion against Parliament. Lambert wanted England to become a military dictatorship again—but he had failed. And Mark did not wish to see a failure; he would rather see the Lambert he remembered.

He rode over a gentle curve of the land and the mile-castle came into view. He at once wheeled the horse back out of sight and dismounted. He had expected to be seen but there was no point in exposing his mount.

He undid the roll behind the saddle and shook out the horse cover, murmuring reassurance as he flung it over the stallion's back, across the holsters that held carbine and pistol. Armed only with his sword, he strode up the incline and paused at the top to examine Lambert's position little more than a hundred yards away.

The Picts' Wall at this point was a low line across the landscape just one or two stones high, but the cylindrical mile-castle built across this line was still recognisable as a Roman sentry post. It had once had an upper storey but most of the turrets and one section of its rounded wall had collapsed centuries before. The rest stood high and solid, however, and provided good shelter.

It looked lonely under the moonlight but Mark caught the momentary red glow of a fire, obscured by rubble at ground level but reflecting off the stonework above—then scattered by whoever hid within. He surveyed the scene. There was no sign of Lambert's horse, which would be behind the ruin or more likely inside it. No creature stirred on either side of the Wall—not even a tree grew up here and none of the outcrops of rock were high enough to give a man cover.

He and Lambert were within shouting distance and also well within range of each other, supposing Lambert had a firearm.

'General! I am Colonel Mark Denton, militia colonel under Governor Robert Lilburne, and I come alone. You have my word, my men are at York. Will you parley, sir?'

Silence. Lambert was either bedded down asleep or awake and angry, for he would know why he had been tracked into the West Riding. All at once, Mark was angry too.

He drew his sword and raised it. 'You'll come out unarmed and meet me or I come in with this. Your choice.'

Silence again. Mark had time to picture the crack of flame from a carbine in the darkness, then saw movement within the ragged fissure in the Roman keep. Next moment a figure walked out onto the glistening snow—Lambert, wearing a cavalry helmet and carrying a sword.

Mark shifted his grip on his weapon and plunged it into the ground so that it stood erect. 'May I approach?'

Lambert took three paces further away from the keep, did the same with his sword, and without a word went back to stand at the entrance.

Mark walked forward. His mind went blank as he strode across the snow, which gave him a certain relief. It was too late to calculate all the risks yet again; he must make of this meeting what he could.

Mark paused six paces from Lambert, removed his wide-brimmed hat and made a deep bow. When he straightened, Lambert in turn removed his helmet and gave a curt nod. The cold at once began to freeze the top of Mark's head, but he thought better of replacing the hat in case Lambert took offence. It had a metal cap called a 'secret' inserted in the felt crown, and with this and a muffler wound so high it covered his ears, he had been able to endure the freezing two-day expedition in search of the man who stood before him.

Without the helmet Lambert looked vulnerable, his soft dark curls crushed to his scalp above the high forehead and his eyes narrowed against the biting cold. A drop of moisture glistened at the tip of the long nose and the full lips were pinched. The voice, however, was as rounded and authoritative as always. 'Whatever you're after, colonel, it's not worth standing about in the cold for. You'll oblige me by mending the fire.'

The two men walked into the shelter together. It was an ample circular space and the stones of its foundations were silted over with 16 centuries of dirt. Lambert's horse, with a nosebag hanging from the halter, stood at the far wall with its ears laid back and nostrils flaring. Of a touchy temperament, Mark thought, like its master. There were hurdles stacked against the wall, to be pulled across the entrance when a flock needed to be kept in. There were no sheep tonight but they had left behind abundant traces from which the fire released a sharp odour.

Lambert must have been resting on an unrolled pack near the fire which at present was a scattering of glowing fragments and ash. His other weapons—a dagger and a carbine—were partly concealed beneath the end of the roll; Mark could see the butt of the gun and the point of a sheath winking in the light of the embers.

He took it all in with one glance before bending to pick up a dry branch from a pile of wood at the rear of the building, avoiding the horse's back legs. With Lambert watching him from just inside the entrance, he scraped the embers together with one end of the branch then cracked it over his knee to add it to the flames that darted up. He went back to the pile to find shorter pieces and crouched to lean them in a pyramid against the other two.

Lambert said: 'You may sit, colonel,' and lowered himself onto the pack roll, where he sat with one knee drawn up and his hands clasped about it.

Mark scraped away sheep droppings with his boot then kicked across a short log that he found next to the pile. The farmer had gone to some trouble to keep up the supply of firewood: trees were rare on the upland, so it must come from coppices in the dales. The nearest forests were over the river Irthing, in Scotland, around Wiley Sike, and a little further north was the vast green wilderness of Spadeadam—no safe hiding place for a general who had beaten the Scots time and again on their own soil.

It was Lambert who asked the first question, in his confident manner. 'Your regiment's in York—why aren't you?'

'I was ordered north, sir.'

'Not by Lilburne! He informs me that you've served him well. But he must be wondering about your loyalties now.'

The statement was dispassionate but Mark stayed on guard, as he always had with Lambert, a man in whom the impulses of thought and feeling moved rapidly, making him a commander of spirit and a very unfortunate man to cross.

'I serve the Governor of York, sir, whoever he may be. If you must know, I was loath to part from my regiment and would rather return to it.'

'Meanwhile you're taking your orders from Monck. And Monck wants to know where I am and what I'm about. What will you say to him, colonel?'

Mark could not help smiling. 'At present I've little to tell. Except that I'd wager you have no thought of entering Scotland.'

'And that's where you've been the last few weeks, I hear. I'll say this for Monck, he knows how to treat the Scots. When you and I were there with him it was with the edge of the sword. What does he expect to achieve by turning his back on them?'

'I don't know,' Mark said truthfully.

Lambert raised his haughtily arched eyebrows, but Mark could tell he believed the statement. It was better to be honest with Lambert. Opinionated and rash himself, he deeply mistrusted men who concealed too much and he took silence, sullenness, stupidity or caution for hypocrisy and deceit. The rather dour piety of Cromwell used to annoy Lambert and so did the Christian humility of Thomas Fairfax: he had preferred their company in battle, when both men turned into demons.

'At this point you appear to know a deal more about me than I do about you, sir,' Mark said.

Lambert shook his head. 'By no means, colonel. When we last saw each other, I had you as Cromwell's man, through and through. But you've lately become Lilburne's man. Until you find out what Monck's up to and then perhaps you'll become Monck's?' There was the faintest sneer on the general's full lips but Mark told himself not to be goaded. Better to foster Lambert's sense of superiority.

'The Council of the North still sits in York, sir, and it ratified Robert Lilburne as Governor after Cromwell died and the Protectorate collapsed. Lilburne in turn confirmed me as colonel of my regiment and there was no change to the officers under my command. My mission in Yorkshire has changed not a whit and neither have my troops. We uphold peace, the law and the pursuit of traitorous royalists. Have you considered joining your forces to Lilburne's?'

Lambert's eyes narrowed. 'Before Monck gets to York? Is there time?' He was suspicious but could not help asking: 'Where is Monck?'

'The infantry crossed the Tweed yesterday morning before dawn. The cavalry and artillery followed. In these conditions, I'd be surprised if they've even got as far as Wooler. And no one travels as fast as you, sir, when you've a will—snow or no snow.'

Lambert suddenly got to his feet, startling his horse. Glancing up at him, Mark could see extreme tiredness in his face and his stance. There was not a scrap of food about and no flask. Had the man eaten tonight, before riding out to this strange vigil over a solitary fire?

'You're forgetting Fairfax,' Lambert said.

'What about him?' Mark cursed Monck inwardly for giving him no chance to talk to anyone except Ralph Knight in the hours between his arrival from Scotland and the fording of the Tweed. He was lacking good information on almost everything that pertained to Monck's move into England.

Lambert said. 'Surely you know Lilburne sent to arrest Fairfax at his home after Christmas? But he'd flown westwards. With as many as he could muster.'

'What is he mounting, an armed demonstration against Lilburne?'

'And myself!'

'What will you do, then, confront him?'

Lambert was roused but not enough to respond to that question. He posed another. 'Why? What would you do in my situation, colonel?'

'Join up with Lilburne as soon as may be.'

Lambert snorted and was about to come out with a retort but hesitated, looking sidelong at Mark. 'Where would *you* like to be at this moment?'

'York, sir.'

It was a truthful statement, and once again Lambert knew it. 'Is York so important to you?'

'It's always been worth having and holding. All through the wars. The key to the North.'

Lambert knew that, for he was a northerner too, born and bred in the Dales. Mark saw a change in his drawn face, a flash of emotion, then the dark eyes were veiled and the lips compressed. He said: 'On your feet, colonel.' As Mark rose he said: 'If I dismiss you now, with a message to Lilburne, will you carry it?'

It took a mere instant for Mark to weigh this up. 'I will, sir.'

Lambert gave a curious grimace, both bitter and elated. 'So be it. Tell him: "True opener of my eyes, prime angel blessed, much better seems this vision and more hope of peaceful days portends than those two past."'

The words meant nothing to Mark, but he asked Lambert to repeat them, then said them back, bowed, and replaced his hat.

Lambert said: 'Farewell. What will you tell General Monck?'

'That I know as little about your intentions as I do about his.'

Lambert laughed, not at Mark but up at the moon, which shed a slanting beam across the general's cheek and shoulder. It gave his face a lurid, ungoverned aspect. There was something wild about the man tonight that put him in tune with this deserted place and unseasonal endeavour.

When Lambert let him go without further comment, Mark did not retrace his path by Gerrold's farm. He picked his way across the southern reaches of Thirlwell Common and headed down towards Haltwhistle through an area called Vallum.

He knew several telling facts. For one, Lambert was no longer a threat to Monck's march. Suspicious of Mark's idea that he might rejoin and reinforce Lilburne, he had declined to be cozened and would continue west and south. Lambert knew his forces were as nothing against Fairfax's, so he would not risk confronting them on the way.

The interview at the fireside had not driven the ache from Mark's bones and now the cold closed in further. It seemed to slice through to his brain, exposing it to the silver blades of moonlight. Lambert was close to unhinged, but in this exalted state he was even more intrepid, more dangerous, than in the moments before his greatest victories. Instinct told Mark that he was on his way back to London, with the men he had hidden at Gerrold's farm.

Lambert was determined to oppose Monck at the place where everything counted, the field where the battle for supremacy over the English people would come to a close. He would get to London before Monck.

Cursing the high-piled snow as he approached Haltwhistle, Mark felt an odd stab of sympathy for Lambert. He even wished that the whole issue could be simpler, cleaner, more honourable. But there was nothing simple about any of it. Except that he was determined to reach London too.

YORK
January 2

The invitation came late on the evening of Lord Fairfax's entry into York, and Lucinda was even more eager than Maurice to accept.

'Why not Fairfax House?' Maurice said. 'Why should Sir Philip play the host?'

Lucinda was debating which gown to wear to this event, a concern of more importance than his. 'Fairfax House! Where his lordship has not set foot in years? It won't be breathable, let alone habitable. Sir Philip is the perfect gentleman to welcome Fairfax. After creating such a spectacle in the Minster, he can scarce do less.'

Sir Philip Monckton, an influential royalist, had gone to York Minster the day before and when the town alarms began to ring had summoned citizens into the cathedral and urged them to set up a clamour to rival the bells: 'A Fairfax, a Fairfax! Fairfax and a free Parliament!' Governor Lilburne meanwhile had been preoccupied by the problem that Fairfax's 1800-strong army was drawn up before Micklegate bar. Pressed on all sides, only too well aware that he had lost control of the citizenry and his troops, Lilburne had opened the gates. Fairfax entered in triumph, Lilburne was governor no more, and the whole garrison went over to Fairfax.

'We must find out whether Fairfax is for the king,' Lucinda said. 'It's all that matters.'

She noticed that Maurice glanced in a nearby mirror, which meant he cared as much about how he looked tonight as she did. He said: 'He may take an age if he likes, working out where everyone stands. If he asks royalists to put all our heads above the parapet at once, we'd best be wary—he has the power to slice them off at one blow.'

'Tonight will all be fulsome greetings and mutual congratulations. You don't think we're capable of mouthing platitudes like everyone else?'

'No!' Maurice smiled. 'At least not you, Luce. There's many a time I've wished you kept a more deceitful tongue in your head.'

Lucinda was in too happy a mood not to see the justice of this. 'Very well, I shall do nothing but drink, eat and smile. In return you may tell me whether I should do so in the blue gown or the rose madder.'

Maurice's smile faded. Their lack of income shamed him, its worst aspect being that he could not help Lucinda to the future she deserved. The Selby coffers could furnish no dowry, thus he had no worthy husband in prospect for her, and her manner of living was cramped and shabby to the point where she had only two gowns fit for important occasions.

'The blue,' he said, 'and Mama's pearls.'

She agreed but did not wear all the ropes of pearls. She had her maid thread the narrowest strand through her black hair and wore no other ornament.

Maurice, handing her into the sedan chair, raised his eyebrows quizzically but she could see that he approved her looks, and without a word he mounted up to accompany her. It was the first time he had left the house for over four months and the short ride to Sir Philip Monckton's would cause him pain. She reminded herself not to stay long if he was suffering.

The great chamber upstairs in the town house was warm, colourful and crowded when Lucinda and Maurice were shown in. There were upwards of 30 guests already, men and women alike exquisitely dressed. The atmosphere was expectant, but as Lucinda received a greeting from Sir Philip and his lady and went on to talk to other acquaintance, she saw that the dismissal of Lilburne would provide no excuse for glee. York had changed hands but the author of the transfer, seated near the fireplace, had a sombre dignity that reminded everyone how the rest of England was governed—by a Puritan regime that had outlawed religious and public festivities and frowned on private ones.

She was not afraid to approach Fairfax. They were distantly connected by marriage: Lord Fairfax's sister Ellen had married Sir William Selby, a second cousin of Lucinda's father. In his younger days Fairfax had moreover been friendly with her father, who was a scholar, and both had made a study of the sermons given in the region around York by pastors and lay preachers renowned for their strong congregational spirit. Thomas was also a writer and translator from the Latin. On a Sunday he and Lucinda's father might travel far to hear a sermon and discuss it afterwards—and if they disagreed, as they did more often than not, it was with relish. They had exchanged books from their libraries, shared sincere protestant beliefs and had worked hard to temper religious factionalism in Yorkshire. The Civil War had driven the two men apart but even the horror of the king's execution had not obliterated her father's memories of Fairfax when he used to be a man of peace and justice.

'He's just written about the king's murder,' her father had said once, leaning his head on one hand and looking down at a pamphlet that lay on his desk. 'He says: "My afflicted and troubled mind for it, and my earnest endeavours to prevent it, will, I hope, sufficiently testify my abhorrence of the act."'

'Do you believe him?' the nine-year-old Lucinda had asked.

Her father had looked at her in sorrow. 'I believe in his penitence. He has also written a poem claiming that if the divine power permitted the king's execution, then we must accept God's will. But can anything be proven, one way or the other, with a poem? Only a court of law could have convicted the king, and parliament is not a court of law.'

As she walked over to Fairfax, Lucinda reflected that she really had only her own father's comments by which to judge him: as a man who had betrayed his own nature by taking up parliament's cause. But her father was gone and events since had given her no easy way to interpret Lord Fairfax.

He noticed her at once and rose from his seat, his hooded eyes widening with pleased recognition. He was lean and stooped and his bow was stiff but this was because of the gout that riddled his frame: he was smiling beneath the pendulous nose and moustache. 'My lady, I see you so little and each time I regret it a little more. You never cease to grow in beauty.'

'And you speak as you ever did: like a poet, my lord. Do you remember when you used to exchange verses with my father?'

He gestured to the stool placed near his chair of honour. 'Pray sit with me, if you will. To be sure I remember, though I would rather not recall my own. Your father translated Virgil and I Vegetius. He possessed the better taste.'

She sat down. 'But you still write, my lord.'

He looked at his hands. He was of a swarthy complexion and illness had yellowed it. His hands were as Lucinda remembered them: long, fine-fingered and beautiful. She had always found it hard to imagine them wielding a sword. He murmured: 'One of the few pleasures left to me. That, and my gardens.'

'Then what brings us the pleasure of your presence in York?' she asked sweetly.

'I wish to ensure the free passage of General Monck to London.' He gave her a shrewd look. 'He has been invited thence by Parliament and it is not the business of this garrison to impede his progress. I'm here to welcome him, and on his departure appoint Sir Charles, my uncle, as governor. You remember him, I think?'

Lucinda nodded and looked around. 'Is he here this evening?'

'No—on the road. He commands one of General Monck's infantry regiments. But there's another absent friend who wishes to be remembered to you. My son-in-law, the Duke of Buckingham. I judged it best that he not ride with us yesterday.'

Lucinda was amused. 'I can imagine how he must have felt about that! How does he fare? And the duchess?'

He looked up and beyond her; others were approaching. 'They're both excellent well.'

'I saw them a month or two ago, at a friend's. Do they live still with you at Nun Appleton?'

He rose painfully to greet the guests who stood behind her. 'They do. I confess, the older I grow, the happier I am to have my family around me. I regret your father, my lady. But I like to think of one consolation: you and your brother were with him until the end.'

She rose without reply, he bowed over her hand and she had no choice but to accept the kind dismissal.

Before supper she drifted over to an alcove where Maurice was talking to their friend Andrew Castlemaine. Castlemaine's stocky figure partly obscured Maurice, who was on a long cushioned chest beneath the window; her brother must already be in pain from putting weight on the injured leg. She greeted Castlemaine and sat down by Maurice.

'Did he say anything?' Maurice asked. He and Castlemaine planned to tackle Fairfax after supper and build on whatever she had extracted from him.

She smiled, keeping her voice low. 'Not much, though he was very sentimental about father.' Maurice gave a snort but she carried on, 'He did tell me he's commanded the Duke of Buckingham to cool his heels at home.'

'Aha,' said Castlemaine, 'so that's why we don't see your favourite here tonight.'

'Exactly,' she said, declining to be teased about Buckingham, who was always very playful with her. 'Lord Fairfax doesn't want firebrands around him just now. I think that's why we were invited—to see how we comport ourselves. If I want to be welcomed to Fairfax House, I've just received a gentle warning to guard my tongue.'

Maurice's cheeks were burning and he said impatiently, 'Then who is he *for*, or are we never to know?'

'At present, he's all for General Monck.'

Castlemaine said: 'I saw Mordaunt the other day and he—'

'Where?' said Lucinda at once. Sir John Mordaunt was a spy and courier for the king, and passed regularly from Brussels and back, but since the disaster led by Sir George Booth she had had no news of him.

Castlemaine gave her a rueful smile. 'My lady, the fewer the people who know that, the better.' He spoke very quietly. 'Mordaunt told me the king has been offering prodigious prizes to Monck and Fairfax over the last few months. Separately, they've turned him down. But they're colluding together, nonetheless. Yesterday was no coincidence. Monck sent to Fairfax before Christmas and they came to an agreement. Whenever Monck started his march to London, Fairfax promised to take York on the same day.'

Lucinda said: 'How does Mordaunt read Monck? Why is he going to London?'

'At the invitation of Parliament,' Maurice said. 'To rid them of the rebels.'

Castlemaine said: 'But Parliament is safe. Sir Arthur Haselrig brought enough troops into London to rout them. Mordaunt told me, their leader crumpled on Christmas Eve. In floods of tears.'

'Haselrig did it?' Lucinda said, and her heart fell. 'The republican?'

'The same. So Parliament sent to Monck thanking him for his offer of assistance and politely demanding that he stay in Scotland. What do you think to that?'

'Well, if he's bound for London,' Maurice said eagerly, 'it can't be for Parliament's sake!'

'It might be.' Castlemaine looked down at his friend with sympathy. 'He might wish to stiffen their sinews and force them to write a constitution as Cromwell tried to do. Monck was Oliver Cromwell's protégé.'

'But Monck fought for the king when he was younger,' Lucinda said. 'He was put in the Tower for it. His whole family is royalist.'

'Including his wife, they say,' Castlemaine agreed. 'No one can guess what Monck is up to. Sir John Mordaunt confessed to me plain, he has no more idea of what's festering inside that black head than the greatest booby alive.'

'In that case,' Lucinda said, 'we'll get nothing out of Lord Fairfax tonight. I'll have to steel myself to eat, drink and be merry.' She turned to Maurice. 'The world is going upside down and us with it. But as long as the wheel keeps moving, it may turn for the king.'

****

George Villiers, Duke of Buckingham, supped that evening almost in silence, while he thought about land. There was little cause to open his mouth as the only other person at table was his wife, Mary, and it was to obtain access to his land that he had married her, a motive of which she was perhaps aware, though it did not matter, since she was still in love with him.

After the king's defeat, most of George's estates had been settled on Oliver Cromwell and had then passed to Oliver's heir. The Buckingham estates, once the richest in England, would never be his own again in their entirety—unless, of course, Charles Stuart returned. All George had gained by marrying Mary were Helmsley, where the fine progeny of his father's famous racing stud were still being bred and trained, and his other lands in the North, which had been granted to his father-in-law as part of the extensive rewards bestowed by Parliament for victory in the war against King Charles I.

George did not consider it unnatural that he should want everything, including the London houses, back in his own name. They were the very reasons why he had returned to England three years before—and a spell in the Tower caused by misrepresentations to Parliament had actually done his royalist reputation some good. His father-in-law Lord Fairfax was, for undisclosed motives of his own, about to give Monck his blessing to descend on London and offer it 'help'. If that help somehow led to the return of the king, then the king would insist that Parliament make restitution to all the gentlemen who had most actively engineered him back onto the throne.

George served himself another capon breast and looked absently around the high, dark-panelled room. Why, when one thought about it, wait until everything played out in London? With things in such a state of flux, York was much the handier arena. The exchange of private property in Yorkshire would scarcely be of great moment to the Parliament right now—perhaps he could get Father Fairfax to enforce some independent arrangements.

And if George could once regain all his property and wealth, why should not the Selbys enjoy their own lands as well? They were held by Colonel Mark Denton, a creature of Oliver Cromwell, who had proved himself the worst scourge to the king's cause in the North. The man had been called to Scotland weeks ago by Monck, nothing had been heard of him since, and meanwhile his regiment had gone over to Fairfax. Amidst such confusion, how hard might it be to tip Denton off his high horse and snatch his ill-gotten lands from under him?

Denton had done nothing to deserve them. They had first been confiscated from Sir John Selby after Sir John's heroic attempt to defend them following Marston Moor, and granted to the infantry colonel who made the capture. That beneficiary had died in 1656, without issue, and Cromwell had asked Parliament to turn the properties over to Denton, one of Oliver's protégés. It was done, and it was a scandal. Denton had already been in full possession of family property around Denton Moor and Swaledale, none of which he managed himself. The Selby lands fell under the direction of his brothers and their stewards, while the Selbys—Maurice, and the incomparable Lucinda—eked out a miserable existence in York.

George knew this mainly from Lucinda herself. It was one of the few delights of his present life to draw her out on her relations and their troubles. They were of the old family that derived from Selby itself, not far south of York, and had over the centuries spread across the North. The war had changed everything in her life. It was tempting to try and change some of it back.

She was deliciously placed: as protection she had merely an indigent, reckless brother; and she was untouched. By rights such a beauty should have married at 15 or so, despite the lack of dowry, but according to Mary, who knew everything that happened within a hundred miles of Nun Appleton, the only gentlemen Lucinda had deigned to smile upon had by sad twists of fate ended up dead or imprisoned.

'But I don't think it's the war that prevents her from marrying,' Mary had said to him once. 'It's her character. She's a dreamer and likes her own way.'

'Do the two quite go together?'

'All I know is, she looked me straight in the eye one day and confessed to being romantic. It made me uncomfortable because I could see she meant to tease me.'

'What, you mean you ain't romantic, Mary?'

'If I were,' she had said quietly, 'I should take care not to let you know it.'

He stole a glance across the table at the plain but dear face, the neat, plump figure that he knew how to bring to melting point in bed. He was of a mood to do so tonight, to wipe out the injury of being kicked off Marston Moor by her father. Then he wondered whether Lady Lucinda Selby regretted that he was missing from York and he imagined taking her by surprise in her street at midnight, cloaked up, and escorting her to her door without a word, just a smile beneath the mask. Her hand in his, her breath quivering in her breast ...

Could he help being romantic too?

MORPETH
January 5

Mark had always found Morpeth bleak and tedious and he was impatient to leave it on the morrow. Monck, having settled his army in and around the town, had allotted him the courthouse, which was imposing and spine-chillingly cold.

'It's an old haunt of yours, I believe,' Monck had said dryly, 'so no doubt it will suit.'

Mark had seconded a few men under Corporal Hales to render the guardroom habitable and slammed the doors on the rest of the edifice. Disdaining to put himself or his troopers in the wretched cots supplied for the guards, he had ordered these thrown into the courtyard to freeze the lice out of them, had the stone floors scoured and fresh rushes laid down, and then had bed rolls brought in and placed in corners out of the draughts.

He was back on Monck's London march, where he wanted to be, but he was discontented with Monck's reticence. Having given his report on Lambert, Mark was not obliged to hang about the general and he had no command until he got back to his regiment in York. He pulled a solid oak chair close to the roaring fire, crossed his boots on a stool and studied the vague pictures that formed and vanished within the flames while Hales and the rest scurried about making sure they all got a meal.

He was on Monck's march—but not of it. He was not colonel of any of the regiments and did not attend the officers' meetings. He thus knew a great deal less about the general's intentions than Ralph Knight. Mark's best chance of finding out what Monck was up to was to question Knight, who had arrived that day to confirm that Newcastle was secure.

It was true that the great crenellated keep that formed the Morpeth courthouse was an old haunt for Mark. He had dragged many a royalist to trial here and made sure that the justices handed down the fines, imprisonment and punishments earned for insurgency. He had always tried to second-guess conspirators and to pounce before they risked their families, their possessions and their lives in some half-baked scheme. Their worst failings were in communication and planning, for they lacked his freedom of movement and the sources of intelligence that he could call upon to thwart them.

Royalist folly in the years after their cause was lost had never ceased to appal Mark. While the king was alive there had been a focus to their last-ditch campaigns to save the crown, but once Charles I was gone and his finest generals had either left the country or been cut down or imprisoned, it should have been obvious that royalists' power to put any significant army in the field had been destroyed. The most dangerous amongst them, labelled 'delinquents' by Parliament, were confined to within five miles of their homes; hundreds of them were stripped of their estates, and none were allowed into London. Yet in every corner of the country they planned insurrection, believing, despite manifest proof to the contrary, that one day their poorly coordinated efforts would stir the people of England into outright opposition to Parliament. Thus they sporadically rose up, found themselves unsupported and were either hanged, imprisoned or beaten into hiding.

Mark stretched his legs before the guardroom fire in Morpeth courthouse and thought of the men he had brought to justice for plotting against Parliament over the last few years. He was glad to have seized them, and the evidence against them, before they committed some foolish or fatal act. The price they had paid for conspiracy was in every case less than they would have paid for high treason. And yet, he thought wryly, not one of them had learnt anything from his hard lessons except to hate him and his kind.

He raised his head. There were voices at the outer door and then the footsteps of a guard coming to report. He glanced at the table, upon which his men had just set a meal acquired from a nearby householder or most probably from several. Corporal Hales, who was Mark's scout, servant and caterer, showed the tenacity of a wolf in all his duties. Tonight, the scent of hot mutton on the bone steamed out from under the largest cover. Mark was about to be accosted before his one good meal in a week; let the visitor beware.

It was Ralph Knight. Mark had no sooner heard the name than Knight's substantial form appeared in the doorway.

Mark rose, welcomed him to the fire and dismissed the men to the table on the other side of the great room where their own meal and tankards of ale were set out. He did not dine with the lower ranks but he preferred his men to share comfortable shelter when he could get it. He would not insist that they sup humbly in one of the icy corners of Morpeth courthouse and in return he expected them to entertain themselves quietly.

'You've eaten?' he said to Knight.

'Not yet. The council went on for an age.'

'Then sup with me.' He nodded to Hales who stood by the table, his hand on a decanter of wine, his usual signal that the preparations were complete. 'Pour two glasses, Hales, then go eat. I'll serve myself.'

Hales obeyed. Mark indicated the seat nearest the fire for his guest and the two men sat down, Knight looking on in admiration as Mark took the covers off the food. 'How do you do it? This is better than the general's fare!'

'I'm making up for my last mission. Lambert entertained me in a sheepcote, without meat or drink.'

Knight gave him a shrewd look. 'But you made a few visits, surely, on the way back. Who to? They didn't feed you?'

'Yes. Let me give you a shank. Help yourself to the turnips; from around here they're sweet enough, even in this season.'

'Thank you, that I know.' Knight had bought land and settled in the North after his marriage, and liked the region. In fact he had a secret ambition to one day hold the parliamentary seat of Morpeth.

Ralph Knight piled his plate, rehearsing more questions and knowing that few would be answered. Yet ask he must, since he had been ordered to by Monck. The general had said in private: 'For a gentleman of Colonel Denton's expedition, Haltwhistle to Morpeth seems to have taken him rather too much time. He must have rested somewhere on the journey and he may have visited someone, though he did not say as much. I'd fain know whom he consorts with, colonel. I'm so situated on this march that there is no commander in history more hot to know men's hearts.'

Knight was of the opinion that if Denton had a heart at all, it was entirely devoted to his own personal strategy, but he agreed with Monck that it was necessary to know it. When it came to detecting and stamping out royalist activities, Denton was the most vigilant and thoroughgoing parliamentarian commander in the North—and he was about to rejoin his regiment. Monck did not intend his army to find itself opposed by rogue detachments.

Knight had privately come round to the view that it was time Charles Stuart returned to England and he was desperate to know whether Monck felt the same. Yet despite being close to the general, Knight had never got a word out of Monck about why he was taking his army south. Knight admired what he had achieved in Scotland because it was in such contrast to the chaos in England, where the army and the Parliament, each split into factions and violently jealous of the other, had lost their grip on the country and its government. Monck clearly intended to restore order when he reached London—but on whose behalf?

Knight almost despaired of getting any clues out of Monck but he had been asked to prise some from Denton, and if he was not to ruin a good meal it might be best to make the attempt at once and get it over with. 'What is Lambert going to do?'

Denton gave him a sidelong, considering glance and the strong curves of his mouth formed a half smile. 'The general didn't give you my report? I can't think why not. Briefly: nothing much. Lambert has between one and two score troops—hardly enough to cause us any grief between here and York, though I did tempt him to join Lilburne.'

'Why?'

'So Monck could clean him up on the way. However, it looks to me as though he's chosen to head for London.'

'What can he hope to do there?'

'What can *we* hope to do?'

'I mean, Parliament won't let him enter town. If he evades arrest he'll be reduced to rustling up disaffected troops on the outskirts.'

'Will Parliament let *us* enter town? The Swordbearer of the City of London arrived today. No doubt you know what message he brought to the general?'

'No one does. Meanwhile Doctor Gumble is on his way to London. And we won't be told what message he carries *from* the general, either.'

Knight watched Denton digest this. The Reverend Doctor Gumble was a chaplain, an intelligent man whom the general had often employed as messenger in tricky circumstances, for Gumble was a devoted friend and steadfastly discreet. Gumble had been dispatched by Monck from Wooler on the 3rd of January, following the receipt of a communication from Parliament on the second. Denton had not been around then, which was why he was fishing for information now.

Denton replied: 'Then it's an even bet whether London wants us or whether we're going there against Parliament and the City's express wishes. We're in an interesting fix if they'd sooner see Monck back in Edinburgh.'

'We? The general is keeping you with us after York?'

'What the general wants from me is not easy to predict. At a guess, however, I would say he may find a use for my regiment. They won't be needed in York: the city's quiet, with no objection to Fairfax's ousting Lilburne. Lilburne was not respected enough as commander in the North. You'll agree with me, I think: he fought well enough in Scotland but he's better at taking orders than giving them. He lacks Lambert's fire and Monck's vigilance.'

This seemed a rather glib statement from a man who had served Lilburne with ruthless exactitude. Knight stabbed at a piece of carrot with his fork, but kept his eyes on Denton's face. 'You don't mind bowing to Fairfax?'

Denton shook his head. 'Lilburne doomed himself by siding with the rebels. Fairfax was ever for Parliament and I've no quarrel with that.' Knight's keen stare did not seem to perturb him and he continued sardonically, 'More so than Cromwell, in truth, who had a habit of throwing Parliament out—for their own good, of course.'

Knight felt a flash of anger at this cynical remark. 'You served Cromwell readily enough. And took the rewards.'

Denton raised his eyebrows and narrowed his eyes with a sinister look that perhaps masked a certain anger of his own. 'I took orders, colonel.'

'Orders or no, you gave yourself a pretty free rein under Lilburne. You covered a lot of country, rounding up royalists. In Yorkshire no corner is safe for them.'

'And you're disposed to consider that unwise of me, given the present climate.' Denton was very still and his deep voice was smooth. 'Tell me, is Monck so hell bent on London because he wants Parliament to bring back the king?'

Knight felt exposed, guilty and alarmed all at once but he came out with the truth: 'I don't know.'

'Shouldn't you find out? Otherwise you'll just be taking orders, colonel.'

'That's good enough for me.'

Denton poured another glass of wine. 'I meant what I said: we all need to know what Monck wants because he won't make it public. It stands to reason he'll keep it from the rest of the country until he gets to London, for if he's against Parliament they won't want him to arrive. If he's determined to sway them to bring back the king, the republicans amongst them will meet him with force—and we'll have Haselrig and his troops to contend with. And if Monck's hoping to make some compact with Lambert and his like—'

'Surely not!' Knight burst out.

'We should consider it from every angle. You can wager that Monck has. I remind you that he hung about on the border for weeks without raising a finger against Lambert. Parleys were proposed and commissions went to London last November—and Lambert let them through. Monck knew Lambert was making forays out of Newcastle and not once did he budge. He waited until you and the other commissioners got back from London and then came to his decisions accordingly. What message did you bring him?'

Ralph Knight, pulling a piece of bread apart, did not betray his resentment at this question. His mission to London, during the time when the army rebels tried to supplant Parliament, had been one of the unhappiest of his career. None of the suggestions that Monck had made in his despatch had appealed to the army rebels while their own terms, which Knight had brought north, had been abhorrent to Monck. Knight was not keen, nor was he authorised, to share any of this with Denton.

He said with a hard smile: 'The general didn't give you my report? I can't think why not.'

To his surprise, Denton gave an appreciative laugh, a short sound deep in his throat that he did not follow with a comment. He pushed towards Knight the platter of dried fruit and cheese that completed the meal.

They ate in silence for a while. Then Knight said: 'I wonder, in all your marauding around the North, that you've never laid hands on the Shadow. From time to time you've got mighty close to him, I hear, but he slips through your fingers.'

Denton shrugged. 'He has an unfortunate habit of warning delinquents when I'm on my way to arrest them. I get there and he's disappeared—and so has the prey. Either he's spiriting them out of the country altogether or he has a little group of them gathered somewhere in secret, panting to make mischief.'

'How does he know where you're going to strike? Could there be an informer amongst your men?'

Denton shook his head. 'My men know nothing until they get my orders to move. No, so far the Shadow has stayed one step ahead by pure guesswork. One day he'll guess wrong and I'll have him. And his friends.'

Knight had the sudden sensation that perhaps he had learned something on the general's behalf after all. For all Denton's coolness, it was clear that he held a grudge against the Shadow and he worked so close to the ground that if he thought there was a dangerous group of royalist conspirators holed up somewhere under the Shadow's protection, it was most likely true. If these gentlemen held any interest for Monck, the general would be grateful to anyone who could put him in touch with them. Knight looked forward to discussing the Shadow and his secret cohort with the general.

It was only later, when Knight returned to his quarters, that he remembered the main point of his visit and realised that he still did not know where and with whom Denton had lingered on his journey across country from Haltwhistle to Morpeth.

****

Monck's army was on the road to Newcastle and the tail end of the labouring columns had not long crossed the Stannington Bridge over the river Blyth. Mark was with the rearguard, near the baggage train, having left the general and his staff in the centre. He had just taken a ride along the entire line of march, snatching his first opportunity to make a private review of the army. He preferred to know with whom he marched and assess how handy they might be under surprise attack.

The road was bordered on the west by the wide tract of forest that surrounded Blagdon Hall and it was from amongst the trees that two shots rang out. The first bullet gouged a red score across the neck of Mark's chestnut stallion, an inch from Mark's fingers, which made the horse scream and rear. The second got Mark in the head. There was a peal like a hundred bells in his ears and he toppled, losing control of his horse. The crown of his head had received a hammer blow, as the bullet glanced across what he wore under his wide felt hat—the secret, close-fitting cap of steel that he preferred to a helmet. The stallion recovered itself and Mark managed to stay in the saddle. His hearing was gone but he swiftly got his sight back. As he raked the scene he caught movement somewhere high amongst the trees—a pale horse was moving away and, even as he watched, it disappeared. He spied no other movement near it but there had been two shots. Almost simultaneous, and from a range of perhaps 200 yards, they could only have been fired from muskets. Marksman number one was already retreating; having seen his target crumple, he must have thought the job done. Number two was perhaps still in position. And reloading.

Behind Mark the baggage train had halted and the infantry unit of pikemen beside whom he had been riding were being roared at by their officers to hold ranks—their pikes and swords were useless in retaliation and it was clear that this was not an attack on the column but an attempt on Mark alone.

Further ahead, a captain of dragoons was yelling at his men to charge their carbines. Mark could not wait for them; he had less than a minute to get to marksman number two before the man put another bullet down the barrel.

The stallion had blood dripping from its mane but sprang into action at Mark's urging, and within seconds they were galloping towards the forest margin. Courageous and with a magnificent turn of speed, like all Mark's horses, it found its footing through the ankle-deep snow and plunged into the trees.

Mark had lost hat and secret, and he felt as though an axe had set itself into his skull. His hearing was faulty and his mind dizzy but he could see well enough to find a way through the woodland along the trajectory of both shots, which he was convinced had been fired from the same spot. Ferns and bracken brushed against his boots. He bent low over the beast's neck, urging it on as the ground began to slope upwards and they entered a broad sweep of beech trees that ascended to the top of a hill. Up ahead must be the vantage point from which the pair had taken aim.

If there were more than two men, if a troop were waiting concealed on the summit for him to run straight into their trap, then he was lost, for even Monck's dragoons could not find him in time to help. He had to count on his attackers being personal avengers, not a rogue regiment trying to beat up the rear of Monck's column.

There were no more shots. His hearing returned as the stallion rounded the side of the hill and Mark could suddenly see across a steep valley to the slope on the other side. At its summit there was a flurry as a horse and rider plunged into a grove. The steed, pale against the white snow, was hard to make out but the rider was distinct, draped in a black cloak and wearing a wide hat, pulled low. He disappeared from view without looking back. Was he even aware he was pursued? Mark cursed, realising he could not use the pistol that was buckled into the shoulder holster before his right knee. If he fired it at marksman number two, supposing he ever saw him, it might bring the first rider back and they would be two against one again.

He was nearing the top of the hill. There were no traces on the snow except those of fox and weasel, and the occasional blurred area where squirrels had been digging for their winter stores. The vantage must be above. Had the second man left it by now, alerted by the sound of pursuit and eager to follow his companion before a detachment caught up with him, or was he taking the chance of blowing Mark out of the saddle as he reached the crest? Unfortunately, his musket would now be ready to fire.

Mark cursed again. From behind him and below came the sounds of dragoons fanning through the trees.

He reached the empty crest—bare rock and a higher outcrop gripped by the thick, gnarled roots of an old oak. He pushed the stallion forward to look down the slope beyond and immediately saw a man running across the foot of the gully below, a long musket in his hand, about to scramble up the far side, which was like giant steps of exposed rock, too steep and slippery for a horse. Mark bent forward to unbuckle the flap on his other shoulder holster.

Sturdy, dressed in cloth and leather and with steel at his hip, the man below wore a bandolier of cartridges. He made such noise as he decamped that he would not guess Mark's presence unless he stopped for breath and turned.

Mark's hand touched the carbine in the other holster and slid over it—if he fired, the first horseman would hear the shot in this amphitheatre of trees and rock. Keeping his eyes on the fleeing musketeer, Mark drew out instead the slim hunting bow that he and his brothers had perfected on their youthful forays amongst the Dales, strung it quickly and nocked a goose-feathered arrow.

He might have got the runner conveniently in the shoulder if the man had not twisted around in the last second and received it through the lower ribs on the left side. He fell without a cry, his boots scrabbling in a patch of snow.

Mark's stallion was reluctant to charge down the hillside but Mark gave it a tap on the rump with the bow and they were off, leaping and swerving among bushes.

The assassin's musket had fallen near an overhanging rock when he spun and fell. He was too crippled by the arrow to reach it. In headlong descent, Mark glimpsed him getting onto his hands and knees and then clawing his way upwards, leaving bright drops of blood on the snow before he collapsed on his front, the arrow still grotesquely in his side.

The stallion jumped a frozen stream at the bottom of the gully and in a few strides reached the prey. Mark shoved the bow back into its holster and leaped to the ground. He had but a moment: already he could hear the dragoons shouting, the scrape of hooves on the crest behind him.

He knelt and put a hand on the arrow shaft. The man screamed. Moustache, hair and beard were badly trimmed, his clothing warm but rustic, his boots scuffed. Even at a distance, the insouciant rider on the pale grey horse had had the air of a gentleman; this was of a lesser breed.

'Whom do you serve?'

'Fuck you.' The voice was shrill with pain. 'You deserve to die. He'll get you next time.'

Mark had one knee on the icy turf, his mouth close to the man's ear. 'He might have done it this time, had he stayed. But he's left you to face me. What do you think on that?' With a swift movement he rolled the man onto his back, and there was another scream.

Mark stood against the light. 'Open your eyes. Look at me. You tried to kill me and I'll know why. Whom do you serve? Give me his name.'

There was a gasp, and the man shot him a defiant stare. 'I'll not betray him to a cur like *you*, Denton.'

The conviction and the look confirmed Mark's first thought: a royalist. Under orders from a fanatic. 'He's forced you into murder and then left you to get out of it alone. You've a horse waiting up there, no doubt. I'll let you reach it and go free when you tell me his name.'

With a grunt of agony, the man struggled away and got into a sitting position which took him a little nearer his musket. Unable to speak, he rested his forehead on one upraised knee. Mark examined him, noting the angle of the arrow shaft. The blood flowing at the point of entry was sluggish. The man's vital organs might be spared and if no one tried to remove the arrow he had a fair chance of making it to Blagdon Hall or wherever his commander had gone.

Mark said: 'I'll not follow you. You may go to hell as you wish. The name.' He took another pace to the side, to block the winter sun from the other's sight and allow him to look up.

In the same split second, the man lunged the other way and got one hand on the butt of the musket. A volley rang out from the dragoons above and bullets peppered neck, shoulders and chest. He wavered for another second, blood spurting from his wounds. Then, as he toppled backwards and his head met the ground, he sought Mark's gaze, with contempt and hatred in his own.

He said on a broken whisper: 'The King's Shadow.'

The dragoons and their captain, having rescued Colonel Mark Denton from ambush, looked down in some pride for his reaction and were puzzled to see him step away from the dead man, lean his shoulders against an outcrop of rock and utter a harsh burst of laughter.

YORK MINSTER
January 11

The great cathedral was packed to hear Edward Bowles preach this Sunday afternoon and Lucinda Selby, seated with her brother a third of the way down the nave, could see that everyone of importance was there, while crowds of lesser citizens stood about, crushed together in the side aisles and around the doors. Her family had once had a boxed pew near the altar but those days were gone. She seldom came to the magnificent building that in her childhood had seemed like church, palace and home of heavenly music, all in one. Instead, she and Maurice worshipped occasionally and in secret at the house of Sir Philip Monckton, who had taken one of the Minster's former deacons under his protection and invited him to conduct clandestine services in various York homes.

Sir Philip was present, attending for the first time since he gathered the citizenry to demonstrate for Lord Fairfax on New Year's Day. Fairfax and General Monck were easy to discern in the central nave. His lordship, the family and attendants were seated towards the front while Monck was halfway back, surrounded by his colonels and guards and other ranks of the army who had marched into York with him during the day. Lucinda had entered the cathedral after Monck took his seat so she had not yet seen his face.

The atmosphere was military and expectant. The general's dispositions were all taken and he had more men, including Colonel Denton's militia regiment, which had been terrorising the North for years. It had been selected for the London march, so Lucinda would soon be safe from seeing Mark Denton in York.

Just as she was thinking this, she spotted him entering the cathedral.

He walked from the main doors along the right side of the nave and paused, looking towards Monck and his fellow commanders; but there was no seating left in that area or near the altar and he swept a glance towards the back, in her direction. He saw her instantly and their eyes met over the wide space with the same shock of recognition she would have felt if they had been mere yards apart. As he always did when they met by chance, he made a short bow as though he were a polite acquaintance, not the usurper of her lands. Then, with that infuriating stillness and attention that characterised him, he took time to examine the throng before setting off back towards the doors and out of her view in order to claim some place that he must have spied behind her.

Lucinda could not wait for Denton to leave York. Let him be gone, before he did any more damage to the cause she held dear. With luck he might never return. He had always made sure that he rode with the conquerors and his reputation as a merciless parliamentarian was legend. Therefore, once Monck reached London, it would be far too late to give that reputation another colour. If Monck were secretly royalist, and determined to sway Parliament and London towards the king, Denton was about to march into the lion's den.

The service began and she tried to attend to it but she was so fond of the old, banned Book of Common Prayer that it jarred on her. When it came to the sermon, she found sitting and listening physically painful. It was beyond her to imagine that anyone could feel closer to God by being harangued, yet Edward Bowles was convinced that the worshippers in the Minster that day desired nothing better than to have their ears pinned to their heads by homily.

He soon moved into pious praise of the Fairfax family, looking innocently over the head of his lordship as he did so, as though he had not long been Lord Fairfax's chaplain and counsellor. He chose as his theme the Fairfaxes as defenders of their neighbours in the North, protectors of both gentry and the middling sort of men. To a large extent this was true: before the wars the Fairfaxes had not been significant landowners and had wielded little influence in court or in parliament. They began their rise after Charles I's gathering on Heworth Moor outside York in 1642 when the king tried to garner support from 40,000 Yorkshiremen for his coming contest with parliament. That assembly had misfired, to the personal risk of the king, who never repeated it. The common people of the North, angry at changes in the cloth trade, began to collect arms and stage riots, one of which almost erupted at Heworth Moor. These discontented 'club men' attracted the attention of the Fairfaxes, who saw in them the basis for a new army that they could train and fund for parliament. Thus they skilfully channelled for their own purposes the one popular rebellion in England.

Lucinda thought about all this as Bowles, in studied rhetoric, presented the Fairfaxes as disinterested upholders of the rights of all Englishmen. He expatiated upon 'God's destiny for this family', implying that they had become leaders by keeping 'the greater good to mind'. He praised Lord Fairfax's guardianship of the army and the people, and edged towards his lordship's refusal to sit as commissioner at parliament's trial of King Charles I in 1649. Eleven years had passed since the king was executed but in that time no wrong had been forgotten by either side. While Bowles heaped praise on Thomas Fairfax's 'Christian humility' Lucinda could feel a shift in the congregation, as though invisible lines were being drawn through the densely packed people. The king's head was a touchstone, bringing men's and women's allegiances to the forefront of every conscience. Suddenly, the nave of the Minster was filled from pavement to vault with hope and hostility, clashing like ethereal lightning.

She glanced at Maurice. He was holding his breath to see whether Fairfax had turned royalist at last and given Bowles leave to say it aloud.

Parliament's supporters around them were waiting too. If Fairfax and Monck declared themselves for the king, word would go at once to London, where at least two armies lay in wait. One was more or less loyal to Parliament and upon its orders might seek to prevent Monck's entry into the city. The other, though weakened by the ousting of their rebellious leaders, could still rally to Lambert—and no one could be more fixed against the return of the king than Lambert. There were scores, perhaps hundreds, of men in the Minster at this very moment who believed in the Good Old Cause and who would sooner maintain martial law for ever than see another king on English soil. Denton, poised out of sight behind her, was one of these men. If they heard that Monck was for the king they could round upon him at once and turn the Minster into a battleground.

And now Bowles was talking of Monck himself: the general's strong hand, the order and peace he had established in Scotland, his ready response when Parliament begged him to lend them his advice in London. Lucinda could feel the tingling excitement these words aroused in the congregation.

She leaned close to her brother. 'Maurice,' she whispered, 'are there enough of us here to protect the general if he's attacked?'

He glanced at her, his eyes gleaming. 'I worked it out with Buckingham: if Monck would only permit royalists to march with him to London we could summon two regiments at the drop of a hat.'

'But are they *here*?'

'Luce, there is no need. This is holy ground.'

'And once we're all out in the streets? By heaven, has no one thought of that?'

'For sure, Monck has. He holds York: you may be safe.'

She closed her eyes. War had come to York when she was a little child and never left it. She lived in a divided city, in a country that currently enjoyed the shakiest government in Christendom. She could derive no security from Edward Bowles's voice as it echoed around the Minster from the high pulpit:

'Our Lord Jesus Christ once said: "I bring not peace, but a sword." For our good, for the good of England, the two great soldiers of whom I speak—and upon whom God looks down today as he looks down on all of us—I tell you, these two great soldiers took that saying to heart. They girded their loins to do their Christian duty. Since then we have endured a time of war, when brother has fought against brother, father against son, over the commonwealth of England. Many changes have been wrought, many a victory won in the name of faith and justice. You see amongst you two leaders who have shouldered every task that their country asked of them. We may humbly ask of God this day: what is the *final* task that it now behoves them to take up? Unto what threshold have they brought us? Is it too much to hope that, at last, it may be the threshold of peace?

'On the death of Oliver Cromwell, Lord Fairfax wrote me a letter that I cherish. In it he said: "The Lord look upon this nation that when we are weak he may be our strength till he hath perfected peace and truth amongst us." We may ask of God today: how are that peace and truth to be accomplished, for a troubled people, whose monarch is in exile across the water?'

There was an intake of breath—a low, collective gasp at this reference to Charles. It did not disturb Bowles; it seemed to give him heart.

'We have with us this day two warriors in England's service. How shall we bear them up, my friends? Why, by faith and witness. By seeking guidance from God's word. This morning, when I prayed for that guidance, my conscience led me to Chapter Two of the Apostle Paul's letter to the Ephesians. Let me expound to you the message of Saint Paul.'

Bowles paused, then proclaimed without book: "'At that time ye were without Christ, being aliens from the commonwealth and strangers from the covenants of promise, having no hope, and without God in the world. But now in Christ Jesus ye who sometimes were far off are made nigh by the blood of Christ.'"

There was a murmur in the cathedral and Bowles raised his voice, repeating: "'*Ye who sometimes were far off are made nigh*!" And Paul says further: "For he is our peace, who hath made both one, and hath broken down the middle wall of partition between us. To make in himself in twain one new man, so making *peace*. And that he might reconcile both unto God in one body by the cross, having slain the enmity thereby."

'Paul says of our Lord Jesus Christ: "He came and preached peace to you which were afar off, and to them that were nigh. Now, therefore, ye are no more strangers and foreigners but fellow citizens with the saints and of the household of God."'

Bowles leaned over the pulpit rail and spread his hands, his jutting, sober figure dark against the lustrous wood behind him, his face white with conviction and his eyes like coals. 'Are we on the threshold of the household of God? When General George Monck leaves this city again he goes on a mission whose purpose is a sacred trust known only to him and his Creator. Before he leaves us, let us ponder the message of the apostle, and by our prayers wish General Monck the strength and blessing to carry out his trust.' He stood erect and raised his arms high.

'Let us allow ourselves to pray that we will no longer be *strangers to the covenants of promise*. Let us dare to recognise that there is *one*, inspired with forgiveness and mercy, endowed with the power to *break down the middle wall of partition* between us and bring us together in peace!'

At this there was a stirring in the ranks of men around Monck. The general alone did not move. Lucinda, staring at the back of his dark head, could make no guess as to how he was receiving Bowles's words, but the preacher went on booming forth.

'Let us consider the portent of the words, *ye who were afar be made nigh*. Let us dare to hope that the time has come for *one new man* to come among us. My sisters and brothers, let us be ready to welcome the new man who will *reconcile* us and *slay the enmity* in England, who will—'

George Monck rose to his feet and Bowles's voice ceased. With no gesture towards the preacher or anyone else, the general stepped into the aisle, turned on his heel and began walking out of the cathedral. He was followed by the entire army contingent. It was so smartly done that their boots on the flagstones of the nave made the only sounds in a stunned silence.

Lucinda held her breath as Monck passed the end of her row. Because he was short, his figure was obscured by the crowd but she could see his profile for a second. There was no shock or anger in it; his heavy features were set in the deepest reserve. However many days he stayed, he would leave York as he had entered it: an enigma. As she watched him go, she saw other men move into the aisle and join the exodus of troops. Colonel Denton was one of them, his look sardonic, as though he had known this outcome in advance.

But he could not have predicted it. No one had had a hint of how Bowles would preach, which was why the Minster had been so packed. It was an event beyond anyone's expectations and it left the preacher silent for a full minute.

Edward Bowles surprised Lucinda. He had come to York during the wars as chaplain in the army of the Eastern Association. Over the years, in the 'godly commonwealth' of York, the city aldermen and Bowles kept the balance of power and the preacher had proved himself an adept politician. Today, he had taken an uncharacteristic risk by suggesting that he knew Monck's secret purpose and by giving it his implicit support. Whereupon Monck had repudiated both sermon and support by walking out. Bowles's position might at present appear undamaged—but priests had been hanged for less.

The minister came to himself, however, and directed the rest of the sermon towards Lord Fairfax, who remained seated amongst the somewhat depleted congregation. Bowles gave a peroration on humility that no one listened to and Lucinda looked up at the intricate vaulting above, hearing only her own heartbeat. Something seethed along her veins so fiercely that she could not distinguish whether it was hope or despair.

FAIRFAX HOUSE
January 12

Mark had never found a way of coping with Lady Lucinda Selby. Her antipathy to him cut through everything rational he might say to himself about her and touched him on the raw. It made it worse that whenever they came across each other—which was obviously far too often for her—she tried to hide her reactions under a studied, urbane manner. This hurt, because it was unnatural to her. With others she was courteous and considerate, and at the same time had a luminous quality that gave her a rare charm, for she was as frank about her feelings as about her ideas. Wherever she was, a lightness and liveliness prevailed in the company. Except when he was by.

He might have tried to avoid their meeting but they were both part of the life of York: he was a high-ranking officer quartered in the city; and she belonged to one of its first families. Now that Monck was in York and intending to stay some days, the city seethed with troops only too happy to enjoy any indulgences that the warm billets, the busy taverns and the biddable women might provide. No other force threatened the walls and there was no need for forays into the frozen countryside. He had at one point wondered whether Monck might send him out again after Lambert, because surprising news had come in that when Fairfax was investing York, Lambert had been seen with a small force at Ripon. Lambert did not advance, however, and there had been no further news of him. Thus Mark had orders to remain in York. He was fated to spend evenings amongst the people who mattered most in the fortress capital of the North and to this circle Lucinda Selby belonged.

On his second night back in town, when he entered the great chamber of Fairfax House on Castlegate, he saw her at once on the other side of the room. It was as though she had sensed his nearness a split second before he appeared, and steeled herself. Her gaze was steady but he saw something flare in its blue depths. Then she turned away.

He moved in to greet the hostess. Lord Fairfax was not yet in evidence; he had been taken ill in the afternoon. The honours were done by his wife, Lady Anne, a former beauty of the noble, Puritan and military family of Vere, who was devoted to her husband and never scrupled to comment on his actions in public. During the king's trial, when Lord Fairfax was censured for his absence from the court, she had cried out from the gallery: 'He has more wit than to be here!'

This scarcely made her a royalist, however. She approved of Mark's rigour against conspirators in the North, and treated him as a neighbour, which in fact he was, since the original Fairfax mansion was at Denton, and Mark's principal home, Lang Scar, stood a few miles out of the little town, on the edge of Denton Moor.

'You've been so long away!' she said with a smile. 'I hope you don't find this a cold homecoming?'

'On the contrary, I find everything in remarkable order,' he said dryly—as though he would cavil with her over her husband's seizing York! 'My regiment is perhaps not so enthusiastic as I am about my return—they apprehend my marching them west after miscreants. However, between ourselves, I should prefer to go south.'

'But you must have many matters to attend to. I'm told you haven't been near Lang Scar for an age.'

'My youngest brother lives there and the others take care of the lands in Swaledale. My place is with the army, Lady Fairfax.'

'So who administers the old Selby holdings?' she said with a sly glance across the room at Lucinda Selby's back.

'Do you see much of her?' he asked involuntarily, and saw a smile of curiosity in Anne Fairfax's intelligent eyes.

'We often invite her to Nun Appleton. She and Mary have a quiet friendship that I like to see.'

Mark bit back another question, concerning Lady Lucinda's attitude to Mary Fairfax's husband, the Duke of Buckingham. How much of a *friend* was he?

Lady Fairfax continued: 'I expect my daughter and the duke here tomorrow. My lord and I shall not be in York for long, I hope. We do miss our family.'

He nodded. 'It pleases me to know you'll have their company, madame.'

'As for the Selby lands ... I hope you don't find them a burden rather than a boon? You must know, when Oliver Cromwell had them transferred to you he didn't consult my lord. Yet I well remember my lord saying to me after the endowment was made: "There goes fine country into fine hands. If the young Selbys must starve, at least they're spared the sight of their heritage going to the dogs."'

He felt a surge of bitterness. *Thank you, madam, for branding me an opportunist.* But he bowed again and said: 'I shall always endeavour to deserve his lordship's good opinion. And I'm grateful for your generosity.'

'Now,' she said, 'I must allow you to talk with the ladies. You've been cruelly deprived of their good society, colonel. Pray accept a glass of wine and consider yourself free.'

She gestured to the servant who was dispensing the wine, gave Mark a smile and moved away. He went over and stood with his back to the chamber, received a glass and squared his shoulders, banishing the hostess's words before he spoke to the woman whom he was supposed to have cheated and impoverished. He must acknowledge her.

Lucinda meanwhile wished she had not come. She and Maurice had been in hopes of probing Lord Fairfax about Monck's intentions, but his lordship was suffering from the stone. Monck was not present, either, though he must have been invited. Perhaps he stayed away on account of Fairfax's illness—or he was already tired of everybody asking about his purposes. Worst of all, Denton was here and would not hesitate to address her and Maurice, preserving meanwhile his usual cold courtesy. It frightened her that one day her brother might lose his temper and pick a violent argument with Denton that would lead to a duel. She also worried that Denton in his perceptive way would unearth Maurice's secrets—his contacts with royalist conspirators or, more dangerous still, the fact that he had joined Sir George Booth's uprising in the summer.

Maurice caught her glance, looked beyond her at Denton, and frowned in anger.

Lucinda shook her head slightly at her brother, then did the only thing that might keep the two men apart—she began walking Denton's way. He was by a sideboard, a glass in his hand, looking straight at her. She kept moving, towards the array of wines at his elbow. She would wait for him to speak. She would answer any inquiry he might make about her family, which would deprive him of an excuse to force conversation on Maurice.

As she drew level with Denton, she glanced up at his intent face. He bowed. She hurriedly took a glass of wine that looked too yellow and thus far too sweet. She felt an eerie sense of danger and had to resist the impulse to retreat. She turned to face the room and remained a hand's breadth away from him, his tall, dark form looming beside her, both of them motionless, as though posing for their portrait. To her annoyance, she was trembling inside.

Silence and isolation seemed to suit Denton. His still watchfulness had struck her on many such evenings, when, after entering a room, he would pause on the margins, his dark-grey eyes narrowed, his face inscrutable, his well-shaped mouth giving the only hint of expression—but whether he felt superior to the company or bored with it, or was contemplating some other distasteful subject, she had never been able to make out.

At last he spoke, looking not at her but over at Maurice. 'May I congratulate you on your brother's recovery, my lady?'

'Thank you. He left the house for the first time last week. He's not yet strong. I'm surprised that you—' She hesitated. She was surprised he was at all interested in Maurice's health, but the question had been polite at least.

He said: 'I remember when he fell sick, last August. A very long illness. You must be relieved that he made it through.'

He had a rich, smooth voice that often lingered over his words as though they contained hidden meanings. She felt that he dwelled especially upon 'August' but would not let that make her anxious. Back then, Denton had been ordered to help smash Sir George Booth's uprising, but his regiment was already engaged on some mission at Hull and by the time he had marched it across the country the insurrection was all but over. Denton could not have known about Maurice's involvement then, and if he had learnt of it since he would have instantly had him arrested.

'I thank God for it,' she said. 'Were you not sent to General Monck in September?'

'No, October. I was summoned to Edinburgh where the general gave me duties that took me across Scotland. I rejoined him a week ago.'

'What can you tell me about him, colonel?'

'Only what the world already knows. A stout gentleman with a frown like Jupiter's and a godlike way of keeping his own counsel. Black hair, black eyes, heavy features and a brooding look; but, at his leisure, as finely clothed and right-mannered a gentleman as you could wish to meet. In fact, very much the person you see talking to Lady Fairfax, by the door.'

She followed his gaze. Monck himself!

'A vivid portrait, colonel, but it doesn't tell me why he's taking his army to London. You of all people must know.'

She was looking at Monck, and Denton did not reply until he had shifted slightly, into her line of sight. He seemed determined that she look up for his answer. When she did, he said: 'No. I do not know.'

His gaze was intimidating but she said: 'And if you did, you would not tell me.'

'That would depend. On a number of circumstances. All at present beyond my control.'

Looking into her smouldering eyes, Mark could see she did not believe him. The miracle of standing with her in outward peace, if not harmony, was already over.

She said, 'Then I shall have to ask him myself.'

'I wouldn't advise it.'

'I don't require your advice.'

He kept his voice low. 'My lady, I'm 11 years older than you—allow me to give you the benefit of my experience. This may look to you like a time of change and opportunity—in fact it's one of danger, to everyone on both sides, whether for king or parliament. The general leads an untouched army but it's not unassailable. Getting it to London, deploying it there and achieving his aims, whatever they may be, is no certain task. At present he has all the cards in his hands and he must hold onto them between York and London. This is the worst moment for anyone else to expose theirs. Especially any royalist.' Her expression was still scornful. He said: 'I see I must be specific. If you encourage your brother into any further recklessness at this point I fear that even your best friends will be unable to protect you.'

'Because they'll all be looking after themselves? That's just the kind of remark I would expect of you, colonel. You judge others by yourself. You're determined to remain with the victors, whoever they may be. Take care. One day you may find you've served the wrong masters.'

He flinched and she saw it. He gathered himself for a last attempt. 'Very well, let us talk of your strategy, since you take the freedom to impugn mine. You credit those nearest to you with the highest ideals and sentiments. You think your opponents driven only by greed and a lust for power. That is no strategy at all, my lady: it is a delusion. For as long as you suffer it, you can be of no use to your friends. If you claim that all the honour is in your camp and imagine that your opponents are not equally true to principle and belief, you do not know your enemy.'

'Thank you,' she said in a shaking voice, 'I know him quite well enough.'

'Not a skirmish, I hope?' said a pleasant voice at Mark Denton's shoulder, and the Duke of Buckingham stepped into view. 'Not on such an evening. Speak no more of enemies, Lady Lucinda—anyone calling himself a gentleman must forever be your friend.' He gave a sweeping bow. 'As am I, of long date.' He drew nearer, ignoring Denton and saying softly: 'Or do I presume too much?'

"You're very good, Your Grace. And ... and most welcome.' Lucinda looked towards the door from which General Monck had moved away. 'You're alone?'

'Alas, yes—my wife doesn't leave Nun Appleton until tomorrow. I've arrived before I'm wanted, something I can seldom resist doing, much to my father-in-law's distress. It's a little habit of yours, too, colonel,' he said with a sly smile, giving Denton his attention at last. 'Though I hear, this time, you almost didn't make it here at all! But I suppose George Monck could have dropped you into a long box and brought you on with the baggage train.'

Lucinda was perplexed by Buckingham's words but still more curious to see how Denton would take his manner. She had never seen the two men together. Though of an age, they were in some contrast: Denton a head taller, with his dark hair lightened at the tips by his campaigns of last summer, dressed soberly but well, standing at his ease and regarding Buckingham with indifference; the duke was resplendent in brown velvets and gold lace, his auburn hair, longer than Denton's, fell in generous curls over his shoulders, and the malice in his lazy-lidded eyes was intensified by his brilliant smile.

When Lucinda realised there was no prospect of Denton's either answering or taking himself off, she asked the duke what he was talking about.

'The attack on Monck's columns, near Stannington Bridge. Colonel Denton was knocked off his horse by a bullet fired from the forest.'

Taken aback, she said to Denton: 'You were shot!?'

'Shot at. I remained in the saddle and pursued the two attackers. We got one but the other escaped.'

'Who were they?'

'We've not identified them, as yet.'

The duke put in: 'I heard that the one who got away was the Shadow.'

Denton's glance sharpened. 'That's the rumour, is it? Then you know more than I do. Excuse me, the general seems to want a word.'

The duke waited until Denton had moved off and then gestured towards a chair set beneath a window not far away. 'What a barbarian that man is. To keep you standing, and force you to listen to what—a lecture?' As he handed her into the chair he said shrewdly: 'He wasn't *threatening* you?'

She took a sip of her wine and waited while he drew up another chair. Denton's words echoed in her head: *If you encourage your brother to any further recklessness ...*

'He seemed ... I felt he was threatening Maurice.'

Buckingham's playful amusement disappeared. 'What does he suspect him of?'

'He said—this is not a time to take risks.'

Buckingham nodded thoughtfully. 'He may be correct, where your brother is concerned. Sir Maurice has proved his courage, I shan't say where.' Lucinda looked at him in alarm and he gave her an angelic smile. 'But it has left him vulnerable. Will you allow me henceforth to take such risks on his behalf?' When she did not answer, he added in a caressing tone: 'And on yours. Nothing could afford me greater honour or pleasure.'

Lucinda looked around the room. Maurice was still with their friends and Denton was near the door, taking his leave of Lady Fairfax. Neither man was looking her way. Tears suddenly blurred her eyes. 'I can't bear anything to happen to Maurice!'

Buckingham reached over, as if to take her hand. They were so angled that no one in the room could see the gesture but she drew back a little to avoid it.

She went on quickly: 'There are dangers for you, too! Perhaps greater ones.' Until this moment, she had never been sure of the Duke of Buckingham's loyalties. Child playmate of the king, a young cavalier in the wars, an impoverished exile, but now husband to Lord Fairfax's daughter and restored to at least some of his fortune … She had heard that royalist agents like John Mordaunt were wary of him.

'I'm oddly placed, I know,' he said with a rueful look. 'But aptly so for many purposes, including yours. You see, for some time I've been trying, by steady degrees, to influence my father-in-law into, shall we say, a right way of thinking. About what may be achieved … across the water … and what may be accomplished in England.' He spoke low and leaned close. To any observer, he and she would appear to be exchanging intimacies. For her own reputation (not for his—the duke's was long past repair) she should not allow the conversation to go on much longer. Indeed, she happened to notice Denton leaving, and the glance that he threw her across the room was chilling. Whereas Buckingham's speeches warmed her like strong wine.

He went on: 'Consider: if the Shadow had put paid to Denton at Stannington, he would have done you a favour.' He saw her start but continued: 'With Denton gone, your family lands would be in the balance again. They could scarcely pass to rest of his tribe—he and his father were the only soldiers amongst them so they can make no claim to the spoils of war. In many a long talk with Lord Fairfax, I've learnt that he deplores your dispossession. At the time, he could do nothing about it: Cromwell prevailed. Now that his lordship is back in influence, now that he's acting like a leader once more, I hope that he would favour the restoration of your lands.'

She had to ask: 'Why was Denton attacked the other day?'

'Rumour states that it was the Shadow who fired on him. Consider, my lady: the Shadow has already helped your family in the most audacious way, I shan't say how. Isn't it more than possible that this last attempt was for your benefit?'

'How can you know this? How do you know any of it?' The Shadow's rescue of Maurice, her brother's journey home as he was spirited across country by the Shadow's henchmen, was their closest secret. Of their friends in York, only Castlemaine knew how he had been saved.

'My lady,' the duke said gently, 'forgive me for hinting at these things. I don't expect you to confirm them. I'd never invade your privacy. But allow me the privilege of confiding in *you*.' He got to his feet. 'May I get you a little more wine? I fear I've startled you.'

'Please.' She handed him her glass. She needed to think.

When he returned, he stood by her chair and, because there was no one by, was able to talk to her without leaning too close. She was grateful for his discretion. She took a sip of wine. 'Your Grace, do you know the Shadow?'

His only reaction was a subtle smile. Facing across the busy room, he murmured: 'Let me say—to you *and to no one else*—I do.'

She looked up in admiration. He had married into the enemy camp and now lived in the household of Parliament's former Lord General. If he had been lending his aid to active royalists ever since he was released from the Tower, he was running serious risks. Because of his connections and his rank he had wide freedom of movement, frequently riding between his Yorkshire estates, where he maintained two racing stables. Moreover, he was a man of fiery impulses and courage. Could Maurice have been mistaken when he judged that Buckingham was not the Shadow? Injured and half conscious, how could her brother have recognised who had snatched him to safety? She might owe a great deal to the man who stood so nonchalantly at her side.

Another question occurred to her—but she could not ask it. She had no need to know the identity of the Shadow and it was safer for the gentleman himself if she did not. She also felt that if Maurice were to discover who had rescued him, he would be mortified. To be helped by an anonymous compatriot brought no shame. But for Maurice's delicate sense of honour, finding that he was under a secret obligation to the Duke of Buckingham would make him uncomfortable.

There was still something she needed to say, however. 'Thank you for your honesty. This will go no further. In return, may I ask you to convey something to the Shadow? Or would that put you in danger?'

'Anything from you, my lady, is a sacred trust.' He added hastily: 'Give it to me at once: Lady Fairfax comes our way.'

'Tell the gentleman, if he has been acting on my brother's behalf, I can only thank him from my heart. Tell him I pray for the day when Selby will be ours again. But I'm not willing to have it back at the price of any man's life. It was lost in battle—should it be regained by murder, I'll not set foot there again.'

She saw the effect on Buckingham: gratification, and intense surprise. But as Lady Fairfax came up to them he made Lucinda a graceful bow and said with a tinge of self-mockery: 'Your wish is my command.'

'And what are you commanded to do, I wonder?' said Lady Fairfax.

'I'm scolded, madam! For not bringing my wife tonight. Mary and I are ordered to attend on Lady Lucinda in the Coppergate as soon as may be.'

'A kind thought,' Lady Fairfax said to Lucinda. 'York will soon seem like home to us again, if we receive such a welcome from our neighbours.'

Thereafter the evening passed without incident. Lucinda failed to meet General Monck, who did not remain long after his hostess told him Lord Fairfax was retired for the night, and the other guests chose not to linger. When Lucinda took her leave of Lady Fairfax, she exchanged a glance with the Duke of Buckingham across the room; the subtle smile reappeared and he gave her a quick bow.

In the coach on the way home, Maurice was silent with exhaustion and she offered no confidences about the two encounters she had just passed through. She felt a confused glow when she thought of Buckingham's revelations. She also reflected that, if her reading of them was correct, she had just saved her worst enemy from assassination. Colonel Denton would never know of her mercy, he did not merit it, and it left him free to enjoy the wealth of Selby. She was left with relief, uncertainty and crushing sadness.

DENTON MOOR
January 15

The vast landscape was still when Mark brought his horse to a halt at the southernmost edge of Denton Moor and looked down towards the road to Knaresborough. The black stallion was blowing hard from the climb. Mark's tall chestnut had more stamina on hills but it was at present back in York, recovering.

The view was different from what he had seen on a fine summer's day, 16 years before; but on this bleak morning, memory transformed it all in his mind and he saw again the long columns of pikemen, the great guns and the horses that hauled them, the troops of cavalry that had told him who was marching from the west to relieve the royalists besieged in York—Prince Rupert, King Charles the First's nephew and his most gifted commander, come to wrest the North from Parliament's occupying forces.

At the beginning of the wars, Mark's father had raised a troop of horse and joined the Fairfaxes against the king so that Mark, 15 and the eldest son, had become his mother's right hand, responsible for the family properties in Swaledale and around Denton Moor. But with one glance at the army below him that day, he had recognised his duty: to warn his father that Prince Rupert had brought his force across the Pennines. Not a word had passed through the district about Rupert's coming and Parliament's army, drawn up around York, could have no idea of it.

On foot and concealed from the enemy below, Mark had raced east, outmatching Rupert's pace and assessing his numbers as he went— 13,000 men, maybe more, sparkling with arms in the June sun. Mark even spied the prince himself, darting along the columns on an Arab the colour of new milk, his immensely tall form and long dark hair unmistakable even from a distance, with his big, white water dog running at the horse's heels.

At a tenant's farm near Askwith, Mark borrowed a horse and a musket. He gave one of the men a message to take back to his mother at Lang Scar and set off across country to Knaresborough. There, through friends of his father, he was able to warn the town, obtain a fresh mount and better arms and move on to the army positioned around York.

Lord Ferdinando Fairfax was one of the three high commanders and Mark's father served in the cavalry regiment of Sir Thomas Fairfax, Lord Ferdinando's son. When Mark reached their position and gave his report, he was commended by his father and the Fairfaxes, and he begged to stay with the regiment. His father, reluctant to send him back into the teeth of Rupert's advance, let Mark remain at his side.

As Mark rode on through brittle snow to Lang Scar, he reflected on the change that his accidental glimpse of the last great royal army had wrought in his life. If he had not been alone on the moor on that summer day when Prince Rupert went by, what might he have become? Whatever else, he had become a man—brutally, at Marston Moor, in the failing light of 2 July, 1644, when the royalist left wing swept through Sir Thomas Fairfax's cavalry and Mark's father was brought down by a pistol shot.

Mark caught sight of Lang Scar, half sheltered by a fold in the moorland. Memory returned, making him catch his breath as he saw the slate roofs and stone chimneys rise into view. He recalled riding this very path, burdened with what he had to tell his mother. No matter that he was announcing victory for Parliament: she had done her best to persuade her husband out of joining the Fairfaxes, and it meant nothing to her that they had managed to turn on Rupert and destroy his army; that York was Parliament's at last; that the king had lost the entire North of England. When Mark told her that his father was dead, he thought for one second that he had killed her too. His mother was a strong, outwardly serene woman, but her grief was so violent, so much like rage, that she lost consciousness.

Mark's three brothers rushed to support her. When she came to, lying on cushions under a window, she looked at once for Mark, her face contorted by horror and reproach. He burst into sobs, threw himself on his knees and took her hand.

'It was quick. It was over in an instant.'

'You were there!' she gasped, her face livid, her eyes brimming with tears.

'I held him. He gave me his sword. I promised to carry it for him.'

She knew at once. She gave a cry, reached out and grasped his doublet with both hands. 'You will not go back! You will not!'

'I must, Mother. You don't know what it was like. The dark and the rain. Half the night, we were losing. The royalists rang the bells in York! And then we turned them and they ran. We cut them down. We won. I have to stay with the army. We must go on, so father … so he didn't die in vain.'

She lashed out at him and told him to quit the room. He obeyed, leaving the others to help her. The next week was a misery, as they endured the arrival of his father's body, the funeral, the burial, the condolences of neighbours. His mother's father, Grandfather Morley, came to sit at the family council where they worked out the management of the properties. It was decided that their mother, who could not bear to remain at Lang Scar, would thenceforth live in the Denton manor in Swaledale, 20 miles to the north, and when her younger sons grew old enough they would help to run the family farms. Mark was the heir but since he would be constantly with the army he must stay in touch with the administration of the Denton properties by letter.

Thus, in one dreadful week, a rift had opened between Mark and the rest of his family. He saw them from time to time, usually at Lang Scar. He avoided the beautiful valley of Swaledale, where he had spent his childhood. His mother rarely travelled down to Denton Moor, though she was here at present to assist at the birth of a grandchild—the first baby of Mark's youngest brother, Nicholas. The rift grew deeper because it was never acknowledged. The four brothers were loyal to one another, shouldered their separate responsibilities under the guidance of their grandfather and did not quarrel over the Denton fortunes when Mark reached his majority, shortly before the old man's death. Their mother buried her sense of loss. But she had never approved the choice that Mark made after Marston Moor, nor did she discuss it. And he could not forget how deeply he had wounded her, nor ever approach Lang Scar without remembering what he had felt when he rode away from it to join the army: that somehow, by his own actions, he had lost father and mother both.

The old, sprawling house was well-ordered and welcoming: the forecourt was swept of snow and firelight glinted within the ground-floor windows. Mark was expected, having sent a message ahead, and the servants were quick to open the great door and line up to greet him in the hall. No matter that he thought of the house as Nicholas's home; they always met him as the master.

His mother, Helen, alone in the principal chamber upstairs, came towards him with her right hand outstretched. He kissed it and examined her. Her hair was now silver, but her large grey eyes retained their clear beauty. He often felt that she knew what he was thinking, but she never pried, which increased his sense of guilt and distance.

'How well timed,' she said. 'Nicholas has a son—born this morning.'

'Margery? And the child?'

'Both well. Nicholas is with them now. I am ordered to send you to them the moment you set foot inside the house. But I told them you may have other ideas.'

'By no means. Will you come?'

She shook her head. 'I've done my part. And I well remember what it's like for a mother on the first day—more than two in the room feels like an army.'

So he went in alone and received a quiet but affectionate welcome from Nicholas. Mark's family did not embrace but Nick's pleasure in his visit was patent.

Mark examined the top of the sleeping baby's head and exchanged a few words with Margery, who was drowsy, contented and not in much discomfort, or so she said. She was a pretty young woman with a lively manner. Today, her languid smile and her tangle of golden hair on the cushions softened her, increasing her attractions and somehow making her seem pure and untouched, as though Nicholas had been consorting all this time with an angel. Mark felt both privileged and excluded.

Margery did not rise for dinner, which the three Dentons took in the great hall downstairs. There they talked in detail about lands and rents, harvests and husbandry. Mark heard about the moorland properties from Nicholas and about Swaledale from his mother, and he answered the questions they cared to put about York and his duties.

When the meal was over, Nicholas ordered the best malmsey to be placed on the table and the three of them took a glass and moved closer to the hearth. Their mother sat in her favourite spot, on a settle near the fire, where she could position herself with her back to it. 'I'm like a cat,' she used to say when they were young: 'Give me a warm fire on a grey day, and I'm happy.' In the past she used to sew or embroider. This afternoon, as the winter dusk came down outside the windows, she sat a little forward, her hands on her knees, watching her sons from under dark lashes that were full and sweeping, like her eyebrows.

At last she said to Mark: 'Have you told us everything? You sound as though you came to say more, but you're hesitating. No need: we are remote and rural—avid for news.'

She had guessed, of course, that he was not there by chance.

'There are two matters: one is beyond my control; the other is a decision I must make—and you may not like.'

'Try us.' She folded her hands in her lap and sat erect and Nicholas looked at Mark in apprehension, his face reddened by the light of the fire.

'The first is, I intend to be with General George Monck when he gets to London. Things are uncertain enough now—once in London they'll be on a knife edge. I've no notion what he's up to but I want to be there, to see him run the hazard. It could turn to war all over again, and a nasty one, for it'll be at close quarters, in the streets and down the river. If the royalists rise in Kent, it'll spread there too.'

He turned to Nicholas. 'You know the terms of my will and they've not changed. But I march tomorrow with Monck, and in view of the risk I felt bound to take a look at it again. The short of it is that I'm minded to alter it. In one particular only, but it affects you most and I'd rather see your opinion of it face to face.'

'How can it touch Nicholas most? You have three brothers, my son, all of them steadfast in the care of your inheritance, all with a right to object if you dispose anything in a way to injure their children.'

'Forthright as ever, mother. So you'll hear what I have to say and give me your view.' But he paused. Days and nights of cogitation had got him to this point and yet at the last instant he was torn. It occurred to him that to own nothing at all would be preferable to having the welfare of so many beings dependent on his choices. He must, in the end, hurt some of them.

'I want to change the part of my will that concerns the Selby lands. They came to me by Cromwell's edict. When I die, if I leave them as Denton property, they're likely to be disputed and God knows to whom they might go. But if I bequeath them back to the Selbys, plain and simple, I think my wishes will be upheld by law—whether it's by Parliament's decree or … anyone else's.'

His mother looked at him in shock but she quickly made up her mind and said to Nicholas: 'Selby is neither here nor there to me. But what about your brothers?'

Mark rose and went to stand by the fire, one boot on the slate hearthstone and his shoulder against the mantel. He said to Nicholas: 'The income's considerable. You've managed the farms well, for all our sakes. Losing Selby would take a tidy sum out of the exchequer. But equally it would rid you of a responsibility. How busy does it make you now, for instance?'

Nicholas seemed relieved to discuss something concrete. 'Much as ever. I told you. The flocks on the hill farms are doing well. We drained Little Widcombe marsh in the autumn and the tenants put their shoulders to the work—come spring we'll have the result we wanted.'

'You don't suffer the obstacles and incompetence they put up at first?'

Nicholas shook his head. 'That's long over. It was all whingeing and no nuisance, in the end. They're as fond of the Selby name as ever, and the young lady comes just as often to visit them, when she thinks we don't know it, but we've had no trouble from tenant or labourer— no theft or fraud, no wilful damage.'

'Lady Lucinda still rides on the property?'

He said it rapidly, and his mother and brother both gave him a glance.

'Aye,' Nicholas said. 'You're disposed to forbid it?'

'I'd like to know what you'd think of the land going back to her—or rather, to her brother.'

Nicholas rose. 'Give me a spell to think on it. It's an odd turn-up, to think of you alienating your own land—'

'The family land, Nicholas,' his mother cut in.

Nicholas said abruptly to Mark, 'What do you fear from this march on London? Do you really think the royalists might get the upper hand?'

'I've no idea,' Mark said, 'which is why I'm going. But I'll tell you one thing—if Charles comes back, half the kingdom will be beating at his door for the return of confiscated lands. If the monarchy is restored, my army record damns me. But it would leave you untouched.'

'You mean inheriting Selby might compromise us?'

'Nick, it already does. Let me change the will and the danger passes.'

'You've made up your mind,' Nicholas muttered.

'You'd be surprised how seldom I have the luxury,' Mark said sharply. Then he said in a more even tone: 'Why not go and see how Margery does? You'll wish to discuss this with her.'

Nicholas took the chance to escape and Mark and his mother were alone. He moved across the hearth to a leather-backed chair opposite her.

She spoke first. 'Those lands were given to you as a reward for service. Are you no longer proud of what you and the army have done?'

He shrugged. 'I don't know that I've ever been proud. Resigned might perhaps be the word.' She looked surprised and he frowned. 'All these years, by serving Parliament I believed I was acting for my countrymen, great and small—a principle you set no store by. Very well, let's judge by the results instead. With the army's aid, Parliament has changed our form of government. Even if the king returns, England is not the same country that it was when his father chose to make war upon it.' She did not comment, so he said: 'How would it sit with you, to live in a kingdom again?'

'I thought you knew. Or have you forgotten in all these years? My desires in life have ever been the same. They are for peace, prosperity and the good of my family and my neighbours. If every household were so ordered, the wellbeing of the kingdom would take care of itself.'

He rose, restless. 'You won't regret it if Charles wins back the throne?'

'Not as much as I regretted the naming of Oliver Cromwell as Lord Protector. And I'll rejoice no less than I did on the day Cromwell died.'

He turned on her. 'Then you can't dispute the restoration of the Selby lands.'

'I could scarce understand your accepting them in the first place.'

This stung but he focused on the argument, not on the accusation in her eyes. 'Think. If I hadn't, to whom might they have passed? We can be sure of one thing: any other gentleman who got his hands on those properties would have held onto them, come hell or high water, whereas I knew I could keep them intact and watch over land and tenants, and wait for an excuse to one day transfer them back to Sir Maurice Selby. When I took possession I had no idea what might happen in Yorkshire between army and delinquents. I could only hope that the right day would come. Mother, I think it approaches. Will you stand in my way if I try to meet it thus?'

'Stand in your way?' she said with sarcasm. 'Who am I? You've always done just what you wanted.' This riled him and he did not answer. Goaded by his silence, she went on: 'Without a word to us, ever.'

'I've come here to debate this with you and Nick!'

'Yes, you've come with as little warning as possible and you'll leave in like manner. You're here to talk of risk and death and wills and everything I *don't* want to hear, in that cold way of yours, as though we were stocks and stones. I'm never to know your thoughts and feelings. And you care nothing about mine. So why come?'

He took a step forward. 'That's not true. I'm here to explain to you my reasons for—'

'Reasons!' she said. 'You've not explained to me the true reason why you accepted Selby! And I'll wager it's the *same* reason why you're so ready to give it back!'

He was baffled for a moment. Then he understood. The violence in his mother's voice and the pain in her eyes came from jealousy. She had spent 16 years believing he never thought of her, or cared. Now she was convinced that he held onto the Selby lands for the sake of another woman. He felt a tightness in his chest.

Her voice rose: 'I can name her, if you won't. What were you planning to do with Lady Lucinda Selby, marry her?'

He burst into painful laughter, then sat down again in the chair and ran his hand over his face. All at once he felt defeated, as though struck to earth in an endless battle from which he could never retreat.

Silence again, as he looked at the floor. He had no idea what kept his mother from railing at him—perplexity, resentment? Not remorse, surely; she need not apologise for getting so close to the truth.

He raised his head. 'It wasn't easy to accept Selby. I knew that if I did, it would make her my enemy. But if I turned it down, I wouldn't be able to keep it safe for her. So I said yes. I had no hope of her anyway—having her hate me would make no difference to my prospects.'

His mother's gaze was fixed on his face. 'But didn't you never think that … in time … she might accept you if it meant she'd have Selby back? You're ready enough to let her come and go about the farms, and you're not shy of her society in York, I hear. Who knows but she might look on marriage with favour if it's to regain her family lands?'

He came out with a curse that made her flinch back. He felt a surge of blood to his face. 'What? Sell herself to me, whom she hates like the devil? You're painting her a strumpet. Think what you want of me, but you'll speak of her with respect, Mother. And when I die, you'll hand back what belongs to her without another insult to her name!'

She gasped. 'I'm sorry. I don't know her and—'

'No, you don't.'

'But you're willing it to her! Away from us! What am I to think?' She burst into tears.

He had not seen her cry since her first piercing grief over his father. But this weeping was different: helpless and forlorn. It tore at him so much that he left the chair, crossed before the hearth and knelt to take her hands.

'Yes, I'm in love with her. But she'd never have married me. I can't win her. All I can do is act for her good, when it's in my power. That's why, if I'm killed—'

'You're not to say that!' His mother freed her hands and put them to his cheeks. 'You're not to die! Do whatever else you like ... give her Selby, throw away Denton and Swaledale for all I care, but don't do that. I won't lose you again!'

She leaned forward and they embraced. The tears stopped, and their breath, so hard did they hold each other. He closed his eyes and the rawness inside him was momentarily healed as though something golden were flowing through him like honey.

'Forgive me,' his mother said, pulling away a little until she could look into his eyes. Her own were mirrors to the firelight, emitting tiny sparks. 'I was harsh to you. I drove you away. I didn't mean to, but once it was done I could never get you back.'

'I'm here. I love you. If I'd only said so.' He wiped a tear from her cheek with his thumb, then rose and sat down next to her on the settle. He fell silent and she did not speak again, both afraid of shattering the fragile entente. He put one arm around her and she leaned her head on his shoulder. They looked into the fire, their minds for once seizing upon the same themes and the same memories—some sweet, some sad—until a sense of peace stole upon them. They were so enveloped in its warm stillness that when Nicholas reappeared, he was able to enter the chamber, observe them from behind and then withdraw without their even realising that he had come downstairs.

NUN APPLETON
January 18

Mary Villiers was rambling around Lord Fairfax's immaculate and leafless gardens with her brother George, not because the grounds offered any attractions on this freezing day, but because Fairfax had asked for her opinion of their design and the old man suffered too much in his joints to accompany them. She and George, wrapped in sables to the eyeballs, were alone, with no spies about them, and talking of General Monck, all of which Mary had been angling for since she arrived at Nun Appleton at midday.

'And where is his road taking him, this Monck of yours?'

'Newark, Market Harborough, Mansfield. He should be in Nottingham any day soon. But he's not my Monck. I wish to God he were.'

'He is: it's just that Lord Fairfax is too niggardly to admit it to you.'

'He interrogated Monck, you may be sure, but all he would tell me in the end was that the general is somewhat perplexed in his politics.'

'It's Fairfax who's perplexed in his politics, and moreover trying to put you off the scent. They've both decided for Charles but they're too devious to declare it to you and me. There you have it: Monck turns coat for the second time in his career.'

'And my lord for the first. You have to respect him for that.'

Mary stopped on a gravel path that led between pollarded limes and said: 'I don't respect him for anything. Our blessed king got the measure of him at Heworth Moor. Thomas Fairfax was a rabble leader from the first. There was a wild group shouting for parliament, and Fairfax came up to His Majesty and put a petition on the pommel of his saddle.'

'He didn't accept it?'

'Of course not. He rode off and nearly trampled Fairfax in the process. A great shame the man lived.'

'If he hadn't, I should be without a wife,' George said lightly. He put a hand under her elbow and they moved on. 'Come, he's given you a civil welcome, for my sake and hers.'

'George, you are speaking of the creator of the Model Army!'

'But he put all that behind him long ago, in favour of scripture and gardening. If you're minded to take a compliment back indoors, look down here under the arbour—see, there's the statue he commissioned of Thomas Goodwin. He was thinking of having one of his own hymns inscribed beneath but he changed his mind. He told me, words on stone should be from the Bible.'

Mary turned her back abruptly on Thomas Goodwin, Oxford divine. 'Your father-in-law's piety is odious and his poetry even worse. An hour ago we were deep in one of his paraphrases from the psalms and I was ready to scream. But Lucinda Selby rescued me with a Marvell piece about gardens. Longer, I grant you, but more palatable, despite the flattery. I enjoy Marvell, but when he gets onto the Fairfaxes he sounds as though he's composing on bended knee.' She set off back towards the mansion. 'By the way, I like Lady Lucinda.'

She left it at that, but it never hurt to issue a warning: for all George's dashing brilliance she could still sway him on occasions. He had been a dear, round-faced, chubby little boy when their widowed mother had married the Catholic Earl of Antrim and gone to Ireland. Charles I had taken all three Buckinghams into his household and treated them with kind affection, but Mary, the eldest by four years, had always known that her brothers' deepest love was hers alone. She felt protective towards Lucinda Selby and George now knew it. If he tried to tarnish that particular treasure, he would have to brave her annoyance.

'He was Mary's tutor,' George replied. When she looked at him sideways he said: 'Marvell.'

'And he had a very apt pupil, I wager. Your wife is as clever and super-educated as her mother, though she's not as showy about it. Your wife I approve; your mother-in-law I have yet to appreciate.'

George held open the door of the kitchen garden and they stepped into the walled enclosure, which still held in its geometric beds a few hints of last summer's munificence.

She said: 'Look, rosemary, like a little forest. Of more use than three Thomas Goodwins put together.'

George said, 'We may well owe Lady Fairfax a debt of gratitude. It's quite likely that she dissuaded his lordship from signing His Majesty's death warrant. She had a dream about a man entering her room with

Fairfax's head in his hand, and woke up crying that it was a merciful admonition from heaven. And so—'

'No! Don't tell me more! I'm sure if I were married to such as he, I'd be having dreams to match. You'll never persuade me they're angels. But be they monsters, I don't care: all I need to know is whether they are on our side.'

'Ah.' It was a visible puff of breath that dissipated in the winter air. George looked across the plots, his eyes glittering under a sheen of moisture caused by the cold. 'Yes,' he said. 'I think he's persuaded himself that if he works to bring back Charles he'll lose nothing by it, and may have something to gain. Achieving the *volte face* of England's greatest living commander will be a jewel in Charles's crown. And Lord Fairfax will have the honour of saving England all over again. I've often told him so these last months, in different but very attractive ways.'

'He won't resile, if Monck falls into some hideous trap in London?'

'He won't.' He took her arm again and turned her towards the house. 'Because *I'll* look after Monck.'

****

Lucinda was at Nun Appleton because she wanted Selby back. It was true that she liked the young Duchess of Buckingham, from whom the invitation had come, but the real attraction of the place was Lord Fairfax. He had appointed his uncle Charles as Governor of York and returned to his estate, but he would not take his eye off military and political affairs; therefore now was the time to ask for his influence in restoring Maurice's inheritance. Ever since the first morning of the year, on Marston Moor, Lucinda had tried to imagine what it might be like to have the army's steel bars removed from her path. Ever since Monck had marched into the city under Fairfax's aegis, she had been dreaming of home.

At Nun Appleton, Fairfax was mellower and his wife had lent her wit and the Buckinghams their warmth and energy to the indoor pastimes. Lucinda had had a pleasant time, but not a very productive one: Fairfax did not share her horror of Colonel Mark Denton and had no wish to deprive a prominent army officer of a gift from Parliament, even if the land had once belonged to an old friend. But Lucinda argued that Selby was her brother's by natural right. It had come to him through the loyal service of their ancestors, one of whom had been an admiral in the reign of Elizabeth I. Lucinda tried this line with Fairfax because connections to the great ones of history weighed heavily with him, which was why he welcomed without a qualm Mary Villiers, the dowager Duchess of Richmond and Lennox, lately arrived from the Low Countries, where, she did not scruple to mention, she had been the guest of Charles Stuart for over a week.

In the afternoon, Lucinda found herself sitting with the duchess in a ground-floor gallery overlooking a rose garden that in this season showed skeletons of plants under slender casings of snow. The Duke of Buckingham had been ready to join them in the mullioned window corner but his sister had put him off in her charming but magisterial manner and the two women were alone.

'I've been speaking to your brother,' the duchess said, 'and he's urgent to go to London. Shall you go with him?'

'But he can't! Our father was proscribed as a delinquent. Maurice is not permitted— Your Grace, what has he said to you?'

'He didn't confide his situation. He told me his feelings. I see: he doesn't have your liberty of movement. But you visit London often? You have family there?'

'I've never been to London in my life.'

Mary Villiers raised her arched eyebrows further but did not comment. Lucinda was not intimidated by her but she was aware of the gulf that stood between herself and this lofty noblewoman who had been raised at court and had become the intimate friend and lady-in-waiting of the queen, Henrietta-Maria. Lucinda knew Mary Villiers's reputation for beauty, elegance and wit, and she admired her; but at 38 the duchess was handsome rather than beautiful, with a waist that filled out her exquisite gown a little too tightly for fashion.

'But *no* family there?' the duchess pursued in her light, pleasant voice. She seemed not to think that Lucinda would mind this cheerful interrogatory. In fact, Lucinda was curious; she had the feeling that the duchess wanted something from her.

'There are Selbys everywhere, but as to London … I think there may be a distant cousin of my father's near the Convent Garden.'

'Oh? An excellent neighbourhood. But I agree with you—too central by far for your brother to venture. Or mine. Last time George was in London he was in the Tower.' She shuddered, and her lids lowered over her dark blue eyes. 'I do wish George would stay here. But my wishes are seldom granted. He tried to get through to Monck, you know—to talk to him openly and offer his support—but the man would have none of it.'

'So did Maurice, and failed likewise.'

'And now they both want to tag along behind him! Heading God knows where.'

'Where do you go, Your Grace, when you leave here?'

'Cobham. I should be there now if it were not for …' The duchess bit her lip. 'Cobham is in Kent; the home of my late husband's family. There are sufficient of us Stuarts there to be very good company for one another. I feel I should go, though I've been weeks away from France and I long for my children.' She went on, as though Lucinda had asked another question: 'No, I detest London now. All our houses are snatched away. George hasn't a roof to put over his head. Wallingford House, York House in enemy hands …' Then she seemed to come to herself and gave Lucinda a look of such kindness that it transformed her face. 'But I mustn't talk to you of loss. Your brother has told me what you suffered. What can be done to recover your lands? If there's anything I can do, I beg you to tell me.'

It was so unexpected that Lucinda was moved. 'You're very good, Your Grace. But the army stands in the way. Cromwell granted Selby to Colonel Denton, when he was commissioner to Major General Lambert—'

'But Lambert has been ousted!'

'Yes, but Colonel Denton is as powerful as ever. He rides with Monck.' She hesitated. 'I did hope that perhaps Lord Fairfax might use his influence for us.'

The duchess sighed. 'Don't deceive yourself. Fairfax has done what he agreed to do; he has secured York. He considers that quite enough for a man in his position, and henceforth will do no more for anyone. He received Monck here the other day, but as far as I can tell the conversations were void of import. Fairfax is simply waiting. He can afford to—we can't.'

The duchess rose to her feet, walked to the doorway and looked down the passage on each side. Then she closed the door behind her and came back to stand near Lucinda and gaze out the window.

Eventually she spoke. 'Monck provides the only chance of His Majesty's return. He's a blank wall to any gentleman who approaches him on the king's behalf, which proves to me that he knows his bargaining power and is not going to relinquish it prematurely. The king has offered him £100,000 which he has refused.' Lucinda gasped and the duchess gave her an ironical smile. 'Indeed. He's clearly hoping for more—much, much more. Once he's in London and can gauge how he might act, and what success he might win without risking his neck too far … who knows how high he will set his fee? At any rate, I've been given the mission of making new offers to him from the king.'

Lucinda looked up at her in astonishment.

'Yes, I,' Mary Villiers said sarcastically, and resumed her seat. 'The men have got nowhere with him; we shall see what a woman can do. My methods will be totally different, you may be sure. I've no intention of running about the country after Monck and I'm not going to approach him directly, for he won't trust a Stuart, much less a Buckingham.'

There was a pause, which Lucinda did not break. It was a revelation that Mary Villiers should be a spy and ambassador for Charles—but it made sense. The duchess was a Stuart by marriage, and had spent her whole life at the seat of power.

The lady continued briskly, 'I'll have to get to Monck through someone who's close to him and has a strong influence with him— someone he *does* trust. The candidates are his brother, his brother-in-law, his physician and his chaplain, all slavishly devoted and ready to run errands for him hither and yon—but I'm afraid such creatures are rather beyond my ken. Can you see me suing to any of these men? No, neither can I. So it will have to be the wife. You realise she's for the king, don't you?'

'I've been told as much, but otherwise I know nothing of her. She didn't come with Monck to York.'

'No, he sent her down to London in December. She sailed from Berwick with their son and bound, they say, for Whitehall.' She looked at Lucinda intently. 'Can you tell me the name of the person entrusted by Monck to escort wife and son to Berwick, arrange for their accommodation there and then secure them a passage to London?'

Lucinda shook her head.

The duchess gave a slight frown. 'But he must be one of these numerous relatives you tell me are scattered throughout the North. His name is Anthony Selby.'

'By heaven! You're correct, he is related—my father's second cousin—but we've never met. His branch of the family quarrelled with ours; a religious dispute. He's Presbyterian—'

'And so is Mistress Monck. She no doubt has a fellow feeling with this helpful gentleman, and the name of Selby must be pleasing to her: it will be doubly so when she learns that Anthony Selby is your cousin. Lady Lucinda, I shall be glad of your company on my return to Cobham, and of your help in London. I can't do this alone and I can think of no one more fit to assist me. I'll need you until at least the end of February and no doubt longer. I imagine you may be spared from York?' The dark blue eyes sped over Lucinda. 'You're ideally situated. Good breeding, good looks, a quick mind, no great household to go to pieces in your absence, and no husband, though it's time someone remedied the last— I'll think upon it for you. Not a single impediment exists to your coming with me.'

Lucinda felt bewildered, but her answer was prompt. 'I have a brother. Before you dispose of my time, Your Grace, consider his claims upon me.'

'Indeed. A very impulsive brother, I'm told.' There was another mercurial change in the duchess's expression and she leaned forward to briefly touch Lucinda's wrist. 'My dear, many a woman sees further and more clearly than the males in her family. The men have done quite enough. This is the time for *you* to act. Believe me: the only way you'll ever recover your family's land is if the king restores it to you. By helping me, you'll be helping His Majesty. When he comes back, his true servants will be rewarded. If I speak to His Majesty, as of course I shall, Colonel Denton's activities in this region will be made the subject of an investigation and trial. He'll be thrown in the Tower; he may even reach the scaffold. In any event, over Denton's dead body or not, you'll regain Selby. Do not come to London merely because I entreat you and the king needs you—come for your own good and the future of your family.'

And this lady called Maurice impulsive! Lucinda's mind flashed over what was offered. Revenge, freedom, Selby—and London, a temptation that came as a surprise. Her voice shook when she answered. 'Pardon me, Your Grace, but you don't know me. What makes you imagine I can help you?'

'I wonder if you're aware—' The duchess stood up, pacing away a little, then turning back. She seemed never to be quite still. 'I wonder if you realise how few true friends the king has—I mean, friends who are prepared to *act*? Conspirators, agents, royal trusts, we have in abundance, here and abroad. But who stays by his side? When I was in Brussels, I counted those crushed, unhappy, impoverished few. On one hand.' There were tears in her eyes. She shook her head with a self-mocking smile, then looked into Lucinda's eyes. 'And you are not unknown to me. After Marston Moor, someone spoke to me of your father. It was Prince Rupert. He said that Sir John Selby was a man of letters, not of war, but nonetheless he rode to the moor before the battle and volunteered. Rupert tried at first to dissuade him but he didn't succeed. He said your father was as brave and noble a gentleman as he had ever met. I have a special sympathy with anyone who endured the horrors of Marston Moor and suffered for it after. And I know loyalty when I see it, because it's rare. Don't try to tell me I'm wrong about you.'

Lucinda could not look away, but nor could she speak.

The duchess said: 'We shall leave York by the river and sail from Hull.'

'Your Grace, Overton controls Hull—he's as ruthless as Lambert or Denton.'

The duchess smiled. 'I've a letter of safe passage from Lord Fairfax. I await only your readiness. How long do you need to prepare?'

'You do me too much honour, Your Grace.'

'I'll be the judge of that. May I fetch you the day after tomorrow?'

'Yes. I have little to pack. I possess two good gowns and neither, I must warn you, is fit for London.'

The duchess gave a mischievous, triumphant smile. 'But *you* are more than fit, Lady Lucinda, and so it will prove.'

NOTTINGHAM
January 21

Mark Denton was supposed to be housed in dilapidated and draughty Nottingham Castle while General Monck occupied the governor's comfortable townhouse, where he held his officers' meetings. This evening, Mark stood near the back of the chamber, leaned against the oak panelling and observed Monck's colonels as the general went through the dispositions for the march to London. The infantry had all been commissioned because of their unquestioning loyalty to Monck, who had purged his officers of anyone he mistrusted well before he left Scotland. Parliament had made its own appointments to his high command at that stage, but he had disregarded them, causing much chagrin. Of the cavalry regiments, Monck commanded two and the third was under Knight. A relative of Monck's, Colonel Clobery, was in charge of the fourth, and the fifth was Mark's regiment.

Amongst the commanders, Mark felt himself to be the odd man out, though this was based on instinct, not facts. Monck still gave nothing away and if any of the hardened soldiers listening to him that evening were in on his secrets, they betrayed no sign. In Ralph Knight's craggy profile, Mark read only respect for the general and for his orders, which were well thought out and fair. Monck put the welfare of his army first but his troops would not be trampling through villages creating nuisance, requisitioning free food and equipment and leaving resentment in their wake. In strategic towns such as Nottingham they would stay long enough for gentry, merchants and populace to feel secure; and everywhere, be their quarters fine or lowly, they would pay their way.

Monck had commanded many a forced march in his time, when speed was of the essence, but he was moving this army down the length of England at a peaceable, almost leisurely pace. In appearance at least, he was not mounting a raid on London, which was a wise precaution, if in fact he intended trying to persuade Parliament to bring back the king. It would ill support Charles's return if Monck and his forces were remembered with abhorrence from Coldstream to Saint Albans.

Meanwhile Monck's secrecy, coupled with his sedate and orderly advance, increased his vulnerability. His most dangerous enemies, such as the deposed army grandees like Lambert and the military republicans within Parliament, had been given ample time to observe his progress. One assassination attempt had nearly succeeded while the army was on the move—on Mark, at Stannington—which had surely proved to Monck what acute personal risks he ran. The real aims of this march were concentrated in Monck's black head and if someone managed to get close enough to put a bullet through it, his army would lose both leader and purpose with one shot. Yet the general acted as though he were oblivious to threat, making no change to the order of march and his position within it. Day by day he presented the same stolid, predictable target to any surprise attack. Mark could only imagine that Monck's private measures for his own safety were more carefully planned. Mark had not been told of them, and not since Morpeth had Monck called upon Mark for intelligence; the general's scouting was done by others. Meanwhile Mark maintained his own network—not too difficult, given the army's slow drift down the country.

When it came time for questions, Mark was interested to hear one posed with pretty convincing curiosity: 'When we get to London, sir, will we be quartered alongside Parliament's regiments?'

'It's rather too soon for me to tell you, colonel. Where we're deployed in London will depend on Parliament's wishes and I don't know those yet.'

Mark waited for Monck to mention that two commissioners from Parliament were actually on the road from London to Nottingham, but Monck said no more on the matter and shortly afterwards closed the meeting. The general would hear Parliament's wishes but it looked unlikely that he would share them with his officers. Mark's scouts had given him the names of these gentlemen some days before: they were Thomas Scot and Luke Robinson, neither of whom Mark knew. As Monck's officers clattered down the stairs he was tempted to ask Ralph Knight if he was aware of the two-man delegation, and watch his face as he answered, but it was only a fleeting idea. The people closest to Monck's secrets were the personal friends, like Doctor Gumble, who had rejoined the general from London three days before.

In the street, they found a coach drawn up outside the doors. Ralph Knight stopped on the stairs, with an exclamation that showed he recognised who was descending from the vehicle. The gentleman looked up, saw Knight and gave a half-smile before turning to his servants with orders about his baggage. He then walked forward as Knight came down the steps and they exchanged greetings.

Mark saw a thin man of medium height, well turned out and with an air of self-importance, though without the brisk confidence of an aristocrat. The encounter on the general's doorstep made Knight feel obliged to introduce Mark.

'Doctor Clarges, allow me to present Colonel Denton, commander of the militia regiment of cavalry. Colonel, Doctor Thomas Clarges.'

Mark's interest sharpened as they bowed to each other. Clarges was Monck's brother-in-law, on excellent terms with Monck, and no doubt bringing messages from his sister and news from Whitehall. Mark could not inquire about the wife and son, since he had met Anne Monck but twice and the son not at all, so he asked the usual questions about Clarges's journey and then completed the courtesies and moved away, leaving Knight to escort the man into the governor's house. He was surprised to be joined by Knight at the corner of the street.

'I'd happily have ushered him in,' Knight said, 'but the general came pounding down the stairs to welcome him. Avid for news, of course. The general's indulgence to his wife knows no bounds.'

'Except military ones.'

'Indeed. He follows his own counsel there. But he lets her speak her mind, by God. You've heard her when she has on what she calls her treason gown?'

'I've never dined at her table. But I hear Mistress Monck makes no bones about being for the king, and has her say from time to time.'

'Oh, unashamedly. The gown's no mere figure of speech. I've seen her appear in it and a right royal hostess she is when she has it on.' He caught Mark's eye. 'She's no scold, for all that, nor a shrew neither. The general gives her no reply except a raised eyebrow now and then. It's my conviction he likes to see the guests in amazement, and he as silent as a monument throughout.'

Near the castle they parted, Knight to go to his quarters and Mark to enter the tavern he had adopted in Nottingham. The tapster brewed a good beer that was often served by a comely wench who had a quiet smile by day and a willing way in the small hours. This evening she was not in evidence, so he chose a single spot not too close to the fire and sat down, ignoring all company in the hot, crowded room, to contemplate what, if anything, he should do about the London commissioners, Scot and Robinson.

Instead, he instantly began thinking about Lucinda Selby.

On his last day in York, he had had to fight down the foolish urge to bid her goodbye. There had, as usual, been nothing he could say to her; all the words were shut inside his head.

I've loved you since I first met you on the bridge. Mark had been on horseback one market day and she on foot with a maid, when a sturdy beggar at the end of the bridge across the Ouse accosted her, looming up and preventing her from going further amongst the throng. She had given the man a coin: a mistake, for he then made a grab for her purse. He was a large, belligerent man and reacted violently to Mark's dismounting and telling him to be gone. Angry himself, Mark had used a wrestling trick to get the man off-balance against the parapet of the bridge, and then could not resist tipping him into the river. There was a cheer from the bystanders, a great splash as he hit the water and a cry from the young woman.

'What have you done?'

Amidst general laughter, Mark had invited her to look down, to see the beggar being hauled out by a bargeman. 'The water this side is only deep enough to take his fall, not to drown him. He'll not bother you again.'

Despite herself, she had laughed, too, her hands before her mouth. 'You're very ready with your help, sir. I must take care not to need it again or I'm like to see someone killed!'

'I hope not.' He bowed. 'May I escort you home?'

'By no means: I am all for peace when I can get it.'

He had mounted up and ridden away without seeking more speech of her, let alone any thanks for the rescue. She was grateful, he could tell, but he sensed a streak of independence under the good breeding and delicate beauty, and a wariness of overbearing men, be they beggars or army officers.

Later he had found out her name and estate. She was 15, unmarried, and a Selby, well above him in rank and upbringing. Because of her father's delinquency, her family had no land to speak of, whilst he was landed and comparatively wealthy—but she would want more in a husband than the ability to tip miscreants into the drink for her.

Like a fool, I've spent five years in dread of your marrying. They had next met at a dinner at Nun Appleton in 1656. By then she was betrothed and Mark was commissioner to Cromwell's major-general in Yorkshire. The prospective husband was a royalist gentleman of good standing, too young to have a record as a delinquent, and on quite good terms with Lord Fairfax, then in honourable retirement. At the dinner, Mark had observed Lady Lucinda and Sir William Upton for signs of mutual affection and seen none, which made no difference to his feeling of desolation. On the other hand he soon learned how she felt about Oliver Cromwell's new means of keeping the English in order. She discussed the major-generals with him freely over the table, with the same play of intelligence and charm that she used with everyone. Still, he could tell that she feared the Protectorate and that he disturbed her. Perhaps she was apprehensive that he would mention the scene on the bridge.

He did not. Later, he had asked Lady Fairfax about Sir William Upton and found that the young man had been Sir John Selby's first choice for his daughter. Lady Fairfax slyly suggested that Lucinda had accepted Upton's hand out of respect for the memory of her father, and Mark had fallen into the trap by saying: 'Surely not. It's my impression she has a passionate will.'

Lady Fairfax had replied with a smile: 'Mine also. Though it's not something the gentlemen usually notice at first glance.' He had accepted this in silence and she could not draw him further.

The next time Mark met Lady Lucinda, the Selby lands had just been bestowed on him by Parliament after the demise of the original recipient, and Sir William Upton had recently died, unmarried, the victim of a riding accident. Mark sometimes speculated what might have happened if the two calamities had happened in reverse order, but found no comfort in that direction. There was a bar on every conversation he had with Lucinda Selby: for him to apologise for receiving the family property would have been ludicrous, and she had too much pride to bear its being mentioned.

To her, all their meetings must have seemed accidental, but there had been occasions when he had lingered somewhere to get speech of her, however barbed the conversation promised to be. One such encounter had been outside the Minster, after Monck had walked out of Edward Bowles's sermon and Mark and the rest of the army worshippers had left with him. The others had dispersed but Mark had hung around outside until the end of the service. He had been absent from York for months; she could not seriously object if he gave her greeting on his return. During the service, he had watched her and tried to catch from the turn of her head the impact that Bowles's ill-advised preachments made on her. At one point she had leaned over and whispered in Maurice Selby's ear. Mark had seen urgency and alarm in her profile at that moment, but the eye had sparkled with the animation that made her so fascinating to him. She was too open, too active to remain in the sidelines of the coming struggle—she would want to help her cause, carry messages, even ride into danger.

When Lucinda had walked out of the Minster she was still with Maurice Selby, and on Maurice's other side was the Duke of Buckingham, who had him in close conversation. Buckingham seemed momentarily more interested in the brother than the sister and tried to draw him a little away, with a hand on his arm and a significant look. Maurice had made a quick excuse to Lucinda and stepped aside, which left her alone for a second.

Mark had walked forward and bowed. She started, received his greeting without her usual urbanity, and for once seemed at a loss.

'Fear not, my lady, I merely wish to bid you good day.' She curtsied and murmured something, and he went on, with the only excuse he could find for speaking: 'And I have a message for you from one of your former tenants, Malcolm Gaines?' She looked surprised, but nodded. 'Gaines recently said to my brother at Denton, and my brother has just made known to me by letter, that you were always greatly concerned about the state of the barns at Little Widcombe in winter. Gaines begs us let you know that despite this severe season the barns are sound, and he also begs leave to assure you that in spring, as usual, he will have great pleasure in sending you two lambs when they're weaned.'

Her voice was low. 'Thank you.'

He cursed himself: she found the conversation humiliating. She would find it even more so if he told her the barns had been mended on his orders. 'I'll make sure your thanks are conveyed. May I also say that you're in as excellent health as you seem?'

'You may.' She lifted her chin. 'Yes, despite everything, you may.' She looked over towards the two gentlemen, and Mark saw Buckingham give a sharp glance across Selby's shoulder. Whereupon, in order not to inconvenience the lady further, he had taken leave of her.

Next evening, he had seen her at Fairfax House and read her a lecture about caution, to which she had refused to listen and which had been cut off by the Duke of Buckingham.

Sitting in the Spread Eagle in Nottingham, Mark swallowed the last of his beer and felt a wave of loathing for Buckingham. A ruthless predator with women, Buckingham fancied himself the friend of both sister and brother, adopting airs of protection that tormented Mark even more than Lucinda's dislike. It was absurd to love her and even more absurd to be jealous of her, but he hated having left her behind in York where there was nothing to stop George Villiers from inveigling himself further into the Selbys' lives—and the duke would never be warned off by his wife who, out of purity of heart or besotted love, seemed to have gained no insight into his character.

Leaving the tankard on the table, Mark went upstairs to the chamber under the eaves that he rented from the landlord, who was flattered that he should prefer the tavern to the officers' quarters in the castle and patronise the prettiest barmaid, a choosy lass whose attractions enhanced the reputation of the Spread Eagle.

Mark also used the chamber for different assignations—with informants who slipped up the back stairs from the yard without the innkeeper being aware and gave their reports.

Today the agent was Stillwell, a cheerful, talkative ex-soldier whom Mark had employed over the years for his effortless ability to absorb news. He was originally from Nottingham, but Mark had left him in York to assess what went on there once Monck and Fairfax had quit the town.

Mark sat under a window that looked down into the coach yard, and Stillwell stood at his ease in the middle of the room, his hat in his hand, and gave a succinct report on the military dispositions in York and the mood as regarded Monck.

'Philosophical, sir, very philosophical. Nary a soul in the street but believes Edward Bowles spoke gospel from the pulpit on the day the general marched in. I'm not saying there are any loyal toasts in the taprooms. But many people have laid the preacher's word to heart and you often hear a whisper about he who was afar coming nigh. As for the council and the aldermen, well, there's a great deal of palaver but no purpose, as far as I can tell, sir, to do anything but wait.'

'What of Lord Fairfax?'

'He keeps house in the country in his old way, with the usual visitors. There's only one has never come before—the Duchess of Richmond.'

'Buckingham's sister?'

'The same, sir. And I heard, from the servant I know at his lordship's, she came straight from Charles Stuart, in Brussels.'

Mark felt a jolt and dropped his gaze. To receive Mary Villiers when the world knew where she had just been sent an unmistakable message: Fairfax considered himself as holding the North for the king.

Mark rose and stared down into the yard. What if a royal landing was imminent? Was Monck's march in fact a diversion? If Charles were on the point of crossing to Hull or Newcastle … But there was no army to meet and protect him. The only available force, apart from the garrison at York, was Monck's, for Charles would never trust the Scots again, however many self-styled royalists might offer to muster an army from the Highlands. Would he take the risk of landing in Yorkshire with his puny company of troops and racing down to join Monck? Surely not: in military terms it would be idiocy and neither Charles nor Monck was a fool.

'Is the Duchess of Richmond still at Nun Appleton?'

'No, sir. She'll be on the sea by now, bound for Kent. She's landing at Margate and going to Cobham.'

'I don't suppose Buckingham's gone with her?'

'No. I'm driven to a non-plus by the duke; I can never guess what he'll do from one day to the next and nor can his servants. The duchess has taken but one guest back with her and that's the Lady Lucinda Selby.'

'What?'

Stillwell met Mark's eye with a sly look. Mark wondered whether he had asked rather too often about what the Selbys were up to and concluded that he probably had. Stillwell was no fool, either.

'Have you any idea why she goes? What does Sir Maurice want in Kent? He can't go up to London from there—he's barred.'

'Sir Maurice is not with the lady, sir.'

'Then what is *he* doing?'

'Their servants are well trained, sir—the most tight-lipped in York. But I know one of their tenants as was, Geoffrey Paget, who keeps a market garden at Saint Mary Bishop, and it seems there was a quarrel between brother and sister, he wanting to come down and offer his services to Monck and she telling him not to put himself at risk. Sir Maurice overruled her and said he wasn't going to rusticate when he could be bearing arms for the king's return, and that was that. The lady's for Kent and the lord for Nottingham.'

'Odds blood,' Mark said, 'I can just see the general commissioning a rampant royalist! It will go ill with Selby if he thinks to swagger it in Nottingham.'

'He's a right good blade, I hear,' Stillwell said diplomatically.

'With but a few hours' experience in battle, and none of command. Either Monck will save his tender neck by sending him packing, or I'll have to take care of him myself.'

****

When Stillwell had gone, Mark went over the picture he had been given of York. It sounded as though the city would remain quiet now Monck was gone. Sir Charles Fairfax was in control and Lilburne was still there, seeking permission to retire to his estate in the North Riding. No charges had been brought against him by York's Common Council of aldermen or by order of Parliament.

When Lord Fairfax had appeared outside the gates on New Year's Day, the aldermen had voted to refuse Lilburne access to the army magazine, and to invite Fairfax's forces into York. With Lambert in flight, Lilburne had no allies to call upon and his own men were more than ready to join Fairfax. In the end he had handed over York with scarcely a murmur. In consequence, he had been offered the private choice of self-exile—across the Channel via Hull—but for reasons of his own he had chosen to remain in house arrest.

Mark leaned on the sill and looked down into the yard of the Spread Eagle, through small panes rimed with snow crystals, and thought of the ill-lit, windowless room in which he had last spoken with Robert Lilburne.

It had been an awkward meeting. Lilburne, who looked old beyond his 53 years, was on his feet to receive Mark, but soon sat down again on a low bench by the wall. There was other furniture about but Mark was not going to sit without an invitation and when this was not forthcoming he stood quietly in the centre of the chamber. He had often found that this readiness to listen and observe disconcerted people; but what, after all, does one say to a man whom one has served with zeal for years and who is now cashiered?

Lilburne was resentful and not keen to talk about himself. By contrast with his brother John, the famous Leveller at present in exile and banned from returning to England under pain of death, Robert's impulses were not political but religious. He was an Independent, of the same beliefs as the Cromwells and most of the Eastern Association army officers, and he had taken pride in the godly order that prevailed in York under his command.

Mark made courteous inquiries about Lilburne's treatment by the Common Council, which were answered with irony but without complaint. Lilburne in return asked what Mark had been doing since his departure for Scotland in the previous year and received brief, accurate answers.

Finally, Lilburne gave a snort and said: 'I never thought to say it, but you disappoint me, colonel. You've just thrown away a lifetime of honourable service, and you come to visit *me*! Who sent you? You're not fool enough to think I'd turn coat as you've just done!'

'I'm still Parliament's servant, sir.'

'Really? You know where Monck's bound and what he'll do when he gets there: he'll coerce Parliament into returning the members who were ousted in '48, the ones who were looking for a compact with the king. You know what they'll do the moment they regain their seats: they'll invite Charles Stuart back to the throne. And you're marching with Monck! I'm surprised you can hold your head up before me, sirrah. I'll be even more surprised if you keep it on your shoulders, should London abase itself before the king.'

'Monck's force is not large,' Mark said evenly. 'Nor are his desires clear. And Lambert and the rest may well be there, waiting for him.' At his former commander's name, Lilburne looked away; a slight flush masked his pale cheeks and his anger vanished. There was loyalty there, painful to see. Mark continued: 'Would you recommend that I join Major General Lambert, sir?'

This startled Lilburne and he rose to his feet. 'He lost the North,' he said harshly. 'What sign is there that he can gain London?'

'Forgive me, but I'd like to know whether you were of a mind with him –whether you supported the rebels and were content to see the army try to govern in Parliament's stead. Or—'

'I served my general. I was faithful to my commander, which is more than can be said of you.'

'That is no answer.'

'And you expect one, when you can walk out that door a free man and tell tales to whomever you choose?'

Mark refused to rise to Lilburne's anger. 'I've no intent to betray you. York was lost before I got back and my regiment was turned over to Monck whether I willed it or no.'

'And you've come to join me in defeat? I think not. Begone. You have no purpose here.'

'I have one: to give you my reverence before I leave. I spent years under your command; you're older and more experienced than I and a soldier of principle. If I ask your thoughts, it's out of respect.' *A habit that I should teach myself to break*, he thought bitterly, but did not utter the words, for Lilburne looked confused.

There was a silence: each man was moved, in a different way.

Mark recalled the message he had promised to bring. 'I also have some words to give you, from Major General Lambert.'

'Lambert!'

'I told you how I parleyed with him at the Picts' Wall. He was as chary of his mind as you, sir, and all he gave me was a sentence for you: "True opener of my eyes, prime angel blessed, much better seems this vision, and more hope of peaceful days portends than those two past."'

The response in Lilburne's gaze was stronger than his anger: it was hope. For a second it gave his eyes the brightness of tears. Mark marvelled at the power of a few words to light up the spirits of this man who had chosen confinement over exile.

They had taken leave of each other without further contest, for Mark realised that Lilburne would reveal neither the meaning of the words nor the source, which must be a tract, pamphlet or poem.

Standing alone by the window at the Spread Eagle, Mark pondered on Lilburne's last lesson to him. It was about hope: how deep it ran; how human its face was; how hotly it could contend, even in secret, against the odds.

BEDFORD
January 28

Luke Robinson had no quarrel with the lodgings he shared with Thomas Scot at The Swan, Bedford, but he objected strongly to Scot. He could share his irritation with no one, for Scot was impervious to criticism and they were both too unwelcome on Monck's march to exchange complaints with the commanders, let alone Monck himself.

Robinson was an alderman of the city of London, with no acquaintance in Bedford, and it was a Wednesday, when no market was held in the handsome town square. He went out, nonetheless, his body rugged up against the cold and his mind in the same ferment that he had suffered every night on the way down from Nottingham, with Scot snoring like a blacksmith's bellows in one corner of a chamber while he tossed and turned in the other.

He gave no excuse to his companion this evening, just set out along the bank of the Ouse (were there any rivers north of London *not* called the Ouse?), his mouth pinched in a grimace that no one in the streets could see beneath the immense muffler his wife had given him on his departure. He needed to commune with himself; it was impossible to talk rationally with Scot, who cared for nothing but the sound of his own voice. A day's journey with the man would have been enough: the past fortnight had been purgatory.

Yet their ideas about their mission had been alike at the outset. Unanimously appointed as commissioners, charged with Parliament's authority for the meeting with Monck, he and Scot had gone forth with greater confidence than either had felt in many a year. They were literally the voice of Parliament, sent to address the general with the pent-up breath of decades of office. Their Speaker was the same William Lenthall who had countered with dignity and defiance Charles I's attempt to arrest five of the members in 1642. The House had in the meantime dwindled through deaths and the failure of recruiter elections; it had been purged in 1648 of those members who leaned towards a compact with the king; it had had to contend with the very army that was once formed to serve them; members had been expelled on several notorious occasions; but remnants had survived. They were a mere rump of a parliament—as vulgar contempt would have it—but they were in power. Members like himself and Scot, who had not allowed distance, fear or cynicism to discourage them from attending the House, must command respect.

Unfortunately, Scot in private was fussy, garrulous and a great trumpeter about nothings. In the Commons, Robinson had listened to him debate about fine points of law or commerce for many an hour, and when the man was named as commissioner he had seemed a good choice. But on the road north, Scot proved himself too cold, too damp, too twisted up by the jolting of the coach to talk about anything except his own ills. When they had finally come upon Monck at Nottingham, Scot had had to stop carping and try to get Monck to tell them why he was marching to London—but Monck ignored him.

For a while the sun, slanting along the river, gave a coppery tinge to the house fronts and businesses that made a pleasant contrast to the iron-grey of the sky, but all too soon the light faded and Robinson had to find his way along the towpath in a blackness that unnerved him. He had passed many an alehouse on his walk, always thinking to see a better one a few steps further on; now he worried that he had tramped too far. Behind him now, there were soft footfalls on hard ground, but each time he turned, the sounds stopped. If there was a stealthy pursuer in his wake, he felt for once that it would be of some comfort to have Scot at his side.

He came to a lane where a lamp in a window threw a feeble light across the ground, and took a quick turn away from the river. He was after an alehouse and company, however rude the locals proved to be. He found it: a place of low windows that showed a long taproom, with one hefty door closed against the cold, and an iron sign creaking above, the name easy to guess from its shape, which was that of a large, heavy birdcage—or a gibbet.

From his lifetime of commerce and high office, Robinson was used to being in the public eye and he liked it when he and his entourage were recognised in the London streets. Tonight he had walked out with no attendants and no intention to impress but he did not expect to enter the Bird Cage without attracting notice; in fact he was rather looking forward to it. He wanted company.

A dead silence fell and he took a calm look at the ranks of avid faces turned his way. He stood out, not just as a stranger, with his expensive London clothes, but as a man of substance and power. No one stared too long and the men around the tables began murmuring to each other again. Except for one table, where a slender young fellow sat with his back to the lime-washed wall, facing a bulky man wearing an abundant dark wig, whose face was hidden.

The young man was Sir Maurice Selby, who had been hanging about Monck's army since Nottingham. Selby was a rabid royalist whom Monck kept at arm's length, but the gentleman had never taken the hint and had even persuaded one of the colonels to give him some kind of task. Robinson was an excellent judge of a crowd and he knew that he and Selby were the only people in the taproom who did not belong in Bedford—except, perhaps, for the man in the black wig.

Selby was looking across the room. He had fine, transparent skin warmed by the nearby fire; as their eyes met, Robinson saw a brighter blush come and go across the prominent cheekbones. Holding Robinson's gaze, the lad sat forward in his chair and with the faintest movement of the lips said something to his faceless companion.

Robinson took a glance at the tapster who was standing behind the wooden counter with a beaker in one hand and a dishcloth in the other, his mouth hanging open in what he meant to be a helpful manner. Robinson stepped forward but watched Selby's table out of the corner of his eye. The companion rose, stooping somewhat under a voluminous cloak that made his height hard to judge. No farewell seemed to pass and the gentleman removed himself quickly through a nearby door.

Robinson was cheered to think that the chilly walk along the riverside might yet yield something of interest. He paused at the counter to order a tankard of the best Bedford brew and headed for the hearth. He left Selby no opportunity to escape; the lad scarcely had time to rise to his feet before Robinson was facing him.

'Good even to you, Sir Maurice,' Robinson said affably. 'I little thought to see a familiar face here. May I ask the favour of joining you, since your friend has left the stool free? He's not returning, I take it?'

The young man's face was composed into the mask that gentlemen could adopt when addressed without the formality befitting their rank. Robinson, who considered his approach quite polite enough, sat down.

As Selby resumed his seat, Robinson said with a jerk of his head: 'Where does yon door lead?'

'I don't know,' Selby said with indifference.

Robinson looked up as one of the taproom servants placed a tankard on the board at his elbow. 'This is from a maltster called Farre, I'm told. You're not sampling a local brew?'

Selby raised his wine cup. 'No, mulled claret.'

'Claret! This is a right humble place from the outside, but it has some surprises within. Who were you talking to so cosily here?'

'I hardly know. We exchanged but two words. I'm engaged on purchases for Colonel Knight. Horses. Two of the cavalry regiments are under strength.'

'Ah.' So Monck had fobbed Selby off onto Knight when he came rattling down from York breathing fire for Charles Stuart. 'Strange place and time to meet a horse trader. Or does he have a stable full of nags somewhere yonder?'

'I'll find out tomorrow,' Selby said.

'You're meeting again?'

'He knows what I'm after. If he has anything to offer, he knows where I'm lodged.'

'With Knight?'

'Yes.'

'Ralph Knight has made you an officer, then?'

'No. But he's glad to command my knowledge of horses. I was trained to ride by the Marquess of Newcastle, the greatest horseman in England. My reputation, in York at least, is second only to his.'

Robinson, no great horseman himself, took the boast philosophically. 'And I hear you're a bosom friend of the Duke of Buckingham, who has the finest stables in the country. But is that your dearest ambition, Sir Maurice? To swell General Monck's cavalry train?'

'Why so many questions, Master Robinson?' Selby said. 'You're weary of putting them to General Monck?'

'Monck!' Robinson gave a short laugh and took another sip of ale. He enjoyed sparring with clever youths. 'Scot and I have had nothing out of Monck. He's content to accept Parliament's escort to London but he won't discuss what he'll do when he gets there.'

'Rather, sir, he's escorting you! With 6000 men.'

'You mean we're hostage to his army?' Robinson shook his head. He could tell that Selby was startled at his frankness but to him it brought some relief, enhanced by the smoothness of the ale. 'Sir Maurice, whatever secret ambitions are housed in the bosoms of our countrymen in these tender times'—he had the not unpleasant sensation that he was sounding like Scot—'the fact of the matter is that Parliament is in power. Even if the king were to return, Parliament would still rule England. Government has changed since the day when your father spent his courage trying to defend your home against Cromwell.' He smiled into Selby's intense blue eyes. 'Monck knows that, as do the members of Parliament. If he is to get to London with his 6000 men, then he needs Scot and me in his carriage with him every inch of the way, whether he opens his mouth or not. We are his sanction, we are his protection, as surely as he is ours. Who knows how many men there are in England who'd like to see Monck cut down before he gets to journey's end? But to stop him, they must attack us, who travel with him—the representatives of Parliament. Who but a fool would miss the gravity of that, Sir Maurice? I'm sure the general doesn't.'

'You're not impregnable.' Selby looked down at his empty wine cup. 'If he were to declare himself for the king, there are fanatics in his own army who could ride by and put a bullet in him whether you were in the carriage with him or not.'

'Is that why you're tagging along, Sir Maurice, to arm the general against assassins? Perhaps you know something Parliament doesn't, about his intentions in London.'

Selby did not reply, but a fleeing expression on his face suggested: *If I did, I'd not tell it to you.*

Robinson sighed and said kindly, 'You are, if I may say so, somewhat young and untried to judge of men like Monck. He takes great care of his own neck, believe me. He's a stickler for loyalty—in those below him. His own loyalties, of course, are what his career has shown them to be— variable. I may tell you, he's asked Scot and myself to gain Parliament's permission for you to enter London in his train, should he be permitted to enter the City.'

'Me?' Selby flushed, and he fixed Robinson with surprise and hope.

'Indeed. Meanwhile, Sir Maurice, remember that if the general extends you favours, he no doubt expects services in return.' *Such as exchanging information with conspirators in low tavern houses en route, perhaps.*

'Are you … are you prepared to make a representation to Parliament to allow me to enter the City?'

Robinson sighed again. It depressed him to see gentlemen of Selby's spirit and youthful ideals drawn in to support Monck, who would grind them up like gunpowder if it suited his hidden designs. Without knowing the merest twist of Monck's thinking, this youngster put himself at the general's mercy.

Robinson suspected he would find few allies in support of Parliament's rights in Monck's army. But while he marched with it he could at least keep an eye on the more volatile elements, to snatch glimpses of what Monck's servants and spies had in hand. And he might be able to dissuade at least one promising young man from putting his head on the block.

He said: 'I know your situation, Sir Maurice. Your father was rightly declared a delinquent but you've never been actively involved in support for Charles Stuart. Parliament might therefore be persuaded to think it unfair that you should have—ah, *inherited*—the label of delinquent. You have after all lost enough already: your ancestral lands.'

'But not my name.'

'Or your reputation.' Robinson went on: 'I've not yet discussed this with Thomas Scot but I shall, and when we reach London I should be happy to vouch for the honourable conduct to which we have both been witness. I believe Master Scot will join me in making the request to the Council of State that you be permitted to enter London.'

'I'm … obliged to you!'

Robinson saw with amusement that Selby hardly knew whether to be grateful or not. He had been given sanction to accompany Monck to the seat of power, and perhaps to attend whatever negotiations the wily general had in mind. He had been offered free entry into London, where no doubt he intended to petition for the return of his lands. But he had also been handed a caution: *Reveal yourself an active royalist, and you'll never get there. Monck or someone else will stop you first.*

****

After Robinson had taken himself off, Maurice bought another cup of spiced wine and consumed it slowly, savouring the excitement that surged along his veins with the warm liquor. To have Robinson guess his allegiance was unfortunate but Maurice had given him nothing concrete to go on and they might talk again, which would teach him a bit more about Parliament's attitude to Monck. And their meeting had been preceded by another, much more momentous, with Sir John Mordaunt, the king's spymaster in England.

It was Mordaunt who had approached Maurice, not the other way around. A coded note from the Duke of Buckingham had arrived that morning, naming the rendezvous. Buckingham had offered his services to Monck but had been rejected, whilst Maurice was by the general's side. Mordaunt was desperate for information to take back to Brussels. Maurice could give him no more clues about Monck than any other observer might have done, but he was glad to see that Mordaunt was impressed with his situation: marching with Monck's army and actually lodging with Ralph Knight. Moreover, the king would soon know that Maurice had taken part in the rebellion in the West and had escaped—through the ingenuity of the mysterious King's Shadow—without being betrayed. He was now an accredited spy for the king!

He had been impressed with Mordaunt, who was a tireless traveller and a passionate advocate of the king's cause. Mordaunt had come quickly to the point: he wanted Maurice in his network, the first purpose being to examine Monck and his associates closely. Maurice asked for and got intelligence in return—about royalist enclaves in Kent, where Mordaunt had just been.

Maurice had warned Mordaunt the moment Luke Robinson came into the tavern, giving him time to get away. Sir John had said quietly as he left: 'A fruitful encounter, Sir Maurice, which we'll repeat. Expect my note.'

When he left the taproom himself, Maurice used the door Mordaunt had taken, just to see where it might lead. It gave onto the Bird Cage's ample stable yard. The night was pitch black and there were no lights in the rooms behind the gallery over the yard but at the far end of the stables there was a flicker near an open door. Perhaps a groom was tending a horse in the furthest stall or watching beside it.

Suddenly, a figure that he had failed to notice in the gloom detached itself from the stone wall to his right and walked away towards the faint glow, beckoning him in silence with a gloved hand.

Maurice started. The gentleman's shoulders were hunched under a long cloak, and he wore a long wig as black as the night. Mordaunt.

Maurice followed him into the stables. There was no groom with the immense stallion, grey as a thundercloud, which stood in the shadows beyond a small lantern hanging from a partition. The figure stopped, turned and stood straight so that Maurice became aware of broad shoulders and considerable height. What arrested his gaze and stopped his breath, however, was the black mask across nose and brow.

The King's Shadow.

He waited for the voice, though, just to be sure. It came, and its richness and depth reminded him of his pain-racked ride to safety on the shoulders of this very stallion. He recalled Lucinda's question about the Shadow's manner of speech and noted that tonight it was patterned on that of the high noblemen who belonged about the king, accented only by a slight drawl as though the dialogue were happening at court.

'Well met, Sir Maurice. Excuse the informality. I saw through that grimy set of windows that you've just entertained Sir John Mordaunt and then Luke Robinson—a formidable pair in one night. If you need any help with either, I'm at your service.'

Maurice managed to find his voice. ''Tis the other way about, sir. My sword is yours, and I'll never forget it.'

'I know your loyalty, better than anyone. So you won't mind telling me: Mordaunt wanted to hear everything you could say about Monck, and Robinson was claiming he could get Parliament or the City to let you into London. That was it?'

'Correct,' Maurice said after a second's indecision.

The Shadow gave a curt nod, then slid down with his back to the stall partition and sat on a hay bale, one long leg stretched before him, with the lantern light gleaming on the worn leather of his boot. 'Like Sir John, I've some riding ahead of me before dawn. But I'd value a few words with you first, if you have the liberty.' He gave a slight, ironical smile at Maurice's hesitant look. 'We won't be disturbed or overheard, I guarantee.'

Maurice sat down on another bale of hay and looked across at the disconcerting mask. An insane idea struck him: that he was being addressed by his king. Lean, tall, dark-visaged and clever, Charles was famous for his audacity. On the lonely flight from defeat in Worcester he had been hidden in just such places as this, and the risk of being recognised by his height had forced him into the weirdest of disguises.

'Who are you? I have to know!'

'You will one day. History is catching us up, my friend, and we can do nothing against it.'

'We may do something *for* it!'

'Perhaps. Why do you think Monck is taking his army to London?'

The question was genuine and so differently put from the interrogatory Maurice had received from Mordaunt and the condescending advice from Robinson, that for the first time that night he sat in silence for a while in order to pay another man the compliment of a considered answer.

At last he said: 'Parliament asked Monck not to bring his forces into England, so it's fair to assume that now he's done it and is heading for London, he has in mind something that Parliament doesn't want. That something is likely to be the return of the king.'

He paused, there was no interruption, and Maurice glanced across at the dark, dimly lit figure. This could not be Charles Stuart. No monarch could listen to speculation about his fate with such complete lack of feeling, the full mouth set firm, the eyes within the mask like deep wintry pools.

Maurice went on. 'There are two strong possibilities. The first is that Monck will invade London, defeat and dismiss Parliament, take power himself and bring back His Majesty.'

'If you were Monck, is that what you'd do? How?' Again the questions were dispassionate. 'Parliament has an army, loyal to Sir Arthur Haselrig and well proven in the field. And there's Lambert to think on. He's a republican to his last breath and he can yet pull men to his banner—he'd ally himself with Parliament in a flash if a royalist general tried to take London.'

'It's still a possibility,' Maurice said stubbornly. 'I've seen enough of George Monck to believe he could do it.'

'By putting Londoners to the sword.'

'Yes. If that's what he has in mind.'

'And what's your second possibility?'

'That Monck will get to London—then surround it and use his strengths to parley for the king's return.'

'With whom? All the factions at once? Parliament, the City, Lambert and the rebels, and the Londoners who are ripe for violence? A tall order.' The other man paused a moment, coolly contemplative. 'It's not a military solution. And Monck likes military solutions: they're what he's used to. But what are his strengths, beyond his army—6000 may not be enough.'

The warmth of the wine was deserting Maurice and cold began to penetrate his clothes. But he wanted to stay and keep the exchange going: it was gratifying to be treated as an equal by the man who had saved his life the year before.

He thought aloud. 'If Monck is for the king, and he makes it known, his strength will be increased by everyone who's lying low at the moment. His family in Devon will be behind him, and his former veterans from the war in Ireland. He'll have the secluded members on his side, the ones who were purged from the Parliament in '48—they're still legally members of the House of Commons and he'll cry for their return. And royalists everywhere will take up arms. Mordaunt tells me that in Kent—'

The older man shrugged in a way that gave Maurice a new idea of what he might think of Mordaunt. 'You'll have noticed over the last decade that those who rise up for the king are cut to the ground within days.'

Maurice felt the cold skin on his cheeks begin to glow. 'This time the preparation will be better. It has to be.'

'I agree. And our patience must be the greater, too. If Monck remains as silent and solid as the Sphinx all the way to London, so must we. This is war of a new kind but it depends on an ancient strategy—the concentration of forces.' The Shadow rose to his feet and looked down at Maurice, the light suddenly catching his eyes, which were not black but dark grey. Under the look, Maurice felt as though he had been tested and had passed muster. 'For the last two years, right across the North, whenever an order for arrest has gone out against suspected royalists, they've been warned in time, and they've slipped away into hiding. Or they've been examined by the militia, exonerated and set free. All this time, a force has been gathering in the North. These gentlemen are not numerous but they are trained, led by veterans, in constant contact with their leaders and ready for action. Moreover, since the New Year, they've been on the move. They're travelling south, parallel to us, on secret, well-planned routes.

'If this force is needed in London, it will come to light in the right place, at the right time. I'm sure you know why I'm telling you this. In our lifetime the value of recklessness and bravado is long past, if it ever existed. I believe you have the fortitude to keep your courage cloaked until it's wanted.'

It did not feel like a warning. It was a statement, man to man. Maurice rose too. 'I can guarantee that.'

The other turned away and ran one hand over the massive back of the grey horse. Saddle, bridle and blanket hung over the partition, ready for the Shadow to mount up and be gone.

Maurice had an urge to ask when they might meet again, but said instead: 'There's a third possibility. That Monck is no royalist, but aims to throw Parliament out, declare martial law and name himself Protector for life. Another Cromwell.'

The black mask turned his way, the eyes like smoke within. 'There will never be another Cromwell. That I promise you.'

LONDON
January 29

Lucinda was walking through the upper galleries of the Royal Exchange with Mary Villiers, trying to look as though she belonged by the side of a duchess in this handsome hub of commerce, where the most expensive imported goods shimmered in lavish display. She was choosing velvet—or rather, the duchess was choosing it for her and, moreover, paying for it. Lucinda had no idea what her hostess's income might be and she suspected the lady had little idea either, which seemed no bar to her getting cheerfully into debt whenever she wanted something. Mary Villiers had taken it into her head that Lucinda must be finely dressed on every occasion and nothing was going to stand in her way.

London was dazzling, much more so than Lucinda could have imagined while she lingered at Cobham amongst the Stuarts. She had been glad to enjoy the gentle life of a country estate while Mary Villiers passed on to her influential friends and relations everything that had been said between her and the king. Lucinda had expected to put luxury behind her at Cobham, and to find London grey and forbidding, but it overwhelmed her in a different way. They had arrived up the river by private barge and as they approached amongst a crowd of naval and merchant vessels and Lucinda caught her first sight of London Bridge, and Saint Paul's on the north bank, linked by the steep, tiled roofs of clustered buildings, she had a sensation of the city's splendour that surprised her.

The winter that had held the North in its grip had not been cold enough in London to freeze the Thames over but she saw thick terraces of ice clinging here and there at the shoreline, with children sliding on them, and workmen cutting out blocks to be hauled away and stored for summer, and little orange fires crackling where enterprising folk had set up stalls as though there might yet be a Frost Fair this year after all. On the south bank, the walls of warehouses and inns dropped sheer to the water, and some were built over it on tall, tarred piles. Behind these, dye yards and tanneries sent stinks and steam into the chilly air, and over

Southwark and the Thames drifted a haze from tens of thousands of coal fires, staining the pale blue sky with washes of umber.

The boats shuttling across the river, the activity on its banks, were an invitation to disembark and join in the life ashore. The tall houses built across the arches of the bridge had narrow windows that now and then caught a reflection from the current below and seemed to wink at Lucinda. The stone and the dark timbers of London's architecture, and the cold expanses of river and sky, offered themselves in wintry colours, but Lucinda caught from them a promise of warmth and vigour hidden behind the massive façades.

The walk through the Royal Exchange galleries was her first outing with Mary Villiers. The duchess had taken a house in the Convent Garden on a three-month lease and had spent the first week getting the place liveable and, more importantly, fit to receive callers. Lucinda's distant relative who lived in the area had proved to be from home. His house was empty, as was many a mansion owned by aristocrats with whom Parliament was on unfriendly terms, and the duchess's acquaintance in London was similarly depleted, but none of this dampened her enthusiasms. She had a knack that Lucinda admired: of making any space feel like a home. She got to know her environment by touching it and on the first day had wandered about the great chamber, ignoring dust and cobwebs, her light fingers brushing the wainscoting, the tooled backs of worn leather chairs, the marble mantel.

'We'll make something of this,' she had said with a smile. 'It just needs some colour.'

Colour was what she craved, too, at the Royal Exchange, where she confessed to be shopping for the first time in her life.

She said, fingering a Dutch velvet: 'I might fancy this blue for you. I remember when stuff was brought to the Queen and we chose together, over many a happy hour.'

'I feel guilty that you're indulging me, Your Grace, when there's your new house to furnish.'

Mary Villiers laid down the velvet. 'Nonsense, the house does very well as it is. And it's a long time since I selected fabrics for a home. Hangings and linen? In London, I'd hardly know where to start.'

A silky voice said behind them: 'I can recommend a merchant with a subtle understanding of household cloth.'

Mary Villiers spun round with a haughty look that changed almost at once to studied amazement. 'Lady Elizabeth Tollemache! My word, where did I last see you—Paris or Dieppe?'

'Versailles,' the other said calmly, after a penetrating glance at Lucinda. Her golden hair, light blue eyes and delicate features and clothing were in some contrast to the elegant and imposing Duchess of Richmond, but Lucinda would have been hard put to say who was the more attractive. There was an obvious rivalry between them, betrayed by the duchess's deliberate failure of memory and the lady's quick reminder that she, too, ranked as a guest at the French royal court.

Neither seemed concerned about eavesdroppers on what rather promised to be a royalist conversation, but Lucinda was more cautious. She threw a glance up and down the gallery and was relieved to see that no one was within earshot, not even the seller of Dutch velvets.

The duchess said in her coolest voice: 'Lady Elizabeth, may I present to you Lady Lucinda Selby, who is staying with me. Lady Lucinda, you have the honour to meet Lady Elizabeth Tollemache, the Countess of Dysart.'

'I am indeed honoured,' Lucinda said, and sank into the correct posture.

The countess nodded. 'You're new to London. How do you like it?'

Lucinda rose, wondering what it was about her appearance that so clearly spoke the provincial.

It was as though the countess guessed her thoughts. 'Ah, I frequently sense things about people, so I know you won't mind my frankness, for you're a frank creature yourself. Let me phrase it another way: are you here in London for a purpose or for amusement?'

'Both,' Lucinda said, and smiled.

The countess raised her beautifully arched eyebrows. 'Both?'

'Both,' Mary Villiers echoed, with an approving look at Lucinda.

The countess gave an easy laugh, not in the least discouraged by their reticence. 'I'm certain we'll have much more to say to one another in the right surroundings.' She turned to the duchess. 'You're lodging where?'

'I've taken a house in the Convent Garden.'

'Ah, not very far from me. One of your neighbours is a tenant of mine—Edward Ford.'

Lucinda repressed a start: Mary Villiers had told her that Ford's dwelling, set back from the piazza behind a perfect forest of a garden, provided a meeting place for royalists.

'We have yet to meet,' Mary Villiers said with perfect truth. 'You were about to let me know about a draper?'

'His name is Ambrose Martel. He can lay hands on fine fabrics that rival what I see here, and there's the added comfort that he brings samples to me, which saves me from traipsing all over London. When next he pays a call, shall I direct him on to you?' There was a pause, and the countess continued: 'I warn you, he comes and goes bearing nothing but cloth. He's not the kind of person to whom one would entrust any other kind of commission. Quite the opposite, in fact. When he's about, I advise you to talk about fabrics and nothing more.'

'I'd scarcely think of conversing about anything else, with a draper!' Mary Villiers said. 'Do you live in London at present, or Richmond?'

Elizabeth Tollemache gave a vague gesture. 'I wake up every morning with a different idea about where I'll spend my day. I live on whims and fancies! I must blame that on the atmosphere of this time and of this city, which is most peculiar, don't you think?' She addressed this question to Lucinda.

Lucinda said: 'I haven't been in London long enough to judge how people live here. Do you really consider Londoners to be so ... volatile?'

Elizabeth Tollemache gave her a subtle smile. 'Yes, confusion is the order of the day. But that order may change, and sooner than we think.' Her birdlike glance just encompassed the duchess as she went on to Lucinda: 'I should like to see you one day, when I can be sure of having the right friends for you to meet. I may send a message to you at the piazza?'

Lucinda said faintly: 'You're very good, your ladyship.'

'That's settled, then. I bid you good day.' She made a reverence to Mary Villiers. 'Your Grace.'

The duchess inclined her head without a word and Elizabeth Tollemache swept on. A moment later she had reached the top of the stairwell, sailed down it in a billow of silks, and disappeared.

The duchess beckoned to the stall holder and made a purchase of the blue velvet. Further down the gallery she bought some pearl-coloured tissue and inquired of the merchant whether he had heard of Ambrose

Martel. They left with Martel's address and crossed the busy courtyard of the Exchange towards the duchess's carriage and her attendants waiting in Threadneedle Street. It was a cold day though sunny, and Lucinda was impressed by the number of merchants standing about on the cobbles, huddled into a group or conversing in pairs under the colonnade, conducting the business of import and export outdoors, as they had always done. This thriving centre of commerce had an ebullience that outdid even the most animated market days in York.

'I must declare,' she said, 'that I like London very much! Especially when you give me such good reasons to enjoy it, madam.'

The duchess replied briskly: 'I was glad to see you take the measure of the Countess of Dysart.'

'I'm not sure that I did. She puzzles me.'

'You're quite right to be cautious.' The duchess entered her carriage and Lucinda followed. When they had settled themselves opposite each other, with their skirts spread comfortably, the duchess gave the order and the vehicle moved off. 'In vulgar circles Elizabeth Tollemache is rumoured to be a witch; in our own she's known to be skilful with herbs and magic.' She caught Lucinda's glance. 'Yes, magic. It's said she can divine truths hidden to others. I can never decide whether she's an out-and-out charlatan or simply deluded. She's a very untrustworthy woman, whichever side she happens to be on.'

'So you don't believe in her magic, madam?'

Mary Villiers shivered. 'My dear lady, I can't afford to. I've been a toy of fate all my life. My only defence against omens and portents is to give no countenance to the dark arts. I must deny it all, if I'm to be of the slightest use to my family or anyone else.' Her voice fell on the last words and she looked down at her hands, smoothing the left glove over her fingers with her right hand.

It was the first time Lucinda had seen her vulnerable since the confessions at Nun Appleton. It had never occurred to her that the Duchess of Richmond and Lennox was to be pitied; she always appeared so much the mistress of her existence. Sympathy made Lucinda say: 'If an invitation comes from her, then of course I … we … shall refuse it.'

'By no means!' The duchess looked up. 'I knew I'd cross paths with the Tollemache sooner or later. She happens to be the lady patron, or the resplendent hostess, or the good fairy'—the duchess chuckled, all her easy humour restored— 'of a group known as the Sealed Knot. You've heard of them?'

Lucinda nodded. Sir John Mordaunt had spoken of them to Maurice. She knew no names, only that they were in direct communication with the king.

'Their gathering point in London is the house of Edward Ford—the Countess of Dysart's tenant. If she gives us an invitation it might be to meet them, and I should have no objection. They are six very different gentlemen, not to be all esteemed alike, but one of them is a relative of mine and another something of a friend.'

'Have you been to any of their meetings?'

'No, I've never seen the necessity. Indeed, I've never seen the necessity of the Sealed Knot! I gather Elizabeth Tollemache likes to preside when they're together. I have the impression they're united by a love of mystery and they meet more to talk than to act.'

'You don't expect them to be of any help to you over George Monck's wife?'

Mary Villiers laughed. 'Not in the least. We'll have to take care of all *that* ourselves.' She looked at Lucinda brightly. 'Last week, Parliament confirmed George Monck as commander-in-chief of the army in the three kingdoms. As befits her standing, his wife now occupies the apartments known as the Prince's Lodging in Whitehall. Can you imagine what the interior of our king's palace must look like, after 18 dismal years of occupation by an army of upstarts?' Her eyes dimmed and her voice altered in the kind of mercurial change to which Lucinda was now accustomed. 'It used to be my home. I can hardly bear to think how derelict it must be.' She roused herself. 'If—when—His Majesty returns, Mistress Monck will have the daunting responsibility of making sure the palace is fit to house him. Considering her origins—a washerwoman, I declare!—she will be completely at a loss and incapable of rallying help, let alone making decisions. She needs someone to tell her what must be done. She needs a grand plan, cleverly worked out and ready for action. She needs help *now*. And I shall provide it.'

Lucinda said: 'Is that why you want to consult Ambrose Martel?'

The duchess nodded briskly. 'Martel and others.'

'You don't think Mistress Monck may already have advisers in Whitehall?'

'Such as who? That master spy, John Thurloe, who answers to the Council of State? Or the captain of the parliamentary guard? My dear, the King's glorious palace has been given over to plotters and poltroons for nigh on two-score years. All men, and none of them with an ounce of breeding or culture. Returning Whitehall to civilisation is a monumental work. It has no chance of success unless it is begun by a woman.'

****

Mark Denton was in London on a special mission for Monck. This did not mean the general showed him any particular approval—in fact he had grown more taciturn with everyone. After Nottingham, Monck ceased to hold officers' councils. With his army he remained alert and decisive on all military matters but silent on his purposes. In public, when delegations poured into the towns as the army passed through, he received them with courtesy but was as unforthcoming as he was with his men. Mark observed this with irony, especially when he was ordered to attend all civic and political meetings, a task he could have done without.

Mark was never asked to contribute—just to stand by and, as he sardonically said to Knight, 'act the ogre to frighten the children'. His fearsome reputation as a scourge to royalists in the North reached far into the Midlands and it aided Monck's pro-Parliament countenance when he was faced with vociferous collections of country gentlemen and townspeople, all hoping he was marching to London to achieve a 'free parliament'. Monck already had Parliament's commissioners, Thomas Scot and Luke Robinson, at every audience. Colonel Mark Denton was an extra discouragement to any party who was dissatisfied with the Rump and wanted it to name the day for a long overdue election. And his presence was meant to dash the hopes of those petitioners who dreamed that on arrival in London Monck would at once insist on the secluded members of Parliament being recalled to the House. Mark Denton's obdurate figure was a dark reminder of the regicide Oliver Cromwell and his Commonwealth, which Parliament had pledged to uphold. So far on his long march to London, Monck had given no hint that he would influence Parliament to do anything but stick to their guns.

Day after day at places like Mansfield, Market Harborough and Dunstable, Mark had witnessed Monck receive mayors, aldermen, councillors and landed gentry, watched him listen impassively to their grievances against the Parliament, and then dismiss them without a crumb of comfort for their cause.

In private, however, something else was going on. After deputations had gone away disconsolate, Monck would more often than not send them a letter by despatch rider. As soon as Mark caught onto this he decided he must see at least one example of the covert correspondence. He chose his moment after a torrid day at Market Harborough where Monck had faced a deputation from the Lord Mayor, aldermen and Common Council of London. The spokesman stated that the Council desired the return of the secluded members to the House. Commissioners Scot and Robinson rejected the plea at once, shouting down the aldermen in their outrage. Monck's heavy features stayed imperturbably grave and when he spoke at last, it was in support of the commissioners, much to the Londoners' horror. An hour or two after the delegation set off on their journey home, empty-handed, the letter that Mark had predicted was despatched. He set out, alone and in secret, to capture it.

It was a swift operation. The despatch rider, an ensign in Monck's superbly disciplined army, had a false sense of his own security and he did not consider himself to be riding through enemy territory. It was early evening and he was meant to deliver the letter in the dark, in the town where the deputation made its first halt on the road to London. In the fading light, on a deserted bend in the highway, Mark surprised him from behind, giving him only a few seconds to understand that he was under attack and no time at all to draw a weapon.

Mark was clad like a travelling merchant and riding his favourite mount which, though one of the string of horses capably looked after by Corporal Hales, was quite unknown to the army. For good measure he wore a mask under the hood of his cloak and spoke not a word as he unhorsed the cavalryman, smashed him to the ground behind a stand of bushes and bound wrists and ankles with tight cords.

The letter was in the breast of the man's buff coat. Mark forced him to lie face down, put a boot on his neck for good measure and broke the seal on the single sheet of paper. The message was brief and contained no change of attitude on Monck's part, but the tone was more friendly than that of the afternoon's exchanges. Monck said that he feared the gentlemen might have found little satisfaction in the meeting and went so far as to regret this. He confirmed that he was proceeding to London as

Parliament's servant but revealed that he did have a purpose on arrival—he hoped to see ere long 'a settled condition of the Government'. Mark smiled cynically to himself: the City was free to make what it might out of that ambiguous statement. Monck concluded by looking forward to discussing such matters again with the Council in London and meanwhile suggested: 'proceed in your intentions'. In other words, the whole issue was still open—whereas, in the presence of the commissioners, Monck had wished it to appear closed.

Mark had folded the letter up and shoved it into the rider's buff coat, then cut his bonds. At the point of the man's own pistol he signalled for him to mount the cavalry horse that had been waiting wearily for the men to finish their business, and sent both on their way with a sharp smack across the beast's rump.

From Dunstable, George Monck wrote a letter to the Speaker of the House of Commons, William Lenthall. It asked for the withdrawal of the entire London garrison into the country: he wanted no troops in London but his own. Mark heard this from Ralph Knight, who got it from the letter bearer, a fellow colonel.

It was also in Dunstable that Monck got the bad news from the despatch rider that his message to the City men had been intercepted and read, though delivered nonetheless. Was it coincidence that Mark received his special mission from Monck on the same day? After being tied to the general's side during the march through the Midlands—where Monck could keep an eye on him—he was now to hand over his regiment to his major and do Monck's bidding in the City. He accepted, of course, knowing that he had no choice and that this might be another subtle test of his loyalty.

Mark was not at home in London but that did not mean he knew no one there. He had served in England's army with distinction for 16 years and his contacts extended widely. He had met Ambrose Martel several years before while attending to military matters in Liverpool, from which the merchant's brother ran a fleet of trading ships. The two Martels had been spectacularly successful under the Commonwealth. They had thriving companies in the City, Portsmouth and Liverpool and received support and favours from the most powerful men in the Rump Parliament. Ambrose Martel had been one of the first 'silken independents', who with Oliver Cromwell's blessing had replaced the old order of London merchants and founded enterprises that flourished under the Lord Protector's aggressive policies on British trade at home and abroad. There could be no more passionate advocate of the present Parliament than Ambrose Martel, which was why Mark was now seated in the man's great chamber, enjoying a cup of excellent sack and listening to all the reasons why Monck should never have been allowed to advance on London.

He heard them calmly and with attention. His appointed task was to gather the true attitudes towards Monck amongst the army, the City and certain members of Parliament, and to take this information back to the general. Monck obviously considered he had chosen his observer well: knowing Mark's allegiance to the Commonwealth, he could be sure that any criticism of his supposed aims would be frankly passed on. Before Monck set foot in London, he was determined to know the real feeling for and against him amongst people of degree. And so was Mark.

Mark said: 'You really apprehend he'll be wanting to make changes to government? He's commander-in-chief of the army, not of Parliament.'

'Of course he wants changes! Haven't you read the odious pamphlet that he broadcast all over London?'

'Yes, but it's been exposed as a forgery. The ideas in it—'

'To bring back the secluded members, by force!'

'—are not Monck's. That trash was printed by a mischief-maker. I have that from Monck himself and I believe him.'

Martel was a thin man of 50, bald and sallow-faced, with intelligent hazel eyes. He considered Mark narrowly, his uneven teeth displayed in a deceptive smile. 'You're close to Monck, then?'

'No. No one is.'

'Then I'm surprised you march with the black toad.'

'I was surprised not to see you with the aldermen's delegation in Market Harborough. You might have come to a proper judgment of him there.'

'No, I guessed in advance what he was playing at. I knew he'd deny them and lie to them without scruple. And I'd no mind to be one of them—I didn't agree with a syllable of what they put to him!' Martel gave a dry chuckle. 'Pack of fools. Questions, questions.' He tapped the woven covering on the table with a bony forefinger. 'The only question worth posing is this: will the merchants of the City make more money by the present government or by a new one under the king? The answer is simple: the present. My fellow merchants don't know when they're well off. But I do and I continue to build my wealth on it.'

'There's many a strong man in the City complains of the taxes that Parliament puts upon you.'

Martel gave a reedy laugh. 'Since when did we *not* complain of taxes? That's the East India Company men for you, swearing great Goliath oaths. But consider this: they'd never thrive as they do if the Commonwealth hadn't disrupted the old merchant companies and opened the way to fresh talent, and promoted the colonies, and thrust the Dutch aside to give us overseas trade such as England's never seen.'

'And strengthened the navy to back it up.'

Martel nodded. 'Well said.'

'Though they've no funds to pay the seamen. And all the army officers I've seen in the last couple of days are telling me there's no pay for the soldiers either. Where's Parliament going to get the money for that? Heavier taxes, I surmise.'

'Did I not say, there'll *always* be taxes? And they cannot be worse than Charles's ship money in the bad old days—he screwed the whole country for it!'

Mark smiled. 'It's a pleasure to hear straight talk. I don't get it in Monck's company. How does the Common Council take such speech from your mouth?'

'Ill. Very ill. I scarcely attend. I've pulled my head in and put it to better use about my business.' He shot Mark a keen look. 'Don't misunderstand me. Whatever storm breaks on Monck's arrival I shall weather it. If the republicans can't stay afloat in Parliament I don't intend to drown with them. I take my sightings by the Commonwealth, as any thinking man in the City ought to do, but I'll set my own course if I must.'

'Do you advise others to do the same?'

Martel snapped: 'Who's asking? You or Monck?' When Mark merely raised his eyebrows the merchant went on with asperity: 'Come now, you announced this as a friendly call but from the first word it's been questions, questions on your side and all the answers on mine. Time to tell me what you want in London, colonel. I'm blunt with you because of your record as a soldier—one of the best. I expect you to be equally blunt with me.'

Mark took another drink of Martel's sack and considered his reply. He said: 'I'm after information. In a few days' time I'll be entering London with my regiment, under Monck's command. I owe it to myself to find out what sort of reception we'll get. My loyalty to the Commonwealth is well known. Too well known for some—there was an attempt on my life three weeks ago, just north of Newcastle. Well-aimed shots while I was in the line of march—so at least two people didn't want me coming south.'

'By my troth!' Martel said. 'Who fired on you?'

'We got one of them. On his last gasp he said his commander was the King's Shadow.'

'The king's devil more like. I've heard of him.' Martel paused for a moment, then said: 'No further attempts?'

'No.'

'Well, I should consider London pretty much the best place you could be, for the nonce. Of course there are royalist enclaves here, but they'll be lying lower than ever in the present crisis.'

'You consider it a crisis? Already? Monck's army isn't here yet and there's no knowing whether Parliament will let us enter.'

'London is a tinder box. If Monck doesn't strike it alight, Londoners will do it themselves.'

Mark was about to reply to this when a servant came in with a message for Martel, and stood waiting while he read it. It was written in red chalk on a small piece of paper, and when Martel laid it thoughtfully on the tabletop, Mark could see that it held simply a title: the Duchess of Richmond and Lennox.

'Speaking of royalists … no, of royalty!' Martel murmured, his shrewd eyes alight with curiosity. 'First I've ever heard from her! No appointment, no previous note, nothing. But at my very door and requesting entry, with a companion.' He looked up at the servant. 'Who's with her? Heaven forfend, not her brother, the Duke of Buckingham?'

'A young lady, sir.'

Martel said to Mark: 'I should be loath to have our meeting interrupted, but—'

Mark put down his empty glass and rose. 'It's time I took my leave.'

'Thank you for your patience. One cannot refuse one's door to such as her.' Martel rose with a smile and said to the servant: 'You will show Her Grace and the lady up, with all courtesy.'

Mark moved towards his hat and sword, which he had placed on a chair just inside the room, but Martel said: 'Stay a moment. Unless you object to greeting the duchess? I have a question to ask you.'

Mark bowed his head slightly. 'By all means.'

''Tis in two parts. Is Monck manoeuvring to bring back Charles Stuart? And if so, how can he possibly succeed?'

'To the first part: I don't know. No one does. To the second part, another question: why do you consider the task so difficult?'

'Because there are too many parties at odds. Parliament, Parliament's army, the Common Council, the City, the people of London. Provoke them into open conflict and you'll have riots, bloodshed and chaos. Agreement on any matter, let alone the return of Charles Stuart, will be the merest dream.'

A rustle of skirts and an intake of breath at the doorway told them that they had been overheard. The men turned together and saw an exquisitely dressed matron with red-gold curls, and a dark-haired young woman with brilliant blue eyes who was unknown to Ambrose Martel but painfully familiar to Mark Denton. Lucinda Selby.

****

Lucinda was so shocked to see Denton that she hardly took in the merchant. Denton was equally surprised, indeed more disturbed than she had ever seen him, and he quickly dropped his gaze. He had not changed –his mouth still had the firm confidence that he always showed—but she knew *she* had changed, at least on the surface, and was glad of it. She kept her composure while he raised his eyes again and took in her fine clothing, the expert styling of her hair and shoes. Her posture was meant to show that she was at her ease, though she shivered inside.

Meanwhile Mary Villiers was taking over the occasion in her insouciant way. 'Pray forgive the stealthy approach—I had no notion of creeping up on you, Master Martel. I blame the softness of your rugs.' She gestured with a slim white hand to the floor behind them, covered with good Norfolk matting in the normal way, but overlaid in several places with eastern carpets. 'A new fashion?'

Martel simply said: 'Your Grace; my lady,' and bowed.

Mary Villiers nodded, her cheerful glance taking in both men as she replied to Martel. 'It is of fashions and fabrics and possibly furbelows that I am come to speak with you. If I overheard anything of a political nature, I have already forgot it, and so has this good lady, whose business is the same as mine. That is: practical, domestic, but in the service of beauty. May I present Lady Lucinda Selby?'

Martel bowed again and introduced Denton, who bowed also, without a word. He avoided Lucinda's eye and looked instead at the duchess, who had a knowing smile on her face, which made it quite clear that she knew as much of his history as she cared to know, including his possession of the Selby lands.

It was impossible for Lucinda to stay silent any longer. Her voice overrode the merchant's as he was about to speak. She said in the most neutral voice she could command: 'Colonel Denton: why aren't you with Monck's army?'

'I'm assessing troop accommodation in London, on the general's orders. My visit here was informal and I'm just away—no need for it to interfere with yours.'

'Pray don't hurry,' the duchess said, sweeping into the room at a gesture from their host. 'I'm here for advice about cloth and for all I know you may have something to contribute to my research.' She gave him a mischievous smile. 'And surely you won't run away at once from valued acquaintance? Lady Lucinda,' she went on, turning to Martel, 'is a native of York, or rather, of an estate nearby. As are you, I believe, colonel?'

'Indeed,' he said with a characteristic frown. 'But what we have in common also divides us. Land.'

Lucinda looked at him in astonishment. This answer hardly covered the enmity between them. *Everything* divided them, from their deepest loyalties to their highest visions of the future. The duchess, too, was momentarily taken aback. She continued to examine him closely, as though there might be more behind his direct utterance than he wished to express.

Martel, having sent a servant for refreshment, now begged the ladies to sit down. Lucinda did so, but saw that Denton remained standing, undecided whether to withdraw. She could at least ask for news of Maurice before he left. 'My brother rides in George Monck's train, colonel. I've had no letter from him recently—can you tell me anything of him? Have you seen him lately?'

'Yes, my lady. He's of some assistance to the cavalry commanders—he has a good eye for a horse. I've come across him once or twice but we've spoken little. When I last saw him he was in good health and spirits.'

Denton said this dispassionately and kept his gaze on Lucinda but, aware of the duchess's scrutiny, he changed his stance so she could only read his face in profile.

Martel had shown the duchess to the chair of honour at one side of the fireplace and was seated opposite her. At this point he leaned forward and said: 'Your Grace, I beg you to let me know how I may serve you.'

'I've taken a house in the Convent Garden and I plan to refurbish it. But I live mostly in France and I've no idea what's available here. Once, where grandeur and elegance were required, I knew how to spend money to good effect. But in London today, I'm at least a decade behind the times. Your knowledge of cloth was recommended to me and here I am.'

'By whom, may I ask?'

'By a lady to whom elegance is second nature. And on whom grandeur,' the duchess gave a subtle smile, 'may one day be conferred, who knows? Now, what can you show me?'

Lucinda noticed that the word 'money' had already put a light in Martel's eyes, and they brightened again as he said: 'I'm most honoured, Your Grace. My goods are in warehouses on the Thames but I've found it helpful to display samples in the storerooms downstairs. If you consent to accompany me there'—he flicked his fingers at a waiting servant, who opened a door to another stairwell—'believe me, you will not be disappointed by quality or quantity.'

'Just what I desired,' the duchess said, rising briskly. When Lucinda moved, she waved her down and said: 'I'm content to wander in Master Martel's treasure trove and see what pleases me. I shall send for you when I need you.' She glanced from Lucinda to Mark Denton. 'You are neighbours, after all. You must have many another piece of news that you'd like to exchange.'

She walked away after the servant and Martel was only too happy to follow. Lucinda felt annoyed but suddenly realised that the duchess intended her to interrogate Denton about Monck—having one of his colonels in the room must seem too good an opportunity to miss.

However, he got in first. 'May I ask why you're in London, my lady?'

Again the question was too personal but this time his tone was not so blunt. In fact if he were another man she might almost think him nervous.

'I'm here at the invitation of the duchess. It's her first time in London in many years and most of her friends are absent. I've found her very kind and … stimulating'. He looked eager for her to go on, so for once she explained her feelings to him. 'I suffered from the confinement of York. Almost as though I were under house arrest. This is like an escape.'

'By heaven,' he said, 'surely your existence was not so dismal!'

It would hurt her pride to complain to him, of all people, so she said more lightly: 'It lacked colour. And that's just what her grace provides. She started by ministering to my needs and now she's concentrating on her house.'

He was observing her, as though he were looking at a painting. 'You've chosen well. Forest green becomes you.'

Too intimate again, to talk of her gown! She rose from the chair and moved away.

When she did not reply, he said: 'And are there other reasons for your coming, beyond fabrics and fashions? I must accept that we're neither true neighbours nor friends but I've known you long enough to be aware of your spirit. London may be an escape but, pardon me, let it not be a danger to you. There are people all over this city with wild petitions and dreams of change. When the time comes, a host of them will be shattered.'

She turned to face him. He must not guess the duchess's mission at Whitehall. 'I bring no petition, colonel, and my dreams were broken when I was a girl. I'm here out of curiosity—to see the fate of this nation reveal itself in the next few weeks. If I'm ever to understand the England in which I live, here is the place to see its true colours emerge.' He narrowed his eyes and looked at her doubtfully. 'You think it a strange desire, for a young woman?'

'No. But you are following this … apparently idle … pursuit … in the company of a prominent member of the royal court. She obviously considers herself untouchable but Parliament will have its spies out after her and, therefore, after you. You must realise that she and her brother skate on very thin ice. What is she doing in London?'

'You may ask her yourself.'

'She'll brook no questions from such as me.'

She tried another angle. 'You said you're here under Monck's orders. As a spokesman to Parliament?'

'No. Amongst other commissions, I'm to consider where my regiment might be quartered, should the general be permitted to enter London.'

'And when do you think that might be?'

'It depends on Parliament. So I can't give you a date. But I can send you word of the place, once I get to quarters.' Lucinda looked at him in confusion. Why did he imagine she would want to know where he and his troopers were billeted! He caught the look and grew paler suddenly, as though he had spoken in error. But he continued nonetheless. 'Before the week is out, the situation in London will have changed radically.'

'So soon!' she exclaimed. He had as good as given her a date after all.

'At present, I have some credit with those in power. Should you find yourself in any danger or distress, I beg you to contact me at the address that I'll send you. You need give me no reasons or explanations—a simple request for help will bring me to your side.'

In her astonishment she gazed at him in silence for so long that he went to the doorway and picked up his hat, cloak and sword before returning halfway across the room. She could not read his clouded grey eyes. But his promise had been sincere—his deep, compelling voice had convinced her.

'You confuse me, sir. But I must thank you for the offer. It ... I trust it was well meant.'

He made her a low, graceful bow and left.

BARNET
February 2, Morning

Hugh Peters was preaching at the abbey church in Barnet and George Villiers, Duke of Buckingham, was there to hear him, seated near Monck and his officers. George was convinced he had made the right decision to catch up with Monck but he no longer wanted to join him; he felt safest as a free agent. Even if the general entered London unimpeded, he was cautious about trying to sneak in himself. All the same it would have been thrilling to adopt some entertaining guise and beg hospitality at Mary's Convent Garden house or—if she refused to have him so near the delectable Lady Lucinda—he might find a room at Edward Ford's. But during his last time in London he had been locked in the Tower. Until he knew Parliament's mood better, the city was no place for the Duke of Buckingham. His own mansions were quite inaccessible. The one he preferred above all, Wallingford House, was still occupied by top ranks of Parliament's army. Oh for the day when the world righted itself on its axis and military upstarts like Mark Denton were consigned to outer darkness!

Hugh Peters, not only famous for his rhetoric but suspected of having been one of Charles I's two heavily disguised executioners, announced that he was taking a verse of Psalm 107 as his text. *And he led them forth by the right way, that they might go to a city of habitation.* Being a poet, George was alive to many interpretations of this theme and he amused himself with them while Peters thundered on in tortuous vein, thoroughly bemusing the congregation. Peters had once been an eloquent advocate of Cromwell but had fallen out of favour with the military dictatorship, which made his homily as ambiguous as his loyalties.

George happened to be attired as a humble townsman. His neighbour to his right, no doubt an Independent like Peters, had come armed with his bible. With a friendly nod he passed it to George at one point, setting a forefinger beside verse 16 of the same psalm: *For he hath broken the gates of brass, and cut the bars of iron in sunder.* This was easily applied to the gates of London—but would Monck need to batter his way into the City and did Peters intend accusation or praise in his sermon?

The last halt on Monck's long march had been at St Albans, where the general had finally got his reply from Parliament about the quartering of his army. In the meantime, George Villiers had received a coded message from his cousin in the Sealed Knot, letting him know that Parliament was in fierce debate as to whether Monck's forces should be allowed into London and whether Parliament's standing army should be banished to country quarters before the general marched in. The most militant republican in the Rump, Sir Arthur Haselrig, had stormed at the Council of State for hours, exhorting them to refuse this request. But it looked as though Haselrig would lose the battle and see all his troops widely dispersed. This had decided George and he'd left his wife behind with the Fairfaxes and set out to keep himself on hand for whatever happened in London. The moment he caught up with Monck he made discreet contact with Maurice Selby to learn the general's mood.

George now knew from Selby that Monck had not spoken to his officers about the details of Parliament's message. But the march from St Albans to Barnet spoke more loudly than words. All Monck's forces were now concentrated around the town. Tomorrow, Friday the 3rd, they expected to march into London.

The tedious preachments over, George slipped away to a packed tavern in the main street, the Goose and Gander. Sir Maurice Selby kept him waiting rather longer than he liked for this rendezvous and also irritated him by taking an age to recognise him from the other side of the taproom—but at least this boded well for George's disguise and the abundant black wig over his auburn hair.

Selby gave a quick bow and sat down opposite him with an excited look. 'Your Grace—'

'Perdition!' George snapped. 'Remember to address me as Fletcher!' a playwright of whom he was fond. 'What in Hades is happening? Yon preacher encourages the belief of everything and nothing.'

The absence of George's usual good humour prompted Selby to sit up and take a more considered tone. 'I have it through Knight: Parliament will welcome the army. The lodgings of the former troops are swept clear and ready to receive them.'

'And the City?'

'Grows louder against the Parliament but distrusts Monck.'

'You're going to show your face amongst them?'

'My access to London has been confirmed by the commissioners,' Selby replied.

This statement caused the duke a pang. Selby, younger than he, almost untried in action and of infinitely lower rank, was at present the better informed and had total liberty of movement! George hid his discomfiture by taking a sip of some stale ale that the Goose and Gander obviously considered good enough for one of his apparent class. 'And where will you lodge?'

'With Ralph Knight's attendants.'

'Rather public, should anything go awry with our cause.'

'In that case I've been informed of a safe house where I can go privily.'

'You're not speaking of my sister's house in the Convent Garden?!'

Selby looked horrified. 'No, of course not! No, another direction entirely. A verbal message came to me through Sir John Mordaunt … from … the King's Shadow.'

George started. 'You're in contact with the Shadow?'

'Yes. I encountered him by chance in Bedford. He told me to expect a message and it arrived yesterday, through Mordaunt. I now know the address of a house on the outskirts of London that gives shelter to gentlemen of our persuasion.' Selby looked around the room and continued in an even lower tone: 'Mordaunt offered two major pieces of information that should give us all heart. You'll know one of them—what Mordaunt calls the ghost army?'

George said: 'I haven't spoken to Mordaunt lately.'

'I see. Well, the Shadow has masterminded the approach of a loyal force who've been in hiding in the North. They're mustering to the west of London as we speak. They're armed and ready to act, and they're lodged with families of the utmost discretion. The other good news is: the secluded members are afoot! They'll be ready to take their appointed places the moment the opportunity strikes.'

'But Monck made a great pother about them and said they're to keep to their homes. He's given them no hope of a return to Parliament.'

'Nevertheless, the staunchest are on the move to London.'

'Privily invited by Monck, then?'

'No, Mordaunt told me the messengers who've urged the members to come, and promised them safe haven when they arrive, were sent out by the King's Shadow.'

'He's everywhere! Who the devil *is* he?' George said with equal curiosity and envy.

'I thought you knew him! Lucinda told me so, before she left York.'

George searched Selby's gaze. *Did she also tell you I implied that I was the Shadow myself?* It was a most inconvenient lie, and if Selby knew of it he would fiercely disapprove of George's playing the romantic with his sister. Seeing no suspicion in the young man's gaze, however, he risked a reply. 'That's strange—I don't remember discussing the Shadow with Lady Lucinda. Have you told her about meeting him in Bedford?'

'Of course not. As if I'd put something like that in a letter!'

George relaxed. 'I must say, judging by his actions, he seems to have a particular interest in your family. Yet you've no idea of his identity?'

Selby blushed slightly. 'Damn me, I don't. Goodness knows where he springs from—he seems to range over the whole country.'

'You put your trust rather readily in a complete unknown.'

'I'm in no doubt that he once saved my life!'

'Granted,' George said affably. 'But shouldn't you check out this house he's offered you? What's the address?'

Selby looked at the duke in consternation. 'I was … I was sworn to secrecy.'

'God's blood, sir,' George said with a brilliant smile, 'you may tell *me!*'

Selby shook his head, embarrassed. 'No one is to learn it. Not even my sister.'

George gritted his teeth. 'Which means the Shadow knows everything about you, and you not a jot about him. Secrets can be sold. To the highest bidder. Who at present would be John Thurloe, latterly of the Council of State. Have you no fear of denunciation?'

To the duke's surprise, Selby laughed. 'In these times? Thurloe has weightier things to mind. I'd be small fry to him, whatever tall tales anyone might tell about me.'

WHITEHALL
February 2, Afternoon

As soon as Mary Villiers had heard from Lucinda how soon Monck would be in London she had written a note to Mistress Anne Monck at Whitehall, requesting to pay her a visit. Out of flattered surprise, curiosity, political opportunism or all three, Mistress Monck granted the favour, naming Thursday afternoon, no doubt to give herself time to make due arrangements.

Their barge was propelled up the Thames by four oarsmen and commanded by an officer sent as escort. Also in the barge were two large canvas bags packed with luxurious cloth: samples provided by Ambrose Martel and other merchants eager to indulge the duchess's sophisticated tastes. The women were well rugged up against the cold, sitting side by side and keeping their voices down so that the escort could not overhear.

As they approached Whitehall, the duchess said: 'You interrogated Colonel Denton to good effect about Monck's movements. We're seeing this woman at the right moment. Her husband will be at her side within days and what we say will be fresh in her mind when she reasserts her influence over him.'

Lucinda replied: 'I wish I could have asked the colonel more questions but he left in a hurry.' She had not recounted all of her conversation with Denton—it had been far too personal. And his lecture about royalists staying out of trouble, if she passed it on, would not be gratifying to the duchess, who seemed to have complete confidence in her own schemes and might resent any idea that she placed herself or Lucinda in danger.

The duchess looked at her sideways. 'Against his inclination, I'll be bound, considering how he admires you.'

Lucinda looked at her in astonishment. 'You're quite mistaken!'

Mary Villiers said with a sad smile, 'I am not mistaken in such matters. It's a skill I'd rather not have: seeing into people's hearts has caused me great pain over the years and very little joy.'

Lucinda said: 'Excuse me, Your Grace, but I would defy anyone to look into Denton's heart. He doesn't have one.'

'I never mistook a man yet where his affections were touched. And I have never seen a human creature deeply in love and able to conceal it for ever. It always bursts forth, at the most catastrophic moment.'

Lucinda would have laughed at this but the duchess's tragic expression prevented her. Instead she said with conviction: 'Mark Denton cannot be in love with me. You must understand, it's quite impossible.'

The sad smile was still there. 'And what about you?'

Lucinda did laugh at this. 'I'm delighted to inform you that I'm in love with no one.'

The duchess looked at the high walls of the great palace that sprawled along the shore above them. The sight seemed to hurt her. 'I hate coming here. I knew it would be terrible. But Anne Monck is our best hope and here she waits, to preside over our fate.'

They were approaching the wharf below the Privy Stairs where they had permission to land. Lucinda could see a group of soldiers lined up on its blackened planks under which the river ran smoothly, creating sinuous ripples around the piles. They had come by water because the Prince's Lodgings, so named because they traditionally housed the heir to the throne, consisted of extensive apartments poised above the waterside; Mary Villiers had told Lucinda they would have a shorter walk there than from the immense courtyard within the palace gates on the far side. The rowers and their master, serving as an escort on the Thames, had been sent on behalf of Anne Monck. In the past they had been the king's watermen—now they were at Parliament's command.

The barge turned towards the wharf and Lucinda looked up at the tall buildings with their terraces and crenellated roofs. Perhaps Anne Monck was looking down from a window in one of the turrets—unless her closet was in a turret, which was a likely place for it. Lucinda tried to find humour in this thought and failed. 'Your Grace, you must tell me how you wish me to act in Mistress Monck's presence.'

The duchess turned to her. 'As your true self, otherwise I shouldn't have brought you. But if any surprises occur, take your cues from me. You understood perfectly at Martel's, when I left you alone with Denton. We shall see what we can accomplish with Anne Monck, together or separately.'

'But how frank do you intend to be with her, Your Grace?'

'That depends on whether she's alone or not. If she is, she's a fool and we'll have to take that into account. She may be queening it briefly in this place but she's under surveillance by Parliament and its spies—no doubt they're in every corner.'

'So she needs one of them by, as a shield against suspicion?'

'Indeed. But I doubt if she's a fool. I've heard she has a certain bold, practical wit, so we must expect company. Of the worst kind.'

Lucinda would never have admitted it to Mary Villiers but she found Whitehall intimidating. Entirely administered by Parliament, which housed a host of officials within its labyrinthine halls, it looked as much like a village or a stronghold as a palace and Mary Villiers had told her it rivalled both Versailles and the Vatican. 'Oliver Cromwell used to live here, didn't he?'

'And died here, God be praised. Beyond, in the Cockpit, looking over St James's Park.' The duchess's voice was distant.

'Can we see His Majesty's lodgings from here?'

Mary Villiers pointed up to the left of the stairs. 'Between those two turrets. I fancy we shall be taken behind, so you will see nothing of them except through the windows that look down into the king's garden.'

'We don't go near the Banqueting House?'

'I pray not!' The duchess visibly shuddered. After a while she continued in a strained voice: 'Buckingham, my father, was murdered in a Portsmouth Street. My second father was murdered here, on a scaffold outside the Banqueting House. My husband James chose to share his captivity until the very end. It was a miracle that he escaped the same fate. All three had a high courage that I can never, ever hope to have. Nonetheless, I must enter here today.'

The boat glided neatly alongside the wharf and the master handed up a pass to the guardsman in command. The man checked the seal, an order was given, the barge was tied up and the two noblewomen were respectfully helped ashore.

When they moved forward again, up the sloping wharf and a steeper set of stairs, they were flanked by foot soldiers armed with pistols and halberds. Lucinda felt a hollow dread as she listened to the tramp of their stout shoes on the ancient timbers and stone. For her whole life, her movements had been restricted by Parliament and its army. If she entered the palace today alongside Mary Villiers, intimate of princes, lady-in-waiting to the dowager queen of England, she was displaying her unequivocal loyalties before those in power. What if they defined this as treason?

Suddenly the duchess took hold of Lucinda's wrist. She whispered: 'My lady, what am I doing? *You* are not obliged to enter here! At Nun Appleton I begged for your help—and you gave it. All along you've shown me the companionship of a friend. How can I ask more?' She stopped and Lucinda halted too, upon which the escort gave the soldiers an order and stood staring at them both.

'You've been most kind—'

'And amply repaid.' The duchess released her gently. 'If you prefer, I shall do this alone and you may turn back and wait in the barge.'

'Your Grace, I did not come all this way to desert you at the sticking point.'

Mary Villiers gave a quick smile, nodded and walked on. Behind them followed two watermen bearing the cloth.

As their little party was guided through the vast complex of buildings on the way to the Prince's Lodgings, Lucinda noticed that the duchess's face became paler and paler, so she walked a little behind her, thinking she needed a few private moments to withstand this fraught return to the home of her childhood and youth.

Lucinda looked critically around them as they passed up the stairways, searching for signs of neglect, but it was only when they were ushered inside that she could see how much the character of Whitehall must have changed in the last 18 years—from the splendid to the worn and functional. No surface, whether of stone, wood or weave, had been maintained to its original standard. The halls echoed, for they had been stripped of furniture that was now crowded into the bureaus of officials or gathered around guardroom fires. In the once handsome reception rooms, no paintings or hangings decorated the walls. Probably the private chambers were better appointed but they were closed to view. When Lucinda did catch sight of the king's little courtyard garden from a gallery, she thought it unkempt and forlorn.

'The Privy Garden is ten times larger,' the duchess murmured. 'Beyond the Stone Gallery, in that direction.' She pointed ahead to their right. 'I wonder if it's a thicket now or a desert? But we won't see it. We must turn soon, back towards the river.'

They did so, and a minute later entered Anne Monck's apartments—disconcertingly, through a guardroom. Then they were in a very long gallery with a generous row of windows overlooking the Thames, and Anne Monck was before them.

As Mary Villiers had predicted, she was not alone. The greetings were made—the duchess being given precedence, Lucinda was glad to see—and they were faced with a blowsy matron in a crimson dress and too many pearls, and a dark-browed man with a fleshy countenance: John Thurloe, until recently Secretary of the Council of State.

Thurloe showed no surprise at meeting them and after the introduction waited for one of the ladies to speak first. When no one did, he said deferentially to the duchess: 'I happened to be paying Mistress Monck a visit—my bureau is within the palace—and she mentioned that she was expecting this honour. I trust you had smooth passage upriver, Your Grace?'

'Thank you, yes.' She turned to Anne Monck. 'And thank you for receiving us, madam. It is many years and a great many things have passed since I last stood in this place.'

Anne Monck gave a little toss of her head, which made brassy curls bob around her face. 'And I'll warrant you see many a change here!'

It was the self-satisfied tone as much as the words that made Mary Villiers recoil. She took a step backwards and gazed around the high-ceilinged gallery, then said, as though bewildered: 'Where are all the paintings?' She put a hand to her temple, swayed—and Lucinda realised that she was about to faint.

Thurloe, too, was quick to see what was happening and they stepped forward to take an arm on each side and guide the duchess to a chair.

'Your Grace?' he said in genuine concern, then to Lucinda: 'Can you support her? I'll bring a glass of wine.'

The duchess's eyelids fluttered as Lucinda said softly: 'Put your arms on the rest and bend your head towards your knees.'

The duchess obeyed and Lucinda glanced up to see Thurloe approaching with a glass of wine and Anne Monck frozen in the background; she had not moved from the middle of the room.

The duchess raised her head, took the glass and murmured her thanks. Lucinda looked at her with dismay. All the courage Mary Villiers had said she lacked had brought her to this spot—but shock now revealed the sensitive woman beneath all the ebullience and wit. She looked earnestly at Lucinda, her eyes brimming with tears. 'I'm so sorry, my dear. This place once had a beauty that I cannot bear to describe to you.' She said to Thurloe, with the ghost of a smile: 'I apologise. I don't know why I should complain about the paintings—I knew quite well they wouldn't be here.'

'There was none here when I came, neither!'

All three of them turned to Anne Monck. She had a square, determined face and it was impossible to tell from her expression whether this statement was intended as comfort or defiance.

Thurloe chose to believe the former. 'Madam, is there a suitable bedchamber where her grace may retire and rest for a while?'

'Yes, of course there is. Any number. I'd just have to check about the linen. Housekeeping in this place is like running a barracks, stables and a blessed camp all in one—I never seem to get on top of it.'

All Anne Monck's extraordinary remarks were universal; she did not address any directly to the duchess and it occurred to Lucinda that the situation was simply too much for their hostess. This was confirmed when Mary Villiers handed the glass to Thurloe and rose slowly and gracefully from the chair—Anne Monck retreated a step and beckoned to a servant as though she needed an ally by her side.

Mary Villiers said: 'Pray don't disturb yourself, madam, I shall recover. I'll just take a walk by the windows—it's cooler there. Don't mind me,' she said with a reassuring smile at Lucinda. 'I'll return in a moment.'

Thurloe said at once: 'Would you care to take my arm, Your Grace?' Lucinda was surprised to see both admiration and sympathy in his face and it occurred to her that if the duchess had set out to disarm Thurloe from the beginning, she could not have done better.

'Thank you, no—I shall be all right by the windows. I used to stand there on a chilly day like this, watching snow fall on the river.' She walked away.

Anne waved at her servant. 'Go open one of the panes along the end there—only a crack, mind, or the whole place will be froze like an ice fair.'

Thurloe was still holding the glass. He said to Lucinda: 'Would you care for some wine yourself, my lady?'

'No, thank you.'

He stepped away two paces to put the glass on a dresser and returned. 'I fear the duchess has caused herself much distress by coming here. Could it not have been avoided? Would you care to explain her purpose?' He glanced at their hostess. 'I'm sure Mistress Monck will be glad to hear it and to know whether she can oblige you in any way.'

Anne Monck took this as a cue to draw closer and look Lucinda in the eye for the first time. She even said: 'If it please you, do sit down.'

'Thank you.'

Lucinda chose the chair beside the one the duchess had occupied and Thurloe, without invitation, took one opposite, a plain chair with a smooth leather back. Other chairs in the gallery had tooled backs in the Spanish style: they might well have been part of the original furniture. Lucinda examined the rest of the room as she pondered her reply. The walls were lined with linen-fold oak that had darkened with age and was disfigured by faded patches where paintings from Charles I's priceless collection had once hung. The dressers, chests and tables were even darker, almost black. There were not enough of them but those that remained were handsomely carved. A generous fire leaped in the magnificent fireplace and the light winked on pewter and silver placed about the room, but no gold dishes were displayed, there were no rich carpets on the wooden surfaces and no cushions below the casements. Blue drapes along the immense rank of windows were faded at the edges where they caught the light and darkened by smoke within the folds.

Anne Monck had her eyes on the bulging canvas bags that the watermen had deposited just inside the principal doors. 'So, what have you brought me, my lady?'

'Linen and other fabrics that her grace hopes you'll be pleased to look at.'

Anne Monck started. *'Linen*? Why?'

Lucinda cringed inwardly: if the lady chose to be offended, the visit was already a spectacular failure. Mistress Monck had begun life as Anne Clarges, a London farrier's daughter, and had first met George Monck when she was a washerwoman at the Tower and he was imprisoned there as punishment for fighting on the king's behalf in Ireland. But she had not scrupled to mention linen herself, a moment ago, so the word need not always be taken to refer to her career in laundry.

Lucinda took a breath. 'Her Grace would be glad to have your opinion of the fabrics. She thought they might interest you.' Anne Monck looked unmollified, so Lucinda went on: 'She has taken a house in the Convent Garden, you see, and it's in much need of refurbishment and colour. She has begged samples of the best merchants.' She included Thurloe in her glance: 'I'm sure you'll know of Ambrose Martel, for instance.'

Thurloe nodded. 'Her Grace will get sound advice from Martel, and the finest quality.' Like Anne Monck, he had a puzzled look. They were both waiting for her to get to the point.

'Preparing a London town house with luxury and style is a labour of love to Her Grace. I've had great enjoyment seeing her do it. And then the other day she remarked to me that you, madam, have just such a prospect ahead of you, and on a much, much grander scale.' When Anne Monck still looked blank, Lucinda said: 'All London knows that you'll shortly welcome your husband to Whitehall. He'll be here at the behest of Parliament and I'd be very surprised if Parliament didn't want these apartments furnished in the first fashion and to a standard worthy of the commander-in-chief.' While Anne Monck was mulling this over, Lucinda noticed Thurloe give a slight nod. She aimed the next question at him: 'Perhaps Parliament has already made provision for the reception of General Monck?'

'An interesting coincidence.' Thurloe's gaze probed Lucinda's. 'It's been my pleasure this afternoon to inform Mistress Monck that the Council of State has voted funds to cover the general's needs at Whitehall. Not only for the household—the main responsibility of our good hostess—but his regiment and his retainers; everyone whom he quarters within the palace.' He turned to Anne Monck. 'The duchess's intervention may save you a great deal of time and effort over the next few days.'

'Intervention!' Mary Villiers had rejoined them. She said to Anne Monck: 'I came simply to share some ideas and to hear what you think of the samples. I have permission from the merchants to leave them with you—whatever you decide, you can deal with Ambrose Martel and his like from today. I shall give you their names and directions and they of course will come to you.'

'I make no promises about trading with them! I hope you've given no commitments about what I might or might not buy.'

Anne Monck was still offensively wary. Lucinda wondered whether she was like this because of John Thurloe or the duchess.

The duchess said in a bright tone: 'No promises have been made—in fact I've mentioned neither your name nor Whitehall to a single draper. My conversations with them have been about my house in the Convent Garden. If you decide to deal with them, the initiative will be yours alone. Or, if you prefer, I shall leave at once.'

This took them all by surprise. Thurloe got to his feet. 'Your Grace, are you well enough?'

'I'm quite recovered, thank you.'

'It pains me to think that your visit has been so discomfiting. May I beg you to stay a little longer? It would give me great pleasure to make you some small amends.'

The two exchanged a long glance. Thurloe obviously wanted her to linger—but why?

'What exactly do you propose, sir?' The duchess had regained her aplomb and looked ready to fence with Thurloe on whatever ground he might choose.

He said: 'You've been bitterly disappointed by the lack of paintings here. I sympathise with your appreciation of fine art and I regret as much as you do that most of it is gone. But not all the Whitehall collection is dispersed—there are still some treasures in the better appointed bureaus. Mine is but a short walk away. Would you care to accompany me?'

A flush of pink came to the duchess's pale cheeks. She seemed touched by the offer. 'Which paintings do you have?'

'Portraits, in the main. By Van Dyck, Holbein and Honthorst. In fact, there is one of your late husband the duke. Of course, you mustn't let me press you if viewing it would give you pain ...' But he offered his arm.

She murmured: 'You are most considerate,' and took it.

With an expectant smile on his full lips, Thurloe said to Anne Monck: 'Excuse us for a moment, madam,' and nodded to Lucinda before moving away.

The duchess inclined her head but avoided looking at Lucinda, which was as potent a signal as any that she would now have to deal with Anne Monck on her own.

To her surprise, it was easy at first because of the lady's loud enthusiasm for the samples that were soon spilling from the canvas bags.

With the duchess out of the room, her awkwardness disappeared and she relaxed into the role that she had defined for herself at the outset—housekeeper of these grand apartments. Lucinda, perforce a housekeeper herself from an early age, did not find it hard to draw her out or to discover her greatest passions—her husband, her son and the military life.

Mistress Monck was immensely proud of the general and his towering achievements, and referred to him constantly by his rank. Praise for him reflected upon herself and on their son, Christopher, whom she called Kit and who at that hour was with one of his tutors, a scholar recommended by John Thurloe. She elaborated happily on Kit's qualities and his prospects which were now among the best in the land. And when she spoke about the challenges of being a military wife—surviving behind the scenes of battle after battle; making the best of the travel, the shortages and the quarters; feeding family and servants; receiving the officers; supporting the commander through victory and retreat—Lucinda discovered the real woman whom Monck had made his mistress in prison and then, when he was widowed, had chosen as his second wife.

Forthright, energetic and with an obvious flair for organisation, Anne Monck could make a home for her family wherever she happened to be, and was glad to do it. The dumpy body in the crimson dress strode forcefully around the gallery, trying different fabrics in various lights, with Lucinda in her wake. It came as a surprise, therefore, when the conversation abruptly swerved from the domestic.

'Now,' Anne Monck said, turning from the furthest window with a swathe of Dutch velvet over her arms, 'tell me why you're here, my lady, if you please. This is the best corner for it—no doors for Thurloe's men to snoop behind.'

'To talk about Whitehall.'

'Nonsense! The duchess has a message for me or for the commander-in-chief and you'd best hand it over quick, before Thurloe comes back.'

'I spoke truth. Think: today you're planning to receive your husband in this palace—one day soon it must be ready for the king.' Anne Monck's light blue eyes widened. 'Isn't that your dream—to serve the king? To foster his return and receive his gratitude for it?'

The eyes brightened further, then narrowed. It was obvious that Anne Monck had been expecting something rather more tangible by way of a message—or payment. But Lucinda was not authorised to mention the £100,000 that the king had previously promised Monck and nor did she know what the current offers might be. What they needed was another meeting with Mistress Monck in which the duchess could talk to her freely. It was obviously not going to happen today.

Lucinda said,: 'We are here to call upon your allegiance, Mistress Monck, which is known and deeply appreciated. We've heard that you've spoken for His Majesty's return to the general himself, many times and with great eloquence. However, if you tell me that we're misinformed, I apologise.'

Anne Monck jerked her arms under the length of velvet as though it prevented her from putting her hands on her ample hips. 'Aye, indeed I have. A fine wife I'd be if I didn't give him a straight answer when he asked my notions! And I admit to the habit of talking sense to anyone else who needs to hear it, at my own table. But stay—' She raised a forefinger beyond the folds of fabric. 'Before I parted from him, the commander-in-chief said: "Nan, not a word on this until we meet again, as God is my judge, and the world's to hear not a jot from your lips upon it." And so I gave my oath. Consequently, make any demands you like, I cannot answer them.'

Lucinda flashed: 'One does not serve one's sovereign by *demand*!' She felt crushed and angry. If Anne Monck refused to speak of the king and her husband in the same breath they would learn nothing about George Monck's intentions. And there was no hope of asking the woman to influence him for the king.

Anne Monck placed the Dutch velvet carefully on the chest under the window, flung a glance up the empty gallery and turned back to Lucinda with her characteristic, self-satisfied smile. 'Come. I put a bar on *speaking* of it. But I don't say I won't *listen* if you choose to have your say.'

Lucinda just managed to quell an impulse to walk away. She thought quickly. 'The hopes of this kingdom rest on your husband's shoulders. No one else can bring about the return of the king. This puts you in a position of influence that no other woman in this country possesses.

Everything you do, whether at home or in public, has a bearing on the future.'

Anne Monck's eyes grew wide again. She was hearing the truth—and it seemed that she had just realised it, with a mixture of pride and awe.

Lucinda went on: 'You cannot speak. I understand. How long you remain silent on this subject is your decision entirely. May I simply ask this—may we beg that when you *are* in a position to speak, when you judge us worthy to hear what the general intends with regard to the government, you will send a secret message to the Duchess of Richmond and Lennox at the Convent Garden? If your husband will gladly receive a personal letter from the king, we will be honoured to pass that message on.'

Footsteps could be heard and there was a murmur at the outer doors as the guard registered the return of Thurloe and the duchess.

Without a word, Anne Monck bent to pick up the velvet and walked the length of the gallery to meet them by the fire. Lucinda followed, moving through the white, wintry light of each window until she stood in the glow of the flames, noting the colour on the duchess's cheeks and regretting the disappointment she would cause her on the swift return downstream.

Mistress Monck said comfortably: 'I must thank Your Grace again for the fine cloth. I've had a right good time, trying the pieces in every corner.'

'Please keep them, then,' Mary Villiers said with a smile, 'if you find them useful.'

'With pleasure. I'll keep this piece with the rest,' she said, draping it over a chair back. 'But Lady Lucinda tells me you like the colour particular. For that reason, I promise to send it back to you. Within days, or a week at most.' She turned so that Thurloe could not see her expression and held Lucinda's eye with an earnest look. 'At the right time. You have my word.'

BARNET
February 2, Night

Mark Denton had finished his London report to Monck. The night was far advanced and he had not yet eaten supper but he was in no hurry to end the longest conference he had ever had alone with his commander. As he sat by the fire in Monck's chamber with a beaker of mulled wine, he reflected on the army's achievements during the month since the freezing New Year in Coldstream: the unopposed crossing into England; the end of the threat from Lambert; the securing of York and the North; neutralisation of Parliament's commissioners; the progress down the country; the welcome given by gentry and towns folk every step of the way. It did not surprise Mark to see a suppressed excitement in Monck's bearing as he listened to the recital of how Londoners were likely to receive him. Nor did Mark miss the motive behind his pointed questions—which for a strategist like Monck had to be nervousness, if not alarm, about what would happen on the morrow. Despite the general's almost trouble-free arrival outside the city, there was no guarantee what would happen once his forces entered it.

'So every man and his dog has an idea of what this army is to do in London,' Monck muttered, 'and none of them match.'

'There's cohesion enough in some quarters.' Mark replied. 'Consider the advocates of a free parliament—the people who talk the loudest. Their aims are clear: Parliament must re-admit the secluded members, name the date for new elections and replace themselves with a larger, more representative body. Everyone takes for granted that that body will pass a bill to recall Charles Stuart.'

'Are there any of that persuasion in the present Parliament?'

Mark considered Monck for a moment, wondering why he asked a question to which he knew the answer. Perhaps the general felt the situation called for thinking out loud. About damned time!

'A paltry few, if any. But that won't matter if the secluded members are called back. It'll give them a majority and they'll name the date for elections.'

'And the City?'

'You got their measure from the delegation to Market Harborough, sir. Most of the silken independents are thoroughly sick of Parliament and want the dead wood thrown out. The merchants of the old school want the same, which is the only way they'll ever be represented in the House of Commons again—at the moment there's but one member for London.'

'They seem to be provoking Parliament in a most intemperate way.'

'True, sir. Which gives the apprentices strong excuse for riots—'

'Against Parliament?'

'Against anything you care to name. There's a rebellious spirit abroad and it springs up in a multitude of ways, for good and bad causes or none at all. The city guards are called upon to cool it down but, depending on the issue, there's the risk that they too will mutiny in consequence.'

Monck frowned. Setting the streets alight must be the last thing he would want upon the morrow. 'And Haselrig's army? Do they share his republican temper or are there divisions amongst them, too?'

Mark said carefully: 'I found their talk somewhat opaque, even amongst the officers I know best. They're discontented with being banished to the country, of course—but I don't know whether the defence of Parliament is very close to their hearts. It's just possible that they've been sent out of range, not because the Council of State thinks they'd clash with you, sir, but because they might choose to join you.'

Monck's frown blackened. 'You've evidence for that?'

'None. Except that Parliament's not paying the troops.'

'And they think I might?' Monck gave a snorting laugh, then threw Mark a saturnine look. 'Any sign of Lambert?'

Mark shook his head. 'Parliament has let him hang about London unpunished but he never shows his face and no one knows where he lodges. I don't think he'd be the first to make a move, if it came to a fight.'

'Who *would* be the first? The gallant cavaliers for Charles Stuart? You've told me very little about them.'

'Because they're of little consequence, sir. The people who are dreaming and yearning that you'll declare for Charles are far more numerous than the earls and sons of earls who are creeping about waiting to get their aristocratic fortunes back. They're people of every degree and every trade, rich and poor. They once trusted Parliament and its army to end the war and restore peace and prosperity. Well, they've got prosperity, if they could only see it, but no peace. They've been held beneath the sword for 20 years and their only help, as they see it, is the restoration of a representative parliament under the king.'

'Why the king, necessarily?' Monck said, as though it was the question that haunted him most.

'People need leaders, sir. They looked to Parliament for them but it's let them down, and what's more turned the army against them. It's not in the nature of the English to be run by the military. People want their leaders to come from the body politic. They want elections and they want the highest in the land—the king—to stand guarantee that those elections will be regular and perpetual. The only figure on their horizon that looks like bringing that about is you. Sir.'

Monck said with sarcasm: 'My oath, a fine summary! And all this you got from what Londoners have been saying to you?'

'No. From what they didn't say. From what they feel, in the heart, and they're not ready to reveal. Yet.'

'The heart.' Monck looked at him keenly. 'This is the first time in all your years of service that I've heard such speech from you. If I could see into your heart, colonel, and descry how you feel on these matters, what should I find?'

Mark was suddenly tired of caution, patience and endless deception. 'I had intended to wait until you finally revealed your own purposes, sir, before telling you mine. But what the hell, ask me now.'

Monck opened his mouth, then shut it and stared into his mulled wine. At last he said: 'Thank you, colonel. I think we'd both do best to sleep on what's been said tonight.'

****

As once before, at Coldstream, Mark was lodged overnight with Ralph Knight, in a house a few doors down from Monck's. This time, however, he had a room to himself, under the thatch. As before, he was too exhausted to eat and threw himself fully clothed on the bed, expecting to fall asleep at once.

Sleep did not come. There was far too much to think about. On the swift ride back from London in the evening he had regretted having to leave the city. The potential for unrest thudded beneath the surface of everyday duties and tasks, like muffled drums. In the capital, where opposing forces often came into open conflict, riots could change the course of history.

In 1642, a few hundred enraged citizens battering at the gates of Whitehall had been enough to convince Charles I that the palace was unsafe for him and his family. His musketeers had dispersed the rabble and restored order—but he fled from London and the war began.

During Oliver Cromwell's reign, Parliament was frequently exposed to angry demonstrators bearing petitions. The crowds that clustered outside the doors of the House were loud and threatening; the guards who defended it, and the members within, could be trapped for hours or days almost in a state of siege.

Now the whole of London was on tenterhooks about Monck and his army. Everyone felt they had something to gain or lose by his actions once he marched in, and no one could guess what those actions might be. Mark had had an urge to stay overnight and send Corporal Hales to Barnet with the report that Monck had requested. But he had had no time to write it down and he was under orders to deliver it himself, without fail. So he had taken the next best course and left Hales behind in the city, to be his eyes and ears on this crucial night and to gallop to Barnet and warn him if unrest threatened.

To Mark's mind the most vulnerable target for discontent would be the Speaker of the House, William Lenthall, the man who had defied Charles I when he tried to arrest five Members of Parliament just before the outset of the war. A faithful and long-serving member, Lenthall had presided while the governing body dwindled to the meagre Rump that was still clinging to the vestiges of its power. People who cried for a free parliament or, on the contrary, wanted the Rump to cleave to republican principles and make sure that monarchy was irretrievably dead, might menace Lenthall from outside the gates of Somerset House, the Speaker's palatial residence on the shores of the Thames. They might even try to overcome his guards and invade it. Thus Mark had found Hales a handy post on the Strand, some way east of Somerset House, and his corporal was spending a night there—sleepless, like himself, and alert for possible trouble.

Midnight came and Mark heard a clock strike somewhere in the unfamiliar house. Since he was wide awake he allowed himself to think of Lucinda Selby. How he wished she had not placed herself in the thick of things and with such an ally as the Duchess of Richmond! He knew no evil of the duchess, who, in a lifetime of devotion to Charles I and his queen, had never misused the influence she possessed as a lady in waiting. Cunning women of the court could amass fortunes by promising to gain the monarch's favour for others—but Mary Villiers had always acted with integrity and was uninvolved in politics. Parliament knew this well, which was why she had not been designated a delinquent. Her husband the duke had likewise been unimpeachable. His relationship with his cousin the king had been guided by a strong sense of honour and he had managed to give him rational advice without being a war-monger. When the king was Parliament's prisoner, turning this way and that to bargain for the throne, Richmond had voluntarily shared his captivity and given him advice and comfort without conniving at Charles's many shameful deceptions. But the Richmonds' own honour prevented them from seeing how dishonourably—and dangerously—other members of their famous families might act while plotting to restore the monarchy. What was Mary Villiers doing in London? Whatever it happened to be, it could risk Lucinda Selby's life.

Mark lay staring into the darkness and remembering the far too brief conversation he had had with Lucinda at Ambrose Martel's. It had been a heady experience. He had been able to bathe in the steady clarity of her blue eyes; to relish her melodious voice, which never lost its vivacity no matter how hard she tried to control it; to watch the changing colours in her perfect complexion as she listened, with much less annoyance than he had feared, while he tried to persuade her to pull out of the duchess's schemes and accept his protection if they went awry.

She was not good at hiding her reactions: he'd seen that she not only believed his offer but was momentarily touched by it—and despite himself, this aroused his hopes, or at least his dreams. For the first time he wondered whether there was a chance that they might both emerge from this crisis and find peace. Like a fool, he imagined them together at Lang Scar, where her brother's properties would be restored and Mark would at last lay down his sword and take over the management of his own. They would create a home in a landscape that had seen much bloodshed and sorrow but was nonetheless dear to them both. Out of conflict and suffering, joy might arise.

He imagined more: it was impossible not to. Her body entranced him and her face haunted his dreams. The thought of seeing her every day and tasting the most intoxicating of pleasures with her every night made him burn with desire. But if Charles came to the throne, the marvellous future that he pictured for them would never unfold. Her connection with Mary Villiers would put Lucinda out of his reach for good. When the royal court reconstituted itself, one of its stars would be the Duchess of Richmond. She had already shown Lucinda great favour; with the return of the king, she could bestow another gift—a splendid match. York and the North might never see Lady Lucinda again. Marriage would anchor her in the charmed circle of the king's intimates and she would leave London only in summer, to sojourn on her husband's noble estates in Kent, Surrey or Devon …

The duchess took a proprietorial care of Lucinda and, at Martel's, Mark had had the uneasy sensation that she saw straight through him as they spoke. Her glance as she left the room had been satirical: '*I may safely leave her alone with you, colonel: she is not for you.*'

Of late, everything Lucinda Selby did took her further away from him. Yet he was more in love with her than ever.

****

All at once, the main street of Barnet came alive. There were hoof beats, the sound of running feet, shouted alarms. Mark sprang up and snatched a glimpse into the road. A small, noisy party had arrived at George Monck's door. Whoever it was had already dashed inside and guards were flying up both sides of the thoroughfare, waking the officers. Mark lit a candle from the embers in the fireplace and placed it on the mantel. Then he straightened his clothing, sat down on the bed and ran both hands through his hair. Downstairs the street door opened and he heard Ralph Knight's calm, unhurried voice. But the sound of his boots on the stairs sounded urgent.

 There was a knock and Knight opened Mark's door and stepped in without ceremony. 'Good, you're up. The general wants us all now.'

'What, the first officers' council since Nottingham? In the middle of the night?'

'Yes, and that's all I know. Waste no time!' Knight turned on his heel and clattered back downstairs.

Mark put on his thigh boots and sword, splashed water on his face and blew out the candle. Two minutes later he was in the chamber where he had last spoken with Monck. A few extra chairs had been brought in to accommodate the officers, who were all present. The room was charged with excitement—for once they looked like hearing some of Monck's ideas and even, should action be required, sharing them with the men they commanded.

However, their focus was not Monck, who stood silent by the fireplace, but Parliament's commissioner, Thomas Scot, who had clearly entered in haste, for he was still wearing nightcap and night shirt.

When the door closed behind Mark, the general began. 'Mister Scot has news from London, gentlemen.' He nodded at Scot. 'In your own words, if you please.'

'Rebellion!' Scot's eyes were staring, as though a dire scene were playing out before his eyes.

The officers exchanged glances and Monck said quietly: 'By whom and against whom, sir?'

'It's mutiny! Against the government! The Somerset House regiment is up in arms and a mob is rioting in the Strand.'

'Is the Speaker at risk?'

'With hundreds at the gates—of course he is!'

Monck turned quickly towards Mark, who stood just inside the door, his back against the panelling. 'The guards regiment and its commander—what's your judgment of them?'

'Infantry regiment, sir, not full strength but enough for guard duty. This surprises me. Their commander's experienced and seems well able to control his men. Somerset House has a massive courtyard and fine barracks—he keeps a company within the gates under a seasoned captain and the rest without. If it's the men without who've mutinied, they may still mean no harm to the Speaker himself. And to invade the courtyard they'd have to break down the gates and tangle with their comrades inside.' He said to Scot, 'Have the gates been breached?'

'How do I know?' Scot cried.

'It depends what they've mutinied *for*. Are they violent against the Parliament or just determined to be paid? Midnight's a weird hour to take up arms on either score, given that the paymasters and members are all abed and oblivious.'

When Scot seemed too overwrought to answer, Monck said to him with some impatience: 'What are the cries in the street? Whom do they rally to?'

'Charles the Second and a free parliament!' Scot said angrily. 'Does that sound traitorous enough to you?'

'And what are Parliament's wishes? I presume that's why you're here—to convey them,' Monck said calmly.

It occurred to Mark that Monck thought he might trip Scot up at this point, if the commissioner had rushed to report the calamity without exact directions from the Council of State.

But Scot was very prompt with his reply. 'That you march in at once to restore order! The government of England is without an army while you and the rest of its troops remain outside London. Apprentices have massed to support the mutineers. The city is in the grip of terror and anarchy. The time has come for you to keep your promise of aiding Parliament in its most need.'

'Thank you, Mister Scot. I shall ask you to remain during our meeting, in case any of the colonels has questions to put to you.'

Despite Scot's painful experience of Monck's extreme reticence to speak or act as Parliament desired, this took the commissioner's breath away and he sat down abruptly on the last available chair.

Meanwhile Monck spoke ponderously to each of his colonels in turn. Mark watched their faces as they replied, and privately commended their cautious advice. This night gave a tempting opportunity for Monck and those he commanded to accept Parliament's invitation, march into London under cover of darkness and impose their absolute will upon the city and government. When Londoners woke up tomorrow, they could be at the mercy of whatever policy Monk and his cohorts put in place. But the colonels' remarks were dutiful and to the point. If any of them were for Charles II and a free parliament, they were not about to reveal it at this juncture.

The infantry colonels all tended to think the disaffected soldiers should be disciplined sooner rather than later. The cavalry colonels had differing views. One was alarmed that apprentices had joined in: they were young and would willingly throng the streets until dawn, which might send the situation out of anyone's control. Two were worried about deploying their troops at night in a city that was unknown to many—what if confusion reigned and the populace of London misinterpreted what the army was doing, thus destroying its reputation in a few hours? Another thought it best to wait for a letter from Parliament instead of acting on

Thomas Scot's information—which of course incensed Scot and brought an enigmatic smile to Monck's face.

Mark, the last to be questioned, was still searching for a non-committal answer when there was a knock at the door and a guard entered. Monck glared at him but he said boldly enough: 'Begging your leave, general, there's a Corporal Hales below, from Colonel Denton's regiment. He says he has a message for Colonel Denton that cannot be delayed, be the colonel in conference with you or no.'

'Indeed,' Monck said with heavy displeasure. He said to Mark: 'Get rid of him.'

'With respect, sir, I left Hales in London, on watch near Somerset House, and he was to ride to me if any trouble flared up. Will you permit him to make his report? He will have the latest information, without a doubt.'

Monck's eyes narrowed. That evening, Mark had made no mention of positioning Hales to keep watch in the Strand. But his motives were surely self-evident now.

'Bring him up,' Monck said to the guard.

Corporal Hales displayed all the military composure that Thomas Scot had not. If he was daunted by facing the full complement of army command, he didn't allow it to damage his delivery. Monck left the questioning to Mark and everyone in the room was given a clear picture of the mutiny and its progress.

Hales's summary was equally graphic. 'So it's not the whole regiment, sir—a couple of companies at most. It sounds as though it started about pay but then someone got it into their head that they were strong enough to make trouble about Parliament and things moved down the Strand. Next minute there were 'prentices all over the place and they were calling for the downfall of the Rump. Then half the crowd started calling for Charles the Second and the other half for a free parliament. I lingered on the edges of the crowd and tried their temper by saying I was an infantryman and would rather serve under Monck than Parliament, whereupon a great cry went up for you, general, saving Your Grace.'

Hales drew himself up, ready to brave a reprimand, but Monck said at once, in a dispassionate tone: 'Were any threats made in my name?'

'Not that I heard, general. To be frank, I don't think most people knew what they were shouting in the end; it was a confounded din with no sense to it.'

'You judge the Speaker is safe?' The question came from Mark.

'When I left, sir, his gates were still barred and the commotion had moved well down the Strand.'

'Where were they all heading?'

'I'm not sure they were going anywhere. Because the infantry met no opposition but their commanding officer—'

Monck said: 'He was present? I should hope so! He's William Lenthall's son, after all.'

'Yes, general. I didn't spy him but someone told me he had men in there battling hand to hand, to turn them back. So, with no one else to fight, the mob were brawling amongst themselves, some for the Rump and the rest for the City and the 'prentices … And when I judged I'd seen enough, I obeyed orders and came to make my report to Colonel Denton.'

'Thank you, Hales,' Mark said. He scanned the room. 'Any more questions?'

'Yes! What are you going to do about this?' Scot said to Monck.

Monck ignored him and addressed Hales. 'Corporal, you're dismissed. Not another word on this to anyone except Colonel Denton.'

'General.' Hales saluted and marched out.

'It's late, gentlemen. Or rather, far too early. I won't keep you.' Monck scanned their faces with the same impassive stare that he had directed at them while they were giving their thoughts on the mutiny. 'Get some sleep. Later this morning, we move out at the appointed hour. I shall inspect the army at Highgate as arranged and thereafter your orders and dispositions are in every respect those you've already received. I bid you goodnight.'

Everyone rose except Mark, who was still on his feet by the door, and a red-faced Thomas Scot, who seemed rooted to his chair. Mark received a glance from Monck that commanded him to stay and Scot, waiting no doubt to read the general a diatribe about ignoring Parliament, was chagrined to see he would have a witness.

He rose, took a single step towards Monck and said with venom: 'And what message am I to take to the Council of State?'

'With my deepest respect to the council, please inform them that this army will enter London on the hour and by the route previously arranged.'

'Leaving chaos meanwhile!'

'Mister Scot,' Monck said with a weary smile, 'one may see Londoners brawling in the streets at almost any time. I see no reason to rush there this morning for such a common sight.'

Scot marched out, his eyes aflame and his nightcap bobbing in rhythm.

When the door closed, Monck said to Mark: 'Does Corporal Hales often undertake the kind of work you gave him tonight?'

'His duties are varied, sir. He tends my string of horses, he's an efficient courier and an even better scout. He's been in my service for years and is a soldier of some talent. As you see.'

'Then I have just one question before I bid you goodnight. Why is that man a mere corporal?'

'I'd have liked to promote him to sergeant and then ensign, long since. But that would have given him more men to command and I couldn't put that responsibility on top of his other tasks.'

Monck looked at him shrewdly. 'And when he makes ensign one day, whose flag will he bear?'

Mark grinned. 'Yours, sir.'

CONVENT GARDEN
February 8

Lucinda Selby was trying to curb her restlessness by sewing a piece of silk-thread work that Mary Villiers had abandoned in disgust.

The duchess had said: 'The moment I get a needle in my hand I have the overpowering urge to open a book.' She now had a volume of poetry in her lap but was gazing through a casement at grey sky.

Lucinda would have liked to ride or take a walk down to the Thames, or go into the City to look at merchants' wares, but there was noise, unrest and the constant threat of violence in the streets.

She said: 'I'm grateful for this work. I'm used to activity and none of the things I do at home are possible in London. Not that I object,' she added hastily, 'to sharing the luxury of your beautiful house.'

Mary Villiers smiled, put aside the book and rose. 'You're as discontented with idleness as I, but much more polite about it.' She drifted over behind Lucinda's chair and leaned forward to inspect the image, which was of a finely dressed lady presiding over the planting of a herb garden. 'How very green. You're doing well with the face—I didn't have the courage to attempt it. It's too square—horribly reminiscent of Mistress Monck's.'

'Why is there still no word from her? She gave you a promise last week and I thought it a four-square pledge at the time.'

Mary Villiers sighed and moved away. 'She's avid for cash and consequence, and since we can offer her neither, her attention is elsewhere. When I set out from Brussels, I begged His Majesty to give me something in writing, some concrete offers for the general. But he was reluctant. Monck had already refused to read his first letter—the cheek of the man! And if His Majesty puts anything on paper there's the danger to the recipient and the bearer. He told me: "It's like putting my seal upon someone's death warrant for treason."' Lucinda shivered, and Mary Villiers continued in a self-mocking tone: 'Just as well I carried nothing to Whitehall, therefore. I should make a very inept conspirator, as I manifestly proved. John Thurloe didn't even consider me worth interrogating when we had our tête-à-tête in his chambers—we only talked about art. He showed me a miniature of himself as a youth. Fortunately I was able to admire the frame.'

Lucinda smiled. 'Perhaps Anne Monck is too busy just now, surrounding her husband with luxury.'

'And he is too busy giving speeches!'

Lucinda continued sewing.

The Friday before, Monck had come into London along Gray's Inn Road and entered the Strand by Chancery Lane. He and his regiment proceeded to Somerset House where they were courteously greeted by the Speaker of Parliament, William Lenthall. When the duchess received word that all this was happening only a few streets away from her house, Lucinda had suggested they go and watch the army's progress back down the Strand towards Whitehall. The duchess had refused at first, as beneath her dignity—but, not liking to disappoint Lucinda and full of sudden curiosity, she changed her mind. They went on foot, cloaked and muffled against the cold, with two grooms in their wake.

The duchess had a right to be nervous: the riots only a short distance away the night before had been tumultuous and neither woman had gone back to sleep until the sounds of conflict faded. But there were no rowdy stragglers to disrupt Monck's grand occasion. The long parade, sparkling in pale winter sunlight, was cheered by the crowds on either side of the thoroughfare. The bells of St Paul's and of nearby churches pealed merrily as citizens swarmed out of the nearest gate in the city walls, Ludgate, to see the man they hoped would take the merchants' side against the Parliament.

Monck looked as sober as Lucinda remembered him from York; the only showy things about him were his fine horse and a richly embroidered belt worn over dark clothing. His men were impeccably turned out and the very picture of discipline. The general's officers rode behind him and Lucinda at once saw Mark Denton amongst them. As he passed by on a tall bay stallion he looked keenly at people in the crowd, and it gave her an uncomfortable frisson to think that he might spy her. She drew her hood closer about her face.

'Your admirer is clean-shaven today,' the duchess had murmured teasingly. 'We can see his lips better. And haughty curves they have, by my troth. He must have a devastating smile.'

'I've never seen him smile. I doubt he's capable.'

At last the parade had moved further down the Strand, leaving them to walk safely home, full of anticipation about Monck's next moves. But so far these had been confusing to all and encouraging to none.

Monck, his own troops and retainers moved into Whitehall where he inspected every aspect of their quarters and appointments before being reunited with his wife and son.

Next day, Lucinda learned without pleasure that Mark Denton was also lodged at Whitehall, in the Horseguards Barracks: a note was delivered to the Convent Garden house, containing a polite greeting, the address and his signature.

Monck was invited to the House that day to be thanked for his 'signal and faithful services' and was asked to take the oath of allegiance that the other members of the Council of State had already agreed to, declaring that England should never be governed 'by the House of Lords or a single person'. He begged leave to consider it and left it unsigned.

On Monday the 6th, he gave a speech to the House which neither criticised nor challenged its members. Lucinda and the duchess, reading it next day from a pamphlet bought in the Convent Garden, could see nothing to suggest that Monck disagreed with the Parliament on anything.

I know all the sober gentry will close with you, if they may be tenderly and gently used; and I may be sure you will so use them, as knowing it to be their common concern, to expatiate, and not narrow our interests; and to be careful neither the cavalier nor the fanatic party have yet a share in your civil and military power ...

Lucinda looked up from her thread work. 'Being one of the cavalier party, I am sorely wounded by Monck's speech on Monday. But I think if I were a City merchant I should be quite appalled—for I got no mention at all!'

'I hear from Dorothy Chiswell that the Common Council has lost trust in Monck.' Dorothy Chiswell was Mary Villiers's tailor, hired on the recommendation of the Countess of Dysart; she was a sensible, talkative woman, who had proved a fount of knowledge on what went on in London's centre of commerce. 'The mayor has not invited him to the Guildhall and neither he nor his officers have set foot inside the gates of the City. Meanwhile the merchants are screaming for a full and free parliament. I heard a slip of a boy screeching below my window this morning, an apprentice I suppose, and do you know what his words were?' The duchess laughed sardonically. '"Kiss my Rump!" What do you think to that?'

'Does it sound as if the noise in the streets just got louder?' Lucinda said uneasily.

'I hope not.'

They both started when a servant appeared in the doorway. 'Two gentlemen beg leave to wait on you, Your Grace. Sir Maurice Selby and a Mister John Fletcher.'

'Maurice!' Lucinda leaped to her feet.

'Good Lord,' the duchess said. 'Bring them to us if you please.' When the servant was out of hearing she said to Lucinda, 'Your brother—and mine, unless I'm mightily mistaken.'

'Were you expecting him?'

'No. I never have any idea what George is up to. He's the most unpredictable man alive. Were you expecting Sir Maurice?'

'No! I didn't even know he was allowed into London. Oh, I do hope they came discreetly.'

'As hugger-mugger as you could wish, dear lady, muffled up in a drab coach.' The Duke of Buckingham paused in the doorway, wearing a black wig, a tall-crowned black hat and a long cloak that he unwound gracefully from his shoulders to reveal a fine brocade doublet and breeches. His practised eye took in every detail of Lucinda's appearance. 'How wondrous you look, my lady. It is a sublime pleasure to see you.' He beamed at the duchess, said 'Dear sister', and made them both an elaborate bow.

Maurice Selby, entering behind him, looked at Lucinda across the duke's bent form and gave her a smile of mixed amusement and affection. The duke went forward to kiss Mary Villiers on both cheeks and Lucinda ran into Maurice's embrace. He held her tightly for a moment, then put her at arm's length to examine her. His eyes shone. 'I've never seen you look so well.'

'Nor I you!' There was no trace of illness in his bearing. After his weeks in the saddle on Monck's march, his skin had lost its pallor and he looked fit and strong.

The duchess held out her hand and Maurice bowed and kissed it. She said: 'I'm very glad to make your acquaintance. Your sister is delightful company; I see I may expect no less of you.'

A few weeks ago, Maurice might have found this speech a little intimidating. Today he smiled and said: 'My sister owes all her present fortune to you. If I can repay your favours by any service, I beg you to ask it of me.'

The duchess smiled back. 'Very well, you can tell me what you know of George Monck. We've been puzzling over him for days without the slightest result.'

Lucinda burst out: 'But Maurice, is it safe for you to be here?'

He smiled. 'The parliamentary commissioners secured me a permit.'

'Which I on the other hand do not possess,' the duke said. 'But nothing could have made me give up the chance of seeing you.' He was facing his sister as he spoke but his gaze was on Lucinda.

'Then let us all drink, eat and anatomise George Monck.' The duchess waved them to a table and sent a servant for refreshment.

As they shared their stories of the last few weeks, Lucinda wondered whether the duchess would describe the meeting with Anne Monck. When she did so, Lucinda gained the impression that George Villiers was a little jealous of his sister's efforts on behalf of the king—and secretly glad that they had come to nothing so far. In return he reported on the Fairfaxes and the situation in York, which was pretty much as they had left it in January. The most dramatic news was Maurice's—his meeting with the King's Shadow in Bedford. This was such a surprise to Lucinda that she exclaimed and glanced at the duke, but he did not meet her eye. From Maurice's description of the Shadow it was soon obvious that the mysterious cavalier was a stranger to them all.

Lucinda plied Maurice with questions about where he might have come from, and his appearance. When she asked about his voice, Maurice laughed. 'All I can say is that he was fine-spoken and had a sort of courtier's drawl. As for the quality of the voice—I can't say. I haven't your musical ear, Luce. At times I had the feeling I'd heard it before—apart from the first time I met him, of course—somewhere closer to home. But now he's nearer London; maybe *in* London.'

'Can you add anything to the picture of this amazing gentleman?' Lucinda said to the duke. She had a right to tease him: he had once hinted that he was the Shadow himself.

He shook his head ruefully. 'Our paths haven't crossed of late.'

'I should prefer to complete the picture of Monck,' the duchess said briskly. 'I have a horrid feeling we've not seen the worst of him yet.'

'I think what he's doing today qualifies as suitably diabolical,' her brother said.

'What?'

'You don't know?' Maurice said. 'I don't see it as an absolute catastrophe, Your Grace, but the truth is bad enough. The City mistrusts the general and well they might, for he's doing Parliament's bidding. The merchants have lost patience with the Parliament and declared they'll have no dealings with it, and pay no taxes, until they have due representation in the House. Parliament's responded by ordering the arrest of eleven members of the Common Council and they've asked Monck to carry it out.'

Lucinda exclaimed: 'On what charge? Not treason! Heaven help them.'

The duke shrugged. 'They're bound for the Tower, whatever the charge. The City's declared that no one hostile to their council shall pass through the gates. So Parliament's remedy to *that* is to order George Monck to pull down the gates, break up the portcullises and sweep away the posts and chains. And your commander-in-chief'—he poked a forefinger at Maurice—'has said aye to that, up boys and at 'em. That noise you hear in the street? It's Londoners finally getting the measure of Monck.'

Both women looked at Maurice in consternation. The duchess spoke first. 'Can this be true?'

He sighed. 'I'm afraid so.'

'Maurice, this is the army you marched with!' Lucinda said. 'Have they called on you to join in?'

'I have no commission, Luce. And now that we're in London my duties are over, though I'm still lodged by Ralph Knight. I agree, it's a grave turn of events.' They all looked at him as he gathered his thoughts. Lucinda was struck by how much he had matured in just a few weeks; she suddenly felt that Maurice's summary of the situation would be more worth having than the duke's.

Finally he said: 'Up until now Monck has had the spirit of the army with him but today he bids fair to lose it. All his senior commanders protested against Parliament's orders and when the general said they must be obeyed, they refused point-blank to lead their men to the task. I have this from Ralph Knight, one of those who refused. Of course Monck's command carries the day and companies have been sent to demolish the City gates and make the arrests. But no colonel consented to do it—junior officers are in charge. Oh, except for Colonel Denton, who at this moment is tearing Ludgate apart.'

The duchess put her head in her hands. 'No wonder we haven't heard from Anne Monck! Her husband is the devil himself.'

George Villiers reached out and put a hand briefly on her neck. 'Don't despair, Mall. What did we ever expect from Monck anyway, but empty gestures? The country's ripe for change and this proves it. Why don't we see it as a chance to move for the king? Listen to the people in the street calling for the downfall of the Rump! Parliament's just made its worst error by taking on the City. If there were king's men in town at this instant, I vow they'd gather all London behind them and carry the day.'

Lucinda exchanged a glance with Maurice. 'You said this isn't a disaster. How could it be any worse? A few streets from here'—she pointed eastwards—'Mark Denton's men are smashing up Ludgate. Monck and his army have turned on London.'

He shook his head. 'It looks bad, I know. As though he'll never be our ally and never was. But he still hasn't said anything about his intentions. What if he's waiting, to get the true mood of London? Letting its passions play out, seeking the right moment to show us what he really has in mind?'

'What I have in mind,' the duke said in his suave, agreeable voice, 'is an appointment with the Sealed Knot.' He rose from the table and scooped up his cloak and hat, which he had thrown on a chair. 'It couldn't have been arranged at a better time. The conference is but a short step up the road,' he said to Maurice, 'in a secure house in the piazza. Their lordships have invited you?'

'No,' Maurice rose also. 'And I don't think it would be wise for me to meet them yet. There are hotheads amongst them, I hear. In my somewhat tricky situation, I'd prefer men of a cooler variety—like the King's Shadow.'

'Oh, hang the King's Shadow,' the duke said equably. 'Seems to me he dillies and dallies as lamentably as George Monck.'

When the men had taken their leave, the women sat looking at each other in despair. Lucinda could tell that the duke's thirst for action worried the duchess. 'You don't wish you could call on the Sealed Knot? The Countess of Dysart as good as invited you there.'

Mary Villiers shook her head. 'I could never keep a straight face, watching her preside. She sees herself as a rare breed of conspirator—do you know she was once a friend of Oliver Cromwell? As a spy, of course, or so she claims. No, I think poor George will be disappointed in them. They won't want to make any decisions amidst such dreadful uncertainty and frankly they'd be mad if they did.' She put a hand to her brow. 'And now I have a headache. I'll lie down for a while.' She gave Lucinda a troubled smile as she left the room. 'Your brother is quite correct. There really is nothing else to be done just now but wait.'

Lucinda was relieved to be alone. She sprang from her chair and went to the casement. On the seat below it was her abandoned thread work, which she turned upside down so as not to see the square-faced woman and her dreary herbs.

She had not been quite truthful with the duchess when she thanked her for giving her the work to do. Now that chaos had come to the city, she did not find this refuge in Convent Garden an improvement on her own in York—it was more like a prison. She looked down into the street and realised she was better able to read the mood of the passers-by than when she had first arrived in London. People were walking too fast and looking about them warily. There were groups of apprentices hurrying by, sticking close together—clearly not bound for work, so perhaps planning protest and mayhem. There were fewer coaches; it was not a day for aristocrats or the gentry to drive about to visit one another in this fashionable quarter.

The duchess was convinced that the streets were dangerous and the only place to be was at home. But Lucinda did not have Mary Villiers's talent for waiting.

She envied Maurice his freedom of movement and his proximity to Monck, even if the general proved a bitter disappointment. She envied George Villiers his meeting with the Sealed Knot, for at least there they might decide on action. And if she could attend, she might hear more about the King's Shadow, who seemed by far the most effective agent for the king.

The duke's disparaging comment as he'd left the room showed that he, too, admired the Shadow—and was jealous of him. She sensed that her own zeal for the Shadow had increased the duke's interest. As they talked she had been very aware of the glances he bestowed on her, unnoticed by the duchess and Maurice.

And meanwhile Mark Denton, who had in an extraordinary moment actually offered her help, was more obdurate then ever against her cause. How absurd it would be to turn for advice to the only colonel in Monck's army prepared to carry out Parliament's vile bidding.

She had an impossible urge to ride out of the Convent Garden on the little mare that the duchess had hired for her and somehow find a solution to the impasse. But there was nowhere she could think to go, and no one to see.

****

George Villiers enjoyed the meeting with the Sealed Knot. It took place in a comfortable house tenanted by Edward Ford, who was not present, and owned by the Countess of Dysart, who was. Radiantly aware of her own beauty, the countess was a subtle hostess who allowed each guest to take the floor when he chose; fixing her attention on him, she made him feel like the only man in the room. George, who was encountering her for the first time, was not deceived by her manner, for he detected a sharp mind at work behind the angelic blue eyes.

William Compton, brother to the Earl of Northampton, was not in London, which did not displease George. Compton had a strong sense of his own importance and strove to assert himself even in the presence of a duke, which George had always found tiresome. He preferred the company of his cousin Edward Villiers, and of Lord Loughborough, and Baron Belasyse—the last two, like Compton, were seasoned commanders from the king's armies and George had a sincere respect for their military experience. Also present were the Earl of Bedford and another veteran, Sir Richard Willys, the only man in the room without a hereditary title. In the absence of Compton, Willys talked rather too much, trying to direct affairs. George could see from the others' expressions that they liked this no more than he did—and no more than the Countess of Dysart, who very soon took her gracious leave and slipped away to her home, also in the piazza.

George was sorry for her departure but not unhappy because his mind was full of Lucinda Selby. What a spectacular temptation Mall had created by giving the lady the clothes and surroundings to set off her stunning beauty. Mall could hardly expect George to resist it; no warnings could keep him away now.

Of course, Mall would try to line up a great marriage for the lady if Charles's court was restored—someone with estates and consequence enough to keep her in the inner circle. Lady Lucinda would become a prize for an ancient and grateful cavalier. Before that happened it would be a sin not to introduce her to the gratifications of the flesh. She might never have more bliss in the rest of her life than he could give her. He was a veteran himself, damn it! Along with her quick ideas and impulses she had a freshness that belonged to someone untouched and vulnerable. Her first man should be an accomplished lover, practised in the amorous treatment that he longed to provide. The sole problem was getting her out of that house, in which Mall had her trapped like a butterfly in honey.

His contribution to the meeting was to give his own view of Monck which, being a mixture of his sister's and Sir Maurice Selby's, was ambiguous. His cousin Edward, always wary—if not alarmed—by any public show of force against the royalist cause, said: 'The plain fact is that Monck has got all the troops out of London but his own. Now he's been asked to show who they're fighting for—and it's Parliament. So placed, he's unbeatable. Do we have anything like the force required to lay siege to London? No.'

Belasyse frowned at Edward. The baron's mane of golden hair was grizzled but his well-muscled body still had a warlike bearing. His loyalty to Charles I had been heroic and he had paid for it more than once with imprisonment in the Tower. The war had cost him dearly in bail and fines as well, not the least being £6000 for his last release and a security of £3000 so he could keep his estates in Yorkshire. Parliament had granted him a pardon in 1652 and he was a free man, but he had continued to work secretly for Charles II, in the Low Countries and in England. At a fit and strong-minded 45, he qualified for Mall's list of likely husbands for Lucinda Selby—except that he had married for the second time only the year before.

Belasyse said: 'I agree, that's the military situation today. But it's not cast in iron. Let's see what it looks like tomorrow.'

Sir Richard Willys seemed ready to carp at this but Lord Loughborough cut him off. During the wars, Willys had once been given the governorship of Newark by Charles I, but in a disagreement between the king and Prince Rupert, Willys had taken the prince's side and been dismissed. The king had appointed Belasyse as the new governor and Willys had held the grudge ever since.

'You don't want a siege,' Loughborough said. 'You want a swift onslaught and capitulation, like Rainsborough's attack in '47. London was his in a matter of hours.'

Bedford shook his fair head. 'Rainsborough had cannon. Where are ours?'

'They can be found,' Loughborough said calmly. With his long nose, pursed lips and arched eyebrows, he looked more like a languid courtier than a former commander for the king. 'But not at short notice.'

'Who knows what the Shadow may supply?' Bedford said. 'He's assembled a secret force around us—and they're well-armed.'

'You think one of us should respond to his invitation, then?' Loughborough flicked a speck from the slashed sleeve of his dark-brown doublet then ran his gaze around the room.

'I beg your pardon?' George said.

'We've heard from the Shadow, through Mordaunt. He'll be at a deserted hunting lodge in Coldfall Wood tomorrow at four o'clock in the afternoon, and he'll wait there an hour in the event that one of us wishes to meet him.'

'Is the lodge really empty, though?' Edward Villiers said. 'It might not be safe.'

'And why should we go to meet him?' Willys said, affronted. 'It's he who should be suing to *us*.'

Belasyse said: 'I know the lodge. That part of the forest is Melford property. It was built two generations ago but the present earl doesn't hunt.'

'Then I know it, too,' George said. 'Chased deer there with my brother, aeons ago. Why go all that way just to see the Shadow?'

Lord Loughborough said: 'He's manifestly on our side and may have some ideas about joining forces.'

'But we don't know his identity. All I can confirm for sure is that he has no direct communication with His Majesty,' said Belasyse, who did.

'He can't possibly be one of us,' Willys said. 'Low country gentry from the North, if that.'

The others forbore to remind Willys that by birth he was scarcely one of them either. But George's lip curled and Willys saw it.

'Agreed,' Villiers said. 'Either he comes to us or no meeting.'

It was then that a plan, glorious in its simplicity, burst upon George. He said: 'I'm in the position to do you a favour. I'll go, get a look at this fellow and bring you my impressions. Won't commit you to a thing, you'll know who he is and what he's up to, and it will give me something to do with my time.'

Loughborough, Bedford and Belasyse exchanged approving glances. Edward Villiers, relieved that no Sealed Knot member would be going to the rendezvous, said: 'Upon my soul, a neat solution.'

Willys, however, took offence. 'Sir, are you the person most suited to this role?'

This impertinence caused a flush on George's cheeks that had nothing to do with Edward Ford's malmsey. He said with unmistakable steel in his voice: 'What, you don't trust me, sirrah?'

There was a cold pause in the room. Everyone looked at him with alarm—his reputation as a duellist was legendary.

George could see Willys was struggling with violent emotions. Was he about to progress to downright insult? Of what might George be accused? Quite a lot, considering. Foremost, of course, would be quarrelling with the king and marrying into the Fairfax family.

Then an odd expression crossed Willys's face—a mixture of mortification and cunning. He said: 'I bow to my companions. If a majority agrees that you should meet the King's Shadow, then so be it.'

Belasyse raised his glass. 'Thank you,' he said directly to George. 'We'll await your report.'

Loughborough, Bedford and Cousin Edward raised theirs.

'Done,' Willys said stiffly.

****

The conference broke up shortly after this decision but Willys stayed behind to finish the decanter of wine and think how fortuitously tonight's doings had played into his hands.

He had always loathed the Duke of Buckingham, for his careless exercise of privilege, his sheer magnificence and most of all for his arrogance. George Villiers had sailed very close to the wind for the last few years, risking conviction for treason from both sides of England's conflict. If the meeting with the King's Shadow turned out to be a trap, if it went wrong in any way and ended in arrest or even death, it would be no more than Villiers deserved.

Willys had similarly poisonous feelings about the King's Shadow, who had taken it upon himself to prosecute the king's cause without seeking a scrap of intelligence, let alone permission, from the Sealed Knot. Having royally ignored them, he now deigned to talk with one of them—no matter who—alone in the thick woods outside London. If he was ready to put his head on the block by doing so, Willys did not object to Parliament's capturing him.

To let the Council of State know about this opportunity presented no trouble to Willys, who for years had been in covert communication with its former Secretary and spymaster, John Thurloe. In 1652 he had passed on information to Thurloe about an assassin who was stalking the streets of London, hunting down former officers in Parliament's army. In return, he had received a guarantee that his estates in Cambridgeshire would not be confiscated by Parliament, nor would he be persecuted as a delinquent despite his conspicuous service for Charles I. Since then he had taken care to feed scraps to Thurloe about the Sealed Knot's contacts without ever identifying its members or giving away major royalist secrets. Thurloe had acted upon them all and remained utterly discreet about their source, thus ensuring that Willys had an unblemished record with the king.

He now stood in an advantageous position, whether king or parliament should come uppermost in the conflict. Apparently Thurloe was due to be reinstated as Secretary of the Council of State. Willys continued to communicate with him under a code name, so any leakage to the other side he could simply deny, claiming that the losers were reduced to slander.

His message to John Thurloe would be brief. In their usual cypher, he would give the time and place of a meeting between the King's Shadow and ... an unknown. The capture of the Shadow alone would raise Willys's stakes high with Thurloe: credit enough for his present purposes. And if the Duke of Buckingham ran afoul of the troops that Parliament despatched to the meeting place, so be it—but Willys was not prepared to provoke so grand an enemy. There was no need to give the duke to Thurloe on a plate. The Shadow would do.

With the malmsey warm inside him, he took up hat and cloak and prepared to walk home and encode his message.

WHITEHALL
February 8, Night
February 9, Morning

Mark was the last of the officers to return to quarters after the destruction of the City gates. Others had sardonically handed out pieces of iron from the debris and told their men that these were medals that the army gave for brave service. There had been shouts, insults and threats from the populace at Ludgate but Mark had quelled the protest and kept the men at their work. He was unsure who was the more disgusted by it—himself or they. But they obeyed because in the years they had spent under his command they had learned to carry out many an unexpected task without question. They trusted his leadership, even if the only soldier amongst them who knew his underlying purpose was Corporal Hales.

The palace on his return rumbled with a tension that emanated from the Prince's Lodging, Monck's private quarters. As news from the streets rolled in and Monck's intimates and contacts gathered, the military, political and domestic commentaries became intertwined. Mark heard from Ralph Knight that at different hours Monck had been approached about the outrages on the City by chaplains Thomas Gumble and John Price, the physician-general Samuel Barrow, his brother-in-law Thomas Clarges and, last but certainly not least, his wife Anne.

Their argument was unanimous: Monck had destroyed his credit with the City and proved himself a creature of Parliament. And Parliament was now held in hatred by the whole of London—which provided due occasion to move against it.

Clarges had always been strictly discreet about the services he performed for Monck but today he unburdened himself to Knight for the first time. He revealed that in the morning he had told the general that 'there was no way to redeem his reputation, but the very next morning to return to the City with his army and declare for a free parliament'. Monck had cautiously declined to act. Clarges had renewed the assault in the afternoon, saying it was vital to retrieve the good opinion of the City as soon as possible. Anne Monck joined in this heated exchange.

Mark's conversation with Knight was taking place in the Horseguards Barracks, where he had a room overlooking St James's Park. He had offered Knight a chair but he himself was restless, pacing by the dark, uncurtained panes to get a view of London that might not be his for very much longer.

He muttered: 'So he's spent all afternoon scowling at his household. I wonder he hasn't called an officers' meeting to do the same to us.'

Knight smiled. 'He hasn't called us because he knows we'll agree with Clarges and the rest.' He paused, then examined Mark's face as he said: 'Well, perhaps not all of us.' Another pause, then he said with a hint of nervousness: 'If he asked you whether this army should declare for a free parliament, what would you say?'

'I'd say yes.'

Knight's expression wavered comically between consternation and excitement. 'Good God! That's the opposite of what he'd be expecting.'

'Is it? I don't know what he might expect—he's never sought to know my purposes. I'll open my mouth when he opens his.'

'He's never asked me for mine, either. But he has a comprehensive idea of them. Yours, on the other hand, are a conundrum.' Another pause, then Knight continued with caution: 'Do you remember the meal we had together in Morpeth? The general wanted me to find out whom you might have visited on your way in from Haltwhistle, but I never did. Are you prepared to tell me now?'

Mark leaned against the embrasure of the window. 'Three royalist families that I'd had my eye on for some time. Don't ask for the names.'

'Well, did you make any discoveries? Plan any arrests?'

'No.'

'Why not?'

Mark pushed himself away from the window. 'Because timing is important. Action without timing is pointless.'

At that moment Knight's adjutant brought an order from the general: Knight was required at an officers' meeting.

'Is Colonel Denton to be present?' Knight asked.

The adjutant shook his head. 'It's yourself, colonel, along with colonels Lydcote and Clobery.'

Knight rose and exchanged a long glance with Mark. 'I suddenly have a strong wish that you could be there.'

Mark laughed softly. 'I think we both know the event, do we not? God speed to it.'

The summons next morning came before six o'clock and Mark was barely awake enough to be surprised. This time the officers' meeting was packed with colonels, lieutenant-colonels and majors.

Monck on these occasions would often lean back in a chair and chew tobacco while he listened to his officers. Today he was on his feet before them. His stocky form seemed heavier, his frown more gloomy. His eyes, examining each in turn, were as black as the pre-dawn sky.

'I have listened to you, gentlemen, about the execution of yesterday's orders in relation to the City gates and I have heard that it was grievous to you. I understand also that many sober people in London fear that further force will be offered to them by this army, on Parliament's orders. They conceive themselves to be cruelly punished for desiring the speedy filling up of the House and elections for a free parliament—both of which you have argued to me as vindication of the liberties of the people.

'This, gentlemen, is a day of extremity on which we must act with decision. And we do so according to the groundwork of our undertaking which is, I repeat, the just liberties of the people.

'After this meeting you will assemble the regiments in St James's Park. The army will then move to Finsbury Fields and draw up there, well outside the walls of the City. From thence I will send a request to the Lord Mayor, respectfully desiring that army command be received at the Guildhall where we shall render our support to the City with regard to the election of a full and free parliament.'

They were stunned. He had spoken—at last. But no one exclaimed; it seemed to dazzling to be true.

'You now have a weighty task. I invite you to speak to the dissatisfactions that you have pondered on these months past—or, mayhap, for many years—with the present Parliament, especially concerning its treatment of the representatives of the people and of the army. The main points will be gathered and the Reverend Price'—he indicated his chaplain, who was seated at a desk in the corner before a great pile of writing paper—'will render them into a letter that will be carried to the Parliament this morning while we are on the march to Finsbury Fields. The letter will be addressed and signed by myself. Such of you as solemnly approve it will also sign.'

The time had come for their voices to be heard, recorded and broadcast to the government—and they were all silent, overwhelmed.

In his pragmatic way, Monck ignored their confusion and began eliciting views. One by one they rose to speak.

Mark, perched on the corner of a table to one side of the assembly, listened with keen attention while his mind sped to the results that might come crashing in that afternoon. The City could be so disgusted with Monck that they would refuse him entry, let alone a friendly reception. What would the general do then—breach the gates, this time with his whole army? Parliament would be incandescently furious when they read the letter, that was a given—but would they despatch commissioners like Scot and Robinson to negotiate with Monck or send an instant despatch to Sir Arthur Haselrig and bring in all the troops from the country?

Soon, however, what was said in the room made him forget the immediate consequences.

The letter would be one of consensus, which was impressive in itself. The main grievances were: that the House of Commons was not representative of the nation while elected members were excluded from it; that this Parliament refused to call elections or dissolve; and that it had mismanaged the army in London by failing to punish rebels like Lambert and their supporters in the House. The demands were: that Parliament issue writs for elections, to be sent out no later than the 17th of February; and that it name the date of its own dissolution.

Hereby the suspicion of your perpetuation will be taken away and the people will have assurance that they shall have a succession of parliaments of their own election which is the undoubted right of the English nation.

The letter ended with Monck's intention to draw his forces within the city walls, 'to compose spirits and beget a good understanding in that great City'.

John Price read the letter aloud and Monck signed it. The general then beckoned his officers forward in order of seniority: eight colonels, two lieutenant-colonels and five majors.

When it was Mark's turn, the general gave him a veiled look. 'You've kept a considered silence during this meeting, colonel, as is your right. It is also your right not to sign this letter, if there is aught that you cannot approve.'

'I approve every point and would gladly put my name to it.'

The general's black gaze widened.

'But I may serve you better by not signing. To be blunt, none of us can doubt that Parliament will react to this with offence, bitterness and anger. Spokesmen from Parliament will beleaguer you, all hot to change the army's mind.'

Monck thundered: 'And you'd fain do the same?'

'On the contrary. General, I command one of your regiments. Parliament knows that well and it knows even better the services that I have rendered to it throughout my career. If I do not sign this letter, misguided people may imagine that I would lend a receptive ear to the messengers who will harangue you on Parliament's behalf. For a convenient way to shut them up, you may like to kick them on to me.'

Monck's laughter, a rare and raucous sound, echoed around the room. 'Stay your hand, then, colonel, stay your hand.'

Mark stepped away and watched the others sign: Lydcote, Clobery, Hubblethorne, Reade, Knight, Randers, Redman, Morgan, Barton, Johnson, Smith, Prynne, Nichols, Bannister. He thought of the endless petitions spurned in the past by the pitiful rag-end of a parliament that was the only government England possessed. He thought of the thousands of names, signed with urgent hope, on all those rejected pages. There were but a few at the end of Monck's letter. But when it reached the Rump it could not be brushed aside.

CONVENT GARDEN
February 9, Morning

Very early on the day after Monck's assault on the City, the Duchess of Richmond and Lennox received a letter from the dowager queen of England in Colombes. Henrietta-Maria begged that Mary return to France, to succour her dear friend and attend on her own 11-year-old son, Esmé, who was unwell.

The duchess read the tender and effusive letter with pain and self-reproach. At the end of it she raised her white face to Lucinda and said: 'Esmé is seriously ill. I must go back. I should never have left.' She held out a page with a shaking hand. 'You see here? This comes to me by ship and that very ship sails back this morning, on the tide. So wonderful a friend, to wish me comfort and to make sure I receive it, at such a distance.'

'I'm so sorry. How does your son suffer?' The duchess had often spoken with concern about the health of both her children. She had travelled to Brussels to find a physician to send to them at Colombes and would have returned there herself if the king had not persuaded her to travel first to Kent and then London on his behalf.

'Esmé has that weakness of the heart that has always terrified me. Mary has a fever. I pray it is nothing like those I used to undergo when … and that my husband …' She dropped the letter in her lap and put her hands to her temples.

Lucinda went over and sank to the floor at the duchess's knee. 'Madam, calm yourself, and we'll prepare for your departure. Of course you must go. In a few days—think, a few days only—you will be with your loved ones. Nothing else matters.'

The duchess put her palms on Lucinda's cheeks. 'But how selfish I am; I'm abandoning you! And there's not even time for me to find George and say goodbye to him.'

'You're leaving me in luxury and ease,' Lucinda said lightly. 'Of which I may soon grow tired, in which case I shall take myself back to York.'

They both rose, the duchess embraced her, and they set about packing.

Mary gave a great deal of thought to Lucinda's situation and was adamant that she should remain in London. The house was at her disposal and the servants would stay on. Lucinda was to request that Sir Maurice Selby move in with her at once, something he would no doubt be very willing to do, since his duties for Monck's army were over and he was no longer under the command of Colonel Knight.

As she was driven with Lucinda to the docks, Mary said: 'This coach and your mare also remain at your disposal. When you choose to travel back to York is entirely up to you but I should be grateful—and so will His Majesty—if you will stay in London until you receive a positive answer from Anne Monck. You need not visit her again—I don't think that would be wise. But if Monck is willing to receive a letter from the king, she will send you the package of Dutch velvet and you will then send a piece of it to me—no letter, just the cloth. The courier knows his business. You'll contact him through my head groom, as I told you.'

'You're showering me with benefits, Your Grace, and for such small recompense to you!'

Mary took her hand. 'This is not a small thing that we ask. For the king to *know* that Monck is ready to negotiate is the lynchpin of this endeavour. Charles will never write personally to him until he is certain. And Monck will never commit himself fully until he has that letter. Will you do this for us?'

Lucinda bowed her head in consent.

The leave-taking was affectionate. Standing on the dock while a breeze across the Thames tugged at her bright curls, Mary Villiers was suddenly cheerful. 'I wonder,' she said, 'whether His Majesty will sail up the river when he comes home, or ride in from Dover?' She smiled at Lucinda. 'I shan't be here to witness his return, unless the queen braves the voyage—and she hates the sea. But you will see it. Imagine the day when he marches into London.'

'I should like you to see it! I should like to see you walk into Whitehall and make it your own again.'

Mary chuckled. 'Mine? Mine was but a small corner.' She was watching the longboat pull into the dock, ready to row her across to the small trading ship anchored in the stream. 'Do you know, when I stood at the casement in the gallery that day, I realised that I sat beneath that very window when I taught Charles to play chess? Over many a sunny afternoon.'

'Those days will return.'

Mary sighed. 'But it's a different game, isn't it?'

When they had embraced for the last time, and the boat had taken the duchess to the ship and the anchor had been cast off, Lucinda continued to stand on the dock and watch as the ship's sails were set to catch the breeze. As the vessel glided downstream, she spied a small, blue-clad figure poised amongst the officers on the poop deck. The figure raised a gloved hand in farewell.

Lucinda thought that, for the rest of her life, if anyone were to speak to her of a person with a loyal heart, she would know what was meant and measure them by Mary Villiers.

****

The moment she got home to the Convent Garden, another letter was handed to her. Delivered anonymously to the servants an hour before, it was a single, folded sheet with a blank seal, addressed to her in a gentleman's firm and elegant hand.

May I beg your ladyship to do me the honour of conferring with me in secret? I have important news to impart about Selby, your fortunes, and your brother's future. At two in the afternoon today, I shall await you at a disused hunting lodge in Coldfall Wood, indicated on the map below. I can hope for no reply to this note and, if you choose not to attend, I can only beg you to forgive my presumption in suggesting it. Allow me to assure you that the meeting place is secure. I shall attend alone and I respectfully encourage you to do the same. Your security is precious to me. No one could have greater care of your safety than your humble and grateful servant, now and ever, the King's Shadow.

She read and reread it. Could it possibly be genuine? The haste worried her; why could he not have written the day before, or the *week* before, to give her time to reflect and make arrangements? She checked the hour: if she left quickly she could get to the rendezvous, but there was no time to find Maurice and ask him to come with her.

There was no mention of Maurice or the Duke of Buckingham, the only two people now in London with whom she had ever discussed the King's Shadow. Surely neither could be privy to this or she would have received a message from them.

And if it were a joke or a trap, who could have written it? No one except her brother, the duke and Mary Villiers knew that she had ever heard of the Shadow.

She checked the map, drawn in ink by the same confident hand that named the villages, paths and landmarks. Coldfall Wood was part of a forest that stretched across the north of London, beyond Muswell Hill. If she were mad enough to go there, she ought to take the coach to the edge of the wood with an armed coachman and a groom who would ride her mare thus far. Then she could speed on horseback alone to the meeting place. But there might be trouble on the way through London; even though she would skirt the City, it might take far too long to get through the clogged streets in a vehicle. The only swift way was to ride, as she used to do over the moors in Yorkshire which, she had always been told, was neither ladylike nor safe.

So how could the Shadow ask her to do it? She read the letter yet again. He had written to her because his news was urgent. There was something she should know, about Maurice, herself and Selby—and she must learn it quickly.

He expected her to trust him: and indeed, hadn't he given her powerful reasons to do so? He had saved Maurice's life and made sure his participation in the Booth rebellion was never known. He had attacked Mark Denton and, according to the Duke of Buckingham, had done so for her sake. This meeting, too, was for her benefit and protection.

Your security is precious to me. No one could have greater care of your safety than your humble and grateful servant, now and ever, the King's Shadow.

In their own ways, he and she fought for the same cause. He was part of her life; he had long occupied her thoughts and dreams; yet she had never met him. She could not bear to remain timidly at home and let this chance go by.

COLDFALL WOOD
February 9, Afternoon

Mark was on the way to the Melford lodge in Coldfall Wood, eight miles north of London. He knew the lodge well and sometimes used it as a refuge for hunted men, but he moved them on next day—it was too easily exposed to surprise attack. Today it was a meeting place, and the encounter might be over in minutes or hours, depending on who turned up to it.

He planned to be there by two o'clock, to cope with any surprises—so he had time in the saddle on the way to consider this most bizarre of missions.

The march to Finsbury Fields that morning had taken place without incident and Monck had sent Thomas Clarges on a placatory embassy to the Guildhall. The mayor at first refused to have anything to do with Monck, so Clarges called on alderman Luke Robinson, who was in favour of conciliation, and more talks ensued outside the Guildhall. While the army waited all morning, news came of outrage and vituperation in the House when the letter was read. However, it seemed members were wary of censuring Monck or sending too hostile a response. Eventually they despatched Thomas Scot to him with a letter of thanks for 'securing the City'!

At midday, still with his army outside the gates, Monck had received an interesting piece of intelligence from the Council of State, and summoned Mark.

'You were prescient, colonel, when you spoke this morning about your unblemished record in Parliament's armies. I have a mission that will suit you better than listening to the rantings of Thomas Scot!' He grinned. 'There is an arrest to be made, of a traitorous conspirator that the Council of State has long hoped to capture. You will take however many troopers you consider necessary and ride to a hunting lodge in Coldfall Wood, which is north of here, beyond Muswell Hill. We have certain intelligence from former Secretary John Thurloe that at four this afternoon, the King's Shadow will keep a rendezvous there with an unknown gentleman. A splendid opportunity, colonel, to annihilate the bastard who tried to kill you at Stannington Bridge! You will arrest the Shadow on the spot, identify the other gentleman and use your judgment about arresting him also. You will then convey the Shadow, or both, to the Tower for interrogation.'

Mark's first reaction had been crippling disbelief, which he managed to hide by turning away and running a hand over his face. He should be accustomed by now to reversals of fortune but this one was so spectacular that it was almost ludicrous. He had a crazy impulse to laugh and an even crazier urge to tell Monck to go to the devil.

But he had accepted because he could see that Monck would insist: the general was at present bullying Parliament—all the more reason to do an inexpensive favour for the Council of State, in trifling compensation.

The preparations were made; 20 men had ridden out behind Mark, including Corporal Hales with a spare mount, as usual; and here they all were, nearing the forest on a chilly grey day when not a bird sang amongst the bare branches.

Mark was riding Skipton, a stallion born and bred in the Dales—a tall beast, grey as a thundercloud, which he normally reserved for his longest and most dangerous journeys. For an instant, he had an absurd feeling that this was his last.

****

The moment had come for Lucinda to enter the forest. The long ride up to Finchley Common had not been easy, for the hired mare was evidently unused to such excursions and had turned ill-tempered and jumpy. Leaving the city streets for country lanes had been a relief for Lucinda and she relished the broad trails across slopes and heathland where the people who watched her pass were herders of sheep or cattle, and the way to higher ground ahead was always clear. But the mare was used to picking her way through bustling streets and the empty upland made her nervous. Lucinda had to forget the wild hopes that were sweeping her to journey's end and focus on controlling her mount.

She wore riding clothes made for her by the duchess's tailor, Dorothy Chiswell, and fashioned so that she could ride astride. Over these was a long cloak with a deep hood which was constantly blown down upon her shoulders by the sharp winter air, but she also had a woollen muffler and fur-lined gauntlets. She knew she presented a strange figure—a fine lady, unaccompanied and riding a rather plain horse—but once she left the staring townspeople behind her and her path took her past hedges, fields and coppices, she recaptured at moments the exhilaration she used to feel when rambling across the moorland and pastures of the Selby farms—as long as she could prevent the mare from putting a hoof in a rabbit hole.

The edges of Coldfall Wood were marked by an earth wall and ditch, shaped to stop herds from straying into the forest from the common land. Lucinda urged the mare across and found the path marked on the map. She could see a long way into the trees because the undergrowth was low—she noticed St John's wort, wood anemone and speedwell clustered around beech trunks that looked black against the grey of more distant hazel. The forest here would provide excellent hunting, since game would be easily visible amongst the trees. She spied none today.

There were coppices further in; timber had been recently cut, and logs of hornbeam lay ready to be hauled out by oxen. But there was no one working on this dim afternoon. From here, Melford lodge should not be far ahead.

The branches above her were bare and let in some light but as she went in deeper and rode through oak groves they seemed to tangle more closely together, smothering the sky.

She glimpsed the entrance to a glade ahead, fringed by straggly growth, and urged the mare forward. Next second, a man stepped out from behind a bush and flung up a hand. The mare screamed and reared, and Lucinda tumbled out of the saddle.

It was a moment of sheer panic. The man's strong arms caught Lucinda before she reached the ground but the mare screamed again and galloped back through the trees, its hoofs thundering on the icy ground.

Blinded by her cloak, Lucinda fought to get her feet on the ground and fend off the man. He set her on her feet, gripping her shoulders. 'Great God, what have I done to you? My lady, forgive me.'

He let her go and she swept back the cloak to see the Duke of Buckingham standing before her. She took a step away, and he looked at her with earnest supplication.

He said: 'I never so misjudged a horse in my life. I caught sight of you coming; I guessed that mare was about to bolt, and I thought to calm her. I am ashamed and miserable—and delighted that you consented to come and are safe.'

Lucinda felt as though she were still upside down and falling. 'You ... you were *expecting* me?'

He gave her his most brilliant and boyish smile. 'Yes, I admit I was. I would confess anything and everything to you. There's not a friend of mine, however dear, who could demand the half of what you may demand of me.'

She retreated another step. 'Then tell me: how did you know that I was coming?' A thought struck her. 'The Shadow. Did he ask you to be here?' A strange confusion came over her. She realised she had been moved by the idea of meeting the Shadow alone.

'No. Do sit down.' He gestured to one side of the path. Amongst the bushes she saw a fallen log over which he had thrown his voluminous cloak. 'I shall allow you to recover. I shall explain myself, unto the last detail, and pray don't spare me if you wish to scold.'

His warmth and playfulness were the same as ever. So was his appearance: he had not come in disguise today. She sat down, but she felt desperately impatient with him and herself. 'How did you know I was coming?'

'I *hoped* you were coming,' he said softly, 'because I wrote you a letter.'

She gasped. '*You* wrote it?'

'Yes. I'm an incorrigible fraud when it comes to you. You and only you. But I promised to explain and I implore you to hear me.' He took a deep breath. 'It was the best excuse I could invent, to tempt you out of my sister's house. I wanted a few stolen moments with you. No more than that. Don't be shocked, don't be fearful. I meant what I wrote: you are precious to me. No one could have greater care of your safety than your humble and grateful servant, now and ever.'

The disappointment that she was not to meet the King's Shadow was intense. But her astonishment and annoyance with the duke were greater. 'Nonsense. You exposed me to any number of risks by asking me to ride here alone. And now you've robbed me of my horse! What were you *thinking* of?'

He took her gloved hands, but she pulled them away. 'You. You don't understand what an extraordinary woman you are. From the moment I met you, I worshipped your passion and your spirit. Mall thinks you're suited to the insipid indoor life, but I've always known you better. I wanted to give you an experience that would take you beyond all that. A taste of hazard and adventure. My lady, I am a poet—if this is all rather *too* poetic, forgive me. But I was convinced that if I wrote you such a letter, you would respond in kind, and you would do so without a word to my sister. And I was right, was I not?' He gave her his charming, sympathetic smile.

'I did not inform her, no. But only because she has left London for Colombes. Esmé is ill and the queen has sent for her.'

He sat back. 'Great heaven, and she didn't tell me!'

'The letter came early this morning and she sailed on the tide. She's written you a note. If I'd known you were going to be here, I could have brought it with me.'

He ignored the jibe. 'How bad is Esmé? He's always been a sickly child.'

'Your sister fears for his heart and the queen is very alarmed about him.'

'When you meet Henrietta-Maria,' he said thoughtfully, 'you will find her a capricious and demanding old creature who knows that a strong show of emotion will always bring Mall to her side.' He rose. 'I must hope she exaggerates Esmé's condition for her own ends.' He looked down on Lucinda fondly. 'But this leaves you quite unprotected. It will not do. Allow me to offer you my devoted services.'

'Thank you,' she said coolly, and rose to her feet. 'Your sister has invited Maurice to stay at the Convent Garden. I sent him a quick note before leaving and I told him where I should be this afternoon.' When he did not meet her eye or reply to this, she said: 'Maurice will stay with me for as long as I remain in London.'

'Which is for ever, I hope.' He resumed his cloak and offered her his arm. 'Come, I want you to see the lodge. The King's Shadow *does* use it as a meeting place, you know. Much of my reprehensible letter was pure truth.'

She was still deeply annoyed with him, but Coldfall Wood began to seem dark and menacing, and she wanted light. She took his arm and they walked out into the clearing, on the far side of which stood a timber building with a gabled shingle roof, small windows and a wide-open door. Grazing the meadow before it was a white, very beautiful Barbary stallion that lifted its head and whinnied at the duke's approach.

'I had intended a much more dignified welcome for you,' he said ruefully. 'The lodge is not uncomfortable inside and I brought wine and cakes. But then I wanted to see if you were coming, and strolled along the path ...'

She stopped listening, riveted by the scene spread out before her—the lodge, his horse, the secluded glade. She had been tricked into an assignation.

She dropped his arm. 'I thought you were a friend.'

'I am!' he said in surprise. 'Whatever happens to you or to me in the future, I wish us always to be close.' He examined her face. 'Are you cold? Let's go inside; it's a trifle warmer. There's even a fire built, but I shan't light it, I'm afraid—the last thing you want is to draw attention. No one will ever know you've been here with me. This is our secret.'

She stopped several paces from the door. 'I am not going inside that place. I demand that you find me a way back to London immediately.'

'Of course! Sans Souci will take us both.' He waved his hand towards the stallion. 'But there's no need for haste. We have an hour of blissful solitude—and then ... you may leave in peace and I shall decide whether to wait for the Shadow or not. He actually comes at four.'

'He really *is* coming?' Lucinda could feel her face glow.

'Yes, he has an appointment with me, as ambassador for the Sealed Knot, at four o'clock. But, forgive me: it is not necessary for me to keep it. It occurred to me, with emotions that I tremble to confess, that I would much rather keep this one with you.'

She took a step away from him, but stopped because it brought her nearer the lodge—which no doubt had a bed in it, or a rough straw mattress on the floor. She shuddered at her own folly. 'Then I shall wait for him. Alone.'

He did not move. He stood at his ease, examining her tolerantly. There was a gleam in his heavy-lidded eyes and his small but handsome mouth was slightly pursed. 'My lady, that is impossible. If anyone finds out that you kept this tryst with me, you are compromised. I could try denying it on your behalf but'—he gave a wicked smile—'with my reputation, who would believe me?'

She was overcome by hurt, confusion and fear. 'Why are you determined to ruin me?'

'Good God, I just explained—I'm not! The opposite is true: I adore you. I would never harm a hair on your head, much less your name. All I want to do is make love to you and, for the rest of my life, to have a care for your welfare. Take pity on me.' He stepped closer. 'You are a jewel that I could never have hoped to possess. Except, if you can find it in your heart ... this once ... today ...'

****

Mark led his troopers to Coldfall Wood from the south. A few yards from the margin he brought them to a halt and, in the ensuing pause, he heard a distant noise that put them all on the alert—the sound of a horse galloping through the forest. As far as he could tell, it was heading not towards them, but westward.

Corporal Hales tipped his head back, listening as the hoof beats faded. 'Would that horse have been somewhere near Melford lodge, colonel?'

'Perhaps.' It crossed Mark's mind that the gentleman intending to meet the King's Shadow might have arrived at the rendezvous early, suffered from second thoughts, and departed. If so, it would be the first convenient thing to happen on this most ridiculous of days.

He beckoned Hales further towards the trees and the corporal handed the reins of Mark's second horse to one of the troopers and rode up to him, out of earshot of the rest.

Mark said: 'We're here to arrest one man, perhaps two. The one we want is the King's Shadow.' He threw a glance into the woods, then back at Hales, whose eyes were like saucers. 'Yes. Interesting, isn't it?' He gave a sarcastic grin. 'I'm going in alone. You'll keep the men here until I rejoin you, or until I give you the signal. One shot.' He touched the carbine in his horse's shoulder holster. 'The moment you hear that, ride straight into the wood towards the lodge, then fan out. To anyone trying to escape, you give the order to halt. If they don't, bring them down.'

Hales was appalled. 'Alone, sir? You don't think—?'

'No, I don't think.' Mark gave him a hard stare. 'In circumstances like this, I obey orders. You'll do the same.'

'Yes, colonel.'

When Mark entered the woods, along a track he knew well, he smoothed a hand down Skipton's neck, asking for quiet, but the stallion's weight and strength meant that his hooves still reverberated on the cold ground.

What Mark wanted was to find the lodge and the clearing deserted, but as he drew within a few hundred yards he developed the unmistakable feeling that they were not.

He pulled Skipton up, dropped off him and left the reins dangling. He already bore his sword, powder horn and shot for the carbine that he slid out of the holster. He skirted westwards for a while, then headed towards the lodge by a different trail. It had been used that day, by two horses. Only one horse's tracks went out. He cursed in his head.

Then he heard a whinny nearby.

Near the edge of the clearing, despite the hardness of the ground, there were indications that people had trod here very recently. He couldn't see the lodge yet. He moved off the path and began to circle amongst the trees. A fringe of bushes concealed him from whoever stood about ten yards away, talking softly. There were muffled exclamations, then longer speech from a deeper voice. A man and a youth, perhaps.

He was five yards away from them when he found a concealed spot that allowed him to observe them.

He recognised two of the figures at once: the Duke of Buckingham and the horse grazing nearby—a magnificent white Barbary that Mark had seen once before, disappearing into the woods after the assassination attempt at Stannington Bridge. So *Buckingham* had fired on him.

The recipient of the duke's attention was not a lad but a woman, who was crushed in his arms. And struggling frantically. Then she managed to wrench her head away from the cruel embrace and let out a scream that penetrated Mark's soul—Lucinda Selby.

****

Lucinda used everything: her fists, her knees and her teeth. But that excited him, and he ceased to be the man she knew. He was impervious to attack. He crushed his lips to hers so hard that she thought her neck might break. Fear flashed in her mind and she knew that if she hurt him it would provoke more violence, which would come upon her tenfold. She turned her head and screamed, willing the sound to go for miles, to reach out through the empty forest, in the mad, mad hope that someone would come.

Next moment, Buckingham was hauled off her with such speed that she staggered. She regained her balance and gasped at the sight of Mark Denton, who had the duke in a fierce grip. Denton forced him onto his knees before her, one hand on the neck and the other twisting the left arm high between the shoulder blades.

Denton was looking not at her but at his victim's bent head. In a deep, ferocious snarl he said: 'Beg her forgiveness, or by God I'll kill you with my bare hands.'

Buckingham was panting. 'I'll have you executed for this.'

'Not before you grovel.' He smashed Buckingham's head against the ground and held it there. 'Beg her forgiveness!'

Lucinda was trembling. Even in his cowed state, the duke terrified her. In fact, they both did. So it still seemed part of the nightmare when she heard the muffled voice say: 'I beg your forgiveness, my lady.'

Denton wrenched him to his feet and fixed burning eyes on Lucinda. 'Did he hurt you?'

She felt battered and bruised but the horror was over. She wrapped her hands around her chest, took a breath and fought for control. 'No. I'm all right.'

Denton said savagely in Buckingham's ear: 'Thank your god that she is!' He shoved him away and the duke flailed the air to stay upright. 'Go! Never come near her again.'

The duke stood straight, his forehead bloody and his face distorted with humiliation. He put a hand to his sword hilt.

Denton said brutally: 'I won't stoop to duel with you, Buckingham.' He pointed to the south. 'I've a troop at the ready, waiting to arrest the King's Shadow for conspiracy—along with anyone else who happens by. Go, and save your filthy neck.'

There was no hesitation. Buckingham ran. Without even glancing at Lucinda, he sped to his horse and vaulted into the saddle. Rider and steed thundered out of the clearing in a whirl of black and white.

Lucinda watched him go, aghast at his treachery. At the same time, she felt dizzying relief. She turned to Denton. 'You rescued me. Thank you, thank you! He's a monster.'

He narrowed his eyes. 'Then why are you here?'

Her gratitude turned to shock. 'My God, you don't think I came to meet *him*?'

'Who, then?'

She began to tremble. Her lips were swollen and her neck bruised from Buckingham's assault. She felt ready to sink to the ground, but she had to stand firm and make a decision. Denton had just saved her from being raped. Did that give him the right to know whom she had planned to see—the King's Shadow, who even now was riding to keep the rendezvous, unaware of his danger?

She sought help in Denton's eyes, those dark-grey eyes that were so often guarded when they looked at her. At this moment there was something vulnerable in his open gaze. It was almost as if he was afraid of her answer; as though it had the power to hurt him; or make him despise her. By heaven, did he think she was here to meet a lover?

'I'll tell you the truth. The Duke of Buckingham wrote me a letter that tricked me into meeting a gentleman here today. A king's man. He did not arrive. Forgive me, but I will not give you his name.'

'Ah.' He stepped closer and murmured it for her. 'The Shadow.'

She said nothing, but he read her face. His reaction astonished her. His eyes flooded with recognition—and tears. Then he closed them and turned his head away. She stood nonplussed, looking at his strong profile.

He said quietly: 'You must leave.' He turned and walked away. 'You'll take my horse.' At a few paces off, he put two fingers to his lips and a long, low whistle rang around the glade.

Lucinda jumped, afraid for a second that this was the signal for his troop to come storming through Coldfall Wood. She waited in aching suspense.

He remained with his back to her, listening, and eventually they both heard the sounds of a horse galloping through the trees.

Denton came over to her. His gaze was opaque and his voice brisk. 'Are you fit to ride?'

'Yes. Thank you. But—'

A gigantic stallion burst into the clearing, slowed to a trot and stopped a yard away, its long black mane swinging over its forehead and its breath misting the cold air in great gusts.

'His name is Skipton. Don't be nervous of him. He'll look after you. Quick, mount.' He cupped his hands for her to step into and lifted her into the saddle. He gathered the reins, pressed them into her hands and looked at her earnestly. 'The King's Shadow is not at risk today. You have my word on that. When you've gone far enough, I'll make a signal, one gunshot, and my men will join me.' Through the thick gauntlets he squeezed her hands tightly, then let her go and pulled a carbine from the shoulder holster.

'You're giving me your horse!'

'You may keep him.' He stepped back.

'I shall have him returned to you.'

He gave her an ironical smile. 'As you wish. You know where I lodge.'

He had come with his cavalry, to capture the Shadow and the king's man, but he had let Buckingham ride away. He knew that she was part of the same conspiracy, and he was letting her go!

'Ride,' he said urgently, grabbing the reins beneath the horse's mouth and turning him in the direction from which she had come.

She cried: 'Why are you doing this?'

He moved to stand beside her while Skipton stamped and chewed the bit. 'Because I love you.' He hit the stallion's rump with the flat of his hand and it sprang away.

THE GUILDHALL
February 9, Evening

Luke Robinson was sitting on a bench with Thomas Scot at one end of the Great Hall in the Guildhall, between the colossal papier mâché figures of Gog and Magog, the legendary founders of London. Having been fashioned in the time of Elizabeth I they were, close up, a little the worse for wear. So indeed was Scot, though he was talking with unabated energy. Robinson, frayed into dazed tolerance by this extraordinary day, let him rattle on because he detected that this was Scot's valiant attempt not to burst into tears.

They were almost alone in the huge, cavernous hall, with its 5ft-thick walls and tall, clustered columns. The army commanders, the mayor, the aldermen, the throng of officials, the clerks and the masters of the livery companies had all dispersed to mark in their own way the conclusion of today's momentous business.

From outside, flooding in like a mighty tide over Scot's stream of unhappy words, came the crescendo of Londoners in bacchanalian celebration. The whole city, outside the gates and within, had given itself over to joy. Bonfires raged in every neighbourhood, on almost on every corner, shooting sparks into the winter air. There were plenty of watchers to make sure they did not become a danger, for every citizen, old or young, seemed to be on the streets tonight, gleefully roasting rumps of beef, or poking potatoes into the embers, or dancing to sweet music while thousands of impromptu suppers sent smoke and fragrance spinning towards the starry sky.

Strangers drank toasts to one another and passers-by were dragged into the circles of light without question as to their allegiances or beliefs. There were no enemies tonight. There was no caution or fear: the cries that went to heaven, arrowing up through the clamour of the bells, attracted no censure or punishment—they were free.

Scot said fiercely: 'I don't know how you can sit and listen to these abominations and *smile*!'

'It's an amazing thing, friend, to witness a city so united.'

'This is the death of the republic.'

'Thomas,' Robinson said, touched by the misery in Scot's voice, 'we did not have a republic.' *We had a coterie of old men clinging to the shreds of power.* 'We had a company of brave hearts who lost their chance to create one.'

'There are still soldiers who know how to fight for the good old cause!' Scot rose unsteadily to his feet.

'Not in London. And not immediately outside it, either,' Robinson said dryly. 'I do not believe Haselrig's troops capable of changing the situation and it would be folly if they tried.' He rose, too, and put a hand on Scot's shoulder. 'The good old cause was government by Parliament. It still is. You and I will be replaced—but the Parliament will be renewed, in every sense of the word. It will be filled with freshly elected men, younger men with a sense of purpose that is better founded than ours because they are freely chosen by this nation.'

'We've failed!' Scot exclaimed. 'We're thwarted in everything.'

'But we still have this country in our hands. There are important affairs to attend to. Our responsibilities do not end until we dissolve. We may have two months of fruitful activity before us.' He took Scot's arm. 'I for one should like to hear what London has to say about its new destiny. Will you walk with me and join the crowds? You deserve a rest from anxiety. Can't you let your cares fall to the ground for just one night?'

'We'll be recognised,' Scot muttered. 'And vilified.'

Robinson said: 'I agree, this afternoon was torrid.' While Monck was waiting to be received by the mayor, crowds had converged on the Guildhall, avid for news. Robinson and Scot, sent from Westminster to bargain with Monck about his letter before he could reveal it to the City, were afraid of being attacked. Later, in discussion with Monck, two of the colonels had roundly abused the commissioners as hypocrites and toadies. Monck rebuked his officers but calmly repeated his demand to Parliament: writs for elections must go out on the coming Friday.

At five o'clock in the afternoon, Monck was finally admitted to the Guildhall. He spoke to the Common Council, told them of his letter to Parliament and said what was in it, and a short time later the astonishing news was broadcast in the streets.

When Scot reached the wide steps outside the majestic medieval building, he stopped and drew his cloak tightly about him. 'I can't conceive why you wanted to creep back here.'

Robinson took in the throng of revellers stretching across the square and into the thoroughfares beyond. It was hard to believe that this was a

Sunday. 'We had a long march with Monck, all the way from Nottingham. I have a mind to witness journey's end.'

Scot snorted. 'Don't expect me to consort with this foul rabble. If I hear another word about the "just liberties of the people", I'll vomit.'

'Then thank God your duties to them will soon be over.' Robinson stepped smartly down and walked away into the crowd.

****

Mark Denton was on a long settle near the fire in one of the taprooms of the Triple Crown tavern in Gresham Street by the Guildhall, which had been recommended to him by Ambrose Martel, alderman of the livery company, the Worshipful Company of Drapers. Three imperial triple crowns hovered in the central shield of the company's arms, painted on the wainscoting above Mark's head; sunbeams issued from each, in happy reflection of the dancing fire that warmed the packed room.

He and his troop had entered the City some time after the repercussions of Monck's letter to Parliament spread out through London, at first as ripples, then as a torrent. Mark had reported to the general at the Bull's Head tavern in Cheapside. The news that the King's Shadow had not been captured brought neither surprise nor censure from Monck, who was busy arranging for his army's billets in the city and posting guards at possible trouble spots. Mark asked for permission to deploy his militia regiment in groups of four throughout the City to prevent public brawls. He had given the men their orders: they were to entertain themselves as they wished but to consider themselves on duty if they came across any disturbance. He would be at the Triple Crown for the night, if anyone required further orders.

He had then sent Corporal Hales out to gather Londoners' reactions to the news that there would soon be a full and free parliament—though the rowdy cries and cheers that filtered into the taproom from Gresham Street told him quite enough. The City was alive with euphoria.

In reality he had sent Hales out so that he could be alone and not obliged to talk. Not that he had said much after his troopers had galloped to Melford lodge: he had sent them all out again to search Coldfall Wood from end to end. While he waited, he had checked the building, found Buckingham's arrangements and only just resisted the urge to smash the bottle of wine against the wall. Instead, he sat down and drank it.

On the way back to the City, he and his men had ridden the route he calculated Lucinda Selby would have taken, starting from Finchley Common. In the villages, out of earshot of his men, he had made inquiries to see whether she had passed through, for she and Skipton were conspicuous enough to attract notice. She had been observed in several places, for which he felt achingly thankful.

He had even retrieved the hack that she had ridden to the rendezvous. It had wandered witlessly as far as the outskirts of Fortis Green, where a canny field worker had taken it as a prize of fortune. The man had marched with it straight into town, where there happened to be a market. It was not horse-market day, however, so when Mark spied the mare in solitary splendour in the town square, with a covey of potential buyers around it and a lady's saddle on its back, he had wasted no time in having the labourer arrested for theft. With two burly troopers to carry out the interrogation, the man broke down and confessed to having found the mare. Mark handed it to Hales, released the thief with a stern warning, and they rode on. The mare was now in the stables of the Triple Crown—and he would have it delivered to the Duchess of Richmond's house on the morrow.

He felt sure that Lucinda Selby had reached home long since. Despite Skipton's immense size and strength, he was a lamb in a good rider's hands and Mark had every reason to know she was a superb horsewoman. Still, the state in which he had sent her away tore at him: shattered, trembling and bewildered.

He had told her that he loved her.

His breath caught every time he thought of it. Yet he had had to say it—it was the only reason she would believe for his springing two royalist conspirators from a parliamentary trap. And she *would* believe it, because of his emotion when she wordlessly admitted she had a rendezvous with the Shadow. The poignancy of that realisation had overwhelmed him, and he had not been able to conceal it.

To speed her flight, he had told her the Shadow was not at risk. What would she make of that? She would know he spared the Shadow for her sake—she could not possibly guess at any other reason.

She was loved by the man she hated. What would she make of *that*?

Today she had learned to hate another man, the Duke of Buckingham, and she was wildly grateful to have been rescued from him. But she had other protectors: the Duchess of Richmond and her brother Maurice. If her pride allowed her, and if she was not afraid to mortify the duchess and prompt her brother into a catastrophic encounter with the duke, she would turn to them for guidance and support.

Tomorrow she would have no more need of him. The relationship between them would revert to what it had always been: a blank.

As to the rest, he still had her land and she had her just resentments. That situation could not change; the present was the worst time to try handing Selby back because Parliament was in crisis, with far weightier matters to consider than the return of confiscated property.

Hales reappeared and Mark gestured to the settle on the other side of the table and beckoned someone over to serve. He said to Hales, 'The brew here is tiptop. Being in the centre of commerce has its advantages.' He said to the tapster: 'Two tankards of the malt.' When the man had gone, he realised he had only half finished his first tankard, so he took a gulp and set it aside. 'Anything to report?'

'No, colonel. Except jubilation and jollity.'

'None of Haselrig's men sent to suborn ours?'

'Not yet.' Hales's eyes were shining with an ebullience that he was struggling to keep in. But he said nothing more until his own tankard was before him, whereupon he raised it and exclaimed: 'At last, colonel. *At last*!'

Mark raised his. 'And against all the odds. You've never failed me. Thank you.'

Hales blushed and his eyes shone more brightly. 'The lads can hardly contain themselves.'

'Indeed? I hope they do, for your sake and mine.'

Hales looked down at his ale, on which the foam glinted in the firelight. 'I think they would take it as a favour to … to … hear a word from you, colonel.'

'What? They have their orders.' Hales obviously considered this too short an answer, so Mark added: 'And I gave them permission to rejoice. What else is wanting?'

Hales stirred the foam with a broad forefinger. 'They've heard that the other colonels addressed their regiments whilst drawn up before the Guildhall.'

Mark gave a bark of laughter. 'I'll wager they did! No doubt half of them were practising to stand for the next Parliament.' Hales looked offended at the laughter, so he went on more quietly: 'What I heard this morning, while that letter was being written, cured me of speechifying for good. You may tell the lads that, if you like.'

Hales murmured: 'Do *you* not rejoice?'

Mark shifted on the settle. It was painful to think of Lucinda Selby, but it was painful *not* to think of her, every minute. Nonetheless, he owed his men—and particularly Hales—more concentrated attention on this night of nights. He wrapped his hands around the tankard and sat for a long time in silence.

Finally he said: 'Do you remember Coldstream ... that bastard of a frozen place? You may tell the lads, the name Coldstream will be remembered for generations. That's where the march began on New Year's Day. This army will long be honoured as the one that marched from Coldstream with Monck, the length of England, without bloodshed, to achieve a full and free parliament.'

'But some of the lads are afeared we've turned *against* the Parliament and will be reproached for it.'

'And many of them are far too young to remember this: in 1642 Parliament raised an army for its protection. For 18 years, our soldiers have fought for that cause. When Oliver Cromwell usurped power he forced the army to subdue the country, but that was never our true purpose. Monck has brought us to our finest victory. The time fast approaches when none of us will be needed—for the regularly elected parliament of a free people wants no protection. If it please God, when the legitimately elected members take their places in the House, the war is won and we may lay down our arms.'

Hales looked startled at this vision of the future.

Mark said: 'What will you do then? Is that bonny miller's lass in Hull still waiting for you?'

There was nothing of the miller about Hales, except for his pale skin, that never seemed to tan and was set off by very dark hair and brown, alert eyes. Elsewhere he was all soldier—well set up, with broad shoulders and capable hands. There was a faint line of crimson along his high cheekbones. 'Yes, she is, praise be.' He swallowed a draught of ale and gave a cautious smile. 'And you, colonel? What will you do? Go for Parliament?'

Mark shook his head. 'God spare me from that—and the country!' He sought the words. 'What I'll do is ride up to Swaledale and find the woman who once told me that the greatest blessing in life is peace. And then I'll be home.' He raised his tankard. 'To peace, Hales. Some day soon, it will be upon us, at last.'

CONVENT GARDEN
February 10

Lucinda roamed from room to room of the duchess's rented house, waiting in trepidation for her brother. Maurice had received her note the previous afternoon and had sent a brief reply, thanking the duchess for allowing him to take up residence and saying he would do so on the morrow. He said that stupendous events were about to occur in the City and he must be there to witness them. He had ended with stern advice that Lucinda stay indoors meanwhile, a brotherly caution that made her cringe with annoyance—and also with something close to shame.

She had lied to Buckingham when she told him Maurice knew of her meeting in Coldfall Wood—in fact she had written to him only about the duchess's kind invitation. She had told the story to remind Buckingham that he could not treat her as he no doubt treated his mistresses, for she had family to monitor his behaviour to her—and so did he. But the lie had been useless against his onslaught.

She had ridden to Coldfall Wood on the strength of that diabolical letter, without a word to anyone—taken off alone and on horseback in the way that had always made Maurice anxious. She used to laugh when he insisted that it was not ladylike to do such things. Well, apparently there were other men who thought the same, the Duke of Buckingham being one of them. When he cynically wrote to her in the Shadow's name, he must have told himself that if she came alone to a secluded meeting place, on a quite unsubstantiated request from an unknown man, she put herself beyond the bounds of acceptable behaviour and placed herself in his hands. As he pointed out, simply by arriving there she had compromised herself.

Ah, but the punishment for her error—if one claimed it as error, and not as her personal right to act as she saw fit—was monstrous and could never be justified by moral argument. She told herself that she had done nothing to be ashamed of, and the duke everything. But still she felt tainted, to the point of wishing that she needn't say anything at all to Maurice. Yet he had to know. She might be frightened that he would provoke a duel with Buckingham, but she could not let him go in ignorance of the duke's villainy. Buckingham might chose to attack either or both of them again, out of humiliation and spite. Maurice must be warned.

Lucinda went to the mullioned windows in the great chamber and looked down into the street. On the far corner was a pile of cinders, the debris of a bonfire that had cast flickering light onto the façades of the grand houses, while people danced on the cobbles below. There had been no need for her to venture out—London's revels had come to her. Last night, people had waved to her when she stood behind the panes. One wag had offered her a piece of the enormous rump of beef that was being turned above the flames. She had seen men and women go down on one knee to give thanks for their hope of the king's return and she had felt something of their excitement.

But she did not feel like one of them. The ground had shifted and she hardly knew where she stood. The encounters in Coldfall Wood had distanced her from the person she used to be. She was a royalist—yet she had been attacked by an intimate of the king. She was dispossessed and knew exactly who to blame for it—but her nemesis had saved her from rape, injury and ruin. Because he loved her! Lucinda swept away from the window and back into the room. In all the confusion, this was a truth she had to accept—she had seen it burning in his eyes.

She had no one to help her confront whatever happened next. Maurice would always protect her—but that was precisely the problem! The duchess—well, Lucinda was thankful that the duchess must by now be in France. Mary Villiers loved her brother and was tolerant of his faults, but this would mortify her if she heard of it and rupture the friendship she had shown to Lucinda. She would never want to see her again. And Mark Denton ... was in love with her. How strong his passion must be, to inspire the terrifying rage he had unleashed on Buckingham. How profound, for it to overcome his orders and his principles when he found her in danger, and drive him to set her free. She could not call upon a love like that again, unless she returned it.

****

Mark waited in a lane behind the piazza of the Convent Garden for rather longer than he wished that morning—he had a very full day ahead. Parliament were debating desperate measures to get rid of Monck, such as putting the army under commission, which would remove its commander-in-chief. Meanwhile Haselrig's men were infiltrating London, bent on spreading mutiny amongst the general's rank and file.

At last a gentleman slipped out of the back garden of Edward Ford's house and strode confidently towards Mark, who was concealed within an archway further down. The lane was otherwise deserted.

Mark stepped into sight and put his hand on his sword hilt. The other stopped in his tracks. Clearly faced with one of the military, he pondered whether to defend himself. He looked past Mark's shoulder, trying to see how many others he might have to contend with.

Mark studied him: broad-shouldered, with a mass of fair hair to his shoulders, going grey; and the kind of bearing that had been described to him more than once when the king's stalwarts were being discussed. This had to be Baron Belasyse, the one Mark preferred to intercept—Belasyse was by reputation the most formidable of the six members of the Sealed Knot.

'My lord, I've a few words to exchange with you. Here might be best for you, in terms of concealment. But this can be as public as you wish. Your choice.'

Belasyse kept his eyes on Mark's hands but his own did not move. 'I have nothing to conceal. And no wish for any exchange. I don't know you, sirrah.'

'Colonel Denton, York militia regiment in General Monck's army. You'll listen to what I have to say. Two days ago you received a message from the King's Shadow suggesting a rendezvous at Melford lodge in Coldfall Wood, at four o'clock yesterday.' He saw Belasyse turn pale with astonishment and continued. 'Yesterday morning, General Monck received information about the meeting from the Council of State. A message was sent through John Thurloe with a demand for the Shadow's arrest. A company was despatched to Coldfall Wood, led by myself. The Shadow did not make the meeting but the lodge had been prepared for it. I don't know whom you chose to represent you, but the Duke of Buckingham was observed near the wood at around two o'clock. If he had kept the appointment, we would have arrested him on the spot. He and the Shadow might both have been imprisoned for treason.'

'Are you done? You're talking to the wrong gentleman. None of this farrago has anything to do with me.'

'Oh yes it has. No one knew of this meeting but the Shadow himself and whoever was with you when his invitation was delivered. The information was betrayed to Thurloe. It can only have reached him through one of your party. The person who betrayed you is clearly not the Duke of Buckingham, who rode to the rendezvous in good faith. It has to be a fellow conspirator. Your lordship, you have a double agent in the Sealed Knot.'

Belasyse looked even paler than before. 'Why do you tell me this?'

'So you can root him out before he completely destroys your usefulness to the king. And I suggest this to you—the King's Shadow is unlikely to contact you again, so you must act henceforth without his collaboration.' He turned and walked away.

****

At ten o'clock a package arrived for the Duchess of Richmond and Lennox, from Whitehall. Lucinda had it brought up to the great chamber, unwrapped it on the table in the centre of the room and draped the contents across the tabletop, almost with reverence. It was the swathe of lustrous blue velvet that she and the duchess had left with Anne Monck. There was no message and Lucinda almost missed a single object that the lady had slipped between the folds: a red rose. This was February, so no doubt it was a bloom from last year. Dry and blackened at the edges, its abundant petals had been pressed to retain their shape. The rose had meant something to Nan Monck, and when Lucinda picked it up gently and sought its fading scent, she suddenly had a hint of the emotion that the lady must feel now that her husband had proved himself England's greatest ally in the king's cause.

Anne Monck's gesture meant that Monck would now respond to a letter from Charles II. Lucinda sat down and wrote the duchess's address on a sheet of her best paper. She signed on the other side and tears stole down her cheeks.

As directed, she wrote no message. She cut a small corner from the velvet, folded the paper around it and sealed it, then had the head groom called up, the man who would take the message to the courier. Lucinda handed him gold from the drawer of the desk, gave him his instructions and sent him on his way.

The next claim on her attention was the return of the mare that had carried her to Coldfall Wood the day before. She was so amazed that she ran down to the courtyard to catch the man who had brought it in before he rode away. He was a cavalryman, short and grizzled, with gnarled hands and a weathered face. He was just about to mount up again on his own horse when she approached him from across the yard, her silk skirts gliding over the cobbles.

He let his horse's reins drop and stood in shock as she halted in front of him, then bowed awkwardly. 'Your Grace!'

'The duchess is not at home. I just wanted to know—who sent you, and how was the mare found?'

'Colonel Denton, ma'am.' The man's Yorkshire accent moved her. He was one of her countrymen, who by his age must have been in a northern regiment since the war began. 'He saw the mare at a market in Fortis Green and vowed that it rightly belonged to the Duchess of Richmond and it were our duty to return it. Beg pardon, ma'am, but I must shift m'self—I were ordered not to tarry.'

Behind her the grooms were leading the mare away. 'You will thank Colonel Denton for me. And you may take his stallion back to him and thank him for that also. I have it here in the stables.'

'*His* stallion, ma'am?' The man was incredulous. 'Which one? He rides the black today—must be one of t'others, if it's his at all.'

'I tell you it belongs to him. A huge grey, by the name of Skipton.'

He held up his hands, palm outward. 'Them's not my orders, ma'am, and any road, no one touches Colonel Denton's horses but Corporal Hales. The colonel has a better string of horses than the general even! It's more than my life is worth to go near yon beast. I'll pass this on to Corporal Hales, ma'am, but begging your pardon, there's nowt else I can do.'

She let him go and went to inspect the mare, which seemed delighted to be in its stall and was already snatching hay from the feed net. Its tack was likewise in good condition. Watching the animal munch contentedly, Lucinda realised that all evidence of her catastrophic ride to Coldfall Wood had now been eliminated by Denton, provided the Duke of Buckingham kept his mouth shut—and Denton had given him crushing reason to do so. Relief and gratitude brought her close to tears.

In her overwrought state, she jumped when she heard the clatter of hooves again from the courtyard—but the rider was Maurice. When she stepped out and saw him, all the nightmares about what she would say to him disappeared. He dismounted and she ran into his arms. The tears came, and he noticed them, but he judged them by his own elation. He laughed and swung her off her feet, spinning her around the yard. 'At last!' he said. 'At last we know what was inside that black head of his. Honest George Monck lives up to his nickname!'

She took his hand. 'Come upstairs. I received something today from his wife. I want you to see it.'

Their reunion was so happy, she hardly needed to say a word. Maurice gave her a glowing account of the events of the day before, which he had witnessed at the side of Ralph Knight. 'I believe he could become a friend to us. He has land in the north and he'll be seeking to get into parliament, to represent Morpeth. You'll like him.'

'What did you do last night? Did you eat roast beef?'

He laughed. 'I did, as a matter of fact. It got very late and I was wandering about alone, and ran across Luke Robinson in East Cheap. He looked so pinched and out of sorts that I told him he was hungry and bought him a meal at a good place called the White Hart.'

'The parliamentary commissioner? You kept strangely mixed company, all in one day!'

'And thoroughly enjoyed myself.' He took one of the cakes she had had brought to the oak table under the window. 'What about you?'

'I kept mixed company too. And it was horrible.' He looked startled and she said: 'I can bear to tell you about it, but only if you don't interrupt. Please remember no harm will come to either of us because of it, and as you see I'm safe and well. Do you promise to listen?'

He dropped the cake, sat straight and glanced around the room as though danger threatened.

She put a hand on his wrist. 'Maurice, if you love me, hear me out, and then we'll talk about what to do.'

In as calm a voice as she could command, she told him everything. He was not a patient listener, but she did not allow his exclamations to divert her from the story. When she got to Buckingham's sudden appearance in the wood, he leaped to his feet and began pacing the room. She tried to describe the attack without emotion but her voice shook and her own horror was reflected on her brother's face. He was stunned by what had happened next: Denton's violent intervention; Buckingham's flight; her miraculous escape before the troopers thundered through the wood.

At the end she said: 'Denton let me go free. I asked him why and he said it was because ... he loves me. I rode home on his stallion. He even said I might keep it! And this morning he had that stupid little mare returned to me. And the King's Shadow was safe. He swore it to me, and I trust his word.'

Maurice was hardly listening any longer. He slammed his fist into the wall. '*Buckingham*! I'll have his liver and lights.'

'I wish I could take his own sword and run him through. But if we did, it would all come out. My ... imprudence. My shame.'

He rounded on her in fury. 'Shame? *None* attaches to you. I will *never* let anyone shame you. You're a Selby and beyond reproach.' He looked around the room again, his face distorted. 'Villiers is a reptile. I don't know how you can remain in this house.'

Lucinda rose. 'If you want to go home, Maurice, I shall pack at once.'

Some of his fury fell away. 'He's gone to Nun Appleton. He's running all the way to Yorkshire. Perhaps it's best if you're here, as far away from him as possible. He sent me a note yesterday evening. Now I know why.' He took a piece of paper from inside his doublet and opened it. He said quickly: 'That message that he invented, from the Shadow—do you have it?'

She fetched it from the desk and he examined the seal on the outside. 'It's blank. The Shadow hardly ever puts pen to paper but Mordaunt tells me that when he does, he seals it with the image of an oak tree. And he never signs his name.'

He turned the sheet over, spread it on the velvet-covered table and laid Buckingham's note beside it. The handwriting was identical. The duke had written:

Sir Maurice,

On this day of days it would have pleased me to celebrate in your company, with my sister and yours, but I feel it my urgent duty to convey in person what I know of Monck to Sir Thomas Fairfax and his family, and to my wife, who is ever anxious for my safety. I expect to be some time at Nun Appleton, but will return to London before the glorious event occurs to which we have devoted our courage and our lives. Kindly convey to your sister my assurance that the Selby family commands my deepest respect and I shall always have a care of your fortunes and your honour. Your most affectionate friend, George Villiers.

Lucinda felt a blaze of anger as she read, but she concealed it from Maurice. She walked away from the table and went to the casement while he read the other letter. As he finished it, she could hear him cursing under his breath.

To preempt his comments, she said: 'In that specious note, he pretends he never saw me yesterday—he pretends not to know the duchess has left for France.'

'The coward! He thinks to slide out of this without the breath of an apology.'

'He did apologise to me. Denton forced it out of him. He made him beg my forgiveness.'

'And did you give it?' he said angrily.

Perhaps the reproaches were to come now—because she had ridden off alone to a dangerous meeting. If she had not done so, none of yesterday's disasters would have happened. But nor would they have happened if the Duke of Buckingham were not a scoundrel! She lifted her chin. 'No, I did not.'

He threw the note on the table beside the other. 'Look at this trash. He's the Duke of Buckingham—he can do anything he likes. He expects to injure us to the last degree and get away with it.' He looked at her in dismay. 'Have you written to his sister about this?'

'No! I thought you would feel as I do. No one else must know—this is between you and me, and the most dishonourable man it has been my misfortune to meet.'

He looked at her beneath lowered brows, then his gaze softened. 'And you're the bravest woman I ever met. What would you have me do for you?'

She stepped forward, took the papers from the table and went to the fireplace. 'I should like to forget the follies and failures of yesterday, and remember only the triumphs. I want your permission to throw these in the fire.'

He hesitated for a long, agonised moment, then said: 'You have it.'

She cast the letters into the flames and they shot instantly up the chimney in showers of sparks.

Then they sat down and discussed Colonel Mark Denton. Maurice at first did not mention Denton's extraordinary reason for letting her go. He concentrated on the strategic aspects—Denton's confirmation that the

King's Shadow had indeed arranged a rendezvous at the lodge; the revelation that Monck's army somehow knew of it in time to lay an ambush. Finally he said: 'The Sealed Knot! Buckingham was with them the day before yesterday, and he told you he was at the lodge on the Knot's behalf. But he went there early, because of you. Someone in the Sealed Knot told the secret of the rendezvous to Parliament. It can't have been Buckingham! One of the six is a traitor.'

Lucinda felt guilty that she had missed this inference. She had been dwelling too much on Denton's rescue of her and not enough on the train of information that had brought him there in the first place. 'But which one?'

'Mordaunt told me that Compton is not in London, Belasyse spends most of his time with the king in Brussels, so he may not be in town either. The others are Edward Villiers—'

'Who'd surely not put his own cousin at risk!'

'Sir Richard Willys, and Lords Loughborough and Bedford.'

'Perhaps I could consult the Countess of Dysart.'

Maurice shook his head. 'We must stay well out of this. I'll inform Mordaunt, without any mention of you, of course, and he can talk to Compton.'

Silence fell, and Lucinda realised Maurice was not going to speak of Denton's reason for letting her escape. She could understand his confusion and reluctance, because she felt them herself.

She said tentatively: 'How much simpler this would be if I owed my freedom to the King's Shadow and not to Denton.' When Maurice did not reply, she said: 'Did you see much of him on the march?'

'No, we avoided each other. At least, I avoided him, and I think it was mutual. This supposed passion he has for you: if it had been simmering for years, surely one of us would have seen a sign of it! So it must be a recent affliction.' He looked at her closely. 'But you've only met him once in London, at Ambrose Martel's.'

Lucinda flared up. 'Do you find it *amusing* that he's in love with me?'

He was contrite at once. 'No, Luce—I find it disturbing. When it comes to you, he's prepared to play a double game with the army. He was supposed to arrest anyone who had a rendezvous with the Shadow, but he let you go. And he parted with his horse, what's more, and then said he'd spare the Shadow—as though he did it for *your* sake. But what if ...' He got up and began to walk about the room. At last he stopped and said: 'I wish I'd kept a sharp eye on him when we were on the road. Then I might be able to guess what he's up to. What if he's playing a double game altogether, now the march is over? What if he's seizing opportunities to ditch his loyalty to the Commonwealth and seek favour with our side—before it's too late, and his record condemns him in the eyes of the king?'

Lucinda said: 'He's nothing like that! He's not a feather in the wind, he's a man of principle! I might have hated him, but I've never despised him.'

He studied her. 'Do you plan to return the horse?'

'Naturally. I tried to do so today, but his man wouldn't take it. He said Skipton can't be handled by anyone except the corporal who looks after Denton's string.'

'I'm not surprised,' Maurice said gloomily. 'His horses are the best in the army. Which is Skipton: the black, the chestnut or the bay?'

'None of those. He's dark grey. And he's huge. Riding him was like being astride'—she smiled at the memory—'a thundercloud!'

'I've never seen Denton on a mount like that.' Suddenly he said, in quite a different tone: 'Show the beast to me.'

Maurice was intent and silent when they went downstairs. He strode so fast across the courtyard that she had to hurry to keep up.

In the stables it was almost dark; the winter sun was setting. Lucinda asked for a lantern to be lit and the groom hung it opposite the stalls where her mare and Skipton stood, eyeing each other through the rails.

Maurice loved horses and had been schooled in horsemanship by a master, the Earl of Newcastle. She had never seen him study an animal with such awe. He did not approach or run his hands over it; he remained quite still as he took in the great head, the large eyes, the magnificent musculature. Then he said: 'Great God, I know this stallion. Twice seen, never forgotten.' He turned to Lucinda and said in hushed tones: 'He belongs to the Shadow.'

Lucinda gasped. 'That's impossible. You must be mistaken.'

He shook his head. 'I was on this horse's back when the Shadow brought me across the Pennines. He was in a stall when I talked with the Shadow behind the tavern in Bedford.'

'Then what is *Denton* doing with him?' Maurice was silent for so long that she said in a whisper: 'Describe the Shadow to me.'

'Lean. Tall. As tall as the king, which is why …' Maurice ran his hands over his face and back through his fair hair. 'He was masked and wore a black wig, so I can only vouch for the eyes and mouth. The eyes are grey. The mouth is … ironical. Sorry, I don't have your gift for description. The chin is … clean-shaven.'

'Oh, Maurice, you're telling me nothing!' Lucinda glanced around to make sure the groom had not emerged from the tack room, where he had gone after lighting the lantern. She hissed: 'What about his voice? No, don't give me the answer you did last time: close your eyes and *listen*.'

After a while Maurice said: 'My God.' She waited. 'He changed his accent. He did it perfectly—I'd never have guessed he's not a nobleman fit for the court. But the quality of the voice is identical. It's deep and cool and lingers over words—as though he's sneering at you or himself. No, not sneering, mocking. He doesn't suffer fools gladly.' He opened his eyes. 'You know whom I'm talking about, don't you?'

She could hardly say it. 'Denton.'

'Yes. Denton is the King's Shadow.'

The truth overwhelmed her. 'How did we not guess? Maurice, this is just like you. To recognise his *horse* today, when all that time ago you might have recognised the man!'

'How could I? The two identities are radically opposed. He stands for the reverse of everything the Shadow believes in.' He paced before the stalls, his boots swishing in the straw. 'I was wrong about Denton—he must have changed his mind about the government, but not lately—it would have been years ago because that's how long the Shadow has been operating. But he had to work undercover because the major-generals had the upper hand, all over the country. He said to me … the Shadow said to me'—he gave a soft, helpless laugh—'I still can't comprehend that they're the same man! He said something like this: "In our lifetime, the value of recklessness is long past. I believe you can keep your courage cloaked until it's wanted."'

'And you have,' Lucinda said. 'So has he. By heaven, so has he.'

BRUSSELS
February 16

Charles was playing billiards with Philip Stanhope, Earl of Chesterfield, and hoping to win a princely sum from him in the next few minutes. Chesterfield could well afford to lose—he enjoyed a colossal fortune and could not at present spend it in London. He had fled England in January after killing a man in a duel, and had come to Brussels to seek a royal pardon for the crime. Charles had given it readily; whenever Chesterfield appeared at Charles's impoverished and truncated court in the Low Countries, he pledged his person and his purse to the king and proved an entertaining companion. In his lively 20s, an inveterate gambler and a keen pursuer of women, Chesterfield fitted well into the circle of Charles's younger supporters, who, with no physical battles to fight in the royal cause, could be forgiven the drinking, gaming and whoring that whiled away their idleness. Charles had almost despaired of giving them something meaningful to do—and then came Monck's progress down England and the outlook had brightened for all those in exile.

Chesterfield was not the only recent arrival from England. Lately, members of prominent families had been turning up in Brussels and seeking audience—single gentlemen, usually, but sometimes accompanied by their wives, and Charles had noted with amusement and gratification that the ladies were mostly beauties of the glowing English variety that he had sorely missed: their blushing cheeks were modest, but the eyes were not.

Chesterfield's horror of the dour Puritanism enforced by the Parliament had driven him into a sexually inventive lifestyle made even more piquant by the secrecy required. Like Charles, he had a preference for young, high-born women with spirit, a taste for luxury and a sense of fun, and from the way he described London, it was pullulating with them. Charles was particularly taken with the sound of Barbara Villiers, a penniless first cousin once removed of Mall and George Villiers, but brought up by the Earl of Anglesey. Anglesey had clearly been a lax guardian, for Barbara had turned herself into a courtesan very young. She was now a delectably experienced 18-year-old, newly married to a fellow named Palmer who was about to bring her to the Low Countries and pledge his allegiance to Charles.

He did not question Chesterfield closely about her, however, since Chesterfield had patronised her himself, and it was beneath a king's dignity to appear to follow skirts that had been lifted by an earl. Should Barbara Villiers take his fancy when she turned up, he would require no one's collaboration to conquer her.

Once Charles won the game of billiards, he got rid of Chesterfield and everyone else in the room in order to receive Sir John Mordaunt. The news from London was extraordinary and he needed Mordaunt, his most communicative agent in England, to confirm it for him. When Sir John appeared, another begged admittance, and Charles was heartened to receive Baron Belasyse as well.

They made their obeisance and he stepped forward so that they met halfway across the room. He did not try to keep the eagerness out of his voice. 'You're a thousand times welcome! You must tell me about last Sunday, for we have been told it in fragments, and no matter how we piece them together they will not make a whole.'

Belasyse said: 'Your Majesty, the whole is greater than the parts. In sum, London clamours for your return.'

'And the way is open for the nation to do the same,' Sir John Mordaunt said. 'General Monck and his officers demanded that Parliament name the date of free elections and it will do so tomorrow. The secluded members will be readmitted, the republicans will be outnumbered and the new parliament is expected to restore the monarchy.'

'So much achieved!' Charles exclaimed, and then his voice fell. 'And so much still to be done. Can Monck hold Parliament to all this? He needs to keep control for weeks. Can he do it? Surely that would be some kind of miracle.' He walked restlessly away from them.

'Your Majesty,' Belasyse said with a tremor in his voice, 'I wish for your sake that you had witnessed what we saw in London last Sunday, for it would not only have reassured you, it would have given you joy.' He said more emphatically: 'General Monck is not alone. He has the army, the city and your people behind him. There is the miracle.'

Mordaunt said: 'They fell on their knees in the street and gave praise to God for the return of their king.'

Charles turned to them again. 'Then tell me everything. Describe all the details, every part of this miracle. I want the whole of last Sunday to pass before my eyes.' He smiled sardonically at their expressions: they could not tell whether he was overwhelmed by their news or by fresh doubts. 'No one shall disturb us—you have a captive audience for as long as you wish. Make the most of it.'

****

In bed much later, he lay alone, contemplating the shifting images of the day when George Monck stood up for London against the Parliament. Despite Mordaunt's and Belasyse's enthusiastic accounts, he still could not believe that Monck's deft turning of the tables would lead him to the throne. The capital seemed far away and tainted with tragedy, loss and humiliation for his family. Yet these advisers, whom he had learned to trust, would have him believe that the mood in London was shared all over the country. He was loved and needed—what, after years of being shunned by every nation in Europe, starting with his own?

He was prepared to believe that Monck was in control of London, but the man had not come out plainly as a monarchist. Consequently, the most influential leaders in Charles's cause were not publicly in support of Monck and there might well be dissension amongst them. Belasyse, for instance, feared treachery within the Sealed Knot: royalist secrets were being leaked to Parliament and as yet Belasyse and Compton had not been able to identify their source. And Mordaunt did not have a full grasp of the royalist cause across the country. For some time he had been reporting to Charles about the activities of a singular agent who operated mainly in the north, called the King's Shadow. Recently, the Shadow had moved south and begun contacting all the secluded members in preparation for their appearing once more in the House. Mordaunt had noted this at one remove because the Shadow had declined to work with any other conspirators for the king. At last, he had got in touch with Mordaunt and arranged to meet someone from the Sealed Knot—but the rendezvous had been prevented by parliamentary troopers and the Shadow, having escaped arrest, was continuing as a free agent. If these were examples of how Belasyse and Mordaunt prosecuted Charles's rights in England, anything might happen when he set foot there. Despite everyone's assurances, he might cross the Channel into chaos.

Then a letter came. Because he had ordered that all correspondence must be brought to him at once, whatever the hour, he read it in bed by the light of a candle. It was from Mall Villiers, uncoded:

If it please Your Majesty,

We have wept so many bitter tears together, and you have suffered my painful frankness on so many occasions that I know you will believe me at once when I state that glorious news from England has just made me weep for joy. If I were younger and my cares in Colombes less dear, I would take horse at once and gallop to you with these tidings—but my courier will speed this message to you more swiftly.

You asked me to sound George Monck. I did so, through the person who stands closest to him, because I believed that only when he revealed his heart would we truly know the man and his purpose. Today I received absolute confirmation that he will respond with glad allegiance to a letter from your hand.

You will know by now, as I do, what happened in London last week. Yet to my perception and yours, the event is capable of many interpretations. Let your conviction rest lightly upon the event, but firmly on the heart of George Monck, because that heart is yours. The message that came to me today seals it: through Monck's agency, and by the grace of God, you are saved for England.

My tears have wet the paper—forgive this scribble around the edge! But I have done with crying: I shall smile until you set foot in England and then I shall laugh with happiness.

God keep you home, Your Majesty.

With deepest respect from your humblest and happiest servant, Mary.

The message ended with a butterfly, sketched in red chalk on the bottom right corner. He kissed it, blew out the candle, sank back into the feather mattress and began to lay his plans.

WHITEHALL
February 21

Mark Denton was reporting once more to Monck. Every time he did so, he wondered whether it might be for the last time, but the general always seemed to find another mission for him and he could never think of anything to do but comply. Thus he stayed faithful to a private vow of serving Monck until his final purpose was accomplished. He had lived for months with the hope that the general was England's best chance of attaining just government, and he would stick with him.

As for his own fate, it was as ambiguous as ever. Paradoxically, his reputation as a rigorous parliamentarian had made him extremely useful to Monck, especially when the general needed to show an orthodox face to Parliament. Because of Mark, Monck had been able to deal with Lambert without needing to arrest him; keep Scot and Robinson at his side without either offending them or releasing any crucial information; create a plausible impression of obeying Parliament's orders even when told to demolish the City gates. Meanwhile, at crucial points when Colonel Denton might be considered inimical to the general's moves, Mark had been given tasks that took him well away from the action—such as the attempted capture of the King's Shadow. Mark had suspected at the time that Monck was interested not so much in the Shadow as in carrying out the Council of State's wishes, and when he reported that the prey was still at large, Monck's only comment had been a wry smile.

The latest mission put both of Monck's strategies neatly to use: it was the recall of the secluded members from Devon. These men, all victims of Pride's Purge in 1648, had been sustained over the years by Monck's brother Nicholas, who lived in Devon, and had recently petitioned Monck in the belief that he would support their return to the House. While on the march, the general had steadily rejected such overtures in public, and in private he had been very circumspect, as Mark had discovered when he intercepted one of his letters. But the day after the Rump was symbolically roasted in London, Monck had summoned Mark alone to a room in the barracks and ordered him into the West. Seated under a window on a very grey day, he had explained his tactics.

'I have the inconvenient benefit, colonel, of being the best obeyed where I am the most respected. The secluded members in Devon have listened faithfully to my strictures over recent weeks and I seem to have so dampened their eagerness that they will be the last to come to London and claim their seats. My brother has made great efforts to convince them that I have changed my mind and now advocate their return—but some of them need stronger persuasion, and they need it urgently. You have distinguished yourself as the most obdurate defender of Parliament in this army. When the Devonians see that your mind and loyalties have been reversed—when they learn that you, a high-ranking officer of integrity, now support a full and free parliament—they can have no lingering doubts about my principles. Are you prepared to canvass them on this ground?'

'I obey your orders, sir, on whatever ground you choose.'

George Monck's black eyes narrowed, as though he found this too glib. 'Really? You will scarcely deny that while serving under my command you have pursued your own political purposes, without a word to me!'

'No, I do not deny that.'

Monck gave an audible sigh. 'Just as I have long suspected. Then I want an honest answer to this: have you ever covertly disobeyed me in order to prosecute your own ends?'

'No,' Mark said at once. Then, after a slight pause: 'With one exception. When you told me to arrest the King's Shadow, I did not carry out the order.'

For the first time, Monck looked nervous as he put the next question. 'Why not?'

'Because to capture the Shadow, I would have had to arrest myself.'

This hit Monck so hard that he got to his feet. His suspicions had clearly never taken him as far as this. For a moment he could not speak. Finally he said incredulously: 'What about Stannington? You're not about to claim you fired upon yourself?!'

'I've since learnt that the attack was part of a private feud. The gentleman who led it told his musketeer that he was the Shadow, to give him an excuse for assassination.'

Monck glowered. 'By heaven, this is a heavy confession, colonel. The King's Shadow has been in operation during the entire time that you have nominally been serving under me!'

'I have served you meticulously. At the same time, your accusation is true. Therefore I'm ready to resign my commission if you find fault with anything I've done under your command.'

Monck took a step towards Mark, who remained seated. 'Your men! Have you suborned them all? Take care how you answer or I'll have you and them for mutiny!'

'Corporal Hales is the only other man in England besides yourself who knows that I am the Shadow. And I have never given Hales any order that contravenes yours.'

Monck shook his head. 'You're a conspirator for the king, across the whole country, and not a soul knows your identity?'

'That is correct, sir. And I would prefer things to stay that way. If you think differently, and decide to expose or cashier me, I have no right to protest. But if you're prepared to deploy me, knowing my loyalties better than you did before, I await your orders.'

Monck was still frowning. Above all, Mark detected, he was angry with himself —for never guessing what one of his colonels had been doing for so long. Exposure would of course reveal a crack in the general's leadership—not an attractive move at this point during the parliamentary crisis. Monck said abruptly: 'As the Shadow, you've already been in contact with the Devonians, I presume?'

'Yes, sir, by messenger. My letters are sealed with this ring.' He reached into an inner pocket at his breast, took out a gold seal ring and handed it to Monck. It was set with a blood-red carnelian into which was cut the shape of a spreading oak tree. 'In our correspondence and through my network I urged them to join other secluded members in safe houses set up around London.'

Monck handed the ring back and sat down once more, as though it had taken the seal to finally convince him. 'And their response?'

'As you say, sir, they await your express permission to travel to London—which I'll be glad to convey in person, if your orders remain the same.'

Monck said slowly: 'I chose you because I considered you the best man for the job. Now that you've spoken freely, my mind is made up. You will make the journey to Devon and confer with my brother. I shall give you a list of the gentlemen you are then to see.'

'Thank you.' Mark rose to his feet.

Monck stayed seated. 'How long does this double identity continue, colonel?'

'Until the King's Shadow is no longer needed.'

'And when will that be?'

'The date is not easy to predict.'

'It never has been, has it?' Monck stood up. 'In the meantime, your secret is safe with me. With one exception. You may not be aware, but the King's Shadow has a fervent female admirer in London and she lives not far from where we stand.'

It was a moment of confusion for Mark, who felt his cheeks glow. Like a fool, he was unable to reply.

Monck continued, with a knowing smile: 'The lady in question is my wife. Will you allow me to share this stirring intelligence with her? You have my pledge that it will go no further.'

Mark had bowed his consent, with bitterness in his heart. It should have been a comfort to reveal himself at last to Monck and, moreover, to go unpunished for all his subterfuges. But somehow it made them even more burdensome.

****

Now he was back in the same room, very early in the morning of 21 February, having confirmed for Monck the good news that the important Devonians were amongst the 73 secluded members who were due very shortly to attend on the general at Whitehall. It was none too soon, as Monck explained.

'While you were in Devon, colonel, the Parliament finally drew up writs for the elections, but on reading them I judged that the qualifications required for new members were too restrictive. In my estimation, no parliament elected on those lines would be sufficiently representative of the people. However, yesterday Parliament went ahead and asked the Speaker to sign a warrant for the issue of the writs. I am relieved to say'—he smiled as though at a personal achievement, which perhaps it was—'that William Lenthall took learned advice and refused to sign the warrant. He declared that he ran a risk of being sued at law if he approved elections on that basis—any secluded member whose seat was filled by another man would have the legal right to take the Speaker to court.'

Mark felt no need to comment on this piece of reasoning, and remained silent.

'For the good of the parliamentary process,' Monck went on seriously, 'it is vital that the members who were illegally ejected from their seats in 1648 be restored. Those who are still living and in health must be readmitted to the House. It is crucial to the nation that they amend the Act of Qualifications and give their consent to new elections. In the meeting this morning I shall sound their hearts before they return to office.'

'You're hoping to escort them to the House today?'

'I'm hoping you will do so, colonel, with the Adjutant-General and a contingent of the parliamentary guard.'

Mark rose and stood to attention. 'I shall be honoured.'

'In the meantime, while I consult with the members, my wife will have the pleasure of your company. Thank you for accepting her invitation—she is eager to see you.'

Mark bowed, murmured something more about being honoured and was dismissed.

During the hour before he was due to attend on Anne Monck, he sat by the window in his empty quarters and looked out over St James's Park, through a corner of which he would escort the members on their way to the House. They would all have to keep their wits about them, and he would put his guards on high alert, because they were to take Parliament by surprise—and its reactions were quite unpredictable. He would draw his contingent up outside, with the guards that were already there to protect the sitting members. Those in the House would raise a protest when the other members entered but they would be outnumbered by 73 very determined gentlemen who were quite convinced of their rights.

He believed that the statements that Monck had just made about representation in government were genuine. It was true that the secluded members all wanted the ultimate return of the king, but in summoning them to London and reintroducing them to the House, Monck was not staging a royalist coup. Violent assumption of power, within the House or without, would leave Parliament and the people with no bargaining capacity when the king returned. Instead, it would clear the way for a totally unconditional monarchy where the king held the upper hand—and that was not Monck's intention. If it had been, Mark would never have marched the length of England with him.

If the secluded members were able to peacefully take their places in the House, Parliament would be strengthened rather than humbled and London would have a grand excuse to rejoice for the second time in 12 days.

For Mark, spending those days on the mission to Devon had been worthwhile. He did not regret his absence from London during the curious period of hiatus after the roasting of the Rump. The only event he was sorry to have missed was the return of his stallion, for Lucinda Selby herself had ridden Skipton to the Horseguard Barracks on the 12th of February.

He pictured her, riding with a groom through the busy streets from the Convent Garden to Whitehall and taking much greater care of Skipton's progress than on the day when she fled Coldfall Wood in panic. At the barracks, she had asked to speak to Mark, and was received by the major of his regiment. Politely asked about her purpose, she asserted that Skipton belonged to the colonel and that she was delivering the stallion herself because of his value. The moment she learned from the major that Mark was not in London, she had mounted her mare and left.

Skipton was in perfect condition, if rather restless. Mark had spent a few minutes with him at first light, trying to decide why Lucinda had returned him. To say thank you, once again, for the rescue? He shook his head. An encounter like that would leave wounds that could only heal in silence and retreat. It had taken courage for her to return Skipton; she must have done it out of duty, to keep the promise that she had given as she prepared to ride away into safety. No doubt she had been relieved at not having to deal with him when she arrived at the barracks. She might also be thankful that the Duke of Buckingham had gone to Yorkshire; this had at least prevented any confrontation between her brother and the duke. There were no rumours of it in London—Mark had asked Ralph Knight about Selby and been told that Sir Maurice was currently living in the Duchess of Richmond's house in the Convent Garden. Nothing more was being said of either brother or sister.

Because of Mark's intervention, she was safe and untouched. He told himself that he could do no more for her until he was able to return the

Selby estates to their rightful owner—a transaction that required the return of Charles II.

****

Lucinda alighted at the wharf below the Privy Stairs and was handed ashore by a guardsman, just as she had been three weeks before. Everything else about this visit felt very different, however. To begin with she felt no shyness or unease at being there alone. The invitation from Anne Monck had not surprised her, as the woman had a right to be thanked in person for the inspiriting message she had sent on the 10th of the month. Much had happened since then, so they could talk more freely, and Mistress Monck would be spared the anxiety of trying to behave in seemly fashion before an august lady of the court.

As Lucinda was escorted up the flights of stairs and through the endless buildings, she realised that she was no longer in awe of Whitehall. It still belonged to Parliament and the army but, because Mary Villiers had first introduced her to it, she could now see it in her imagination as the king's palace, as though its new grandeur were just the blink of an eye away.

It came as a shock, therefore, to turn a corner with her escort and be confronted by the tall, ominous figure of Mark Denton.

Her two guards halted and all four of them remained stock still at the end of a long, vaulted corridor into which Denton had just stepped from a doorway. He looked startled and Lucinda sensed that his disarray was greater than hers. To her surprise, she felt no great embarrassment on seeing him—instead there was a surge of excitement. She was looking at the face of the Shadow.

He collected himself and bowed low. 'My lady. Well met.' He straightened. 'This gives me the chance to thank you for returning Skipton. I very much regret I wasn't here to receive you the other day.'

His voice was as smooth and deliberate as ever but somehow it no longer concealed his emotions from Lucinda. From its rich timbre, as he lingered over the words *I very much regret*, she sensed a depth of sorrow that he had always been able to hide from the rest of the world. In that instant she remembered that he loved her, and her gaze fell. She murmured: 'They told me you were gone to Devon.'

'Yes. I returned yesterday afternoon. But I'm interrupting you. Where are you going?'

'To see Mistress Monck.'

There was another startled pause, and she looked up.

He said: 'So am I. Allow me to escort you.' He looked at the two guards, one at each side of her, and cocked his head curtly towards the entranceway behind them. Without a word the soldiers brought their heels together, spun round and disappeared.

Lucinda was in no hurry to move. They were alone in this deserted corner of the palace with no one around to eavesdrop. There were so many things she was tempted to tell him—for one, that she knew he was the Shadow. And she had a host of questions to ask, but Coldfall Wood fell between them like a tangled barrier, a topic she dared not discuss. She sought for one that had no barbs in it. 'You know Mistress Monck well, I presume?'

He shook his head. 'I've met her twice, but not dined with her. Whatever the campaign and wherever she lodges, she has her favourites among the officers—and I've never been one of them.' He gave a sardonic smile. 'I suspect that today's invitation signals a change in my social fortunes.'

'Are we to dine? At this hour? I thought I would be nibbling on something and taking a glass of wine at most.'

'Mistress Monck's ideas of hospitality are lavish—at least ever since she became the wife of a general. Her origins, her education and her past have not fitted her for the position she holds, so she compensates with excess. As you probably noticed when you called on her with the Duchess of Richmond.'

'How did you know about that?'

He looked away, down the corridor. 'No matter who runs Whitehall, my lady, it is still the biggest gossip-warren in London.' He gestured. 'We go this way.'

She walked at his side. 'Well, I can tell you that when we visited her, the entertainment was Spartan.'

He gave a soft laugh. 'But I wager she was generous enough with what you were after—information about her husband?'

'You seem to know my purposes before I even think of sharing them with you, sir. Allow me to wager something about you. You have just conducted some of the secluded members from Devon to London.'

'Indeed.'

'Why?'

'I was ordered to do so.' With a sidelong glance he recognised her dissatisfaction at this short answer and went on: 'The general expects to introduce them to the House today. But until he does, it cannot be mentioned to anyone else—even his wife.'

She felt her cheeks glow. He had shared a strategic secret with her, for the very first time.

They reached the low flight of stairs under the arch at the end of the corridor. He took two steps up, then turned to offer her his hand. She gave him hers and he held it until they came to the landing above.

'You might have been glad of Skipton on the journey to Devon,' she said as they walked towards the Prince's Lodgings. 'I deprived you by not returning him sooner.'

He shook his head without meeting her eye. 'I told you, he was yours to keep if you wanted him. He's never been fond of army life. He was born and bred in the Dales and he likes best to roam free on the moors. As you do, on occasion.'

Yes, on the land that was once ours. But she did not say it. She was too entertained by his comparing her love of freedom with that of his horse. She said lightly: 'He was very well-mannered with me. I congratulate you on his training. But I'm certain he would prefer your company to mine.'

'I'm not so sure. I paid him a visit this morning and I could swear he gave me a look of reproach.' He smiled at her without a trace of mockery, though it lingered amusingly in his voice.

She laughed, and just as she did so a sergeant stepped out of the guardroom at the entrance to the Prince's Lodging and came to an abrupt halt at the sight of Colonel Denton.

Denton said in repressive tones: 'The Lady Lucinda Selby,' the guard hurried ahead, and they were announced and shown through the double doors.

****

Mark well knew why Anne Monck had invited him to visit—she wanted to observe him for herself now that she had been told he was the Shadow. Thank God, Monck had forbidden her to say so to anyone else. If they had been alone she would have probed to her heart's content: as it was, the presence of Lucinda Selby put a stop to her talking about the

Shadow openly. Why the lady had asked Lucinda at the same time as himself was not quite clear, but he had no private objection. He had been disarmed by the surprise encounter in the vaulted corridor, and he treasured even more the chance to sit opposite Lucinda and watch her respond to the mistress's conversation, which began with enthusiastic commentary on George Monck's many victories.

The hostess did most of the talking and they both listened courteously, which did not prevent Lucinda from exchanging a humorous glance with him now and then as more and more dishes were piled on the table. It was a collation that might have made someone a very hearty breakfast or dinner. They ate off strenuously polished silver plate and the wine was superlative.

When Anne Monck abandoned the subject of her husband and began praising various items about the room, he noticed for the first time that it was luxuriously appointed. There were also portraits that he had previously seen in other parts of the palace, and the mistress boasted that there were more in the long gallery that looked down on the Thames.

Lucinda Selby was admiring the picture of a gentleman with long, red-gold hair and an intelligent face. He wore the Star of the Garter on his slashed doublet and by his side sat a lanky wolfhound gazing up with a worshipful look. She asked the hostess, 'Who is that?'

'James Stuart, Duke of Richmond and Lennox.'

'Oh. Is it by Van Dyck? He loved to paint the duchess, as well. I wonder if Her Grace would have liked to see it here when we visited you before? But perhaps ... no ... such memories can be painful.'

Mistress Monck received this very cheerfully. 'Oh, to be sure, she's welcome to see it any time. I don't know who painted it but John Thurloe prized it, so no doubt it's worth a vast deal. I told him it belongs in the royal apartments and he had it took down off his wall and brought in here, as agreeable as you please.'

Lucinda said: 'It was the one in John Thurloe's bureau?' Mark was moved to see sorrow in her eyes. 'She viewed it but never talked to me about it. She holds her husband's memory very dear.'

'And when is she coming back to her house in the Convent Garden?' Anne Monck asked. Then she laughed: 'Oh! When the queen comes to see her son crowned, I surmise!'

Lucinda shook her head. 'I don't know. The duchess's duties are all in France. There really is no reason for her to keep the house on, and I'm afraid she's only doing it for my sake. My brother is keen for us to leave—he's writing to let her know.'

Mark said quickly: 'But where will you go? Has Sir Maurice found you another place?'

'No. I doubt if he can.' Her cheeks grew faintly pink. 'We're not wealthy and London is suddenly very expensive. There's a confluence of people from the country—noble families are moving back into houses they've not used for years. Others are coming to the city to lodge with friends ... but all our friends are in York.'

Mark said irresistibly: 'I hope you'll believe that there are some in London who care what happens to you.'

'Yes,' she murmured, and their eyes met.

'Of course!' cried Anne Monck. 'I shall speak to my husband. Shame on us if we couldn't find a corner for you somewhere.' She added on a jocular note, looking at Mark: 'If only we could call on the King's Shadow—he has many a safe house at his disposal, I hear!'

Anne Monck had mentioned the Shadow several times and on each occasion Lucinda had looked at Mark earnestly, as though trying to read his thoughts. He found it excruciating. He had never expected to regret the work he did on the king's behalf and it was ludicrous to do so when he was in the presence of two devout royalists, but it was as though his activities had created a net that was slowly strangling the life out of him. He was sick of all his secrets—but this was not the moment to dispel them.

****

There had been a number of occasions in the last four years when Lucinda Selby and Mark Denton had been forced to conceal their enmity for the sake of the polite company around them. Today was different, even though the reasons for discord remained unchanged: Mark's possession of Selby; his loyalty to Parliament against the king; his refusal to discuss his true allegiances with anyone. Somehow, for a unique period at Anne Monck's table, they had been able to ignore these thorny issues and talk in a relaxed and random manner, even about the household matters that interested their hostess—finding, as they did so, how similar their sensibilities were in contrast to hers.

When the little party broke up, to the genuine regret of Anne Monck, Mark offered to escort Lucinda as before and they walked back towards the Privy Stairs in silence. To Lucinda, there had been something almost magical about the encounter: the only one during which she had been able to glimpse a more sympathetic man behind Mark Denton's iron façade. She had hardly spoken, afraid to break the spell. Meanwhile Mark was thinking fast about her leaving London.

He could bear the silence no longer. They were at the final corner before the stairs when he stopped her with a touch on her arm, then stepped forward and faced her. 'Forgive me, but there's something I must say. I meant to wait and tell you when I was sure of doing this—I abhor giving a promise I may not be able to keep.'

He spoke with an urgency so unlike him that all Lucinda's warm sense of understanding fell away. 'What are you talking about?'

'Selby. It's always stood between us. I want you to know, and I beg you to tell your brother, that it has always been my intention to restore the estates to you. I promise to find a way.' She was so taken aback she could not speak, so he went on: 'All these years, Parliament would never have consented, and it certainly won't listen to me now—today I'm escorting the old members to their seats and the Council of State will curse me as an apostate. But there is a way, if you agree. Selby will be yours.'

She was trembling. 'If you believe it belongs to my family, how could you accept it in the first place?'

'It was being alienated by law. When Cromwell named me to take it, I realised I had the chance to keep it safe for you and return it when the time was right.'

'But why, why? You might have told Maurice, instead of snatching his inheritance without a word! I don't believe this.'

'How could I tell your brother when the future was so uncertain? It would have been salt in the wound. And I couldn't tell *you* why.' He drew a quick breath. 'I did it because I love you. Don't dare tell me you don't believe that. It's the truth, God help me.'

She was dazed. 'All this time?' It came out on a gasp. He had taken over Selby in 1656 on the death of the first recipient of her father's lands. 'For years?'

Mark flinched. *Since you were 15.* But he could never say it. She was not for him; she had no need to know how he had suffered as a consequence. 'I beg you to believe me and to tell your brother that Selby will be yours as soon as I can make it so. I'm sorry; this is painful to you. I must let you go.' He stood aside and offered his arm. 'Allow me to take you down the stairs.'

She accepted, in terrible confusion. Her enemy had been in love with her all along and had done everything he could to watch over her. He had saved Maurice's life and liberty, and rescued her from danger—and he had preserved their family heritage for them.

'All this you have done,' she said in a stifled voice, 'and received no thanks from either of us.'

'I did it willingly,' he murmured, leaning towards her as they descended the steep stairs.

She glanced below: the private barge was waiting. The oarsmen were on the wharf and there were other figures in a group—guards, no doubt. She saw them as through a haze, blurred by the shimmering river. In a few minutes she would be on the water, speeding away from him. In the past, this thought would have been welcome.

Mark gazed at her profile, imprinting it on his mind. He pressed her hand to his side and said: 'I don't ask for your gratitude. I have no right to claim anything at all from you. But I should hate to lose touch with you completely. Will you permit me to write to you now and then? I shall address the letters to Sir Maurice, of course.'

'Yes,' she whispered. It seemed a very dangerous thing to do but it was impossible to refuse. It was on the tip of her tongue to say more—to confess that she knew he was the Shadow—but her courage failed her. Perhaps they could explain themselves to each other more successfully in letters.

When they were on the wharf, treading the uneven timbers, she kept her hand within his arm, and it was not until they were a few yards from the attendants that she let him go—and realised that the gentleman who stepped out from behind the group and approached them was her brother.

All three came to halt. 'Maurice!' she said in bewilderment. 'I didn't know you were coming to meet me!'

Maurice looked at her sternly, ignoring Denton. 'I was summoned to the palace by Colonel Knight. We've finished our business, so I thought I'd wait for you and take you back.'

Mark did not trouble to speak to Selby since it was obvious the courtesy would not be returned. Nor did he like the coldness with which Selby addressed his sister. It was the first time in weeks that he had seen him, and they had not spoken to one another since Bedford, when the young man had known him only as the King's Shadow. This behaviour was rude but not unexpected. He ignored Selby in return and said to Lucinda: 'My lady, I must return to the barracks. I bid you farewell.'

He bowed and was about to turn away, but she was looking from her brother's face to his, impatient for them to at least greet each other. 'Maurice, what does Knight want you to do? Colonel, did you know anything about this?'

'No.' He examined Selby's expression, which was one of resentment tinged with anger. He was a volatile young man, but Knight had seen potential in him and so, for that matter, had Mark. The best thing he could do was retire gracefully and give Lucinda time to explain the whole matter of the Selby estates in private.

But Maurice addressed him with a haughty air of importance. 'Knight has handed me a commission, in preparation for His Royal Majesty's eventual entry into London. The king, the general and every gentleman of note must be splendidly mounted in the procession, and I've been given the task of finding horses and bringing them to London.' He turned to Lucinda and said with scarcely less pomposity: 'It will take weeks, but I shall do it gladly. The army has supplied the funds. I'll start in the North. We leave for York today.'

Lucinda and Mark exchanged a long, full glance. Then she took a step towards her brother in protest. 'Maurice, the house. We can't just leave like this. The duchess—'

Maurice burst out: 'Buckingham may have it, and good riddance! He's coming back to London. I won't stay a day longer in a Villiers house.'

Mark had had enough. If he remained it would only make Lucinda miserable, and if Selby continued in this vein he would be strongly tempted to throw him into the river. It was obvious that they were about to leave London and there was nothing he could do to change Selby's mind.

'I must bid you good day.' He nodded to the brother and made Lucinda a deep bow. 'God bless you, until we meet again.'

He walked away.

****

Aghast, Lucinda watched him out of sight. Then she turned on Maurice. 'How could you be so disgustingly impolite to him?'

'And how could you let him make such advances?'

'*What?*'

'I've been stood here watching you come down the stairs, clamped to his side. He was all over you! Thank God we're leaving London and I can get you away from him—that man is the devil.'

'How dare you question my behaviour!' Lucinda exclaimed. She glanced towards the attendants who were all looking their way—but she judged they were just out of earshot. 'I was merely being civil to him, which is a great deal less than he deserves, from me *and* you.' She overrode his protest with a cry: 'Have you no gratitude? We are under the deepest obligation to him. We owe your life and my safety—'

'And meanwhile he has Selby. Which he means to keep, for good. Don't you *see*? I hated him too much to guess what he was up to, but I've been thinking about it ever since we realised he's the Shadow. Luce, when he got his hands on Selby he decided it wasn't enough. He wanted you into the bargain. Don't let him trick you into this, I beg you.'

Lucinda put her palms to her cheeks in disbelief. 'You're mistaken. This is horrible. I don't know how you can begin to imagine it. The opposite is true—he always intended to give Selby back. He told me so today'—she pointed wildly—'at the top of those very stairs.'

Maurice snorted. 'How? Parliament will never sanction it. There'll be no restitution of confiscated property until the king returns and any idiot can see that—especially Denton. So before that happens, he plans to be neatly married and have his hands on what he wants: Selby and you.' She looked so stricken that he felt his outrage ebb away. He said with less venom: 'Luce, I had to warn you. I hate to see how far he's cozened you already.'

'He has not cozened me! He told me, today, in all honour, that he will find a way to return Selby to you.'

'To *me*? Are you sure of that? What were his precise words?' She hesitated so long that he said dryly: 'You needn't repeat his sermons of love, I'll take those as read. I should simply like to hear if he mentioned me in the same breath as my family property.'

She closed her eyes and finally said: '"It has always been my intention to restore the estates to you. I promise to find a way ... I beg you to believe me, and to tell your brother that Selby that will be yours."'

'Ah!' Maurice said bitterly. 'Were you not listening? He has my inheritance and the only recompense he plans to make is *winning my sister*, who is as far above him by birth as she could possibly be. Does that sound just, to you? Does that sound honourable? Can you bear the sight of that common double-dealer ever again?'

Lucinda looked at him in despair. 'You don't wish to hear this, but please remember that I've told it, because it's the truth. Mark Denton is in love with me and he also promises to hand Selby back to you. He doesn't expect either of us to be grateful. He has no power over his feelings for me, and the restitution of Selby is a matter of justice which he will carry out, whatever your opinion of him.'

'God's teeth,' Maurice said, 'you care that he's in love with you!' He examined her face and his voice was unsteady as he said, 'Do you love him?'

'I ... I don't think so.'

He said between his teeth: 'What would you reply, if he asked you to marry him?'

She said with sarcasm: 'I should tell him that my brother refuses consent.'

'Rightly so.' He gestured towards the barge and the Thames. 'Let us be gone.'

HORSEFERRY ROAD
April 10

Mark was in a tavern on Horseferry Road, called the Drunken Pony. Situated near the ferry landing, it was popular with travellers and the riverside dwellers of Westminster. The sign hanging over the street showed a horse with its head thrown up in alarm, sinking in water up to its neck. The sign was venerable but locals liked to think of it as a humorous reference to the incident that had happened to Archbishop Laud, whose servants and horses were tipped into the Thames when an overloaded ferry rolled on its way from Lambeth Palace to Westminster during the reign of Charles I. Not a creature's life was lost, but Laud himself was afterwards executed for treason, by order of the king, and his horses' plunge from the ferry was thenceforth considered a portent. The same thing happened to Oliver Cromwell's coach and team in 1656, two years before his death.

Mark often used the ferry to transport his horses: the only other way across the Thames was by London Bridge, and the fee was reasonable. He and Ralph Knight had just crossed with a small troop of cavalry after spending a month inspecting army contingents in the south, under Monck's orders. The provincial militia were required to keep the peace through the elections on 21 April and safeguard the new members, who would form what was to be known as a convention, until such time as the king summoned it as the parliament. Monck had issued orders to ensure the compliance of the trained bands in all the major towns.

He had ample powers to do so. He was confirmed as Commander-in-Chief and also joint General at Sea, and he was a member of the new Council of State. He had been given a personal endowment of £20,000 and granted Saint James's Palace as his residence.

London was boisterously loyal to Monck: the celebrations on the day the secluded members took their seats rivalled those in February. Thereafter, sure of his own officers and troops but faced with unrest in the regular army, he countered by cashiering its most recalcitrant officers. The Council of State itself took care of Lambert: it summoned him on 5 March, demanded £20,000 for his good behaviour and, when he rather naturally could not pay, imprisoned him in the Tower.

On 16 March, Parliament had dissolved itself. One of its last acts was to pass a vote that the House of Lords had a right to form part of all future parliaments. For the citizenry, it was a time of intense preparation for the elections. For the military, it was a time of vigilance and hope.

'Well, I'm bloody glad that journey's over,' Mark growled, drawing a surprised look from Knight on the other side of the table. 'Riding about the countryside telling people what to do—it's all I've been performing in the North for years and I'm weary of it.'

'It beats putting down insurrection,' Knight said equably. 'Those days are over—it's in fashion to be a royalist rebel now. Did you hear Sir George Booth has been given command in Cheshire?'

Mark grimaced. The name reminded him of Sir Maurice Selby, who had taken part in Booth's ill-starred rebellion—and from whom he had heard not a word since he and his sister left London for York. 'Any idea what the general has in store for us now?'

Knight shrugged. 'I've sent a sergeant to the barracks and he's to report back here with any news. Then I plan to get there late, line up some mulled wine and read my book by the fireside. Tomorrow morning's soon enough to find out where we're wanted next.'

Mark threw the book a sidelong glance. 'You'll need more than an evening to plough through that.'

It was the latest by John Milton, who was one of John Thurloe's clerks: a last-ditch attempt to persuade the English to adopt a republican government instead of bowing to 'the new royalised' members of parliament and degrading themselves by bringing back Charles II.

'His argument's plain enough even if the language is somewhat frothy,' Knight said. 'His remedy is for the incoming parliament to be named a Grand Council and rule in perpetuity.'

'What happens as the members die off?' Mark said in disbelief. 'Another Rump?'

'Individual recruiter elections are to be undertaken in three or four stages each time,' Knight said, idly flicking through the pages. 'You're right: I prefer his poetry. I bought this out of curiosity.'

Mark took it from his hands and read the title: *The Ready and Easy Way to Establish a Free Commonwealth*. Then he opened it and recited something at random. '"Let our zealous backsliders forethink now with themselves, how their necks yoked with these tigers of Bacchus, inspired with nothing holier than the venereal pox, can draw one way under monarchy to the establishing of church discipline with these new-disgorged atheisms."' He gave it back to Knight. 'Can you understand any of that, let alone agree with it—or are you a tiger of Bacchus yourself?'

Knight laughed and took a gulp of the Drunken Pony's best ale.

Brooding on Milton's tortuous language, Mark said: 'You're a fanatic of his poetry, correct?'

Knight nodded tolerantly.

'Does this sound at all familiar to you? "True opener of my eyes, prime angel blessed, much better seems this vision, and more hope of peaceful days portends than those two past."'

Knight frowned. 'Yes, it does sound like Milton. But I don't think it's from anything he's published and I have all his editions. Perhaps it comes from a manuscript that's he's recited of an evening somewhere. Where did you hear it?'

'From the lips of a republican, intended for the ears of another.'

'It's a message of hope,' Knight said.

'And the prime angel?'

Knight raised an eyebrow. 'Michael, of course. What are you, one of the new-disgorged atheists?'

Mark grinned. 'Michael—the one with the sword?'

'Indeed.'

'Thank God Lambert's in the Tower, then. And Lilburne's couched humbly at home in the North Riding.'

'They were the two?' When Mark nodded, Knight said: 'Lambert will never give up on the republic, you know.' Getting no reply to this, he said: 'As a matter of curiosity, why did you?'

Mark shrugged. 'I'm not sure I ever have. What I gave up on was a perpetual parliament propped up by the army. What I'm prepared to support in its place is a full and free parliament, upheld by the king. It's not ideal, but it's the best we can do, and the country wants it.' He took a gulp of ale. 'It's time the army bowed out of the whole affair. You know what Monck said last month, in the General Council of Officers. He said nothing is more injurious to discipline than our meeting in councils to interpose in civil things.'

'Hmm. And he said he'd rather lose his life than take the government upon himself. But while Parliament kept on refusing to call these elections, don't you think he might have been keeping an open mind about doing it?'

Mark shook his head. 'He's no Cromwell.'

At that moment, Knight's sergeant reported in from the barracks. To the colonels' surprise, when he came to attention by the table he was breathless and glassy-eyed.

Knight said to him sharply: 'Pull yourself together! What's amiss?'

'Lambert, colonel. He's escaped!'

'What, from the *Tower*?'

'Clean away, colonel. Slid down a silk rope into the Thames and were rowed off by six men.'

Mark said to Knight: 'It sounds too neat. There must have been collusion of some kind in the prison. And whoever sprang him will be joining him soon enough—some of the cashiered officers, no doubt …' He turned to the sergeant. 'Has the general named who's to chase him?'

'The word is it will be Colonel Richard Ingoldsby.'

Mark raised his eyebrows but did not comment. Ingoldsby, who had only recently joined Monck, had been among the regicides who voted for the execution of Charles I. Perhaps Monck was giving him this opportunity to redeem himself. Mark did not envy Ingoldsby: hunting down Lambert would be neither simple nor pleasant.

The rest of the sergeant's news about the troops in and around London was far more encouraging. Unrest was at a minimum and soldiers and citizens together were obsessed by the elections. Anticipation was heightened because everyone knew that Monck was now in correspondence with the king and Monck's relative, Lord Grenville, was acting as messenger to and from Breda in the Dutch Republic, where Charles had lately moved.

Absorbing this from the sergeant's patchy account, Mark could not help thinking about Lucinda Selby's final conversation with Anne Monck before they took their leave from the Prince's Lodgings. The women had been at some distance from him, returning from the gallery where they had gone to look at the paintings recently hung on the walls. Lucinda, in her warm, expressive way, seemed to be thanking her hostess for something and the lady looked moved by her words, the last of which were just audible to Mark.

'It is owing to you that His Majesty has absolute trust in your husband. The duchess told me that nothing would have convinced him so well as your message.' Anne Monck had beamed in reply.

A conspiracy of women—thinking it over, he was prepared to believe that Charles Stuart might have used the Duchess of Richmond as a covert ambassador to Monck, through his wife. For whatever reason, the avenue of communication between Breda and London was open, and from Mordaunt he knew that Lord Grenville was a skilful bearer of the king's personal letters. Monck had as yet committed nothing to writing, which obliged Grenville to get his responses by heart.

'A farthing for your thoughts,' Knight said ironically.

Mark looked up to find the sergeant had gone and Knight had drained his second tankard in silence. 'Sorry. It's my bout—what will you have?'

Knight stretched his shoulders. 'I'm for the barracks, thank you. I'm more weary than I thought. Coming?'

Mark shook his head. 'Corporal Hales went ahead to shake the men up for my return. He's also checking whether I have any letters; if so, he'll bring them here. I'll wait a bit longer.'

Knight gave him good night and left. Mark stayed in his corner with unhappy thoughts. He now regretted having sent a letter to Sir Maurice Selby in York, since he had received no reply. He had only done so to keep the promise to Lucinda and he'd been damned if he felt conciliatory to her stiff-necked brother, so the text had been short and direct:

Sir,

By your receipt of this, your sister will have told you my intentions concerning the Selby estates, which are unchanged. I shall write to you again as soon as I am able to fulfil my promise in that regard. I am conducting a militia inspection in the South for the next few weeks, but any reply may be sent to me at the Horseguards Barracks. Please convey to your sister my deepest respect and earnest wishes for her welfare. Your assured ally, Col. Denton.

What more could he say that either brother or sister would consent to hear? Nonetheless, a host of confidences had built up behind the lines, crying to be written down. He had sealed the letter quickly and sent it by one of his couriers before he ran on with things he would regret. It was only after it had gone that he realised he had used the oak-tree carnelian to seal it. This detail was unimportant, however, since the Selbys could never have seen any correspondence from the Shadow.

The Shadow himself—how long did his work need to continue? He had achieved his purposes in the North, preventing royalist uprisings likely to end in the kind of catastrophe that had befallen George Booth. He had discouraged royalist insurrection around London and proved it to be unproductive, especially now that the desired elections were taking place. Neither royalists who had fought for Charles I in the field, nor their sons, were qualified to stand for the new parliament, but intelligence had it that many were putting themselves forward and looked fair to be elected without official protest. And the secluded members had been readmitted to office and secured the dissolution of the Rump—an event that even the most fervent supporters of the monarchy had scarcely believed would ever happen.

He had a yearning to go on as plain Mark Denton and let the Shadow be swallowed into the dark. He had never planned to make his double identity public, and it was unnecessary to his safety: Monck now knew of it and, along with Mark's recent record in the general's service, that was surely enough to prevent his ever being caught by a backlash against the most zealous supporters of the Commonwealth. When Charles II arrived in England, Mark had no mind to throw himself at his feet and pronounce a catalogue of what he had done for the monarchy—there would be hundreds of opportunists boring the king with their own stories, all the way to the throne.

'Colonel. Begging your pardon.'

It was Hales, standing to attention by the table, with a single document in his hand.

'Thank you.' Mark took it, laid it flat and put his hand over it. 'Anything to report?'

'Nothing urgent, colonel. Except that Lambert has—'

'So I've heard.' He felt suddenly exhausted. 'Is everything ready at the barracks?'

'I have a few things to attend to with the horses, colonel, but your lodging is as you'd wish.'

'Off with you, then. I'll be half an hour.'

Hales disappeared and Mark took his hand off the paper. He had at once known it was a letter, from the elegantly written address. It was not a gentleman's hand—too fluid, too fine. He turned it over and recognised the family crest on the wax seal: a plumed helmet with the visor closed. He broke the seal and tried to keep his fingers steady as he flattened the single sheet of paper out over the pitted and scarred tabletop:

Colonel,

I should be ashamed to write to you without my brother's knowledge, were it not for the injustice he does you in not responding himself. I trust in your benevolence towards our family and I will do my utmost to persuade him to share that trust.

In the meantime I beg you to understand that my brother believes he is acting to shield me—which makes me grieve all the more, knowing that you have acted to protect both of us, and with greater sacrifice.

When I last saw you I should have confessed that I know how much you have done under cover for our great cause but, forgive me, I did not have the courage. Nor do I dare say more, in case this letter is intercepted. Geoffrey Paget of Saint Mary Bishop is taking care of its despatch to you. Should there be a reply, it may be sent to his address.

Your letter confirmed your secret: a friend once revealed to us the symbol by which you seal your clandestine messages. God keep you safe. Your assured and constant friend, L.S.

He kept rereading it. *I should be ashamed* ... a dreadful beginning. But his eye kept gliding on to *Your assured and constant friend* with a sweet jolt to the senses that was stronger every time. Logic told him that 'friend' simply meant 'royalist ally', as in the first line of the paragraph. Who might have told the Selbys that the Shadow's seal was a spreading oak tree? Mordaunt, perhaps. But he didn't really care, and he was incapable of analysing the letter that began to blur before his eyes. The mere fact that she had written to him overwhelmed him utterly—which was sufficient to tell him he would be insane to respond.

ARBURY HILL
April 22

Mark was speeding through Northamptonshire at the head of his militia regiment. They were aiming for a confrontation enjoined upon him by George Monck and he could feel in his bones that, of all the forays in his career, this was the one most likely to get him killed.

The problem was John Lambert. The legendary former general was still at large, had been joined by groups of disaffected soldiers from the counties, and was spoiling for a pitched battle to resurrect the Commonwealth and demolish England's chance to return the king. An even greater problem, to Mark's mind, was that Monck seemed to have lost his nerve in the face of Lambert's audacity and determination.

Mark had not expected to have anything to do with the emergency. Sir Richard Ingoldsby had been despatched from London with an adequate force and gone to Edgehill, where Lambert had planned to make rendezvous with a number of cashiered army officers. Lambert had also been joined by mutinous troops from the regiments that had been dispersed from London to make way for Monck's army in January. Ingoldsby had not caught up with him at Edgehill, but he had stayed on his trail, pursuing him through Oxfordshire and beyond while more soldiers deserted their provincial posts and filtered through to the makeshift army. Intelligence put Lambert's hastily assembled force at fewer than 1000: to Mark, it seemed only a matter of time before Ingoldsby cornered Lambert somewhere and put him to rout.

But Monck had serious doubts. To Mark's surprise, Monck had told the king's envoy, Lord Grenville, that if Ingoldsby failed to stop Lambert, Monck himself would declare for the king, take power in his name, crush Lambert and put England under martial law. To Mark's even greater surprise, he was called to a private meeting and grilled about both Lambert and Ingoldsby.

Mark chose his answers carefully. 'General, you know Lambert as well as I—or better—by reputation and in person. We would agree he is formidable: he has unswerving courage and he's a strategic genius. But in his present situation, how much damage can he do? If he could amass a very large force and inspire every man to go on fighting for him indefinitely, he might pose a threat to the government in time. But I suspect he's already gathered as many troops as he can reasonably hope to get, and Ingoldsby will be a match for them once he's chased them down.'

Monck muttered: 'Is Ingoldsby the commander to do it? He's taking his time! He used to be a staunch Cromwellian—a cousin of Oliver, in fact. What if he's being influenced by the sympathy for Lambert that seems to be springing up all over the confounded Midlands?'

Mark said coldly: 'You put Ingoldsby in command of Colonel Rich's regiment after cashiering Rich. You've given him the opportunity to prove how loyal he is. I had a good talk with him in January after he pledged support to you and on that basis I'm prepared to vouch that he will fulfil your orders to the letter.'

Monck frowned at him, then paced away, perhaps with the recollection that Mark, too, had once supported Cromwell and the Commonwealth but had conclusively proved his allegiance to Monck since.

Mark smiled ironically to himself, but in fact he was disturbed. He had never seen the general so troubled. 'Sir', he ventured, 'the elections are progressing, the City is quiescent, the army is not in revolt and London goes about its business with such composure that one might imagine the Commons and the House of Lords were both in session and the king were already on the throne. Do you seriously believe that Lambert and his puny hundreds can turn all this upside down?'

Monck stopped pacing. 'I tell you, Lambert has to be stopped. I want you to take your regiment and join Ingoldsby. I want you on the spot to give him your advice and make sure Lambert surrenders—otherwise he and his ideas and his forces must be annihilated.'

Mark felt the same dread that had haunted him when he was pursuing Lambert to the Picts' Wall in the New Year, but he tried to banish it and concentrate on detail. 'When we meet up, do I report to Ingoldsby or he to me?'

Monck grimaced. 'You've made your point about Sir Richard. I should not be seen to withdraw my confidence in him, so you will report to him. But you'll tell him I expect him to confer with you when you face Lambert.' He eyed Mark keenly. 'Are you willing to take this on, colonel?'

'I'd prefer you to put the order in writing, sir, so I can hand it to Ingoldsby.'

Monck went at once to a desk and pulled out a piece of paper. He wrote a single sentence on it, signed it, and left it on the table to dry.

When Monck looked up, Mark said: 'I'd also like to ask a favour. It will mean little to you, sir, but it's important to me. It's not a military matter—it's to do with the estate of Selby which was settled on me by Parliament in '56. As soon as the new parliament is elected, I intend to ask it for permission to hand the estate back to Sir Maurice Selby. May I have your support for this petition, in writing?'

Monck's eyes narrowed. It was the first time Mark had not immediately accepted an order—and the only time he had asked a favour. Monck was not used to bargaining, but then he had never needed Mark's experience so urgently. 'I remember Sir Maurice. Colonel Knight speaks well of him and he's combing the country for horseflesh, to good effect, I hear. Tell me why you would relinquish valuable property to him? Has he done you any service that I should know about?'

'No, sir, none. My reasons are private and, I repeat, not military.'

Monck had shrugged, pulled out another sheet of paper and written a few more sentences which he signed with a flourish. He put the second paper on top of the first and held both of them out. 'Without further ado, are you ready to obey my orders, colonel?'

Mark had taken the papers and bowed. 'Yes, sir.'

****

By sending scouts ahead of the regiment and closely following Ingoldsby's trail, he had now almost caught up with both forces, which were said to be roughly southwest of Daventry—and he liked the mission no more than he had at first. The conflict would be ugly, wherever it took place; Ingoldsby would be desperate to force Lambert into unconditional surrender without a clash of arms, because many of the troops facing each other across the divide were old comrades. By contrast, Lambert, who was too fanatical to realise that his cause was hopeless, would be yearning for a fight; to his mind, a final battle for the Commonwealth would cover his name in glory and he was prepared to die for his principles.

Mark had spent his days in the saddle trying to devise a way for Lambert's last stand to end without bloodshed and the only one he had come up with posed significant risk to himself. But he would have to take it or watch hundreds of men lose their lives over a doomed cause.

The intelligence he had received was accurate: the long chase was over. Lambert's forces, which consisted of two wings of cavalry and a small company of infantry, were drawn up on the lowest slopes of Arbury Hill, the summit of which was the highest point in Northamptonshire. His troops were positioned behind a swampy patch of ground leading down to the little river Nene that flowed between the two hosts.

As soon as they came into sight, Mark sent an ensign ahead to announce his arrival to Ingoldsby. As he led his regiment along the northern bank of the Nene, Mark observed Lambert's position to the south. He concluded that Lambert had chosen Arbury Hill because he had been hoping to occupy the higher ground, but woods covered the upper slopes and they looked too thick for easy deployment. On the lower ground, Lambert still had the advantage that if Ingoldsby charged across the Nene, his cavalry would be slowed by the stream and also by the boggy ground beyond it. Lambert would be wanting the fight to come to him, therefore.

Ingoldsby's men were in battle order but the only action was near the Nene, where a group of officers on each side of the stream were exchanging heated words. The shouts echoed confusingly against the side of the hill behind Lambert, who was mounted on a fine white horse that stood just before his infantry. The horse had a Barbary look to it; trust Lambert to get himself an Arabian breed, renowned for its stamina. He wore a dark, highly polished cuirass but no other armour, and no helmet.

When Ingoldsby's escort reached him, Mark beckoned Corporal Hales, who had Skipton in tow. Mark ordered him to lead the stallion to the far side of Ingoldsby's position and said: 'Wait for me by that stand of trees near the water. I shan't be long.'

Mark had the major draw up his cavalry behind the position. 'The regiment remains in reserve unless Sir Richard orders otherwise. Whatever happens to me, you're under his command until this is over. Afterwards you'll march on to Bedford and return to the London barracks along the same route the army took in January.'

He was then escorted through to Ingoldsby, who was about 50 yards from the Nene, in conference with three officers.

Sir Richard Ingoldsby was a short, stout gentleman with a red face and hair like a badger's, gone completely grey rather early for his age, which Mark judged to be in the 40s. At first glance he had a belligerent look but his voice was high and querulous rather than aggressive. He remembered Mark and looked somewhat put out by his arrival, but once he had read the message from Monck he was eager enough to share his grievances about Lambert.

'We've been parleying for four hours! Our terms are generous—if he surrenders, his men may cross to our lines with the honours of war and only the captains taken prisoner. He can see he's outnumbered—and now that your regiment's here, he's lost, whichever way he turns.'

'You don't apprehend more troops coming to his side?'

Ingoldsby shook his head. 'He's threatened us with a tide of men but he's been half the day bogged down with that lot, and no one's appeared to supply him with men, arms, shot or artillery, should he be so lucky. It's Easter Day and the whole country's celebrating the Resurrection—and this is certain as hell not going to be his. But he won't back down.'

'Now we're here, will you try him again with new arguments?'

'Not I! He's insulted me in every way he can contrive for bloody hours and I don't trust myself to exchange a word more. My major here'—he nodded his head towards the tall man on his left—'has borne the brunt, and a nasty time he's had.' He said to the major: 'Repeat to Lambert the glaring truth that we have the upper hand and let's see what he makes of it.'

'You'll mention the York militia regiment,' Mark said quickly to the major, 'but don't name me. Keep him guessing.' Mark turned his horse so that his face was not visible to Lambert, and pulled his wide-brimmed hat further over his eyes.

Ingoldsby said slyly: 'So you won't attempt negotiation yourself, colonel?'

Mark shook his head and said to the major: 'Try him, if you please.' When the man had gone, he said to Ingoldsby: 'I have some experience of Lambert. His opinion of me is such that nothing I could say would move him.' Ingoldsby relaxed a little at this, and Mark went on: 'His pride is too high for this sort of discussion—we could be here until doomsday. With your leave I'd like to try another tack: single combat.'

Ingoldsby was taken aback—his very hair seemed to stiffen in response.

Mark went on: 'His men are in his thrall. His officers are probably begging him to surrender but he'll have none of it. At the same time, he's a man of strong impulses. If he were given a challenge, he'd take it up and distance himself from his forces to do so. You'd have only to observe the combat and the moment the loser falls, take the field by storm. They'll submit in a trice if he's not by to stiffen their sinews.'

'By God, you may be in the right,' Ingoldsby said. 'Yesterday we captured one of their officers, the son of Sir Arthur Haselrig, no less, and he already repents of taking up with Lambert. We let him rejoin the rebels privily and he's promised that his whole troop will yield to us at once if it comes to a fight.'

'Excellent.' Mark was trying to make out the shouted exchange by the river behind him. 'How is your major faring?'

'Lamentably,' Ingoldsby said, then looked at Mark with intense curiosity. 'But who's to issue the challenge? Lambert's one of the best swordsmen in England.'

'That's not your concern,' Mark said coolly. 'All you need do is give me time to arrange it. Continue to parley while I enter the trees over there and cross the stream out of sight'—he pointed to where Hales waited by the river—'and then leave perhaps ten minutes more while I set up the challenge. It will be issued from further up the hill, 100 yards or so from Lambert's ranks. Your view of the combat will be uninterrupted. If the challenger wins, total surrender follows; if the challenger falls, waste no time—charge at full tilt and demand submission at once before Lambert gets back to his men and continues his infernal mischief.'

The major returned at that moment with a long face.

'He said no?' Ingoldsby snapped.

'Every time, sir, he laces his insults with viler language.'

Ingoldsby said to Mark: 'Then we have nothing to lose by employing your device. Except the life of a brave man.'

'What's one amongst thousands?' Mark said. 'The elections were held yesterday, with no hindrance. Today's result, such as I could glean as we chased you across the country, is that royalists will carry the day. Lambert's has gone by; it's time he and the world saw that plain. My regiment is under your command and my major holds it in reserve, awaiting your orders. Do I have your consent to leave the field for a short interval?'

'Go,' Ingoldsby said, 'and pray God we meet again.' He held out his hand.

Mark grasped it briefly and wheeled away.

****

Of the men gathered beside the Nene that day, not a single one ever forgot how the conflict ended. But, strangely, their stories of its beginning differed. Before the clash began, everyone had seen Colonel Denton's York militia arrive with the major at its head, accompanied by a man in a wide-brimmed black hat, riding a black stallion. Denton's men always claimed that this was the colonel himself but they were unable to explain why he left the field after talking to Ingoldsby and disappeared without trace. Ingoldsby's troops believed that he was a courier sent by Monck, and such was their disinterest in him that they failed to even notice where he went after handing over his message.

Lambert's troops, waiting tensely on the far side of the Nene, took no account at all of the movements amongst the opposing commander and his officers—they were concerned only about the fresh cavalry regiment that they could see forming in reserve. The great shock came some 15 minutes later, however—and it was on their side of the river.

There was a shout from behind them, and the whole army turned.

'General Lambert!'

Well up the hill and just before the trees, at a steep angle to their serried ranks, stood a tall, dark-grey horse and rider. The voice sounded again, rich and deep, forceful enough to carry to the front ranks of the army on the opposite side of the Nene. 'Your stated will is to decide this by the sword. So be it. Come to me alone and accept combat to the death.'

Lambert did not move, and his whole force stood equally still. The stranger's appearance underscored the dire import of his words. He was tall, with glossy black hair to the shoulders, wearing a long black cloak and thigh boots. His voice was unaccented and his face unrecognisable under a mask.

'Who am I to fight?' Lambert called, his voice booming against the hill.

At that moment an answer sped around both armies. '*The King's Shadow!*'

The rider's voice dominated all others. 'Your worst enemy.'

'Damn your eyes!' Lambert yelled. 'I've no need to prove myself to you!'

'You'll do it—to redeem your name. Or reveal yourself a coward to this nation. You've lured these men here to no purpose, careless whether they die at your perverted whim. I say again, you're a coward, John Lambert.'

The response was instantaneous. Lambert cried to his officers: 'Stay here!' He put spurs to his white Barbary and tore up the hill towards the Shadow.

The Shadow dropped from the saddle, flung his cloak to the ground and with a slap on the big stallion's neck, sent it back into the trees.

In stunned silence, both armies watched the opponents converge. The picture was only too clear. The ground on which they would meet was uneven—a grassy slope marked by sheep trails and studded with boulders. Their defence was also unequal—Lambert wore a cuirass over battle dress while the Shadow simply had a grey buff coat over doublet and breeches.

But the swords were matched. The Shadow drew his when Lambert came level with him. Lambert leaped from his horse and his own sword flashed from the sheath. They were long, heavy-cavalry weapons, tempered countless times in battle. Lambert smacked his horse on the rump and it bolted further up the hill, where it remained against the backdrop of trees, a white shape on a green ground.

Lambert wasted no words—he flew with such fury at the Shadow that the other only just had time to bring up his sword to parry the thrust. The two men smashed together and fell, with the Shadow beneath, and a groan rose from the hosts below.

Next moment the Shadow somehow thrust Lambert's weight away, slipped out and was on his feet with sword ready as the other rose.

There was a collective gasp when Lambert flashed again into the attack; as the swords clanged, the watchers could almost taste the sparks of his hatred.

In the heat and crowd of battle, such an exchange between master swordsmen would last less than a minute. On this wide ground, with nothing to impede them and no one else to fight, death might come just a little later. Watching them with their hearts in their mouths, the opposing sides came to the bitter conclusion that Lambert had a slight edge. Because he wore a cuirass, the Shadow's classic target ought to be the neck, but Lambert's defence was impeccable and he was constantly moving to higher ground to increase his odds.

The Shadow was taller, leaner and more agile than Lambert, and fought relentlessly to get under his guard and to the limbs in order to maim and then kill. At one point he managed to turn the fight so that Lambert was driven downhill, almost back to the point of his first onslaught.

The bright light of the chilly spring day flickered on the sword blades and on Lambert's steel back-plate, over which the dark curls at his neck hung damply. Both men had ridden hard for days and both must be feeling the effects—but they were still attacking hard. The end would come not by the power of Lambert's thrusts or the Shadow's speed but when one of them made a mistake.

Lambert snatched the high ground again, forced his opponent back—and the Shadow stepped onto the tangled mound of his own cloak, forgotten in the grass. He kept his balance but wavered for a fraction of a second. Lambert struck like lightning and his sword went through the Shadow's buff coat and out the other side.

There was a gasp from the men below; Lambert withdrew the blade and the Shadow crumpled without a sound and lay still.

There was a pause during which no one moved or spoke. Then Lambert bent forward, his sword poised, and stretched out the other hand as though to remove the Shadow's mask. No one knew whether it was a dying word from the Shadow or simple respect for his victim that stayed Lambert's hand, but he stepped back, faced downhill and raised his sword high in victory. All could see the blood that darkened the blade.

Into the stunned interval, Sir Richard Ingoldsby roared: 'Charge!'

At once, his cavalry surged towards the Nene. Lambert's men turned from their leader as he sheathed his sword and ran up the slope towards his horse. Their infantry centre did not move but a troop of horse broke ranks and came forward across the swampy ground to halt a few yards from the stream. They were Haselrig's. Just as Ingoldsby's front line of horse came splashing across the river, the opposing cavalrymen drew their pistols and fired into the ground.

They were immediately surrounded by a party of Ingoldsby's men, and the colonel himself pushed on with the rest, crying 'Surrender!' to the static lines of infantry and cavalry beyond.

Once horsed and aware of the disaster below, Lambert scorned to flee. But it was over in a few minutes, even before he could rejoin his untouched and disarmed troops. He rode down amongst them like a whirlwind, ignored everyone but Ingoldsby, and pushed across the damp ground to confront him. His horse's fine legs, spattered with mud, sank up to the fetlocks in the trampled mire. He was in a fury—the same rage that had sent him flying against the Shadow. But Ingoldsby held his ground without giving him the chance to fight, and steadily demanded his submission. When at last he gave it, his sword was taken and he was moved across the Nene under guard.

It was then, when all was secure, that Ingoldsby sent a party up the slope to recover the body of the Shadow. But there was nothing there, not even the discarded cloak. A spattered trail of blood led into the trees where some claimed to have glimpsed a second man and three horses during the combat. It seemed that the man had thrown the Shadow's body over the saddle of the great dark-grey stallion and led it away.

Ingoldsby did not speculate; in fact he declined to discuss the action on the hill at all. He was about to escort Lambert back to the Tower and report to Monck on a duty well performed. His orders to his officers, and theirs to the men, were to make no mention of the Shadow or the meeting in single combat. He could hardly be blamed for wishing to underline Lambert's humiliation in the eyes of the army and the public—the victory over the Shadow must not figure in the tale of Lambert's capture.

But the soldiers knew what they had seen, and so did the country folk who observed the confrontation from afar and marvelled at the turns it took. Thus the story sped from Arbury Hill into the hinterland and in less than an hour it reached the towns of Daventry, Towcester and Northampton. Long before the army got back to London, it had travelled there and become legend. To the end of their days, the veterans of the fabled general's last stand would tell how the King's Shadow lost his life to Lambert.

NORTHAMPTON
April 23

Lucinda found Northampton more agreeable than she had expected. Maurice had insisted they must give his prize horses a spell of grazing over Easter, on land belonging to an acquaintance, Sir Richard Rainsford. There were 25 splendid steeds in Maurice's collection and through contacts among the gentry he intended to add more between Northampton and Bedford, their next stop on the way to London. This had been a pleasant break in their journey, enhanced by Sir Richard's victory at the elections, which they had celebrated on Easter Day. Rainsford and the other representative of Northampton, Francis Harvey, had already left for London, where they would take their seats in the Convention parliament on the 25th. Further good news had come into town the night before—John Lambert had been captured by a Colonel Ingoldsby not far from Daventry, so the last armed insurrection against the king was over.

She and Maurice were lodged in upper-storey apartments in the best inn, which looked over the town square. Buoyed up by his successful purchases and backed by funds from the army coffers, Maurice was in excellent temper, living and spending as though Selby had never been wrested from him. However, the estate was the one topic that always put him out of sorts with Lucinda. For many days after the receipt of Mark Denton's letter in York she had tried to convince her brother that it was proof of Denton's integrity, but he persisted in believing that it was a sham. She reluctantly decided that Maurice's pride was involved, just as it had been when the Shadow rescued him after Booth's uprising. He hated to feel under an obligation to a man whom he had despised for so long, and he preferred to believe the obligation did not exist.

After writing her secret letter to Denton, Lucinda no longer spoke about him to Maurice. And in any case, there was no fresh news to convey, for he had not replied to her. Every day in York she had yearned for a message to come through Geoffrey Paget, and every day she had castigated herself for her disappointment when it did not arrive.

It should have been a relief to be home but her obsession with Denton created an undercurrent of frustration in all her habits and tasks. Now that the Duke of Buckingham had returned to London—where apparently he was to be seen strolling about in full Garter regalia—she could receive his wife at the Coppergate; she would not allow her hideous memory of George Villiers to destroy that friendship. In return she was invited to Nun Appleton, where her reception showed that none of the Fairfaxes had any inkling of the duke's obscene behaviour in London. But she no longer felt at ease there.

The Duchess of Buckingham had inquired rather wistfully about the duke's cousin, Barbara Villiers. 'Have you met her? Is she very beautiful?'

Lucinda had hesitated. Mary Villiers, who had allowed the girl to visit Convent Garden just once, had pronounced her 'a real little madam' after she left, but Lucinda could hardly repeat this to a relative by marriage. 'She paid one visit to the Duchess of Richmond. She has good looks and … an air of … of sophistication. She asked a great many questions about the king but the duchess insisted on talking about poetry, which was a little mischievous of her. Mistress Palmer yawned and looked bored, and left quite soon.'

The story was greeted with a humorous smile.

However, despite Lucinda's seeing other friends in York, it had seemed dreary and disappointing, and she was eager for London.

On this bright morning in Northampton, she had arranged to take a walk in the town square with Maurice, who was visiting the stables to check on their carriage horses. When he entered her chambers, he looked shaken, as though something were seriously amiss.

'What is it?' she said. 'No equine ailments, I hope?'

When Maurice was disturbed or angry, his light blue eyes seemed very pale. 'We didn't get the full story about Lambert yesterday evening, but it's all over town today. You won't like this news, and I'm sorry. Lambert fought the King's Shadow before the battle, and killed him.'

She said in disbelief: 'There was no battle! It was an abject surrender. *The Shadow*? What could he have had to do with it?'

'It's the truth. He challenged Lambert to single combat and Lambert ran him through. Whatever the official report says, more than 2000 men saw him die.' He looked contrite. 'I must tell you, I regret that he's dead. Denton ... the Shadow ... I confess I admired him.'

'No!' It felt as though the cry tore something out of her—a passion she had never acknowledged, a dream she had never known she held.

Her ears rang, her breath failed her and she found herself on her knees.

Maurice started forward but she stopped him with an outstretched hand. 'Leave me alone!' Her voice came out thin and expressionless, but her eyes warned him away.

He hesitated a moment, then left the room. When he closed the door, she crumpled forward, her forehead against the floor.

Yesterday, while she was celebrating the outcome of the elections that Mark Denton had done much to bring about, he had been a few miles away, fighting his last battle. He had perished, with no reward or honours for the unknown services he had performed for the king. He was gone: a true heart lost, without farewell.

****

Mark awoke in a strange room, without a clue where he was. Despite his peripatetic lifestyle, this hardly ever happened; he was normally in control of his situation from the moment he opened his eyes. Perhaps it was pain that caused the bewilderment, hazing the edges of perception. He put a hand to his side where the ache was worst and suddenly he remembered a day and a place: yesterday, Arbury Hill.

The brutal instant came back, when Lambert's sword pierced his coat of buffalo hide and sliced across his ribs. During his subtle balancing act on the fallen cloak, Mark had tried to trick Lambert into thrusting for the kill too hastily and too wide—but the cut had gone deeper than he had calculated and when Lambert withdrew the blade it sliced back through his flesh with such effect that his fall, and the groan as he hit the ground, were fiercely genuine.

Panting, and with sweat pouring down his face, Lambert had leaned over to make sure he had struck the fatal blow. As he fought for breath, Mark had seen the other man's hand come down to tear off his mask. He had summoned his voice, which emerged in a hoarse moan: 'You've done for me. Is that not enough?'

He might have blacked out then, because he remembered nothing more in any detail until he and Hales were riding through the margin of the woods on the eastern side of the hill. Mark aimed to move out of shelter into a lane that led away into farmland, but Hales had said: 'You've gone far enough for now, sir—there's too much blood.'

They had both dismounted and Mark had lowered himself onto a felled trunk of hornbeam while Hales dug in his pack for the equipment he always carried. Hales had helped to haul off the buff coat, which was blood-soaked and ruined. Mark ordered him to bury it in a hollow under a gorse bush along with the wig and mask. Hales had stitched the slash across his side while Mark gritted his teeth and leaned with one hand on the corded bark of the hornbeam, thinking how fit it was to be called muscle-wood and wondering how soon his own sinews would heal.

He tried them now, swinging his legs to the floor and perching on the lumpy edge of the mattress, his arms propping up his bent frame. They would do. He looked around the room, which he did not remember from the night before. Hales had been horrified at trying to ride as far as Northampton—his idea for a hideout had been a nearby village. But Mark had wanted the anonymity of a larger town and had told Hales to choose the most obscure inn. By the looks of the room it was also the dirtiest. But he couldn't bring himself to care much about that. His mind was still trying to grasp that the King's Shadow had neatly ceased to be. He should have felt liberated but at present he felt like death.

He was smiling grimly at this thought when Hales entered the room. There was no answering smile from the corporal, who took injury and illness to heart, especially on campaign, and was nearly as skilful with wounded men as he was with horses. He insisted on examining and re-dressing his work of the day before, and answered Mark's questions distractedly.

'Whose shirt is this?' Mark inquired, eyeing the hempen garment with distaste.

'I got it from one of the grooms. I said we were delivering horses from a livery stables in Hull and we'd fought off a couple of cut-throats on the way. Your clothes are washed and dried and in that bundle by the window, sir. The blood was something terrible, the washerwoman said. I paid her double to keep quiet and dry your things by her own fire.'

'You've done well. Bring me up some food and writing materials—I need to send a note to the general, to say I'm somewhat delayed. The local militia can despatch it.'

'You need to rest and lie low, sir.' Hales picked up his gear and stood over him, frowning. 'This place is abuzz with what happened at Arbury Hill, and though there's no markets today, the streets are full of people from out of town. Best you don't go abroad, sir, if you'll forgive my saying. Everyone wants to know where Colonel Denton disappeared to before the combat began, and if you're recognised, you'll have nothing but lack-wit questions to answer about yourself *and* the Shadow.'

Mark rose carefully and went to the window. Through the filthy, ill-fitting panes he could see nothing but a back alley and a line of crooked chimney-pots. 'I'd as soon take a walk in the lanes. I've no fever—you said so yourself. If I stay put I'll stiffen up and that will make the travelling worse.' He glanced at Hales's disapproving face. 'Come, who's going to know me here? I've hardly ever set foot in the place.'

'Beg pardon, sir, but we've operated often in these parts. And there are strangers to town who might not be strangers to you.' A slight embarrassment came over Hales. 'I must tell you that Sir Maurice Selby and the Lady Lucinda are passing through with Sir Maurice's mighty string of horses. The stable lads are hot to see them. Seems they're having a spell on Sir Richard Rainsford's property.'

Mark sank down on a wooden chest under the window. 'I thought the Selbys were in York.' His brain struggled with the implications. They'd have heard about the fight with Lambert! Did she believe him dead? Then he shook his head. The moment he'd received Monck's order to pursue Lambert, he had sent Lucinda a line from London, sealed with the oak-tree signet ring: *Should you hear of the death of the Shadow, never believe it, unless you also hear the same is true of me.* He could scarcely have made it clearer than that, could he? But he was overcome with the desire to see her.

'Where do they lodge? With Sir Richard?'

'No, at the Fox and Grapes, on the square.'

'Help me dress. I'll go alone and unarmed. No one's going to accost me on the way, Hales, so take that look off your face.'

****

When he reached the square, he paused for a moment, observing the upper-storey windows—rather as the fox in the fable might have eyed the grapes that hung agonisingly within view. Mark had once stayed at the inn himself and knew that the best apartments were behind those very windows. If he went quickly through the hall at the bottom of the main stairs he might reach the landing without having to announce himself to the establishment. Then he could get a passing servant to knock on Lady Lucinda's door.

It worked, and the man he intercepted turned out to be the innkeeper himself. 'Would you tell her ladyship that I have a message for her, from Sir Richard Rainsford?'

The innkeeper looked up at him in some surprise. Mark reflected too late that messengers were not commonly so tall or so peremptory—and that he had just used the Shadow's courtly drawl instead of his own Yorkshire speech. It was clearly on the tip of the man's tongue to ask his name but something in Mark's expression made him think better of it, and he knocked on the door.

Mark heard the faintest of replies from within. The innkeeper opened the door, delivered the announcement from the threshold and asked: 'May Sir Richard's man step in, my lady?'

'Very well.'

The softness of her voice undid him. Why should she respond as he did to the miraculous coincidence of their being in this town at the same time? He felt his temples burn, as though the fever that Hales feared were about to take over. What kind of fool was he, to step into her presence without having a word in readiness to say to her?

He hesitated so long that the innkeeper, waiting impatiently outside the door to eavesdrop on their exchange, gave up in disgust and went thumping off down the stairs.

He entered. She was by the window, looking down into the street. Had she spied him earlier, through the diamond panes, and been thankful to think he didn't know she was here?

He closed the door behind him and she turned.

She gave a shrill gasp and flung one hand out against the glittering window. The spring sunshine poured down over her arm and bare shoulder, rippling across her distorted face. With a cry she stepped towards him, then stopped. Tears burst from her eyes.

He moved forward, appalled, and she shrieked and rushed blindly at him. 'You, you!' Her hands reached his chest, clutching and pulling his doublet and collar. Her voice was high and wild. 'I thought you were dead! How could you?'

He tried to capture her hands but she pulled back suddenly. Sobs racked her body and her hands hid her face while tears poured down her neck and over her white breasts.

All he could say was: 'Don't, don't.'

Finally he caught her so tightly in his arms that they could scarcely breathe. Her sobs turned to high keening sounds ... then sighs ... then silence.

He pressed his lips to the top of her head. 'I wrote to you, to warn you.'

'No you didn't. I never got it.'

'I didn't know you were leaving York.' He made her raise her face, and looked fiercely into the blue eyes that shone with tears. 'I had to do it. I couldn't have brought myself to kill him—he had to kill me. Forgive me.'

'No,' she said, and kissed him.

For Lucinda, the kiss was everything she had ever wanted, and a world besides. Then, into the bliss shot the realisation that there was no mistake—he had fought, and Lambert had run him through.

She drew back in terror. 'You're wounded!'

She pulled her arms from his neck but he caught her around the waist. 'It doesn't matter.' He kissed her again. His lips and his hands were hot, consuming.

Then Maurice walked into the room. 'What's the message from—?' He halted inside the door, his fingers on the latch.

Mark looked over and let Lucinda go. 'Close the door.'

Maurice shut it with a bang and put a hand on his sword hilt.

'There's been enough blood!' Lucinda cried. She snatched Mark's right hand, held it hard with both of hers and said to Maurice: 'I am betrothed to him.'

Her brother stared at them without a word.

Mark put his free hand in his breast and extracted Monck's paper. He held it out to Maurice. 'This is the message. It's General Monck's pledge to support the return of Selby to you.' While Maurice collected himself and examined it, still open-mouthed, Mark looked down at Lucinda. 'When it's all done, you'll want to spend time at your home first, I imagine. Then we'll be married. You'll want to be wed in the Minster. I don't see why not.'

She said: 'You need to sit down,' and guided him gently to a chair.

He obeyed her. 'After that, you may choose between Lang Scar and Swaledale. Swaledale boasts the beauty but Lang Scar is closer to Selby.'

'Maurice,' she said as her brother glanced up from the message in wonder, 'please, we need a physician.' He nodded and went out in a daze, but remembered this time to close the door.

Mark's eyes suddenly filled with dread. 'How can I win a woman like you, when I tell you what's in my heart too late, or not at all?'

'Now that you've let me close,' she said, suiting the action to the words by coming to stand between his knees, 'I know without the telling.' She paused and his grey eyes darkened further. She went on: 'Fighting for so long has hurt you, in more ways than one.'

He drew her to him and buried his face between her breasts. 'Thank God it's over.'

DOVER
May 25

Charles had been on deck since six o'clock. His spaniels had been running wild for hours, fouling the timbers and amusing him with their tumbled mock combat. His attendants and the navy men, including an official from London who seemed to be taking notes in quite indiscriminate detail, were full of respectful cheer, especially now that Dover was before them.

He could feel they wanted to bathe in visions of the future, but all the way over from Holland he had swamped them with anecdotes that went backwards into his past: of exile; defeat; and the turgid beginnings of his father's war. At his request, the ship in which he rode had been rechristened the *Royal Charles*—before, it had been the *Naseby*, named by parliament for his father's most disastrous battle. The ships in which his brothers James and Henry sailed in his wake were likewise reborn.

His faithful subjects were fashioning a new future for him, turning up little images printed in fresh, bright inks, slippery and gilt-edged, from a virgin pack of cards. But the game they played was an old one.

He watched the royal standard wave above the town in glorious sunlight, and the throngs bustle below, their shouts of acclamation stretching across the water, punctuated by peals of bells. From the pier where he would alight, his father had farewelled his mother when she went to Holland in 1642 to raise gold and arms and support for the war, leaving all her children behind except his little sister Mary. Later, along the high, white cliffs near the castle, his father had ridden, waving, for as long as the queen's ship was visible.

Charles had been safe elsewhere with his tutor when his mother sailed away; this was his first view of Dover from the sea. His attendants were offering it up to him like a new card, shiny with promise. But he had another in his mind, equally apt, from his father's time. It was faded and worn, bent at the corners. The Fool.

It was after two o'clock in the afternoon when the admiral's barge was lowered into the water to take him ashore. He was due to disembark into an atmosphere of delirious enthusiasm. Suddenly the air was rent by the most fearsome explosion of cannon fire that he had ever heard. He managed not to stagger away from it, but the dogs were down the companionway in a trice.

He put his hands over his ears and grinned at the luxuriously dressed people around him. The touch of his long, glossy hair around his face was comforting—he was glad that he had taken Mall Villiers's advice and never worn the new wigs. He knew he looked every inch a king: the King of Hearts. Meanwhile in his mental armoury the King of Spades lurked—dark and watchful.

As the barge neared the wharf, he reflected that his mother would at this moment be praying for him at Colombes, with Mall at her side. A wave of melancholy threatened, then he was buffeted by a lively cross-current of emotion from the shore. It was after all only natural that everyone around him should be happier about his landing in England than he was himself. They were falling over themselves to welcome him: all he need do for the next few days was smile and avoid being offensive to any of the major players. The easiest way to do this was to say very little.

This conclusion was immensely inspiring, and there was a dreamlike rightness to everything that followed. On Dover pier he knelt and gave thanks to God for his safe homecoming. When he rose, the first to approach him was George Monck, who got down on his knees several paces away. He was short, rounded man with a black seriousness about him that instantly appealed to Charles, who stepped forward, raised him to his feet and found himself embracing him. *Certes*, he could scarcely make him anything less than a duke after this.

There was an even longer cannonade, and an answering roar from thousands of throats. A great bonfire went up in flames, and Monck told him that it was the first of a spectacular line of fires that would be lit all the way to London to announce his coming.

The numbers of people crowded into the town and along the shore were astonishing, but despite their cacophony they seemed under good regulation and stayed well back. Monck's entourage and the assembled dignitaries likewise gave the royal party plenty of room and none were presented to Charles at this point; they simply made their obeisance if his glance moved their way.

Once he was escorted into the town, there was a reception, of course, and the lord mayor of Dover presented him with a costly bible, which Charles declared to be the thing he loved above all other things in the world. With this rather childish phrase echoing in his ears, he wandered on foot through the main part of the town with Monck, which seemed to be what everyone desperately wanted—to prove that this was all real, he supposed. He had yet to quite believe it himself.

Monck helped: he explained the day's business sensibly and in sequence, revealing as he did so his considerable powers of organisation. The king would shortly make by coach for Canterbury, where everything was in perfect train for his first night on the measured journey to London. Charles was relieved not to be spending it in Dover Castle, which was notoriously bleak and chilly. Of the people crowded behind the barriers—also ordered by Monck—many were noblemen who had travelled down from London in order to ride back in procession and accompany him home. For this impromptu host, Monck had also made strict provision: on the journey they were divided into troops bearing coloured flags, and their lodgings were allocated accordingly.

Charles wondered briefly whether Barbara Villiers might be somewhere amongst the bevies of women of every degree who pressed themselves up against the barriers and devoured him with their eyes. He certainly hoped she would be in Canterbury tonight. In Brussels, where she had gone to pay him homage with her complaisant husband Roger Palmer, at the close of a very determined flirtation she had given him to understand that she would be his homecoming reward on his first night in the country, if he so wished.

Monck explained that, on the way to Canterbury, the Duke of Buckingham was waiting at Barham Downs with seven troops of horse, to escort the king into the cathedral city. Monck had left his own army behind in the capital: they would be paraded before the king at Blackheath by Colonel Knight on the 29th, before he at last entered London. Monck had brought his other commanders to Dover, however, and they formed part of the entourage.

Charles would be only too ready to give audience to these men in the evening, since with Monck's permission they had replied on 2 May to his Declaration to the convention parliament with a vigorous Address of compliance, declaring that he had restored 'a great measure of quiet' to their minds. The Declaration, and a letter to Monck that accompanied it, had been Charles's promise to the people of England: a general indemnity for those who had fought against the monarch; religious liberty to tender consciences; satisfaction of arrears; confirmation of sales of estates to those now in possession of them—all to be ratified by Parliament according to laws of its own enactment. The 1st of May had been the date of the House of Lords' resolution to recall Charles to the throne, and it had been at once confirmed by the Commons.

The loyal, grateful Address presented to Parliament by Monck's highest officers was the last act by which the army would ever take any participation in government. Charles could only applaud them for it.

CANTERBURY
May 25, Evening
May 26, Very early morning

Lucinda had not expected to come to Canterbury for the king's return, and neither had Maurice. These last weeks had been the busiest in her life, because at Mistress Monck's heartfelt request she was bound up in preparations for the king's procession and his accommodation at Whitehall. Maurice meanwhile had been preoccupied with the horses for the parade: he was especially proud of a dazzling white stallion on which the king would make his entry into London. But near the end of the month, Monck informed them that they were both required in Canterbury, Lucinda to oversee the private provisions for the king's comfort and Maurice to escort her there.

It had also been one of the worst months of her life, because she had not seen Mark Denton since Northampton and she had no idea when they would meet again. He had recovered from his wounds, but without her help—he accepted the ministrations of the physician that Maurice supplied but insisted on returning to his inn to make sure that no one discovered he was in town. He said he had no right to delay Maurice in his journey.

So he had left them in the room above the square, with a few words of farewell, and they had departed next morning without seeing him again. A week later, in London, she received a letter telling her he was mended—and that Monck had ordered him to the North. It was time for his militia regiment to move back to York, and he was to join it on the march, at Wellingborough. Once in Yorkshire, he was to carry out the same inspections for which he had been responsible in the south, to confirm that all army contingents and the trained bands adhered to the principles of service laid out by the commander-in-chief. He wrote: 'I am back in the saddle, riding in the opposite direction from my heart's darling. I dare to call you this in a letter, but were I with you at this moment—heavenly wish—I am terrified that you would find me as slow-tongued as ever.'

London felt alien to her now that he was gone, and every time someone mentioned the death of the Shadow, she shivered, as though she had lost him indeed. She was betrothed to a man she only half knew, and they had not had the chance to make plans for their marriage or even decide when or how to announce it. The dream of one day living with him in their native country was a castle in the air, as evanescent as Charles Stuart's dreams of England.

And yet, when she lay alone at night and relived the encounter after Arbury Hill, she knew they belonged together. One kiss, and she was his for ever.

Trying to fill the void of Mark's absence, she laboured every day for the king's return. Nan Monck was astonishing the City with her energy, utilising a crowd of drapers and tradesmen to replace and replenish hangings and furnishings in Whitehall and fill the presses with fine linen. A myriad minor tenants who had camped in the palace for years were banished and their quarters transformed in readiness for the king's household. Joining Mistress Monck in the choice and purchase of cloth, Lucinda was also drawn into the gargantuan preparations for the royal procession which was to take place in expensive splendour. She wrote to Mark:

I shall begin with the sharp end of the proceedings and soon leave off, so as not to faint under the impression of such finery. Major-General Brown is to lead the way with a troop of 300, all in cloth of silver doublets. Then 1200 velvet coats will appear, attended by footmen and liveries in purple. Alderman Luke Robinson, whom I believe you know and who is right glad to take his place in this march, heads a City troop in buff coats with cloth of silver sleeves and very rich green scarves. After these a troop of 150 in blue liveries with silver lace, along with six trumpeters and seven footmen in sea-green and silver ... The king must eventually appear in tremendous magnificence if he is to live up to his white stallion, whose mane will be braided with rank upon rank of golden tassels. I now jump a mile or more to five regiments of the army horse led by Colonel Knight—where I conceive you should rightly be. I warn you, if you are not, I shall neglect the whole spectacle and mope in my corner of Saint James's doing thread work. I love you. I hate being without you.

Whether Mark was recalled to London was entirely up to Monck. Lucinda, who had never spoken to the general or been nearer to him than the width of a room, could scarcely ask him the question. Here at Canterbury, neither she nor Maurice saw Monck at all. A rider had sped from Dover and arrived at three o'clock in the morning to tell the commander-in-chief that Charles's 20 ships had been spied in the Roads, and he had dashed at once towards the coast, in the dark—for the king had written that he would not set foot on land until Monck was there to greet him. Now, at the end of the day, they waited for hundreds of noblemen and their retainers to descend on the city, and for the king and his train to occupy their apartments in the former archbishop's palace.

Lucinda checked the appointments for the king one last time, and set off for the deanery, where she and Maurice were quartered with a city official. It was in the old monastery precincts, near the cathedral's Trinity Chapel; the former archbishops' palace was at the other end of the cathedral, before the entrance to the nave. Every building in the ancient precincts was in use. As Lucinda walked past kitchens and stables, cloisters and lodgings, people scurried about with urgent purpose, some acknowledging her with a curtsey. She admired the cathedral that loomed above them, its soaring towers drawing the eye upward to the darkening sky. At night, from her chamber window in the deanery, she could see the small tower, the Corona, which stood above the shrine to Thomas Becket.

Before the massed stone buildings where the deanery was located stretched a vast square of grass called Green Court, which had been requisitioned for the horses that could not be accommodated in the various stables. On her way across, she often saw Maurice, who had had nothing to do in Canterbury but stroll at his ease about the town and precincts by day and sup with her and the city official in the evening.

Tonight, she saw Mark Denton instead. He rode into the courtyard at the trot, halted at the end of a line of tethered horses and leaped to the ground. He was bare-headed, wearing a travelling cloak, and armed: she heard the distinctive ringing of weapons as he dismounted. The horse was not Skipton. He handed the reins to a soldier, walked away in the direction of the palace and then halted in amazement as she came to him, running.

They embraced and kissed as though no one were watching, and kissed again.

'My heart's darling,' he murmured, and laughed softly. 'What are you doing here?'

'I wrote you.'

'No you didn't. I didn't get it.'

She laughed too. 'What are *you* doing?'

'Monck sent for me to join him at Dover, for the king's landing.' He looked around the vast green, his hand on her wrist. 'Now I'm sent on ahead of him to scope the palace and surrounds. Where are you going? I must leave you here and do his bidding, damn it.'

'Maurice and I are lodged at the deanery, over there.' She pointed. *'You've seen the king?'*

'I walked the streets behind him, with the colonels, at Monck's behest. The general's nervous. I think he's haunted by the fear of some last-minute catastrophe on the way to London—plots, assassination … He's looking for trouble, and for some reason he expects me to find it before it happens.'

'Mark, this place is crawling with guards. There'll be no danger tonight. As for the king's quarters, they're in the finest trim because I've seen to that myself. That's why I'm here, also at Monck's behest, and I've more than done his bidding.' She put her hands on his chest. 'I can't believe he's put you into the firing line again.'

He pulled her into his arms. 'Never mind. If the doings at Dover are any guide, the country is in love with Charles, at least for the next week. And he's no fool; he'll keep a watchful eye out for himself.' He smiled into her eyes. 'I hope he appreciates the luxury you've prepared, my love.'

'The rooms are what the Duchess of Richmond would approve—and they're secure. You may take my word. I got the servants to open up all the priest holes and secret doors so I could see they're empty, and stop up the peepholes around the great chamber.' He looked at her doubtfully and she said, scandalised, 'It's true! It's done. I give you leave to check for yourself.'

He gave her another kiss, long and hard. 'I must go. Perhaps I'll see you later tonight at the palace, if it all goes on for hours. Or tomorrow, if Monck gives me leave.'

She watched him stride away amongst the horses, soldiers and grooms. When he disappeared she looked up at the cathedral, thanking God for this meeting. She dared not ask for more, or for blessings on the journey home, because it had not even begun.

****

It was a night of wonders, far beyond anything the enormous assembly around the king had dreamed of for so long. The king was delighted to be in Canterbury, where the acclamation in the streets almost rivalled that of Dover, despite the late hour, and the cathedral bells rang joyfully. He would attend there on both days, tomorrow and Sunday.

He was pleased with the palace and gave audience there ceaselessly once he had taken a meal at the archbishops' banqueting table. Loyal noblemen, many who had fought for him and his father—and many who had not—were permitted to crowd into the great hall and receive his notice. There were spoken requests and written petitions for favour, all of which he received with a tolerant smile.

He was expeditious: next day he would choose his Privy Council and it would meet in his presence for the first time. At the cathedral tomorrow afternoon, he would make George Monck a Knight of the Garter; the insignia would be hung around Sir George's neck by the king's brothers, the Dukes of York and Gloucester.

He was magnanimous: he asked to meet the commander-in-chief's senior officers and when the colonels made their obeisance—including even Colonel Mark Denton, once a staunch Cromwellian—he praised them for their unswerving loyalty to Monck and the impeccable comportment of their army. 'You know,' he said, 'of my promise that all who serve in England's armies will henceforth by Parliament's decree serve in the royal army.' He gave an ironical smile: 'As for your soldiers, I believe they will rejoice to have any arrears in pay made up to them forthwith.' He then looked at them solemnly and said: 'As for you, I could not ask for braver or more diligent men to serve under the royal standard.'

There was music and the presence of cultivated and beautifully dressed noblewomen, and therefore clever and happy conversation, though none of the dancing that his little court had enjoyed during the celebrations in the Hague before he set sail from the port of Scheveningen. Lucinda, introduced to the king's chancellor, Edward Hyde, learned that the king had danced at the Hague with his sister, Princess Mary of Orange, and been farewelled at the port by the Queen of Bohemia, his aunt. He had also received a mountain of costly presents, including a bed worth £7000 and linen worth £1000 more. Lucinda hoped that Anne Monck would not hear of this too soon or she would feel dreadfully outshone in her arrangements.

Maurice attended and was allowed to kneel and kiss the king's hand. He withdrew soon afterwards to make way for others, and smiled at Lucinda across the room. She knew he would not have asked any favours on this overwhelming occasion. The same quiet pride that her brother felt prevented her from making any approach herself.

Lucinda had no trouble avoiding the Duke of Buckingham, who was easily visible because of his extravagant clothing, which he wore with his usual flair. He, too, was very careful not to look at her or Maurice. Dismissing him from her mind, Lucinda thought of his sister instead. Looking across the hall at the king, she remembered the Duchess of Richmond and thought what far-reaching results had arisen from the three women's meeting in the long gallery above the Thames at Whitehall.

'Good morrow, my lady,' said a smooth, deep voice beside her. 'After midnight, and the revels continue.'

She turned. 'I've been looking for you.'

'I've been lurking elsewhere, as ordered.'

She gasped at his appearance: he was exquisitely dressed in red-and-silver brocade. 'What is this splendour?'

'Borrowed plumes. The king wishes to speak to me later, in private. I'm not looking forward to it.'

'I heard you had already seen him, with the commanders.' He did not reply; he was looking across at the king. She went on: 'What must he feel tonight? I can't help thinking that of all the things he can do now, his most poignant chance is to avenge his father's murder.'

Mark shook his head. 'His original message to Parliament was without rancour. Now he's here, I'm sure he'll punish the most guilty, and some will hang for it. But the rest he must forgive, or neither he nor the country can be at peace. As for how he feels—' He looked at her sidelong, 'I am not the most apt pupil you could have in that regard. I've been observing him for the better part of a day and I would judge him a sad man—but not a vicious or vengeful one. Will that do?'

****

George Villiers was angry—angry enough to seek solace with Sir Richard Willys, whom he would have disdained at any other time. But he could not neglect a possible ally and Sir Richard had proved himself such by fulsomely praising George to the king when the Sealed Knot was being discussed in the royal presence. This was in Sir Richard's interest, of course—he was avid to ingratiate himself in whatever way he could with Charles—but it had provided secret balm to George during the audience, because the rest of it had been a ghastly failure.

He had perhaps seen Charles at the wrong moment: no one could help being cordially disgusted by the sycophancy, cupidity and self-aggrandising lies that most of the king's so-called loyal servants had poured forth the moment they were invited to speak. George could see that Charles was almost at the end of his tether by the close of the evening, and Chancellor Hyde had remarked quietly that the king was nauseated by the most of what he heard from aspiring courtiers. But damn it, Charles still owed more than a few careless and unrewarding words to a peer of the realm who had been brought up at his side, fought valiantly for his crown and had just escorted him with pomp and ceremony to his present haven.

During the audience, Willys had tactfully failed to notice the king's lack of enthusiasm when addressing the Duke of Buckingham, and he did not refer to it now. He went on instead about how glorious the day had been and what benefits would come to the members of the Sealed Knot now that the king was free to show the liberality that he must have spent years longing to bestow on the faithful. When George glanced at him in irritation, he said: 'Forgive the overflow of my humble gratitude. I expect little reward for myself. It adds much more to my satisfaction to see those I respect and honour receive their bountiful due from His Majesty.'

George had never noticed any respect and honour emanating from Sir Richard—he was convinced Willys disliked him as much as he disliked Willys. But as long as the man professed these flattering sentiments, they might be put to use. The other members of the Sealed Knot could do no good for George just now because they would all be busy promoting their own fortunes with the king. Willys, however, being of a lower rank, could never aim so high. His best bet would be to attach himself to a prominent earl—or duke—and see how far he could get by lending support to his betters.

'Your estates are not confiscate?' George said, trying to sound as though he cared.

'No,' said Willys. 'I am fortunate there, but not in my purse. My losses since the beginning of the war have been enormous—the expenses of exile and service to the king here and abroad have told mightily on us all.'

'And you have borne it faithfully,' George said, ignoring the 'us' and putting a modicum of approval into his voice. He leaned forward and his tone became businesslike. If money was the object next to Willys's heart, they had something to say to each other. 'I may tell you that my estates at the time when they were stolen from me furnished an income of £30,000 a year.'

Sir Richard blanched at this. George had never worn his wealth with any understatement but he knew Willys could not have guessed anything like its stupendous extent.

George went on: 'The value of the lands and properties themselves is of course incalculable, including as they do York House, Wallingford House ...' He waved a heavily jewelled hand. 'Such are the sacrifices I have been prepared to make for His Majesty—along with my sword and my life. Now'—he adopted a tone of lofty resignation—'not even the noblest families can hope for, let alone demand, restitution of estates in the short term. That will depend not just on His Majesty's decisions but on Parliament's. You will have noticed tonight that I let such subjects go by—the king has been importuned enough by the crowd; he scarcely expects like behaviour from his intimates.'

There was a slight change in Sir Richard's obsequious expression, as though he had begun to suspect where the duke was leading. He said cautiously: 'What you apprehend is very true: most of His Majesty's favours will take time to bestow. But some he will confer much sooner—tomorrow, in fact.'

'Yes. Knighthood of the Garter for Monck, and membership of the Privy Council for a fortunate few.' So that they could talk privately, he had invited Willys to his apartments—a decided first. He looked around for a servant, remembered that he had sent them all out of the chamber, and actually poured the man a glass of wine himself. 'The haste of it is remarkable—the very day after His Majesty's arrival! However, there is no escape from it: Monck is to be ridiculously aggrandised and the members of the Privy Council named and assembled.'

Sir Richard said smoothly: 'Am I to congratulate you, Your Grace, on being chosen as a Privy Councillor?'

George shook his head. 'That is not confirmed. But I intend it to be, tonight. The king has retired from the great hall but not to bed—I happen to know he is readying himself for a meeting of another kind ... If I send him a message asking him to allow me into his presence, with the promise that I have valuable information, I believe he will see me. I shall deliver the information—or rather, you will—and when alone with him afterwards, I shall broach the subject of the Privy Council. I must be on it.'

'Information?' Sir Richard breathed. 'Of course I shall be honoured—unutterably privileged—to accompany you, and if there is anything I can say on your behalf, you have my full—'

'On *my* behalf!' George gritted his teeth. 'You will refrain from any such thing, thank you. Your only subject is the Sealed Knot. His Majesty showed great interest in it this evening, as well he might. You are a member, not I, and I wish you to tell His Majesty something that he deserves to know—the name of the gentleman who betrayed the King's Shadow's meeting to Parliament in February.'

Willys's innards turned to ice. 'Why should I know it?' he stammered.

'Why not? You all got the verbal message I sent before I left London. I arrived at Coldfall Wood early—thank God, for there was a troop of parliamentary horse waiting for me and the Shadow. I left quietly and so it seems did he, without our seeing each other. Only someone in the Sealed Knot could have let Parliament know about the rendezvous.' George tapped the table with a forefinger. 'It's time you worked it out and named the traitor. Apart from anything else, Sir Richard, it will make one less gentleman shoving you out of the way and fawning all over the king in front of you. Do you really have no idea?'

Willys searched the duke's expression. He felt sick. Was Buckingham toying with him? Was he about to lead him to the king like a lamb to the slaughter? Or was he doing just as he hinted: sweeping a fellow aristocrat out of the king's favour to reap benefits for himself ...?

Of whom was Buckingham most jealous in the Sealed Knot? Who was likely to be named to the Privy Council before him? Belasyse, perhaps, or William Compton, brother to the Earl of Northampton? But it was no good accusing them—the king would never believe them anything less than loyal.

Buckingham solved this question for him. 'We cannot suspect either Baron Belasyse or Northampton.' Willys felt pitiably grateful for the 'we'. 'And it goes without saying that I cannot doubt my cousin Edward.'

'That leaves Lords Loughborough, Bedford and ...' His voice trailed away. He really felt hideously unwell.

'And yourself!' George leaned back with a hearty laugh. He was cheered all at once by the man's stupidity. For heaven's sake, he would scarcely treat him to a conversation like this if he thought him guilty. Whichever member of the Knot had provided the means to set the trap at Coldfall Wood was not a man of Willys's type—he was a cool schemer with a grudge against the Shadow. Or, more likely, a grudge against himself—and he had tried to use the meeting with the Shadow to get the Duke of Buckingham slammed in the Tower again.

Willys did not look within a mile of making up his mind about whom to denounce. George said smoothly: 'If I can help at all, Sir Richard, my own thoughts tend towards the Earl of Bedford. He's of a sly, envious disposition that has always made me uneasy. And he may well harbour an old, secret allegiance to Parliament. His whole family were solidly for Parliament until well into the war. Many a gentleman who crossed to the king regretted it later, through sheer cowardice, or dismay in the face of defeat. If Bedford secretly looked to Parliament for succour, he would have had to supply them with detail about the Sealed Knot in return. Hence the diabolical trap for the Shadow that almost caught me as well.' He leaned forward. 'If you are ready to let His Majesty know that in your opinion the Earl of Bedford should be investigated, then I feel it my duty to bring you to him. Once you have had your say, you may leave the matter in His Majesty's hands. You will earn his gratitude—and mine, since you are giving me the chance to be of signal service to His Majesty.'

Willys took a gulp of wine and consented. He had no choice.

George relaxed and explained the details of the arrangement—but he did not give them all. His unprofitable time with the king tonight had convinced him that a personal note from him at this hour would get no response from Charles, let alone a private audience. He had decided instead on the simple expedient of a word or two from Barbara Villiers, asking His Majesty the favour of meeting her in private.

Barbara had promised Charles a tryst tonight and confirmed it with him earlier, during the happiest part of the evening, but at the end of it George had come across her in floods of tears and about to depart. She had discovered that she was ill—and by the complicated way she phrased it he knew she was in that injurious time of the month when trysts with anyone at all were out of the question. Her intricately balanced plans had shattered before her eyes, and she was normally such a pert and practised little thing that her distress seemed all the more tragic—George felt genuinely sorry for her. He promised to make her apologies to the king with the most delicate and solicitous tact, and sent her to her lodgings with her husband so no one else should see her pretty eyes rimmed with red.

He had of course said nothing about her to the king, who would be awaiting word from her with some impatience. George knew just how to speak of her regrets and desires to Charles, who would be grateful for his discretion, surely. George would use this gratitude, and Sir Richard's accusation of Bedford, as springboards to his selection to the Privy Council. It was scandalous that he should have to go to all this trouble for a privilege that was his by right—but that was a sign of these uncomfortable times.

****

The king, when Mark was at last summoned to see him, was in a dark mood. He was still splendidly dressed but looked ruffled, as though his time alone since the celebrations had made him restless. The deliberate affability of his demeanour among company had disappeared and he addressed Mark with military exactitude.

'I have heard the woes and tribulations of a thousand gentlemen tonight, all hoping that my return to the throne will resurrect their fortunes. I have not heard yours. I have received a thousand protestations of loyalty and love for the monarch. I have not received yours. I have been given this evening by General Monck a list of persons whom he considers the best to serve me on the Privy Council. Your name is not on it. For these deficiencies, and for the fact that you are by reputation the most rigorous parliamentarian who has ever served in the general's army, I have called you here to give me some frank advice.'

Mark knelt. Whether this was castigation or approval, it seemed the right thing to do. 'Your Majesty. On what do you wish my advice?'

'Rise, colonel. On General Monck's intentions. I gather the country has this year with difficulty made them out. I find myself in the same case.' He went to a table and took up two sheets of paper. 'There are 73 names on this list—73! He handed it to me tonight without preamble or apology and recommended every one of these gentlemen to my notice. I put it in my pocket and said I would always be ready to receive his advice and willing to gratify him in anything he may desire that is not prejudicial to the service he renders me.' He fixed Mark with a saturnine look. 'I am relying on you for an honest answer. What does he mean by it?'

Mark thought fast. 'What is your opinion of the list itself, Your Majesty?'

'My opinion of the gentlemen on it? I know hardly any of them! And of those I do know, only two—two!—have served me in the field.'

'With your leave, what did General Monck say when he handed these names to you?'

'His words were bluntly given. I was not so satisfied with his manner as to recall them.'

'He is not a man of graceful elocution, certainly,' Mark said, and drew the first semblance of a smile from the king. 'Will you allow me to glance at the list, Your Majesty?' The king handed it across and Mark scanned it quickly. 'These are people from all over the country,' he murmured. 'They are not in order of rank or influence, and I think I recognise the hand that wrote them down—that of the general's clerk and chaplain, John Price. They may have been assembled from correspondence, or the general's notes.'

'Hastily got up, then. On that basis, he can hardly expect me to consider any of these gentlemen as Privy Councillors.'

Mark made up his mind and handed it back. 'No, indeed. In my judgment, that was never his intention. These persons have obviously done him real service over the last months and begged him to bring their names to Your Majesty's notice—not for any specific favour, merely so that you should be told of them. Having promised to do so, he has kept his word by handing Your Majesty the list. If it remains in your pocket, his pledge is none the less fulfilled, and he nonetheless satisfied that he has done his duty.'

The king looked Mark hard in the eye. 'In all conscience, that is your interpretation?'

'Yes, Your Majesty. A simple remedy is to ask the general yourself, at a moment convenient to you. He is a plain speaker in these matters.'

The king folded the papers and put them in his pocket. He then walked a few paces away from Mark and turned back to examine him. In quite unembarrassed fashion, he observed him from top to toe, a curious smile on his face.

'The general also told me that you have impersonated your monarch on several occasions, all of them extremely dangerous to yourself. You have not asked for my commendation on this. Very wise.'

Mark cursed Monck inwardly. 'There was no attempt at impersonation, Your Majesty. The regrettable sobriquet was bestowed on me by rumour and was beyond my power to change.'

'Because of the supposed resemblance?' the king said, staring at Mark's face. 'The height, the limbs, I concede. With a wig and mask …' He shook his head slightly. 'But your eyes are darker, and my nose is fatter and longer. When I look in a glass, I see no Adonis.'

'No one has ever accused me of being a handsome man, Your Majesty.'

The king burst out laughing and his brown eyes flashed. 'The general told me I might find a use for you on the way to London—your ingenuity should not go to waste.' He caught Mark's expression and said: 'However, he also told me how creditably you have served as his colonel, which impresses me the more. Meanwhile'—he strolled thoughtfully to the table—'I should like your advice on another document that has just been delivered to me.'

****

It was no wonder that, all over Canterbury that night, there were candles flickering and people astir long after its citizens would normally have been abed and asleep. The miracle had happened: the King of

England was spending the first night of his return to his kingdom, acclaimed, protected and in their city.

His actual safety tonight depended, of course, on the military vigilance around the cathedral and the old monastery precincts, where there was much movement because of the travellers and retainers housed within the walls. The guards set to keep watch through the night were not only lectured on their duty by their officers—they were jolted into alertness many times by Colonel Denton, who seemed to have decided not to sleep this night but instead to prowl the grounds, in and out of the shadows like a lean ghost.

At two in the morning, the sentries at a side door to the archbishops' palace were surprised to hear the bolts being drawn back inside. Onto the threshold stepped an instantly recognisable figure who said not a word to them, but walked out onto the path and strode off towards the cathedral. The men came to attention with a clatter of arms and looked at each other in alarm, wondering whether they should follow him. But he extended a long-fingered hand behind him and waved them back to their post before disappearing around a corner.

The guards at the entrance to the nave had a similar reaction to the sight of their king walking towards them. When he was by the palace, lights from the downstairs windows, where cooks and kitchen hands were toiling for tomorrow's meals, had shown him his way. As he came up the steps to the nave, torches in high sconces on each side of the doors shed flickering light around him. He was dressed as he had been on his journey that day, even to the wide-brimmed hat decorated with glossy red plumes.

He spoke to these sentries, demanding one of the torches and telling them to stay on guard while he was inside the cathedral and admit anyone else who sought to enter, be they lady or gentleman. However, the guards were to ask the names first and, if they were not satisfied, one was to leave the post and escort them to his presence.

Then he swept off the hat and walked into the cathedral.

At night, with the faint light of the stars making grey shapes of the tall windows, it had an eerie grandeur. The shadowed ranks of its columns and the immensely high vaulting above had a powerful beauty that masked the neglected state of the building. He was glad to miss the dilapidation that would become obvious in the light of day.

He held the torch high, taking care that no wax descended onto the lace at his cuff, and candelabras flared in answer at the far end of the nave, before the choir screen, where the holy cross should be. The guards there had come to attention, in the same comical doubt as the others. They were armed with swords, pistols and carbines. If he could see them so clearly, they could identify him without fail.

He called: 'Remain at your post!' His voice rolled impressively between the massive columns and up into the dark vaulting. Then he paced towards them, perversely relishing the bizarre dignity of this lone parade. When he drew level with them, without a word he bore to the right, across the empty transept to the chapel of Saint Michael. Its iron gates were not locked and they yielded with a screech across the uneven pavement.

The chapel held the tomb of a wife of the Black Prince, which had not been defaced, as far as he could tell, and a few alabaster statues, which had. The great stained-glass window was damaged in places. On each side of the altar were sconces, into one of which he thrust the butt of the torch. Then he leaned a booted thigh against the altar rail and waited.

He did not have to wait long. He could hear a visitor being admitted into the nave, and then footsteps approaching towards the transept. There were two people coming, both men. His anticipation flared. If they were armed, despite the alertness of the guards, this could be interesting.

When the Duke of Buckingham and the gentleman at his side stepped through the open gates of Saint Michael's chapel, they saw at once the tall, dark figure looming in front of the altar and fell to their knees with heads bowed.

There was a long silence. The lack of response from the king had a daunting effect; nonetheless, the duke raised a dutiful face and opened his mouth to explain the purpose of the rendezvous.

In the silence, the figure before the altar did not move, but a flare from the torch suddenly lit up the side of the face and highlighted the aquiline nose and strongly sculpted mouth.

'Denton!' the duke said in a fury and leaped to his feet. 'How the fuck do you come here?'

'If I'd known it was you taking the lady's place I wouldn't have come at all. Who is this?' he said in the same cold voice as Willys struggled to his feet in disarray.

When the duke said nothing, Willys gave his name, added the date of his knighthood by Charles I, and launched into a long recital of his service to the monarchy until the icy silence around him made his voice stutter to a standstill.

Denton said to Buckingham: 'Forging a note from a lady and sending it to your king, entering his presence by subterfuge, luring him defenceless here—His Majesty may name all this treason when he calls you to account.'

'I meant no danger. I'm not armed!' Buckingham grabbed Willys's shoulder, spun him towards the open gates and stepped away. 'And neither is he.'

'But I am.' Out of the corner of his eye, the duke saw Denton pull a pistol from the top of his thigh boot and cock it. 'Come back here, gentlemen, and explain. What was it going to be: kidnap, coercion or *lèse majesté*?'

The duke whirled around. 'If that little slut has slandered me to the king—!'

'Careful what you say,' Denton said quickly. 'I don't know her name and the king doesn't wish me to know it. He said she was minded to give him a meeting tonight, but he told her it would be more prudent to save that for London. Having put her off, he was surprised later to receive a note inviting him here. He was naturally disinclined to credit that it came from her. Why did you send it?'

'To obtain a private audience,' the duke said sullenly.

'Your reasons?'

'I'll tell them to the king, not to you, you dog!'

Denton's dark grey eyes narrowed. 'What was your theme, to bring you here with such haste? The Privy Council?' The curves of his unsmiling mouth were contemptuous. 'Well, you've scotched your chances of that.' The eyes turned to Willys. 'And you?'

'The Sealed Knot.' Willys tried to say it stoutly but there was a quaver in his voice.

'For God's sake,' the duke said, 'shut your damned mouth.'

But Willys, who had never met Denton in his life, and was totally unaware of the dire encounter between the two men at Coldfall Wood, saw between them only the enmity of two bitter rivals for the king's favour. He did not see why it must extend to himself. 'I'm here to lay a piece of information before His Majesty. There is something he should know, about a member of the Sealed Knot.'

'Not now, you stupid whoreson,' the duke snarled, and shouldered him across the chapel so that he crashed against the wall. Willys lifted his hands to pry the duke's from around his neck.

Denton was upon them in a second, the barrel of his pistol against Buckingham's chest. 'Back off.' When there was sufficient distance between the two, he kept the pistol trained on the duke and said to Willys: 'Continue.'

Willys squeaked: 'In February, the King's Shadow asked for a rendezvous with the Sealed Knot, in the north of London.' He coughed and tried to bring his voice under control. 'One of our members must have betrayed this to Parliament because a troop of cavalry was sent there to capture him.'

'Yes. Mine.'

Willys looked at him as if the world had just shifted on its axis. '*You* were sent?'

'On a wild-goose chase.' Denton examined Willys with such steely thoroughness that it was almost as though he had forgotten about the duke, though the hand holding the pistol did not waver. 'Didn't Thurloe express any disappointment to you about that? Or name me? Your communication with the former Secretary seems to have been somewhat one-sided, Sir Richard.'

'This is absurd,' the duke snapped. 'The traitor to the Sealed Knot is the Earl of Bedford. We came here tonight to tell His Majesty.'

Denton shook his head and murmured: 'Let's hear the truth instead.' He strolled back to his former position by the altar rail, still so in command that the others did not think to move. He uncocked the pistol and rested it along the flat top of the rail, the barrel pointing in their direction. 'Not long ago, Mistress Monck was supervising the restoration of John Thurloe's bureau in Whitehall—after he had moved out of it, of course. She found some papers that he had unwisely overlooked, and handed them to her husband, who handed them to me with orders to decipher them. I did so and you are perfectly correct, Sir Richard: they were notes from a gentleman about the Sealed Knot. They did not include the one about the Shadow—by their content they seem to be older, going back several years.'

'Who the hell wrote them?' Buckingham demanded, looking daggers at Willys.

'They were all signed with two words in a different cypher that I could not crack. I am no scholar, so I enlisted the help of Colonel Knight, who discovered that they were encoded from the Latin—from Virgil, he thinks. *Debellare superbos.* "To subdue the arrogant." Your Grace, if you stand close enough to Sir Richard Willys and observe the large ring he wears on his left middle finger, even in this light you will see those words engraved upon it.'

Willys ran, then, and neither tried to stop him. There was the thunder of his boots across the flagstones, then shouts, the warning sound of gunfire among the graceful stone columns, a scuffle far off in the nave. Sir Richard's voice, desperately pleading, faded into the distance.

The two men in Saint Michael's chapel did not move or speak. They were locked in a mutual gaze of anger and loathing so deep it was as though neither could ever surface from it.

Finally the duke closed his eyes as the torch behind his enemy's head began to gutter. 'What will you say to His Majesty?'

'That I exposed tonight a traitor and a fool.'

The duke, who was no fool and considered himself far from a traitor, kept his eyes closed and allowed the moment to pass. His future beckoned with as much lustre as it had had before and in London he would seize it with both hands.

Denton slid the pistol into his boot and walked past Buckingham, through the chapel gates and into the shadows beyond.

LONDON
May 29

Lucinda was with Maurice in a hired coach, outside a mercer's shop in Fenchurch Street, East Cheap. It was the day of the king's entry into London, and in a few hours, by the kindness of Ralph Knight, they would watch the royal parade from the balcony of a handsome house at Charing Cross.

'It's a little late to be buying cloth, Luce. There can't be a shred more of silver lace in all London.'

'It's not for the parade, it's for me. I saw a green sarcenet here a month ago and I wish I'd bought it on the spot. I hope she has some left.'

'She?' Maurice looked at the sign hanging above the street. 'It says Christopher Hull.'

'That was her father-in-law, an alderman until he died. She runs the business as he did—in fact even better, I rather suspect. She's such a determined body, I'm in awe of her.' She smiled at him teasingly. 'Won't you come in, and lend me the courage to deal with her?'

'No! I'd rather sit here and look at all this. Do you know, coming through the streets just now, I realise this is what I've been fighting for, all along?'

'What, shopping?'

He laughed and gestured out the coach window. 'This, across the whole nation—people going about their business in peace.' He shifted on the cushion so that he was facing her. 'You see, I thought I was fighting for you and me, for Selby, for Father's memory. I daresay I said I was fighting for the king—'

'And you were!'

'True. But not for him personally. I know now, it was for England.' With a thumb over his shoulder, he gestured back down the street. 'We just passed the White Hart. When I supped there with Luke Robinson in February, with people milling about everywhere, I felt more satisfaction than I did when I kissed the king's hand in Canterbury.' He looked at her keenly. 'Do you know what I mean? I think you do: you never approached him when you had every chance.'

She avoided this with a question. 'You don't mind not being in the parade?'

'No. Knight promised to find me a place but I turned it down. I'd rather witness it than be in it.'

She nodded. 'And I shall be happier to hear tell of the banquet than to share it.'

She and Maurice had been asked to the great feast prepared for the king on his arrival at Whitehall in the evening, which was to be at the Banqueting House. Lucinda had never seen this beautiful building and had no wish to—because it was outside it that Cromwell and parliament had had Charles I beheaded.

'How cruel for the king, to be feasting at the place where they killed his father. I don't think I could bear to sit and watch him do it.' She gave Maurice a troubled smile. 'But if you want to go, don't let me stand in your way.'

He grinned. 'I'll try hard not to let you do that. Go in and leave me to admire Fenchurch Street. If you're too long, I'll be at the White Hart.'

She alighted and went into the shop. The mercer, the widow Alice Hull, had been recommended to the Duchess of Richmond by the tailor, Dorothy Cresswell. She kept a superb stock of English cloth on her premises and was an expert at obtaining luxury imported fabrics. Being a woman, she was barred from being a member of any guild and she had no influence amongst the livery companies, yet she owned her shop and the dwellings above and beside it, and traded as a man would have done, keeping her own accounts, even getting official permission to have her son apprenticed to her.

Lucinda had no sooner stepped inside than Alice Hull approached, walking between the sumptuous displays in her skilfully ordered establishment. A tiny, very fair woman with an exceptionally pretty face, she did not look old enough to be the mother of the lad of 15 who bowed to Lucinda and waited in the background to do their bidding.

'Your ladyship.' Alice Hull gave a graceful curtsey. 'What service may I do you today?' She had a quiet confidence and a steady blue gaze that had disconcerted Lucinda from the beginning, even in the breezy company of Mary Villiers. There was nothing but polite respect in the mercer's demeanour, but at the same time Lucinda had the uneasy feeling that she had been judged and found wanting—made worse by the fact that she had no idea why. Was Mistress Hull a Puritan, who found her constant quest for luxury goods contemptible? If so, it ill became her to sell them ...

'I'm come to look at your sarcenets again. I remember a green that pleased me.'

'Ah yes, the sea green. This way, my lady.' The little mercer showed her to a table spread with partly unrolled bolts in a rainbow of colours. She lifted a corner of one shimmering piece of sarcenet and let it drift across Lucinda's outstretched hand. Admiring it, she said in a wistful, almost melancholy tone that Lucinda had not heard before: 'There will be an ocean of sea green in the procession today. It's the colour of loyalty and thereby a fitting colour for you, my lady. It was also that of Thomas Rainsborough and the Levellers.'

Lucinda understood, then, at once. What she had seen as a personal antagonism was simply the recognition of a political divide. Alice Hull knew she was a royalist. She now knew Alice Hull was a republican.

'Forgive my asking, but … your husband … he fought for the Good Old Cause?'

'And died for it.' Alice Hull let the cloth fall. 'In faith, I lost two men to the war.' With fingers and thumb of her right hand she briefly touched the rings on her left—a plain wedding band, and a lapis-lazuli ring with two hoops of gold. She lifted her gaze to Lucinda and there was now nothing in it but compassion. 'When you love a soldier, there is much to forgive. If love does not put forgiveness in your heart, my lady, best not dare to put your hand in his.'

Lucinda caught her breath. 'I do love a soldier. Are you telling me he's going to die?'

'No!' Alice Hull laid both hands on Lucinda's arm. 'Your pardon—no. Sometimes, when I wear this ring, in memory …' She released Lucinda and smoothed the sarcenet, looking down at it sadly. 'Sometimes I glimpse things about people. You are in love with a man who is very strong, and very troubled. You are troubled too. But love has brought you together. You must trust in that love.'

'I do,' Lucinda said. It was as though speaking the truth gave her new courage. 'Do you … do you see anything of my future?'

Alice Hull lifted her face and smiled. She looked at once tolerant and amused—and there was kindness, too, in her gaze. 'I do see you, on high ground somewhere. You're alone, riding a great grey horse. Make of that what you will—it's all a mystery to me.'

****

Later, Lucinda and Maurice stood on the little balcony in Charing Cross and watched the king go by. There were bright hangings and tapestries on the railings and window sills all around the Cross, where men and women leaned, crying out so that their voices mingled with the bells. There were flowers strewn in the dust below and crowds cheering the brilliant cavalcade. London was decorated from top to toe; trumpets sounded from the procession and music from halls with windows wide open to the street. Every hostelry was hung with foliage and blooms and the Venetian ambassador supplied a fountain that ran with wine all day.

George Monck rode in advance of the king and received the hysterical acclaim of the populace. Directly before the king rode his brother Henry, brandishing a sword in symbolic protection of the monarch. At the beginning of the march, the mayor of London had handed Charles the Sword of the City of London, which he had graciously handed back. He had then ridden through Southwark and across London Bridge to the most deafening welcome the city had ever afforded. Wherever the king passed on his winding route, the crowds who had waited for hours and who would throng there for hours more raised their voices so rapturously that they competed even with the bells and trumpets.

At Charing Cross, it was the same. Lucinda and Maurice watched the focus of the tumult ride by—tall, rigid and solemn on the magnificent white stallion—and took in the incredible sight in silence. The army that had opposed their king for almost 20 years was escorting him in joy and fealty to Westminster, on his 30th birthday.

The cavalry regiments brought up the rear, led by the colonels. Lucinda had eyes for only one of them. He rode a shining chestnut and wore a black hat with plumes. He spied her as he rode by, raised the hat and waved it. She blew him kisses. Maurice frowned at her, then laughed.

When the parade had passed on, she and Maurice could have withdrawn into the chamber to take the refreshments that Knight had supplied, but they lingered above the crowd.

'What a wonder,' she said. 'If I have children, when I tell them about this, it will seem like a fireside tale—as flimsy as silver tissue.' She watched the people below. 'I asked Alice Hull if she were going to see the king and she told me she would take her children to London Bridge this morning to watch him cross. I was surprised, for she's a republican. But she said: "I'm a Londoner; and when London and the king are of a mind, England is on the right road."'

'If she's a republican,' Maurice said, 'I doubt she'd think much of the new parliament.'

'I asked her that, too, and she said: "I approve this parliament. But not the way it was elected." She believes in one man, one vote. And she told me that one day in the far, far distant future it will be one woman, one vote.'

'And you believe her?' Maurice laughed. 'What a bizarre conversation!'

'Maurice,' she said, 'what women think is the stuff of history.' She pointed to the crowds that were cheering the king all the way to Westminster. 'If Englishwomen had not believed in this, it would never have happened.'

****

Later still, Mark Denton joined them. He was supposed to have attended the banquet with Monck and the rest, but as far as he was concerned his duties were over.

When Lucinda greeted him, she made no bones about kissing him passionately, and he wished the brother a thousand miles away. But he collected himself and sat at the table with them while she pressed him with wine.

'You're missing the banquet—why?'

'I've no place there. I've handed in my commission to Monck.'

'You're leaving the army?' Maurice Selby said in astonishment.

'Yes. As soon as I've consigned my regiment to Monck's new appointment. I leave for York tomorrow.'

Lucinda was stung. 'You gave me no notice of this!'

'How could I? I made the decision this morning. As a matter of fact, I was hoping you'd both consent to travel home with me.'

Maurice said with sarcasm: 'I might, if I had a home to go to.'

Mark said in a level tone: 'On the way here, at Rochester, the king asked me if there were any reasonable favour he might grant me. I asked him if you could take over Selby from my brothers and live there until parliament grants it back to you by law. He agreed. You have the king's word, and mine, that Selby is yours, whenever you want to resume it.'

Maurice stood up. For a moment he could not speak; there were tears in his eyes. Then he did something that brought Lucinda to sudden tears as well. He leaned down, placed a hand on her shoulder and said: 'Dear sister, you will be married from home.'

With his other hand, he reached across the table to shake Mark's. 'Thank you. Can you give us one more day to prepare for the journey? I have some concerns about the coach horses.'

****

Later again, Lucinda and Mark were alone on the balcony. Lucinda had brought the festive hangings inside and hung them over chairs in case dew fell in the darkness, but the air was soft and balmy. The Cross was lit by bonfires and figures danced in silhouette around the flames.

Mark put his arm around her and kissed her temple. 'Before you marry me, you must know all my secrets. I have a confession. At Rochester I ruined your chances with the king.'

She decided he was joking. 'What have you done?'

'He must have glimpsed me with you in the great hall in Canterbury. He certainly saw you! He said to me that he had heard much about the Lady Lucinda Selby, from the Duchess of Richmond. Chancellor Hyde had also told him about the author of the furnishings at the archbishops' palace. He asked me if Lady Lucinda was the dark-haired beauty I had spoken to in the great hall. I replied that you were.' He tightened his arm. 'His Majesty said that it would be a pleasure for him to receive you when he reached London.'

Lucinda turned to look at his face, but he was gazing into the throng below. 'And what did you reply?'

'Nothing. I bowed and said not a word. He waited for quite some time and then he laughed at me. In perfect good humour—he doesn't mind in the least to be considered a damned Lothario.' Mark pulled Lucinda to him and said into her hair: 'He knew I was jealous. I always have been. He forgave me. Do you?'

She put her arms around his neck. 'I don't need anything from him. I have everything I want—the shadow and the substance. I have you.'

'Then God save the king,' he said, and kissed her.

Historical Note

I am intrigued that, when it comes to this trilogy, readers show as much interest in the future of my characters as in the real historical world they inhabited, so I'll begin with the destiny of Mark Denton and Lucinda Selby, who are of course fictional. Not long after they married and moved to Lang Scar, Mark was knighted by Charles II and yielded to other people's view that he should stand for Parliament. He was elected in 1661 when the Convention Parliament was successfully returned. He took his responsibilities seriously and was often absent from his Yorkshire estates but Lucinda, the real farmer of the two, managed Lang Scar with flair. They had three children and a long life together. Lucinda got on well with her in-laws, although Mark's mother, Helen Denton, sometimes wondered whether Lucinda fostered too strong a spirit of independence in her children.

I have faithfully recorded George Monck's progress down England and his notorious reticence about his intentions. Historians will always disagree about his true reasons for crossing the border from Coldstream (the village which later gave its name to the Coldstream Guards) on New Year's Day 1660. High office and many honours were bestowed on Monck, who was created First Duke of Albemarle. He continued to serve the monarchy on land and sea, died in 1670 (the same year as his wife, Anne) and is buried in Westminster Abbey.

After Charles II came to the throne, Mary Villiers, Duchess of Richmond and Lennox, returned to England with Queen Henrietta-Maria, who took up residence in Somerset House. Mary's children were Esmé, born in 1649, who became Fifth Duke of Richmond and Lennox but died in 1660, and Mary, Baroness Clifton de Leighton Bromswold (1651-1668). The duchess took up her former place at court, where she continued to exercise her wit and talents, often in a satirical vein, and is believed to have been the pseudonymous poet, Ephelia, whose dramatic poems of love and biting social comment were first published in 1678. Scholar Maureen E. Mulvihill is credited with making the case for Mary Villiers's authorship and for restoring these poems to the canon of 17th-century English poetry.

Mary Villiers married a third time in secret in 1664, her husband being Colonel Thomas Howard, a Roman Catholic. She herself converted, dying a Catholic in 1685, at the age of 63. She is buried in Westminster Abbey.

George Villiers, Second Duke of Buckingham, had a dazzling and unscrupulous career that is not incongruent with his (mainly fictional) exploits in this novel. He was admitted to the Privy Council in 1662 and held high office in ministries thereafter. However, his political manoeuvrings and personal scandals, too numerous to describe here, led to another stint in the Tower and several lapses from power—though when he retired to Helmsley, Yorkshire, in 1684 he was in favour with Charles II. He died in 1687 from a chill caught while hunting and is buried in Westminster Abbey. He left no legitimate children and the title became extinct.

In addition to becoming Member of Parliament for Morpeth, Ralph Knight was knighted by the king in 1660. He purchased the manor of Lethwell in Yorkshire in 1662 and the manor of Warsop in Nottinghamshire in 1675. He died in 1691 and is buried in Firbeck.

John Lambert spent the rest of his life in prison, first in the Tower, then on Guernsey and on Drake's Island in Plymouth Sound. He petitioned the king for release and his wife Frances was permitted to visit him, but after her death in 1676 he lost his reason. He died in 1684 and was buried at St Andrew's Church in Plymouth. His gravesite can no longer be found.

A note on Sir Richard Willys and his betrayal of the Sealed Knot is included after the end of *Farewell, Cavaliers*, the second novel in this trilogy. I took the liberty of having Willys arrested in Canterbury; I may indeed have taken another liberty by lodging Charles II in the archbishops' palace, though the dates and other details of his stay in the cathedral city are accurate.

Thomas Scot was executed in October 1660 for his part in the regicide of Charles I. Among his last words were: 'I say again, to the praise of the free grace of God, I bless His name. He hath engaged me in a cause not to be repented of—I say, not to be repented of.'

Luke Robinson was re-elected to the Convention Parliament as member for Scarborough. He went over to the royal cause, apparently 'bathed in tears', on the reading in the House of Commons of the king's

Declaration of Breda on 1 May 1660. In June 1660 he was however expelled from the House and retired from public life. He died in 1669.

With the exception of letters by Mark Denton, George Villiers and Mary Villiers, all quotes from documents are from the originals. The wording of Edward Bowles's sermon in York Minster is invented but both he and Hugh Peters spoke at the times and places specified, and Peters did take Psalm 107 as his text.

Acknowledgments

I am very grateful to my husband, Bert Hingley, and to generous and knowledgeable friends, especially Rosemary Allen, Mary Morel and Peter Spencer, for reading the manuscripts of this trilogy and giving advice on the treatment of characters and events.

The research for this novel was wide but I include a small selection here. For my purposes, the most useful works on George Monck were *Honest George Monck* by J.D. Griffith Davies (The Bodley Head, 1936) and *General Monck* by Maurice Ashley (Jonathan Cape, 1977). *The Restoration of Charles II* by Godfrey Davies (OUP, 1955) helped me understand the king's time in exile and Derek Wilson's *All the King's Women* (Hutchinson, 2003), threw interesting light on Barbara Villiers. Once again, for meticulous pictures of the times I turned to Austin Woolrych's monumental *Britain in Revolution* (OUP, 2002) and Robert Brenner's *Merchants and Revolution* (Verso, 2003).

The Author

Cheryl Sawyer (the author's maiden name) was born in Wellington, New Zealand, and grew up in Cambridge and Auckland. She has two master's degrees with honours in English and French literature and has lived and worked for some time in England, Italy and France. Research for her trilogy, 'Terror and Awe: England's Revolution', took her around the battlefields of the Civil War in 2005, where she stood at Naseby in the anniversary month of that crucial battle, 360 years before.

While the greater part of her career has been in publishing, her past experience is eclectic. She has been a bartender in Essex; temporary governess to two bright little girls at the Château de Breteuil, southwest of Paris; teacher of English in France and Italy; freelance editor of *The Bone People* by Keri Hulme, winner of the 1985 Booker Prize in the UK; translator of journals by 18th-century French explorers in the Pacific; food and wine writer for *Better Business* magazine in New Zealand; guest speaker at a writers' conference in Reno, Nevada; and, for eight years, opera reviewer for the *Australian Jewish News*.

Her books have been longlisted for awards by the Historical Novel Society (UK) and the American Library in Paris. She now writes full-time and maintains a blog on www.cherylsawyer.com.

Also published by Endeavour Press

The Winter Prince, the first volume in this trilogy, begins in 1642 as a royal duchess and Charles I's nephew, Prince Rupert, fight to save England from the nightmare of civil war. 'A lyrical historical novel ... This is an elegantly written tale layered with meticulous historical detail and highly complex emotions. Beautiful and moving.' Barbara Samuel, BookPage

Farewell, Cavaliers, the second volume in this trilogy, is set in 1652, as Oliver Cromwell tightens his hold over England and his avenger stalks the streets of London. 'A compelling read. I explored a London I never knew existed, full of amazing characters. The scenes in the House of Commons gave a vivid idea of what political power-play was really like during England's revolution ... scary.' Mary, Amazon.com

The Code of Love, the first novel in 'Spying for Napoleon', stages the private battles between an English naval officer and a patriotic Frenchwoman in the midst of the Peninsular War. 'I could not put this book down! Cheryl Sawyer truly makes Gideon and Delphine come alive within the pages. I love the backdrop of the Napoleon story and the excitement of the spy plot.' Arabella Stratton, Amazon.com

The Chase, the second novel in 'Spying for Napoleon', begins with Lady Sophia Hamilton and the enigmatic chasseur, Jacques Decernay, in London on the first of March 1815. It ends at the Battle of Waterloo. 'Fine suspense starring an intrepid heroine ... a tense historical intrigue.' Best Reviews

La Créole is the story of a slave who escapes from Martinique in the middle of the eighteenth century and goes to France, vowing to free her people and take revenge against her Master. 'A magnificent book! This is a bittersweet love story that brings tears to the eyes. It captivates the reader, right through to the breathless finale.' Isolde Wehr, www.buecher4um.de, Germany

Rebel follows aristocrat Viviane de Chercy as she leaves France with Lafayette, to thwart her guardian and elope to the American War of Independence. 'Viviane's guardian, the Comte de Mirandol, is at war not only with the English but himself ... Viviane makes many contributions to the war and goes out singlehanded to save the city of Philadelphia. *Rebel* is a great read!' *Heart's Talk* Australia

17842353R00166

Printed in Poland
by Amazon Fulfillment
Poland Sp. z o.o., Wrocław